JANET
CHAPMAN

ALSO BY JANET CHAPMAN

Charming the Highlander
Loving the Highlander
Wedding the Highlander

Published by Pocket Books

JANET CHAPMAN

THE SEDUCTIVE IMPOSTOR

POCKET BOOKS

New York   London   Toronto   Sydney

An *Original* Publication of POCKET BOOKS

POCKET BOOKS, a division of Simon & Schuster, Inc.
1230 Avenue of the Americas, New York, NY 10020

ISBN: 0-7394-4139-6

Cover design by Min Choi.
Front cover art based on James Randklev/Getty Images.
Back cover illustration by Robert Papp.

Manufactured in the United States of America

To Della,
for being a great sister as well as my best friend.
You might question some of my antics,
but never question my love.

ACKNOWLEDGMENTS

Thank you, Chris Limberis, for helping me make sense of the legal and political systems around here. How wonderful that I can use both *lawyer* and *friend* in the same sentence when referring to you.

And thank you to the gang at Write It/Sell It, Gail and Lance, Jason, Lorin, Marg, John G., Chris F., and all the rest of my extended family from the Writer's Retreat Workshop. A girdle is not the only thing that gives great support!

But most especially, thank you, Chris Goff and Jan Chalfant, my sisters in prose, for the long-distance brainstorming, the pep talks and scoldings, and the many memorable RWA conferences. What wonderful and patient husbands we have.

Chapter One

Using her cane for support, Rachel Foster limped down the steps of the library and headed for her truck, eager to get home and take a long soak in a tub of steaming water. The torn cartilage in her knee was nearly healed, but the rest of her muscles had gotten lazy from lack of exercise. It was going to take a month of kayaking to get back in shape, and Rachel could hardly wait until her doctor's appointment on Friday to get rid of her cane and the stupid, itchy brace on her knee.

She waved at a few friends as she drove down the street that separated Puffin Harbor's small, eclectic assortment of shops from the grassy town park and headed toward her home, which, up until her hiking accident three weeks ago, had been only a fifteen-minute walk away.

But Rachel's smile quickly disappeared as she passed the firemen standing outside the station. She'd yelled at them to be careful when they'd rescued her off Gull Mountain, but they'd just laughed and threatened to drop her. Her glare was answered by whistles and catcalls, with Ronald Pikes waving both hands and shouting something about her taking a hike.

Rachel pulled into her driveway to find Wendell Potter sitting in the swing on her porch, his briefcase tucked under his chin and his eyes closed.

He woke up when she came to a dusty stop beside the porch. He scrambled to his feet as she got out of the truck.

"What brings you here, you handsome old goat? Business or pleasure?" she asked as she slowly mounted the stairs.

He did return her smile, but it seemed a bit forced. Or maybe a bit tired. Rachel leaned up and gave him a noisy kiss on his cheek, realizing that her old family friend and lawyer was getting up there in years.

"This old goat is here on business, I'm afraid," he said, holding the screen door for her as she opened the inside door, then following her into the kitchen. "I'm closing up shop," he continued, going over to the kitchen table and setting his battered old briefcase down.

Rachel hooked her cane over the back of the kitchen chair and sat down, propping her right leg on a second chair, studying him as he dropped into his own chair with a tired sigh.

"You're closing up shop?" she repeated. "But you can't be a day over sixty," she told him, smiling broadly.

"I'll be seventy-four next month, and you know it. What?" he asked, lifting one bushy eyebrow. "You think I'm going to babysit your legal affairs the rest of my life? You've got a sister who can do that now."

"But then what will you do?"

He perked up, shooting her a smile that had surely been a lady-killer fifty years ago. "We bought a condo in Florida. No more Maine winters for us!"

Rachel slapped her hand down on the table. "Good for you! It's about time you spent all that money you've made off us Fosters all these years."

His bushy eyebrows dropped in a mocking glare, and he shook his head at her. "I swear you get sassier every time I see you." He suddenly sobered. "How's the knee?" he asked, nodding toward the cane hanging on her chair.

"Pretty good now. I'm hoping Dr. Sprague lets me get back to work next week."

Wendell nodded approval. "Betty said you tumbled halfway down Gull Mountain," he told her, his eyes suddenly lighting with humor. "Said most of Puffin Harbor's fire department came to your rescue."

Betty was Dr. Sprague's receptionist and an incurable gossip. She was also Wendell Potter's wife.

Rachel covered her face with her hands and peeked between her fingers. "It was so embarrassing. They strapped me into one of those litters and carried me off the mountain." She lowered her hands, her eyes widening as she dramatized her tale. "I was terrified they were going to drop me. I kept screaming at them to be careful, trying to be heard over their laughter. I was dying, and those fools were having a field day."

"That's because they knew you weren't dying." Wendell chuckled. "And every firefighter you've ever turned down for a date had you exactly where he wanted you," Wendell said as he undid the buckles of the battered leather satchel and reached inside.

Rachel's joy at Wendell's unexpected visit suddenly

turned to curiosity when he pulled a small metal box from his briefcase and set it on the table in front of her.

It was an old box, dingy and dented by years of indifferent handling and misuse, the weathered green paint chipped away at the corners and around the lock, exposing the dull patina of rusted cheap tin. Rachel stilled at the sight of the box and fought to repress the familiar weight of grief suddenly welling up in her chest.

She recognized the box.

"What's in it?" she whispered, lifting her gaze to the lawyer she'd known since childhood.

Wendell clasped his hands and placed them on top of his now deflated briefcase. "It's your daddy's strongbox," he said, his bushy gray brows pulled into a frown. "And I can't say what's in it, because I don't know. Frank only gave me the task of keeping it for him."

"When?"

His frown deepened. "Well . . . it was more than five years ago, best as I recall."

Rachel returned her gaze to the box. A good two years, she realized, before the tragedy that had rocked Rachel and her sister's world.

She looked back at Wendell. "You've had this for five years? Why are you giving it to me now?"

The aging lawyer's already florid face turned a deep red. He dropped his gaze and began to fidget with one of the buckles on his briefcase. "I forgot it, Rachel," he said, shaking his head. "Honest to God, I simply forgot I had the damn thing." He looked at her, his liquid brown eyes sad. "There was so much chaos three years ago. So much grief and disbelief. I remembered my duty at that time, but that was before Frank died."

No. It had taken her father two weeks to die from the bullet lodged in his head. Rachel's chest tightened again, this time with heart-crushing sadness. Two weeks of mourning the death of their mother and praying for the recovery of their father. Two weeks followed by three years of trying to understand the senseless tragedy.

And now this. Just when the pain had finally ebbed to a dull ache, Wendell brings her Frank Foster's dented old strongbox.

One last gift from her father.

One final reminder of the destructive power of passion.

"I tucked it away in a storage closet when I realized Frank might live," Wendell continued, his eyes clouded with his own grief. "And then I forgot. I only found it this morning, when I starting packing up the office."

He reached across the table and covered her hand. "I'm sorry. I failed my old friend, and now I've brought back your sadness. But I'm bound by my duty, even though I know the pain it's likely to cause you. Frank wanted you to have this box."

Rachel turned her hand palm up and squeezed the warm, age-bent fingers covering hers. She gave Wendell a grateful smile, then reached out and touched the box, carefully pulling it closer.

Wendell reached inside his briefcase again, but left his hand there as he looked at her, his face washed with concern. "Have you seen today's paper yet, Rachel?" he asked.

"No. Why?"

He pulled out a newspaper and unfolded it, laying it on the table facing her. Rachel read the headline printed in bold two-inch letters across the top: LAKEMAN HEIR FINALLY FOUND.

She stared at it numbly. Unmoving, silent, forgetting to breathe.

"Actually, Rachel," Wendell said softly, "that headline is what made me remember the strongbox. Learning that they'd found Thadd's heir brought it all rushing back. Like you, I thought Sub Rosa would sit vacant until it crumbled into the sea."

Rachel flinched at the sudden pain that lurched at her heart. And that surprised her—that she still felt such a strong love for Sub Rosa.

Nearly as strong as her hate for it.

"That won't happen," she said, picking up the newspaper and unfolding it fully. "We're more likely to witness the Apocalypse than we are to see Frank Foster's work self-destruct. He designed his structures to last until—"

Rachel's words trailed off, her thoughts evaporating like dew at sunrise, as her gaze settled on the face of the man in the large color photo below the headline.

He was . . . arresting.

His eyes captured her attention first; dark, narrowed in laughter as they focused on the child he held in his arms. Eyes edged with crow's-feet, set in a deeply tanned, chiseled face.

His hands—large, blunt, powerful—holding the young girl securely against his shirtless, hair-covered chest. Broad shoulders, sleek-muscled arms, a flat stomach.

Arresting.

The child looked to be about four or five. A girl with riotous blond hair and a cherub face, her tiny hand resting on his cheek as she smiled back at him. She was wearing a bright pink swimsuit, her exposed skin just as tanned as the man's. They were on a sail ship at mooring:

stout ropes, wooden deck, folded canvas sails in the background. A schooner, perhaps.

Rachel read the caption below the picture. "Keenan Oakes," it said, "with his daughter, Mikaela."

Keenan Oakes. Thaddeus Lakeman's heir.

Well, now. It seemed the mansion that stood high on the cliff next door, looming like a brooding ghost, would be brought back to life after a three-year sleep. The storm shutters would be raised. Lights would be seen in the windows again. And people would come. The tomb of Thaddeus and her parents' tragedy would soon be awakened by the activities of the living.

"Hard to believe the man is related to Thadd," Wendell said, breaking into her thoughts. "No family resemblance."

Rachel carefully set down the paper, picked up the strongbox, and began examining it. "Oh, I don't know. Thadd had dark eyes. Where's the key?" she asked, dismissing both Sub Rosa and Keenan Oakes from her mind.

She looked up when Wendell didn't immediately answer.

He was frowning at her. "You have it," he said. "Frank told me he gave you the key years ago."

It was Rachel's turn to frown. "No," she said, shaking her head. "He never mentioned this box or ever gave me a key that I remember." She set the strongbox back on the table and shrugged. "Maybe he gave it to Willow."

"I don't think so, Rachel. Frank left specific instructions that I give this box only to you. He said he wanted you alone to decide what to do with the contents."

Rachel stared at the box, wondering what secrets Frank Foster had wanted kept from his younger daughter, Willow.

She pushed her chair back and awkwardly stood up. Her cane forgotten, she limped to the center island of her kitchen and turned back to Wendell. He'd risen when she had, his eyes concerned as he clasped his brief-case to his chest.

"He didn't say anything else?" she asked. "Like why he didn't want Willow to know about the box?"

"Nothing." Wendell moved around the table, stopping in front of her. "Willow was busy with law school," he reminded her. "You were the one here with Frank, working beside him, building Sub Rosa. You were the daughter of his heart."

"He loved Willow just as much."

"Yes, he did. But the bond you shared with your father was like none other, Rachel. You were Frank's pride, his mirror image."

Wendell set his briefcase on the counter behind her and laid his warm, gentle hands on her shoulders. "Remember, when he gave me this duty, your mother was still alive, and there was no way Frank could have foreseen the tragedy coming. He was expecting *three* women to be mourning his death, not two."

Wendell tightened his hands on her shoulders, giving strength to his words. "But he specifically asked me to not tell Willow or Marian anything about it." He nodded toward the table. "Whatever's in there is between you and your daddy, Rachel. And now I've done my duty," he said with a relieved sigh as he pulled her toward him. "So give this old man a hug and promise me you won't let that newspaper article intrude on the peace you and your sister have finally found."

Rachel leaned into Wendell's embrace and wrapped

her arms around him, hugging him fiercely as she whispered her lie. "I won't."

"That's my girl," he said over her head. "Sub Rosa is only granite and glass, Rachel. Don't blame the house for what took place there."

He pulled away and looked into her eyes, giving her an encouraging smile. "Foster and Daughter Architects designed Sub Rosa, and that's what people will remember a hundred years from now."

Rachel knew everything he was saying was true. It was her heart she couldn't seem to convince. "I lost my own soul there three years ago. And although I know a house cannot cause human betrayal, there's still a part of me that will always blame Sub Rosa."

"That's because it belonged to you and your father as much as it did to Thaddeus," Wendell said, squeezing her shoulders again. "You're not just mourning the loss of three people you loved, you've lost Sub Rosa as well. Tell me, why have you and Willow continued to live in its shadow these last three years? Why haven't you moved, putting all of this behind you?"

"We couldn't. I couldn't," she admitted. As much as she hated the sight of the house where her parents' lives had ended, she hated the thought of not being close to Sub Rosa even more.

"Thirteen years of Frank Foster's greatest work sits next door," Rachel said. "Thirteen years of apprenticing at my father's side. And this house," she added, waving at the kitchen they were standing in. "My first independent design. How could I walk away from the happiest years of my life?"

Wendell's smile returned, warm and understanding.

"Ah, Rachel. You couldn't leave for the simple reason that you will always be your father's daughter. And Frank's soul is restless, child, worrying about your continued refusal to design. It's been long enough, Rachel. When will you start building beautiful homes for people again?"

Rachel turned and picked up his briefcase from the counter, giving it to him along with a wry smile. "When I can figure out how to design homes without getting passionately involved in them."

"That's not possible. Not for you, any more than it was for Frank. Passion runs through Foster veins."

"Passion is what killed my mother, father, and Thaddeus Lakeman," she countered, limping to the door, silently letting the old lawyer know their visit was over. "Passion is what makes a man shoot his wife and friend when he finds them in bed together, and then makes him turn the gun on himself."

"Dammit, Rachel," Wendell said, refusing to follow her. He stood in the middle of her kitchen, his briefcase clutched to his chest. "It's not the same thing at all. Frank's crime and the passion you bring to your designs are incomparable."

He finally walked to the door and stood in front of her. "You're the closest thing I have to a daughter, Rachel Foster. And it pains me to see you locked away in this self-imposed prison of mediocre existence. You're as great an architect as your father was. And what have you done for the last three years? You check out books at the library, collect ten-cent late fees, and read stories to toddlers with runny noses."

"It's rewarding."

"No, Rachel. It's safe. And it's a terrible waste."

"Thank you for bringing me the box." She kissed his cheek. "I'll see you again soon."

Realizing his petition was falling on deaf ears, Wendell reluctantly stepped onto the porch, but stopped and turned back to her. "I love you," he said gruffly.

"I know, Wendell. I love you, too."

He started to turn, but hesitated. "You'll not let the news of Thadd's heir being found upset you," he instructed, his voice thick with emotion. "And you'll be a good neighbor to Keenan Oakes when he arrives."

Rachel shot him a crooked smile. "Afraid I'll fabricate a few ghosts and goblins to scare him off?"

Instead of returning her smile, Wendell narrowed his eyes. "That possibility did occur to me," he admitted. "Give the man a chance, will you? Don't condemn him for having the questionable luck of being a Lakeman. The article said he is Thadd's great-nephew twice removed. That's falling a fair distance from the tree. Keenan Oakes just might be one of the good guys."

Rachel placed her hand over her heart. "I'll be nothing but graciousness personified."

Wendell gave her a quelling look. "Just as long as you know it's not gracious to flood the man's basement with seawater or short out his electrical system."

"That won't happen, because I have no intention of ever setting foot on that property again."

"But you can't expect him to reopen Sub Rosa alone. You're the only one who knows the mechanics of that house. He's going to need your help."

"He's not getting it," she said, alarmed at what he was suggesting. "He can talk to the company that's been overseeing it for the last three years. They have all the schematics and blueprints."

"Hell, Rachel. It took them over a week just to figure out how to close the storm shutters. And another three weeks to drain the tidal reservoir and get the place on line with the public power company. And that was the easiest part of securing the house. The climate sensors kept going off at least once a month for the first year, before a company was found who could handle the problem. And do you know who they called every time that damn alarm went off? Me," he said, thumping his chest. "What in hell do I know about climate control systems?"

"Why did they call you?"

"Because I'm the only contact Thadd's lawyers have here in Maine."

"You never told me Sub Rosa was causing you fits. Why didn't you call if you were having so much trouble?"

Wendell's eyes softened, and he blew out a calming breath before he answered. "Because I couldn't ask that of you," he told her gently. "Not after what you had found the last time you were there."

Rachel's chest tightened again. No, she wouldn't have helped him then. Three years ago she wouldn't have cared if Sub Rosa had burned to the ground.

Now, she was just indifferent. Or so she had thought. But Wendell's reminder of the intricate and sometimes contrary workings of Sub Rosa made her homesick for it. She had loved all the bells and whistles and ingenious innovations she and her father had built into the mansion.

Sub Rosa ran on electricity generated by tidal power. The climate control system rivaled the International Space Station. And everything—from the lights to the storm shutters, the lawn sprinklers to the security alarms—ran from a giant control room in the basement.

Sub Rosa was practically its own living, breathing entity. The loving creation of Foster & Daughter Architects.

She missed it.

And she never wanted to set foot inside it again.

"I can't help Keenan Oakes," she said softly. "Sub Rosa belongs to him now. He'll eventually learn its ways."

"I know, Rachel. I'm only asking that you promise not to do anything to . . . well, to hinder his adjustment."

She shook her head. "I don't begrudge the man his inheritance. I've long since passed the point of caring one way or another." She looked beyond the stunted pine trees growing along the cliffs beside her home, up toward the towering gables of Sub Rosa's roofline. "We've made peace, that great house and I. We're content now to live side by side, neither of us intruding on the other."

Wendell nodded. "Good, then. I'm glad for you." He leaned over and kissed her cheek, then turned and finally walked off the porch to his car. He opened the driver's door, but stopped yet again and looked back at her. "Now make peace with your new neighbor as well, Rachel, because he'll likely come calling once he gets a good look at his inheritance."

"And why would that be?" she asked, glaring at her old friend.

He grinned at her. "Probably because when we spoke on the phone last week, I told him to direct his questions concerning Sub Rosa to the second architect on record."

"Wendell!" she shouted, as Wendell disappeared into his car and started the engine.

He rolled down the window and popped his head out,

his grin wicked. "It's time you rejoined the living, Rachel, my love. And I've been thinking, Keenan Oakes just might be the man to make that happen," he shouted back, just before he drove away in a cloud of gravel and dust.

Four hours had passed since Wendell's disturbing visit, and Rachel was now sitting on the living room sofa, surrounded by the mess she'd made of her home searching for the key to the strongbox. The open box sat on the coffee table in front of her, the contents spilling out of it, the nine-page letter lying half-folded on top of everything. Stunned insensate, Rachel stared at the painting hanging over the fireplace not ten feet away.

It was a beautiful painting, obviously old, technically perfect, of a Scottish castle that loomed out of the mist, standing tall and strong against the battering sea. The small painting had been placed there the day they'd moved in. Her father's prized possession. Her favorite inheritance from Frank Foster. And according to the letter she'd found in the strongbox, worth a small fortune.

The letter also said it had been stolen from a museum in Scotland more than twenty years ago.

The delicate emerald earrings and necklace in Willow's jewelry box upstairs, which had been worn by their mother on special occasions, were worth a staggering $1 million dollars. The letter said they had been stolen from a private home in France more than sixteen years ago.

The bronze Asian statue on the bookcase next to the hearth was sixteen hundred years old, worth $200,000, and had been stolen from an Oregon home almost a decade ago.

The silver tankard, wine-tasting cup, and snuffbox sitting on the piano had all come from a single collection in Germany, eight years ago.

All stolen.

And all of them now in her possession.

The ruby and gold ring Rachel wore on her right middle finger, which had been a gift from her father on her twenty-first birthday, had been taken from London not two months before Frank Foster had presented it to her. At the time of its disappearance, the ring had been valued at $93,000.

Rachel very carefully worked the ring off her finger and gently placed it in the strongbox.

She picked up the letter again and unfolded it, forcing her trembling hands to still enough that she could read the last section again.

Don't judge me harshly, Rachel. I'm not a thief. But I am guilty of being seduced by the beauty, workmanship, and timelessness of Thadd's gifts. If you're reading this, then they're all yours now, and Willow's and Marian's. How you deal with them is up to you alone, though; keep them, discreetly sell them, or toss them into the sea if you can't stand the idea of possessing them. Or simply return them to Thadd, if you wish. He'll understand. He might argue with you a bit at first, but he'll accept them back.

Thadd respects you, Rachel, just as much as I do. You're an intelligent woman with unbelievable talent and a strong, kind, and good heart. Please don't tell the others what I've done. It's hard enough for me to know how deeply I've wounded you with this secret. Don't wound the others with such a tainted memory of me.

*I love you. Every day since you were born, I've
marveled at receiving such a wonderful daughter.
You and your sister are the fruit of a great love between
your mother and me. Never forget that. The passion
I have for my wife is strengthened by the love I have
for my daughters. So instead of thinking badly of me,
remember only the fierceness of my bond to the three
of you.*

*Receiving and then selfishly keeping the stolen art
is my sin alone, Rachel. Not yours or Marian's or
Willow's. And it is a sin I don't wish to see passed
down to my family. Marian doesn't need the heartache
bringing this to light would cause her. And Willow has
hopes of climbing the political ladder, all the way to
the governor's mansion one day. And you, my sweet
daughter, have homes to design for deserving families.*

*Please, Rachel, do whatever you have to, to protect
yourself and protect Marian and Willow.*

Make my sin quietly go away.

And continue to love me despite it.

Rachel wiped another set of teardrops from the letter before she carefully refolded the pages and set it back on the table. She stared again at the painting over the mantel.

Thaddeus Lakeman had collected beautiful and expensive art. Everyone had known that. It was why he had hired Frank Foster to build Sub Rosa—an opulent, powerful venue in which to display his collection. It had taken her father five years to design the great mansion, and another eight years to oversee its construction.

Since adolescence, Rachel had shadowed her father while he worked, adding her own ideas and her own touches of whimsy to the Gothic-like structure. And at her college graduation party, with her still clutching her degree to her chest, Frank Foster had presented Rachel with a full partnership in his newly formed company, Foster & Daughter Architects.

That had been the proudest day of both of their lives.

But now it seemed that she had helped build not only a home to display a world-renowned private collection of art, but an elaborate vault to house stolen art.

Some of which was in her own home.

Rachel looked up at the ceiling over her head. What had the letter said about a hidden room upstairs? She grabbed it back up and shuffled through the pages, skimming the words until she found what she was looking for.

You're going to have to forgive me, Rachel, for tinkering with your beautiful design. But the lovely home you built your family was lacking one small detail. When you and Willow and Marian were visiting Paris that summer, I took it upon myself to rectify your oversight. You've got to be proud of my own talent, daughter, for moving walls and rerouting a bit of plumbing, and still being able to disguise my work— especially from you.

If you take the time to remeasure the rooms upstairs, you'll discover that they don't quite fit your original blueprints. I needed a small room, you see, to keep things in.

Consider this our final treasure hunt together, Rachel, like you and I used to have in Sub Rosa while it was still being built. You were obviously able to find

*the key to the strongbox if you're reading this. Now find
the room.*

   *And when you finally enter my secret door, smile
at my cunning and remember our good times working
together.*

   *Oh, and take note, Rachel, of how I did it. You'll
find one special room in Sub Rosa that echoes the same
design. Just don't let Thadd know that I told you.*

She had finally found the key, once she had stopped
her frantic search long enough to think with the left
side of her brain. The only thing her father had given her
five years ago had been a barrette made up of silver
charms. The charms were miniature architect tools.

All except for the small silver-plated key.

Rachel raised her gaze to the ceiling again, mostly
to keep the tears from streaming down her face. Her daddy
had tinkered with her design.

Moved walls.

Hidden a room.

And kept a terrible secret.

Chapter Two

⊠

Rachel set the plate of overcooked eggs in front of her sister, then carried her own breakfast around the table and took a seat across from Willow.

"Eat," she told her, trying to get her sister's attention away from the newspaper. "Before your eggs get cold."

Willow ignored the petition, instead lowering the paper and staring at her with shocked eyes. "They found him?" she asked in a disbelieving whisper. "After all this time?"

Rachel nodded.

"He's going to reopen the house, isn't he?"

She nodded again.

Willow gave one last look at the photograph accompanying the newspaper article, then picked up her fork and began pushing her eggs around on her plate.

"It was bound to happen eventually," Rachel said into the silence, letting her own eggs grow cold. "A billion-dollar estate won't sit forever without someone stepping forward to claim it."

Willow looked up at her with haunted eyes. Rachel wanted to hug her tightly and never let go, but she gave Willow a smile instead. "A billion dollars in assets and bank accounts, minus the five million Thadd left to each of us. Suppose Keenan Oakes will miss our share?"

"I'm never touching that money," Willow said, her face darkening with anger. "I'm going to give it to the Make-A-Wish Foundation."

"So you've said before."

Willow dropped her fork, pushed back her chair, and stood up. She walked to the island and turned and faced the table. "I'm doing it today. And I'm selling my Lake-man Boatyard stock and giving that money to the College of the Atlantic."

"Then do it. You're going to feel a hundred pounds lighter and five years younger," Rachel promised, speaking from personal experience. She had given her anonymous gift from Thadd away two years ago, to Habitat for Humanity.

"Dammit, Rachel," Willow said through gritted teeth, waving at the paper on the table. "We're just getting our lives together. I don't want him coming here. I don't want Sub Rosa being reopened."

Rachel stood up, limped around the table, and hugged her sister. "Let it go," she said, echoing Wendell's words from yesterday. "It doesn't matter anymore, Willy. You and I have moved on, and now it's Sub Rosa's turn."

She pulled back and smiled at Willow's tear-washed face, giving her shoulders a gentle squeeze. "You have a new apartment to hunt for in Augusta and an assistant state attorney general's desk to clutter up with important cases."

"I can't just leave you here. Not now." Willow suddenly reversed their positions, gripping Rachel's arms. "Come with me. Sell the house and move to Augusta."

Rachel pulled away and went to the stove, taking the cooled frying pan to the sink and running it under the water. "No," she said, concentrating on her chore. "I love this house and Puffin Harbor too much. I'd miss the ocean, kayaking, and walking to the town pier for lobster rolls."

Willow came and stood beside her. Rachel saw that her sister had the newspaper in her hand again and was staring at the photo of Keenan Oakes.

"He's dangerous," Willow said softly. "And he's going to cause trouble."

Rachel arched a brow. "You've decided this from his photo?"

Willow snapped the paper in front of Rachel's face. "Look at him, Rae. I mean, really look at him. Keenan Oakes is part heathen, part demigod, and all man." She shook the paper for emphasis. "There are two types of guys in this world," she continued. "The safe, sweet guy who asks permission to kiss you good night, and the kind who simply pulls you into his arms and kisses the sense right out of you. And this man," she said, pushing the paper mere inches from Rachel's nose, "is not sweet, and he most assuredly is not safe."

Rachel batted the newspaper away, refusing to let Willow see how much her assessment of Keenan Oakes unnerved her. "It doesn't matter what he is," she said, furiously scrubbing the frying pan. "Because I don't intend to even talk to him."

Willow was staring at his photo again. "He'll be on our doorstep within two days of arriving here," she softly speculated. She tossed the paper onto the counter, then stared out the window over the sink. "You have to stay away from him, Rae," she whispered. "You've been so careful, so safe for these last three years." She touched Rachel's arm, making Rachel look at her. "If Keenan Oakes decides to involve you in Sub Rosa's reopening, there's not enough granite in this state to wall yourself up in."

Rachel began scrubbing the already spotless frying pan again. And again Willow stopped her. "How can you watch him reopen it?" she asked quietly.

Rachel smiled sadly. "It will be easier than having watched it sit silent all these years," she said truthfully. She shut off the water and turned to Willow. "I know you probably can't understand that, but Sub Rosa is as much a part of me as you and Dad and Mom. And it hurts seeing it lifeless. Please don't condemn Sub Rosa for being one of the victims."

"I grew up playing there, too," Willow said, her hazel eyes tearing. "But if I see lights in the windows again, I'll be expecting Daddy to come walking down the path looking for supper."

"But when he doesn't show up, it will still be okay," Rachel told her gently. "It's his legacy to the world, Willow. For as long as Sub Rosa lives, so does he. Here," she said, touching the center of her sister's chest. "Frank Foster will always live here, in both of us. And so will Mom, and so will Thadd."

"Thaddeus Lakeman is rotting in hell."

Rachel grabbed her sister's shoulders before she could turn away. "No, he's not. Thadd loved us like daughters."

"He seduced our mother," Willow countered, breaking free and taking a step back. She balled her hands into fists at her sides, her face red and her eyes hard. "He seduced his best friend's wife."

"Yes. Thadd was wrong. But so was Mom. And so was Dad, for killing them and then killing himself." Rachel took a step closer to Willow, trying to drive home her point, which had been an ongoing bone of contention between the two of them for the last three years. "They're all to blame, and not one of them deserved what happened. It was a tragedy, Willow."

Willow covered her face with her hands and shook her head. Rachel reached up and tucked a strand of Willow's rich brown hair behind her ear—but stopped suddenly at the sight of the emerald earring.

"Ah . . . why are you wearing Mom's earrings today?" she asked, looking at Willow's throat for the necklace, but not seeing it. "They're supposed to be for special occasions."

Willow wiped her face with the palms of her hands and took a deep breath. "I'm meeting my new staff this afternoon," she said, grabbing a paper towel and dabbing at her eyes. "I want to look good. And the emeralds give me confidence."

Rachel rubbed her suddenly sweating palms on her thighs. Damn. Now what? She had to get those emeralds away from her sister. She sure as heck couldn't let her take them to Augusta.

"They're a little dressy, don't you think?" she asked, shaking her head disapprovingly. "A bit pretentious, maybe, for a new assistant attorney general?"

Willow reached up and fingered one of the earrings. "You think so?"

Rachel nodded. "Definitely overkill. Why not wear your pearls?" she suggested instead. The pearls had also belonged to their mother, but had been safely passed down for three generations. "They'd be much more professional-looking. More sedate and established."

Willow shot her a weak grin as she reached up to take off the earrings. "This from one who thinks barrettes are jewelry. But you're right. Thanks for saving me from looking like an idiot. Hey," she said, her gaze going to Rachel's hand in search of the only piece of real jewelry Rachel wore. "Where's the ring Dad gave you?"

Rachel touched her thumb to her empty middle finger. Hell, this was getting more complicated than the maze of tunnels spidering through Sub Rosa. What was she supposed to say to Willow when half their cherished possessions suddenly turned up missing?

"I took it to the jeweler to have it cleaned and checked," she quickly prevaricated.

"Oh. Then here," Willow said, handing her the earrings. "Why don't you take these in when you pick up your ring. And take the necklace, too. The prongs should probably be looked at. I'd hate to lose one of the emeralds."

Rachel inwardly cringed as she accepted the earrings. No, she wouldn't want that, either. Not at several hundred thousand dollars a stone.

Willow gave Rachel a quick kiss on the cheek. "I've got to get going if I want to be in Augusta by noon. You'll be okay here alone for a few days? I mean, with Keenan Oakes on the way and everything?"

Rachel stuffed the emerald earrings in her pocket and picked up her cane from the towel rack at the end of the counter. She headed for the door, leading her sister out of the house. "I'll be fine," she said over her shoulder. "And the article said he won't arrive for several more days. You'll be back by then, if only to pack everything for your move."

She didn't stop until she was standing on the porch. Willow, suitcase in hand as she followed her out, still looked worried.

"I'll be too busy to even think about Sub Rosa," Rachel assured her. "I'm going through every room in this house and finding you some furnishings for that new apartment."

"No lifting."

"I promise," she agreed, holding her hand up in a scout's salute. "I'll get a few of the local boys to move the furniture down to the porch."

"Are you sure you're feeling okay, Rachel? Your leg is healing okay?"

"Yes. Why?"

Willow nodded toward the kitchen. "The house looked a bit messy to me when I got in last night. And you went to bed unusually early."

Not that she'd slept, Rachel thought. She'd been awake almost all night pondering the letter, the hidden room somewhere upstairs, and her father's startling confession.

"I'm fine." She stepped forward and hugged Willow, then gently pushed her on her way. "Now go. Have fun, call me the instant you sit at your new desk, and find a nice apartment with good neighbors. And make sure it has a spare bedroom," she said more loudly as Willow set her suitcase in the backseat of her car. "I'm not sleeping on the couch when I come visit."

Willow stopped and turned from opening the driver's

door, shading her eyes from the morning sun as she looked back at the porch.

"I'm proud of you, Willow," Rachel said, her voice husky with emotion. "You know what you want and you've gone after it like a whirlwind. And now you're going to be Maine's youngest, brightest, hardest-working assistant attorney general."

"And do you know what you want?" Willow asked back, just as gruffly.

Rachel nodded. "Yes. And I'll go after it, too. Soon."

Willow still hesitated, then suddenly her expression lifted and she shot Rachel a grin and pointed at her. "I want to put Puffy in the town square this weekend. The townspeople are going to go nuts this time, Rachel, trying to figure out where he came from."

"It's good for what ails them," Rachel said, returning the grin. "And every town square needs a statue."

"But an eight-foot puffin?" Willow asked with a chuckle. "Replacing beat-up old mailboxes is one thing, but putting a big colorful bird in the middle of town is a bit more risky. What if we get caught?"

"We won't. I promise. Now get out of here, unless you want to get fired before you even see your new office."

With a final wave, Willow climbed into her car and drove away. Rachel continued to wave back, waiting until her sister was out of sight before she dropped her hand and expelled a loud sigh of relief.

That was one problem out of the way for the next few days. She pulled the emerald earrings out of her pocket and stared at the expensive green stones. Now all she had to do was gather up all the other problems and get rid of them as well.

She looked up at Sub Rosa. "You might want to put on the tea kettle, Rosa," she softly told the house. "Because it looks like I'll be paying you a visit tonight."

Rachel took a deep breath through a count of four, held it through a count of six, then slowly released it through a count of eight. Determined not to give in to the overwhelming urge to flee to the safety her cozy kitchen, she repeated the process three more times.

It still wasn't working. Instead of calming her, the breathing exercise only made her dizzy. Her heart continued to race as memories flooded her senses: the smell of granite dust mingled with sea mist, the warm brush of stone touching her shoulders, the heaviness of Sub Rosa's brooding weight pushing her deeper into its cocoon.

Rachel leaned her cane against the granite wall of the tunnel and reached down and massaged the neoprene brace covering her right knee. Her entire leg was complaining about the trek up the overgrown path through the woods, complaining even more about her having carried nearly forty pounds of stolen art the entire way.

The pack on her back shifted to one side when she bent over. Rachel shrugged her shoulders and let the pack carefully finish falling to the ground. She followed it, sitting on the warm granite floor of the tunnel, stretching her legs out in front of her, massaging her knee again.

This hadn't been one of her brightest ideas, sneaking in through the cliff tunnel tonight and beginning to right her father's wrong. But it had been the only plan she'd been able to come up with on such short notice.

She wanted this settled before Keenan Oakes arrived. And it had to be settled in such a way that Willow would never discover their father's sin. Rachel knew her sister well enough to realize that Willow's personal ethics would not allow her to simply ignore the fact that they'd unwittingly inherited a small fortune in stolen art. Willow would tear Sub Rosa apart stone by stone, trying to root out all of Thaddeus Lakeman's secrets. And in doing so, she would ultimately ruin her own political career.

Rachel shone the beam of her flashlight farther into the passageway. She was almost to the secret door that opened into the second-floor hall. Rachel's vision blurred with tears as she remembered the horrific images of her last moments at Sub Rosa three years earlier.

The bedroom.

The blood.

The realization, and disbelief, of what she was seeing.

She had seen her mother first, lying across the foot of the bed, fully clothed, blood seeping from her body and running down the rumpled blankets, pooling in a dark puddle so thick the pattern on the carpet was unrecognizable.

And then Thadd, on the floor beside the bed, face down, barefoot but still fully clothed, his body unnaturally still, his left hand outstretched as if reaching for Marian. He had looked untouched but for the dark stain pooling beneath him.

Rachel had run to her mother first and covered the gaping wound in her chest with her hands. She had actually attempted to gather the blood, trying to push it back into her mother's lifeless body. Her screams had filled the room.

She had seen her father across the room then, propped in a half-sitting position against the far wall. His eyes were open. Blood was trickling from his mouth and seeping from the corner of one eye. And higher, oozing crimson from the tiny hole just above his right ear. In the relaxed grip of his right hand was the gun.

Frank Foster's chest had risen on a gasp as she had stared at him, and it had taken Rachel a shocked moment to realize that her father was still alive. Panic had frozen her in place. Blind to her mother's blood on her hands, she'd had enough wits to go to the phone and dial 911. She told the woman on the other end of the line that there had been a shooting at Sub Rosa and she needed an ambulance, and then dropped the receiver.

She'd gone to her father then, approaching him slowly, fearfully, afraid to disturb the fragile spark of life he still held. She'd gently taken the gun from his hand and tossed it away, then looked up and found his eyes focused on her face.

Not just alive. But conscious. Aware.

Huddled on the floor of the silent tunnel, her arms wrapped around her bent leg, Rachel tried to remember what she had said to him. She'd called him Daddy and repeated the word *why* several times, almost as a litany. And while she had cradled him in her arms, wind moaned through the open panel in the wall beside them, sending warm, salt-tainted air swirling into the room to mix with the metallic smell of so much blood. More from habit than thought, Rachel had used her foot to push the panel closed, keeping the secret of the passageways safe.

All these years later she remembered the only words her father had been able to utter in a soft, ragged whisper.

"Ra-Rach . . . don't go Vegas . . . see dancer . . . Norway night . . . fi-find her . . . killed . . . Marian . . . find her—"

They had been the last words Frank Foster had spoken. Rachel had thought for the last three years that he'd meant not to go to Las Vegas—which hadn't made any sense to her at all—and something about seeing a dancer, possibly a dancer in Vegas?

But in the letter her father had left her in the strongbox, she'd learned that Vegas was actually a man named Raoul Vegas, a dealer in stolen art her father had told her to look up if she wanted to get rid of her inheritance discreetly.

Now, though, she realized her father had changed his mind since writing the letter, and had been telling her not to go to Raoul Vegas. She still didn't know what Norway night or seeing a dancer meant, or who it was she should find.

The bullet lodged in his head had stayed there, unreachable by the doctors, and slowly Frank Foster's coma had deepened, until finally, two weeks after the tragedy, she and Willow had made the difficult decision to terminate life support.

Their parents' ashes were floating on the ocean now, forever fluttering on the endless tides of the rock-bound coast they both had loved so much.

Rachel lifted her head and scrubbed at her face with both hands. What had come over Thadd and Marian that they had become lovers? And why had Frank Foster acted so horrifically? Rachel had answered those questions the day she had sat in the hospital and watched the final spark of life quietly drift from her father's body.

And that answer had been passion.

Passion could drive a person to unimaginable heights of greatness, but it could also be destructive.

For her parents, it had ultimately been tragic.

And for Rachel, passion had ceased to exist three years ago.

History, she was determined, would not repeat itself. Every thought, every decision, every action of her life was calculated now. She obeyed society's rules, dressed sensibly, and didn't date seriously. She quietly came to the aid of anyone in the community who needed a hand, but she no longer attended town meetings or allowed her one-time heated opinions to find voice at planning board hearings.

And she no longer designed homes. She did, however, build mailboxes.

After Willow had run over old man Smith's pathetic old mailbox and had replaced it, she had become more aware of the sad condition of most of the mailboxes everyone passed every day without notice. The two sisters had formed a conspiracy then to anonymously replace the worst of the mailboxes in their community. It didn't matter if the owner was rich or poor, Willow and Rachel let loose their imaginations and built and installed beautiful replacements for them.

The results had astounded them. Not only were the recipients of the mailboxes pleasantly surprised to find themselves owners of beautiful works of art, but the entire town had a wonderful mystery that no one was in any hurry to solve.

The mailboxes had become the subject of early morning coffee conversations as folks speculated on who was doing it, why, and when and where the next one would appear. And that speculation was going to explode thunderously the morning an eight-foot puffin appeared in the center of town.

Rachel had found this one careful outlet in which to vent her own potentially destructive passions. It was a safety valve of sorts; Willow had her all-consuming work to pour her heart into, and Rachel had mailboxes. It was rewarding and very safe.

In fact, far more safe than the idiotic mission she was on tonight.

Rachel turned the flashlight beam down to her lap. She pulled the small piece of paper she'd taken from the strongbox out of her pocket and unfolded it.

She traced her father's handwriting, following the neat, bold black numbers that spelled out the master override for the alarms. Of course, the company babysitting Sub Rosa these last three years had changed the codes, probably several times. But these numbers would cancel out their newest sequence.

Rachel sighed and used her cane to help herself stand up. It was time to get going and get this over with. She tucked the paper back in her pocket, then reached down and picked up the backpack.

She should have left the bronze statue for another trip. The damn thing had to weigh fifteen pounds by itself. How many more trips she'd have to make, she didn't know. But the letter had listed quite a few pieces that weren't anywhere in sight, and she still hadn't found the entrance to the secret room in her home.

She hadn't needed to pull out her blueprints to realize it existed, once she started examining the rooms upstairs. Her dad had stolen a foot or two out of all of them, all except her own bedroom. That he had been wise enough not to touch. She would have noticed the missing space immediately.

Instead he'd taken the bulk out of the guest bedroom and the walk-in closet of the master suite. He'd shortened the hallway linen closet and Willow's bedroom by a foot, eking out a good sixty square feet of space, as far as she could tell.

Frank Foster truly was a genius of design, especially considering the original architect would be living in the house. And she still couldn't find the damn door to the secret room.

Rachel started walking deeper into the tunnel. She'd hunt for it tomorrow. Right now she had an old friend to visit, and three-year-old ghosts to face.

Chapter Three

Rachel sighed in relief when the last tumbler dropped into place with gentle precision. She spun the giant lock and pulled open the huge titanium door, revealing the darkness beyond. Warm, climate-controlled air rushed past her as she stepped inside and trained the beam of her flashlight around the interior.

Nearly as large as her kitchen at home, the huge vault was organized with shelves and cubbies and smaller safes against two of the walls. On the other two walls sheet-draped artwork was hung. Every square inch of space had been utilized and was brimming with treasure.

Rachel wasn't impressed. She slid the heavy pack off her shoulders and set it on the floor. She opened the buckles and pulled out the bronze statue, then used her flashlight to hunt for an inconspicuous place to set it.

It didn't belong here with the legitimate art collection, but since she didn't know where Thadd's secret room was, this vault would have to do. Better the contraband eventually be discovered in Thadd's possession instead of hers and Willow's. It would be Keenan Oakes's problem then. The man couldn't very well expect to waltz into a billion-dollar estate without having a few surprises to deal with.

That thought perversely warmed Rachel's heart. Keenan Oakes owned Sub Rosa now, and his great-uncle's legacy was going to rear up and bite him on his butt.

Rachel set the statue in one of the cubbies, then pulled the small painting out of her pack and unwrapped it from the towel she'd used to protect it for the trip here. She pushed the sheets on the far wall aside until she found a space large enough to hang it. She returned to the pack and pulled out the silver tankard, wine cup, and snuffbox next, and gently set them in another cubby beside a vase that looked as old as the earth itself. She pulled the ruby and gold ring her father had given her out of her pocket, set the beam of her flashlight on it one last time, then reached up and dropped it inside the wine cup, flinching at the sound of metal falling on metal.

With a sigh of regret for having given up her father's gift, she turned and dug into the bottom of the nearly empty pack again and pulled out the emeralds.

Rachel clamped her tiny flashlight between her teeth and aimed it at the smaller, sequentially numbered safes. Holding the wrinkled paper next to the lock on safe number sixteen, she moved the dial to match another set of numbers written in black ink. Just as they had on the larger door, the tumblers fell with expected accuracy. The small door opened, and Rachel sighed again in relief.

"Thank you, Daddy, for thinking of everything," she whispered into the darkness. Frank Foster had thoughtfully given her a laundry list of the art she now possessed, along with a list of combinations and codes. He hadn't, however, given her the exact location of Thadd's secret room.

And she had to find it. The letter had also mentioned designs for fishing boats that had been built at the Lakeman Boatyard years ago. Special boats, with hidden compartments for smuggling stolen art into the country.

Designs that likely had Frank Foster's name on them.

Rachel wanted them destroyed. She wanted every last trace of her father's involvement in Thadd's illegal hobby gone.

Rachel shone her light into the small safe and was surprised to see a velvet bag already sitting there. She opened the velvet sack she had brought with her and dumped the contents into her hand. The beam of her light immediately shot out in glowing green ribbons going in a dozen directions.

She reached into the safe and pulled out the second velvet sack and opened it, only to find an exact duplicate set of emeralds.

Well, hell. What did this mean?

They were obviously forgeries. Thadd must have had copies made of the original emeralds. But what were they doing here, in this safe? Surely the lawyers had inventoried this vault shortly after Thadd's death and would have found them.

And they would have known they were stolen, wouldn't they? Wasn't there a database somewhere that listed stolen and unrecovered art? Surely these emeralds would have been on it.

Unless the appraisers had realized these were fakes. It wasn't a crime, was it, to possess copies of stolen jewelry?

Rachel shrugged. She would just leave the real ones with the fakes, and they, too, would become Keenan Oakes's problem.

She used the velvet bag to wipe off any fingerprints on Willow's emeralds, put them back in their bag, and was just placing them in the small safe when every overhead light in the vault suddenly snapped on.

Rachel dropped the other velvet pouch and watched, dismayed, as the fake emeralds tumbled out. She tried but failed to catch them, banging her forehead into the small safe door, slamming it shut with a resounding click. Everything clattered to the floor, including her flashlight and the cane that had been hooked over her arm.

Rachel whirled toward the vault door and saw that several lights in the library had also come on. The raised voice of a woman echoed from somewhere below, carrying up the grand staircase and along the marble hall toward her.

Rachel bent to her good knee and searched for the fallen fake emeralds, scooping them up and hastily stuffing them into the remaining velvet sack.

She stopped then and glared at the closed safe door.

Dammit. She had to get out of here.

The voice of the woman grew louder, along with the tap of heels on the marble floor. Whoever she was railing at was upstairs now and coming toward the library.

Rachel shoved the pouch of forgeries in her pocket, quickly deciding that one set of emeralds was enough to leave behind. She would get rid of the fakes later, and pray it would be years before anyone noticed the emeralds in safe number sixteen were actually real.

She grabbed her pack, cane, and flashlight, and ran

limping from the vault, stopping only long enough to close the huge door and spin the lock. She pushed the bookcase closed, concealing the vault.

Rachel looked toward the hearth on the far side of the room and decided it was out of reach of her crippled knee. She ducked into the storage closet instead, just as the library door swung open.

"I don't care, Kee," the woman shrilled on the other side of the closet door. "You promised we would go to the Renoir party. Then you suddenly decide you just have to come to this godforsaken monstrosity instead. It's freezing in here."

"Jason found the electrical box," the man said softly.

Rachel scrunched herself against the back wall of the closet, unable to suppress a shiver. The man's voice had been low, curt, and thin on patience. But the shrew didn't seem to hear what Rachel could: the quiet building of tension, the ominous calm before the storm.

No, the fool continued railing at the man who could be none other than Mr. Keenan Oakes. Dammit. He wasn't supposed to arrive until Friday.

"I don't know what all the hurry was for," the woman continued. "There's nobody here. You said this place has been empty for three years. Another week wouldn't have mattered."

Rachel silently nodded agreement.

"This might be some grand mansion you've inherited, but it's at the end of nowhere, Kee." Her voice dripped with distaste. "Maine! What in hell is there to do in Maine! It's a two-hour drive to the nearest airport. And this place is filthy. You should have hired someone to come open the house first, and that way we could have arrived *after* the Renoir party."

Rachel pictured the woman waving her hands about the giant library at the dark honey oak bookcases that reached twelve feet high, the heavy, oversized furniture covered with sheets, and the dusty tomes lining three of the walls.

Keenan Oakes still had nothing to say. Rachel decided he either had the patience of a saint or was deaf.

Rachel closed her eyes and covered her ears. A lover's quarrel was not supposed to be a spectator sport.

The woman suddenly snorted. "But this cold, moldering pile of rocks suits your Neanderthal brain perfectly, doesn't it?"

Rachel tried to decide whether the lady was brave or stupid. She wasn't sure she could take much more of this waiting. She was cramped, uncomfortable, and she agreed with the woman—the house was cold. Her right knee throbbed and she ached all over. And she was using every bit of willpower she possessed to keep from sneezing out the dust collecting in her nose.

With the abruptness of a runaway train hitting a mountain, the woman suddenly stopped shouting. "What did you say?" she shrilled.

"I said that was enough, Joan. I told you to wait and come later with Mikaela."

"But I've been planning for us to attend this party for weeks. You said we would go."

"Then go."

"But you're supposed to go with me. All my friends are expecting the two of us."

Joan's voice had lowered to a simper now. Rachel pictured her pouting at Keenan, who stood as tall as a giant and had shoulders as wide as a doorway. Keenan Oakes now had more money than God and looks the devil would envy, if his picture in the newspaper could be believed.

He also had a very stupid girlfriend.

"I said that was enough, Joan. You'll have to go to Monte Carlo alone. Mikaela's due to arrive in a few days, and I intend to be here to meet her."

"Mikaela. It's always Mikaela. Your boat's got a whole crew of babysitters, Kee. She won't miss you for the time it will take to fly to Monte Carlo and back. What's one more week?"

Silence was all Rachel heard for an answer.

"Kee!"

"I asked the driver who brought us here to wait. He'll take you back to the airport," came his softly spoken words through the closet door. "And Joan?"

"Yes?" she asked, her voice suddenly sounding hesitant for the first time.

"Don't bother coming back."

Just for a minute, Rachel almost felt sorry for Joan. But only a minute. Any woman who couldn't handle a demigod didn't deserve one. Rachel thought Keenan Oakes was letting the shrew off lightly. Most men wouldn't be so kind for the assault his ego had just received.

The Neanderthal's manhood, apparently, was quite secure.

The light showing through the crack under the closet door suddenly went out, and the large office door slammed shut with a shuddering bang. Rachel released a breath and listened to the tap of Joan's heels on the hall floor. Keenan was probably walking the banished Joan out to the car on this chilly June night. After all, demigods always had the best of manners—even if that concession to civilization was only a veneer.

Quietly, still a little rattled at nearly being caught, Rachel stiffly got up and opened the closet door. She picked up her cane, then pulled her cap more firmly down on her head while she tested her right knee, stifling a groan as pain shot all the way up her leg to her teeth.

Damn, this breaking and entering was hard on a body.

The big library was once again completely dark, the storm shutters that protected Sub Rosa blocking out what light the fog-shrouded moon was casting. Being as quiet as she could, Rachel used her little flashlight to guide her, hurriedly limping to the huge library door, intending to open it a crack and check her escape route.

Rachel slowly turned the knob on the huge oak door and tried to pull it open, only to find that it wouldn't budge.

But the knob turned easily. She aimed her light at the floor to see if the door was caught on the rug. Nothing. She looked up and gave another frantic tug on the portal.

And then she froze. The beam of her flashlight was shining on a large hand just above her head. A thick, powerful-looking wrist covered with a thin gold watch and crisp white cuff was holding the huge door shut.

Rachel dropped her head and closed her eyes. Keenan Oakes didn't have any manners after all. A shiver ran up her spine. He wasn't saying or doing anything. He was like a giant predator waiting to see what his prey would do next.

Feeling very much like a mouse under the claw of a cat, Rachel slowly turned around and pointed her light at the floor. Scuffed leather shoes with drying grass on them were the first things she saw. She slowly lifted the beam higher, all the while trying to fight down the panic that was making her tremble.

Damn, the man was big. She moved the light along muscled, jeans-clad legs, up over a flat stomach to a broad shirt-covered chest. She stopped and stared at that chest, nearly choking when she tried to swallow. Never had she seen such a formidable man so close up.

With all the nerve she could pull together, Rachel finally lifted the beam of her light above his chest. The man didn't so much as flinch. But Rachel did, all the blood draining from her face.

Keenan Oakes wasn't a demigod, he was a dark warrior with cold Atlantic-blue eyes pinning her immobile, looking at her from a hard, imperious face.

Rachel snapped off her flashlight.

If she didn't start breathing again, she was going to faint. Which she nearly did, when the man slowly lifted one large hand, took hold of her cap, and pulled it off.

Her heavy single braid of hair fell to her shoulder, her barrette hitting the thick oak door at her back with a loud clink, making her flinch again.

"What are you doing in my house?" he whispered, slowly winding the end of her braid around his hand. He tugged, just slightly, just enough to threaten without actually hurting her. "Who are you?"

Rachel couldn't have spoken if she'd wanted to.

His hand on her braid tightened. "What are you doing here?" he repeated, using her hair to tilt her head back.

The only light in the room came from the crack under the door she was pinned against, and Rachel had a moment's thanks that it wasn't enough to see his expression, for surely she would have really fainted then. As it was, his low and threatening voice, the smell of his pure male strength, and the heat of his tensed muscles radiating toward her were enough to make her question what she was about to do.

"Who are you?" he repeated.

Rachel slowly shifted her weight to her weak right leg and sturdy cane. "I am really sorry," she whispered.

And having given that sincere apology, Rachel drove her left knee into his groin with all the force of her weight behind it.

Keenan Oakes dropped like a stone. He fell to his knees with a groan of agony, his hand in her hair going limp and releasing her braid as he moved to cup himself.

The clasp on her barrette popped open and followed him to the floor, Keenan Oakes landing with a heavy thud and the barrette tumbling to the floor with a loud, resounding clank.

Rachel didn't wait to see if he stayed down. She whirled, opened the door, and ran for her life—aware that she'd just enraged a predator who would not suffer this second assault on his manhood quite so nobly.

Her right knee giving her hell for further abusing it, Rachel ran down the wide hall and turned the corner toward the grand staircase that led down to the first floor. She didn't take the stairs, but opened the secret panel at the top of them instead. She stepped into the blackness with all the confidence of someone who knew the passage well and quietly closed the panel behind her.

She took her first relieved breath in nearly an hour, placing her hand over her heart to keep it from jumping out of her chest. She was safe now. No one knew about these tunnels. Their secret had died with Thaddeus Lakeman three years ago and with the architect two weeks later.

Only the architect's daughters knew they existed.

The library had a secret passageway in it, but Rachel had opted to use this one above the stairwell instead. It was a much more direct route for leaving the mansion, much quicker to the outside entrance just above the Gulf of Maine.

Even though she had been caught sneaking around, she was glad she hadn't used the one in the library to escape. Keenan Oakes would have discovered the tunnels then, and Rachel still needed them to be secret.

She had to find Thadd's secret room and her father's blueprints for the boats. And there was still the matter of the fake emeralds in her pocket. Damn. She should have just left them in the vault.

Satisfied that her heart had settled into a steadier beat, Rachel turned her flashlight back on and carefully started down the steps that wound into the blackness beyond the beam of her light. Using her cane for support, she turned left, then right, walking along a narrow corridor that led to more steps. The smell of the ocean slowly grew stronger, and Rachel's spirits lifted.

She had escaped. And though she lived right next door, she doubted Keenan Oakes would recognize her if they did happen to meet in town. He couldn't have seen past the beam of her flashlight, its glare protecting her identity.

She finally reached the entrance to the cave and immediately shut off her flashlight. She worked the hidden latch from memory, opening the iron bars that protected the tunnels from unwanted intruders, both two- and four-legged. She slid through the bushes hiding the gate, careful not to disturb any branches, hearing the well-crafted lock clink softly behind her.

Rachel sat down on an outcrop of granite and slowly massaged her knee. It was throbbing like the devil now. She glared at the cane leaning against the rock beside her. The damn thing was going to be with her another week now, after tonight's little fiasco.

She turned and looked up, trying to see the mansion through the fog, and breathed in the chilly air and let it out with a softly spoken curse. She was going to have to visit Sub Rosa again. Soon. Before Keenan Oakes took inventory of all his newly inherited possessions.

Crouched on his hands and knees on the dusty carpet of the library, Kee took careful shallow breaths, waiting for the pain to ease enough so he could move.

The little witch had kneed him. She had come sneaking out of the closet, apologized, and then smartly taken him down.

Who the hell was she? And what was she doing in Sub Rosa?

One minute he'd been leaning against the desk in the dark, contemplating the fact that he'd just managed to lose another girlfriend, and the next thing he knew, he was watching a small black figure follow the beam of a flashlight across the library floor. Until she had turned around and faced him, he had thought his intruder was a kid—a teenage delinquent intent on pilfering from his new home.

But she was no kid. Not with that head of hair and those big—and scared—eyes. And on her limping escape down the hall, Kee had noticed quite clearly her unmistakably feminine, heart-shaped butt.

He reached over and picked up the cap on the floor beside his hand. The smell of roses drifted upward, and he lifted the black knit cap to his face.

Roses. He'd noticed the same smell earlier, when he had walked from the car into the house. Had his thief hidden in the bushes?

Impossible. Kee knew security systems, and Sub Rosa's system was state of the art. Until he had turned it off at the gate, nothing larger than a mouse could have gotten onto the property.

So where had she come from? And what had she wanted?

"Kee? Where's Joan go— Hey, man. What happened to you?"

Kee looked up to find Jason standing in the doorway with a surprised look on his face. "Did you catch her?" Kee asked.

Jason frowned at him. "Joan?" His eyes widened, and he grinned as he shook his head. "She did this to you?"

Kee finally stood up, the knit cap still in his hand. He held it up for Jason to see. "No, not Joan. The other woman."

"What other woman, boss?" Jason asked, suddenly serious.

Kee stiffly walked into the hall and looked toward the stairs. "Did you come up the front way?"

"Yes."

He turned back to Jason. "Then you must have seen her." He held the hat up again, at shoulder height this time. "A short woman, dressed in black, limping and using a cane. She headed for the stairs."

Jason shook his head.

"Well, dammit, find her! Before she leaves the grounds. I want to know what she was after."

Kee didn't have to ask twice. Jason all but ran in the same direction the intruder had taken.

"And find Duncan!" Kee shouted after him. "And tell him what happened."

That last order given, Kee hit the wall switch, flooding the library with light. He walked to the closet and looked inside, and immediately spotted the crumpled backpack sitting against the far wall. He picked it up and opened it, and pulled out an equally crumpled towel. Other than that, it was empty. He turned and looked around the library.

What had she been after?

Kee shook his head, disgusted with himself. If nothing else, his thief had certainly gotten an earful. She had been sitting in the closet the whole time Joan had methodically listed off each and every one of his impressive flaws.

Which was probably why the lady had been daring enough to take such a dangerous shot at him.

Kee slowly walked back to the library door and looked down the hall in the direction she had run. Where had she disappeared to that Jason hadn't seen her when he came up the stairs? Could she still be in the house?

Kee stepped into the hall, intending to find out, when his foot sent something skidding across the marble floor. He walked across the hall and picked up the object, turning it over in his hand to examine it.

It was a hair clip. Heavy, metal, in the shape of a lobster boat. The light glinted off the colorful enamel.

It wasn't a cheap hair clip, but a finely crafted piece of jewelry. The boat was white and red, with a delicate gold chain wrapped around the miniature pulley that hoisted the lobster traps onto the boat. Several tiny traps sat on the stern, and orange and green buoys littered the open deck just behind the tiny wheelhouse.

Delicate. Precise. Handcrafted.

Kee remembered then the sound of something hitting the floor at about the same time he had.

The hair clip belonged to his intruder.

Well, hell. What sort of thief wore expensive jewelry to a break-in? For that matter, what idiot broke into a house when she needed a cane just to get around?

Kee closed his fist over the clip and adjusted the front of his pants. He was going to ache like the devil for at least a week. His intruder, who'd barely come up to his chin, was suicidal. If she'd missed by even an inch, he might have instinctively retaliated and done her serious harm.

He adjusted his pants again, deciding he still might.

Just as soon as he discovered who she was.

Which he would. She was a local, considering her taste in hair clips. And the reckless lady didn't know it, but she had just crossed the path of a professional hunter.

Chapter Four

Rachel stopped rubbing her sore knee and straightened, tucking her now loose and tangled hair behind her ears so she could hear better. The wail of a siren sounded in the distance, a faint echo trying to pierce the thickening fog rolling in off the ocean.

She captured her breath and held it, and waited, straining to pinpoint the direction. The wail rose in volume, moving closer, traveling at an alarming speed toward her.

"You jerk! You called the police," she growled at the dark mansion above her, scrambling to her feet, groping for her cane. She had to get out of there, back to her house before they searched the grounds. She stumbled away from the hidden entrance of the tunnel, afraid to use her flashlight, even more afraid to get caught. She didn't want to find herself calling Maine's newest assistant attorney general to bail her out of jail. Nor was she eager to find herself facing Keenan Oakes again anytime soon.

And she wasn't sure which possibility scared her more.

The siren's shrill was louder now, pushing Rachel's nerves into a frenzy, quickening her flight. More sirens sounded in the distance, faint but growing stronger, also traveling from the center of town.

Well, shoot. The whole damn police force was coming to the jerk's rescue.

Her dragging right foot caught on a root just then, and Rachel stumbled, falling through nothing but air before painfully landing on the sharp granite rocks and prickly shrubs. She skidded and tumbled several feet before she was able to grab a fistful of rosebush and stop herself from sliding over the edge of the cliff. The tide calmly ebbed thirty feet beneath her, almost silent but for a rain of pebbles cascading into the water.

She couldn't move. Heck, she didn't dare breathe. That had been much too close for comfort.

The mounting cacophony of sirens reached a deafening pitch high on the bluff behind her. Rachel closed her eyes, wanting to weep with frustration.

She didn't deserve this. She was not a bad person. Granted, she had trespassed tonight, broken into Thadd's vault, and assaulted Keenan Oakes in his home, but she didn't need to live through the indignity of being hunted down like a criminal or the humiliation of being carted off to jail in handcuffs.

And she didn't need to fall off this damn cliff.

She was trying to make things right, dammit.

Rachel waited, fighting her panic until she could get her trembling under control. She didn't dare try her breathing exercise again; being dizzy while jutting over the edge of a cliff would not be wise. So she slowly began to count backward from one hundred instead. She was all the way down to fifty-eight before she realized that the sirens were growing weaker, moving away.

They hadn't stopped at Sub Rosa.

She lifted her head and pushed her hair behind her ears, then carefully wiggled backward, away from the edge of the cliff. The sirens had wound down, and the vehicles had stopped at Fisherman's Reach, the next cove over.

Rachel sidled back until she could safely sit up.

The smell of smoke drifted in on the fog, tickling her nose and settling the taste of acrid fumes on the back of her throat. She groped for her cane and found it several feet away, then used it to poke at the ground to find her flashlight. Wood clunked against metal, and she pulled the flashlight closer and picked it up, snapping it on and shining its beam at her feet.

Holy Mother Mary. Her toes still dangled over the edge of the cliff. Yes, that had definitely been too close.

Using her cane again, she hooked the handle around the trunk of a small pine tree and pulled herself farther up the sloping granite until she could grab the tree and work herself up to a standing position. Only then did she take inventory of her aches.

She was a battered mess. Her knee throbbed, her good ankle hurt, and the palms of her hands burned. She stuck her flashlight between her teeth and pulled on the sleeve of her right arm. The beam of light fell just above her wrist, revealing torn cloth and a thin bloody scrape.

It was time to face the ugly truth. As a criminal she was simply inept. Heck, she was self-destructing before her own eyes. There had to be a better way of making her father's sin disappear. His suggestion that she just toss everything into the ocean was beginning to have merit.

But Rachel knew she couldn't do it. Not to a collection of such beautiful works of art. Maybe she could pack it all up—once she found it—and drive the three hundred miles to Portland and anonymously leave it on the steps of the police station. That might be a solution.

But the way her luck was running, she'd probably get in an accident and be found with a small fortune in stolen art in her truck. That would certainly help Willow's career.

Rachel brushed a tangle of hair out of her face with a slightly less trembling hand and blew out a sigh heavy with self-pity. She was stuck with the option of returning to Sub Rosa and quietly finding Thadd's secret room, and filling it with the rest of her dad's stolen possessions.

But first she had to make good her escape tonight.

The scent of smoke was growing stronger, swirling in on the quickening breeze. It stung her eyes and smelled of diesel fumes. An explosion suddenly rocked the air, and Rachel instinctively flinched, only to gasp at the sight of the fireball that rose on the coastline to the east. The fog crackled and brightened with churning, angry orange light.

Rachel stumbled up the shrub-clogged bluff, every ache in her body forgotten as adrenaline shot through her veins again. She reached the bulging headland that guarded Sub Rosa from the sea and watched in horror as the remains of a fishing boat burned on its mooring.

The blue and red strobes of rescue lights added to the laser display coming from the cove. The fog flashed, absorbed, and reflected a scene of chaos.

A faint noise caught Rachel's attention then, high on

the cliff at the base of Sub Rosa. She whirled, suddenly remembering her own little problem and urgent need to get home.

Rachel turned her flashlight back on and more carefully made her way back along the cliff path and through the woods in the direction of her house. It was less than a quarter of a mile, but it was treacherous going, the thickly filtered moonlight offering little help.

Despite being careful and trying not to let panic rush her, she still slipped several times, and fell yet again, landing on her good knee with enough force to start it aching as well. She eventually made it to level ground and the woods that separated her home from Sub Rosa.

She was just within sight of the yellow glow of her porch light when she heard men's voices softly traveling through the swirling fog, making it impossible to tell their direction.

Rachel recklessly quickened her pace. She ran and stumbled along, shutting off her flashlight so she wouldn't give her location away.

The sudden snarl of a dog behind her scared Rachel so badly she went crashing to the ground with a violent jolt, her wrist hitting a tree stump and ripping a cry of agony from her throat.

The next snarl sounded right beside her ear. Rachel twisted and flailed, trying to wiggle away from the beast.

"Back off, Mickey!" a man shouted from beside her. The night fog suddenly glowed with arcing beams of light.

Rachel turned onto her stomach, cradled her bruised wrist in her hand, and buried her face in her arms. "Go away. Leave me alone," she told the men, not looking at them. "Go away."

"Lady? Are you okay?" one of them asked, hunching down beside her.

Hell no, she wasn't okay. Her right knee felt as if it were on fire and was now so intensely painful that she was having to grit her teeth not to scream.

"Go away!" she hissed again, pulling herself into a tighter ball when the man touched her shoulder.

"Jesus, lady. We can't just leave you here," he insisted, again ignoring her plea by trying to turn her over.

Rachel came up fighting. She swung her cane and connected with something solid. The guy leaning over her grunted in surprise, but that was about all the reaction she got. Three flashlight beams glared at her, and she blinked at their brightness, raising her good hand to see, still holding her cane like a weapon.

"Who are ya?" another man asked, hunching down beside her and speaking with a brogue that was almost charming.

Still, she wasn't foolish enough to let down her guard.

"My name is Rachel Foster. I live over there," she told him, using her raised hand to point at her distant porch light.

"This is Sub Rosa land," he said.

Rachel glared at him. "I know that."

"You're trespassing," another man said from somewhere behind his flashlight.

All she could see were his feet, but Rachel turned her glare in his direction. "I am well aware of my property lines."

"Then what are ya doing here?" the man with the brogue asked, reaching for her cradled arm. Rachel turned slightly and tucked it tighter against her body.

"I'm searching for my cat," she told him, staring him right in the eye as she lied.

Not that she knew where she got the nerve. The man looked as if he ate kittens for breakfast. He was positively huge and had a face that belonged on a wanted poster.

"Did Mickey bite ya?" he asked, taking her arm and pushing up her sleeve. "There's blood."

Rachel tugged her arm back again and rubbed her wrist. "No, he didn't bite me. That's a cut from when I fell. Now go away and leave me alone."

Not one of them budged.

"You are the trespassers, gentlemen," she told them, using the term grudgingly. "No one lives at Sub Rosa. And the sheriff keeps close watch on the place, so you'd better get moving."

The two men next to her grinned.

"Well, Keenan Oakes moved in tonight," the second man said as he snatched her cane out of her hand and held it up to the light. "What's this?"

"That's mine," Rachel said, grabbing it back. "Now that we've established ourselves as neighbors, would you kindly leave me alone. I want to go home."

"What about your cat?" one of the men behind the flashlights asked.

"He can just spend the night outside," she told him, scowling into the woods for effect. "It will serve him right."

"We'll help ya home then," the brogue guy offered, reaching out as if to pick her up.

Rachel rapped his hand with her cane. "No. I don't want any help. I just want to be left alone. Go away!" she repeated through gritted teeth.

Both men grinned again. The second man grabbed her

cane, and the first man grabbed her under the arms and had her standing before she could stifle a scream.

"Ya're hurt," he said, still holding her up.

Rachel rolled her eyes. These guys were denser than dirt. "Of course I'm hurt. That vicious dog nearly tackled me. And if you don't leave me alone, I'm going to sue Keenan Oakes for every cent he's got."

He let her go with a chuckle. Rachel barely caught herself from falling, grabbing his arm for balance, and felt solid muscle beneath her hand. She lifted her chin. By God, she would not let these giants intimidate her.

She held out her hand for her cane. The other man handed it to her, also smiling. He nodded as he relinquished it. "We're very sorry about that, Miss Foster. Or is it Mrs.? Is there someone at home who can help you?"

Rachel didn't answer him. Using all of her concentration not to cry out in agony, she carefully turned toward home.

"Wait. Here. Take this flashlight at least," the first guy offered, holding out his hand.

She stopped and turned. "Thank you," she said, taking it from him. If it would get rid of these guys, she'd gladly take all their flashlights.

She briefly shone it back at the group. The dog beside them was huge, dusty gray in color, and nearly invisible in the fog. He was staring at her, his head cocked to the side, watching her with eyes that glowed like pins of starlight. Rachel shuddered and turned her beam on the men.

They were all brutes. And in the shadows of the night, they were every woman's worst nightmare. She forced herself to smile at the lot of them.

"Tell Mr. Oakes welcome to the neighborhood," she said, just before she turned around, gritted her teeth, and started for home again.

Kee stood in the shadow of the woods as he surveyed Rachel Foster's house with a discerning eye. "It looks quiet. She must have gone to bed already," he said to Duncan, inching his way up to the edge of the lawn.

It was a good-looking house, well maintained and sturdily built, sitting on a shallow bluff overlooking the ocean. There was a large barn near the woods in the back, with a motor home parked off to the side. The truck parked in the driveway was a late-model sport-utility vehicle. There was a sea kayak tied to the top of it.

Kee let his gaze roam the grounds, searching for anything that would give him a clue to who else lived here, just in case his background check on Rachel Foster had somehow overlooked a live-in boyfriend. He didn't want or need any more surprises tonight.

Kee knew Rachel Foster was thirty-one years old, the elder daughter of Frank and Marian Foster, and a licensed architect who now worked in a library. He also knew that Rachel Foster knew Sub Rosa better than any other living person.

Guessing the reason for Kee's cautious approach, Duncan chuckled under his breath. "Peter tried to find out if someone was home waiting for her. She wouldn't answer him," he told Kee, his own eyes scanning the area.

Kee shot him a hard look at the reminder that his men had let the woman slip through their hands. "Which means she probably lives alone," Kee said. "Women get in the habit of not advertising that fact." He gave Duncan a

58 *Janet Chapman*

grin. "It's past time I properly introduced myself to Rachel Foster, wouldn't you say?"

"Dammit, Kee. It's two in the morning. This can wait until tomorrow," Duncan said.

Kee stepped onto the lawn. "No. We do it tonight. I want to know what the lady was doing at Sub Rosa."

Kee didn't wait for Duncan to respond. He crossed the lawn and headed for the house, guided by the soft yellow glow of the porch light.

The first thing both men noticed as they approached was that the screen door was shut, but the inside door was not. The second thing they realized was that they could hear soft sobs coming from the dark interior of the house.

Without making a sound, Duncan slipped around to the other side of the house as Kee quietly mounted the porch stairs, both of them drawing guns from the backs of their belts.

Kee silently approached the door. He slowly pulled the screen door open and used his foot to push the interior door wider. He listened for a full minute for any other sounds coming from deeper within the house. When he decided there was no one else there, he eased his way inside, felt for a switch, and flipped it, flooding the room with light. A panicked gasp rose from the floor, and Kee found himself pointing his gun at the woman he'd met in his library less than an hour ago.

She was sitting on the floor of the kitchen, her scared hazel-green eyes the size of dinner plates. Her braid had completely unraveled, and her waist-length brown hair was a wild tangle of curls. There were mud stains on both of her knees and most of her sweater, and pine needles and dirt made a trail across the floor to where she sat.

In one hand she held her cane up as a puny defense, and in the other one she held a small brown bottle that looked as if it came from a pharmacy. Kee lowered his gun just as Duncan stepped into the kitchen behind him.

"Go away," the woman hoarsely croaked, waving her cane threateningly. "Get out of my house."

Kee slipped his gun into the back of his belt, stepped forward, and pulled the cane out of her hand. She gasped in surprise and tried to scoot farther away, but she stopped and cried out. She grabbed her right knee, dropping her bottle of pills on the floor.

Kee hunched down and picked up the bottle, turning the label to read it. She'd been after some pretty powerful pain pills. The bottle was covered with dirt and looked as if Rachel Foster had spent the last half hour trying to open it.

"Get her a glass of water," he said to Duncan as he twisted the cap and poured not one pill, as the directions suggested, but two pills into his hand.

Duncan opened several cupboards before he finally found a glass. He filled it with water and hunkered down on the other side of the woman. Kee took one of her slightly trembling hands and put the pills in it.

Without saying a word, she quickly popped the pills into her mouth and reached for the glass. Duncan didn't let it go, but held it to her lips.

"Thank you," she whispered when she finished drinking, looking down at her lap.

"Tell me what's wrong," Kee softly ordered, turning his gaze to her legs, seeing that the right knee she was holding looked larger than the left.

"I'll be okay in a minute," she said, not looking at him, her voice barely audible. "I've hurt my knee again."

Kee looked at Duncan, only to be surprised by his expression. Duncan Ross, the most lethal, battle-hardened mercenary he knew, was looking at Rachel Foster with all the sympathy of a child watching a wounded pet.

Kee reached over and covered Rachel's hand on her knee with his own. "Why don't you let us have a look at it?" he asked, gently tugging her hand away.

She pushed him away.

"Then let us take you to the hospital," he offered, withdrawing only enough to grab her chin and lift her face.

"No. Go away," she said, staring him full in the face, her gorgeous, tear-soaked hazel-green eyes defiant and determined.

Kee smiled at her as he shook his head. "We're not going away, Miss Foster. Not until you tell me what you were doing in my library earlier."

She gasped and pulled her chin free. "I wasn't in your library!" she hissed, looking as if he'd just accused her of robbing the local bank. "Now get out of my house before I have you arrested for breaking and entering."

Kee sat back on his heels and stared at her. He was amazed. He had her dead to rights. She'd been in his house not an hour ago, and she was threatening to have *him* arrested. He grabbed her chin again.

"You dare lie to me?" he asked in disbelief. "You were waiting in the closet until you thought the coast was clear, and then you came sneaking out and attacked me."

Her eyes rounded, and she tried to pull away, but Kee would not release his hold on her face. She whimpered, paling to the roots of her dirty brown hair as she grabbed at his wrist.

"Kee. Come on, man. Ya're scaring her," Duncan said, moving to intervene.

Kee turned an incredulous look on Duncan. "She's lying. She was in the library," he told him. "I want her to admit it."

Duncan grabbed Kee's arm just below the woman's grip. "It doesn't matter right now," Duncan softly told him. "Ya can battle it out with her later, when she's a more worthy opponent. Let's just make her comfortable."

Kee looked from Duncan to Rachel Foster. She was pale enough to pass out, but her eyes were still snapping at him. He couldn't suppress a smile. The lady had grit.

He let go of her face and gently scooped her up in his arms and stood. She gasped again, hard enough to move his hair.

"Put me down!" she snapped, her eyes level with his. "I'm too heavy. You're going to drop me."

It was Duncan who laughed at that ridiculous statement. "Kee won't drop ya, Miss Foster. Ya're a puny thing," the man thought to assure her.

She turned her glare on him.

Kee didn't wait for her to protest any further. Undecided about whether he did want to drop her pretty little lying butt on the floor—or kiss her pretty little lying lips—he silently carried her around the kitchen island and into her living room.

"I want you out of my house!" she said again, the color returning to her face.

He stopped in front of her couch. "You do seem a bit heavy," he lied. He hefted her in his arms. "You're not by any chance weighted down with booty you stole from my house, are you?"

That accusation changed her expression. "I was not in

your house tonight. I hate it. I hope it falls into the sea."

Kee shook his head, smiling at her mutinous glare, which he could see quite clearly now that Duncan had found the living room lights. "Ah, Rachel, is that any attitude for an architect to have?" he asked, laughing out loud when she gasped again.

"You know I'm an architect?"

"You're Frank Foster's daughter. I was told to look you up if I had any questions about Sub Rosa. That there isn't a nook or cranny you don't know about. If I have any problems with the place, I should check with you."

She closed her eyes. "Then I suggest you burn it down to its foundation," she whispered.

Kee sobered as he bent over and gently set her down. He braced one hand against the back of the sofa and stared directly into her defiant eyes. "I understand why you'd like to see my home in ruins, Rachel. I know the story of your father and mother and my great-uncle Thaddeus. But that doesn't explain what you were doing there tonight."

She stared back at him, unblinking.

"How about if I'm just being curious and promise not to press charges? Will you tell me why you were in the library?"

She dropped her gaze to her lap.

Kee straightened and headed back into the kitchen.

"Are ya sure it's her?" Duncan asked, looking over his shoulder at Rachel as he followed Kee.

"It's her. I'm not likely to forget the woman," he confirmed.

"But how did she get out of the mansion so quickly then?" Duncan asked as he walked to the door and looked toward the cliff path they had used.

Kee also looked toward Sub Rosa. He could barely make out the dark silhouette of the soaring roofline of the mansion. "There must be a tunnel that leads directly out to the cliffs. She'd know about it if there was."

"What are ya going to do with her?"

Kee looked over at Duncan and grinned. "Since it might be Mickey's fault she hurt her knee again, I thought we might start acting like neighbors. We should probably bring her back to Sub Rosa once those pills take effect, don't you think?"

Duncan shot Kee a grin in answer, then sobered. "She'd been sitting on the floor for almost an hour, in a lot of pain. Why didn't she call for an ambulance?" he asked.

Kee waved his hand at the mud on the kitchen floor. "My guess is she didn't want to explain the condition she was in, especially if she thought I had called the police. Being dressed like a burglar at two in the morning and being covered with mud and torn up by rose thorns would be a little hard to explain."

Duncan nodded as he opened the freezer and began rummaging around for some ice. Kee walked to the sink, found a towel, and ran it under the water until it was soaked warm. "Here," he said, tossing another towel to Duncan. "Wrap the ice in that and bring it into the living room." He shot Duncan a grin. "While I try to talk a spitting polecat out of her pants."

He whistled as he walked back into the living room and laughed when he saw that Rachel Foster had succumbed to her late-night adventure and powerful narcotics.

It would definitely be neighborly of him to bring her back to Sub Rosa and give her a chance to finish what she'd started tonight.

Chapter Five

There was an elephant sitting on her knee. There was no other explanation for the heavy, dull, throbbing pain that made Rachel keep her eyes closed as she groaned in agony.

Why did she hurt so much? And not just her knee. Her right elbow burned, her hands hurt, and her left wrist was stiff and aching.

Rachel groaned again when she remembered what had happened last night: her nearly disastrous attempt to return the stolen art, several men with deep voices and laughing eyes, and a very large, scary dog.

And an even larger, even scarier Keenan Oakes.

He had silently entered her home with the stealth of a ghost. One minute she'd been trying to get the damned childproof cap off her pain pills, and the next minute she'd been looking down the wrong end of a gun that had a barrel big enough for a squirrel to hide in.

But that miniature cannon hadn't looked anywhere near as lethal as the man holding it.

The picture in the *Island Gazette* hadn't come close to capturing the real Keenan Oakes. She'd stood nose to chest with the man in his darkened library, and Rachel had known immediately that Thadd's great-nephew was far more dangerous than even Willow had thought.

He hadn't listened to her demands to leave any better than his band of bullies had. Rachel groaned to herself again. He'd come into her house and taken over, popping pills into her and carrying her to the couch before abandoning her there once he realized she wasn't going to admit to anything.

Dammit, he knew she had been in his library.

And he wanted to know why.

Well, she was sticking to her story. Never in a million years would she admit to kneeing the man in his groin. She may be foolish on occasion, but she was not suicidal.

Rachel tentatively moved her shoulders to see what other parts of her body were going to protest. Her groan of agony turned into a startled scream when a rock-solid arm came under her back and lifted her into a sitting position.

She snapped her eyes open and found herself staring into the face of the devil himself. Laughing Atlantic-blue eyes stared back at her.

"Take these. They'll help."

"You!"

His eyes crinkled at the corners, amusement lighting them. Along with something else. Something very male. Keenan Oakes seemed quite pleased with her reaction.

Rachel ignored the pills he was holding up to her lips

and opened her mouth to tell him—yet again—to get out of her house. Then she realized she wasn't on the couch in her living room. She was at Sub Rosa!

She turned back to ask him what she was doing there, but he shoved the pills into her mouth before she could speak. His hand quickly returned with a glass of water, which he all but poured down her throat.

"Don't worry," he assured her, chuckling at her alarm. "It's just aspirin this time. Those pills of yours could bring down a horse, and I'm wanting you to stay awake this time."

He still didn't let her go. He wrapped his other arm around her shoulders and held her up while he used his free hand to arrange the pillows behind her back. He carefully eased her into a sitting position, then straightened.

Not once did he take his gaze off hers. Rachel felt like a doe trapped in the lights of an oncoming disaster.

Panic welled up inside her. She couldn't be here. Not in Sub Rosa. And not at his mercy. She was the daughter of the man who had murdered his great-uncle. She was also the woman who had literally brought him to his knees last night.

She had to get out of there. Now. Even if it meant dragging herself home through the fires of pain.

"Don't even think it," he said softly, his eyes sparkling with challenge.

Rachel realized he'd read her panic and her need to escape. She broke off her stare and looked down at the blankets. "You can't keep me here," she said, her voice sounding firm to her, now that she wasn't looking at him.

"Who's going to stop me?"

She snapped her head back up. He was standing with

his feet spread and his arms crossed over his chest and a lazy, indolent look on his face. The man was no more worried about kidnaping her than he was about the sun falling out of the sky.

Rachel stared at him, seeing him clearly for the first time in full light, without drugs fogging her brain. Holy Mother Mary. Keenan Oakes could be a marauding Viking who conquered all he could see, for all his modern-day trappings. He had to stand six-foot-three if he stood an inch. His black hair was just as unruly up close as it had been in his picture. His face hadn't seen a razor in several days, and still the soft dark stubble did nothing to ease the sharp planes of his face.

He wore a tattered gray sweatshirt that pulled against his massive chest and well-worn jeans that hugged a trim waist and muscled thighs. Rachel wondered dizzily if Keenan Oakes had to turn sideways to walk through most doorways.

She lifted her chin. "I'm going to call the sheriff if you don't let me go," she told him, squaring her shoulders and trying to puff herself up to whatever threatening size she could.

The corner of his mouth lifted. "The phones aren't working. They won't be on until Friday."

Rachel glared at him. It was Tuesday. Or was it Wednesday?

"Then you can just have one of your brutes take me home," she countered, keeping her chin high, stiffening it so it wouldn't quiver.

He slowly shook his head as he unfolded his arms and stepped back to the bed. Rachel pressed herself against the pillows. But she couldn't avoid him when he reached out and took her chin in his hand, forcing her to look at him.

"Tell me what you were doing in my library, and I'll take you home," he said, his voice a whisper of determination.

"I . . . I wasn't in your library," she said hoarsely.

He tightened his grip, ever so slightly. "I'll forget what happened if you just tell me what you were doing there."

Rachel barely stifled a snort. "No man ever forgets something like that," she foolishly blurted out without thinking.

His eyes narrowed.

"I'm not saying I attacked you," she rushed to clarify, pulling her chin free and lifting it again. "But if I had, then you're not likely to just forget it."

He smiled. "What sort of transgression are we talking about, Miss Foster? I don't remember mentioning the nature of your assault."

Dammit. He had told her, hadn't he?

"I-I'm assuming it was nasty," she whispered, trying to sink back into the pillows as he moved even closer. "Since you're so big, and I'm just a woman, and I . . ."

Her voice trailed off the moment his lips touched hers.

And just like her words, her ability to think vanished at the contact.

Oh, God. Oh, God. The man's mouth was not the least bit hard. His lips were soft, unbelievably warm, and so damn sensual, Rachel felt a tingle all the way down to her toes.

He used his tongue to trace her lips while he claimed them, and moved his hand to the back of her head, cupping her gently but firmly, not allowing her to escape.

Dangerous. Lethal. Overwhelming.

Those words kept bouncing around in Rachel's brain, trying to urge her into action. She had to do something. She could not let this guy take such liberties with her mouth.

Rachel pushed at his chest and immediately cried out.

He pulled back and looked down. "Your left wrist is bruised," he said, carefully taking her hand and holding it, his voice utterly clam, as if that kiss had never happened.

Rachel took a bit longer to gather her wits. Yes, she could see the bandage covering her left wrist and most of her fingers. His hand dwarfed hers. It was huge and powerful-looking and so utterly male, it was all she could do not to shiver.

"What were you after, Miss Foster?"

"I wasn't in your library last night," she repeated, this time by rote, still focused on the size of her hand in his.

He sighed, the feel of him wafting over her face, reminding her of his kiss. Her cheeks heated.

"You . . . intrigue me, Rachel Foster."

"Wh-what?" she whispered, snapping her gaze to his. She didn't need to be a rocket scientist to know what he meant. Not after that kiss.

He cocked his head as he watched her, seemingly fascinated by her reaction. "I came to that conclusion just as I finished braiding your hair." He reached up and pulled her braid over her shoulder, watching the end curls slowly wrap around his fingers.

Rachel jerked her head back, grabbing her braid and hiding her treacherous curls in her fist. Their eyes met again, and she became aware of a heat between them so intense, it even singed *his* face with two flags of color.

"You can't . . . you can't . . . you braided my hair?" she finished on a squeak.

He nodded. And then he leaned down and kissed her again. But not her mouth this time. He simply, sensually used those remarkable lips to caress her cheek.

Fire shot all the way down to the pit of Rachel's stomach. Oh, Lord. His causing her bodily harm had just become the least of her worries.

He pulled back and stood up. Rachel saw the light of promise in his steady Atlantic-blue eyes. He winked at her, turned on his heel, and headed for the door.

"Wait!"

He stopped, his hand on the doorknob, and looked at her.

"What—what time is it?" she asked, looking at the closed hurricane shutters on the windows. She couldn't tell if it was night or day outside. The only light in the room came from the bedside lamp.

He followed her line of vision, then looked back at her. "Does it really matter, Miss Foster?" he asked, just before he opened the door and walked out.

Kee stood in the hall, his head thrown back and his eyes closed, listening for any sound coming from the room he'd just left. But all he could hear was the rush of his own blood raging through his body. Kee knew that if he held out his hand, it would be shaking.

Rachel Foster. She'd done this to him—with her snapping eyes that were more scared than brave, with her indignant expression that hid the heart of a very poor liar, and with her wildly curling hair that drove him into a sexual frenzy whenever he looked at it. Hell. He'd been as hard as a stone the entire time he'd worked on getting the tangles out of it.

The lady may have bruised his manhood last night, but she sure as hell hadn't broken it.

Damn. This was not going to be as easy as he'd thought. Rachel Foster may be temporarily in his clutches, but he was the one who was caught. From the moment she'd stood facing him in the library, every damn hormone in his body had stood at attention.

Just before she'd kneed him into oblivion.

It took a brave person to do what Rachel Foster had done. Kee admired her for that. And then she had lied to his men and to him—and right to their faces, by God.

She was going to stick to her story, Kee knew. Neither threats nor kidnaping nor kisses would make her admit that she had been snooping around Sub Rosa last night.

Kee took a calming breath and rubbed his hands over his face, then pulled them away. He smiled as he started down the hall.

The woman was all but brimming with passion. Kee could see it in her eyes and feel it in her body every time he touched her—a sensuous energy simmering inside her that would be nearly untamable when he finally brought it to the surface.

And he would.

Hopefully in his bed.

Kee had already decided, sometime in the wee hours of the morning, that he wanted Rachel Foster.

She would be reluctant, though. She had heard every one of his flaws from Joan—Rachel knew he was an insensitive jerk, a bastard, and a caveman.

But his biggest obstacle was linked to the history of his

new home. Rachel was going to balk at the idea of having an affair with the new lord of Sub Rosa. Daughters tended to shy away from following in their mothers' footsteps, especially when those footsteps had led to tragedy.

Kee didn't care. What had happened between Marian Foster and good old Thaddeus Lakeman was none of his business.

The fact that Frank Foster had shot them both didn't particularly bother Kee, either. That was history. Other than being the catalyst that had brought him here, it didn't really involve him.

He had a tendency to be linearly focused when he was on a hunt. That's what made him so successful in his line of work. He always got his man.

This time, however, his target was female.

Well, so be it. As far as Kee was concerned, the game was officially on. Hell, he'd even been so kind as to warn his opponent this time. What more could the lady ask for?

Kee and Jason and Duncan returned to her bedroom four hours later. Kee nudged Mickey away from the door. "Did our guest try to leave?" he asked the wolf, knowing damn well she had, and that she'd discovered Mickey guarding her escape route.

Mickey looked up with a lupine grin, then trotted down the hall toward the stairs.

Kee opened the door to find Rachel sprawled on her back, her arms thrown over her head, one leg hanging out over the edge of the bed. He hadn't lied when he told her they were only aspirins he'd given her, but it seemed the lady was still suffering from a narcotic hangover.

"Is the lass awake?" Duncan asked, stepping into the room, Jason right behind him.

Kee looked down at Rachel and softly shook her. He turned back to his men and shook his head.

Jason stepped closer. "You've got to wake her up. The cellar's flooding at the rate of a foot an hour," he said, his voice laced with impatience. And frustration. Kee knew that Jason was more mad at himself than at this newest crisis they were facing.

"We've tried every damn valve and switch we can get our hands on," Duncan added, also walking up to the bed to peer down at Rachel before he looked back at Kee. "We can't stop it. The subbasement's nearly full. In another hour this damned overdressed tomb will be floating off its foundation."

It was a good thing Kee was watching his houseguest as Duncan spoke or he would have missed it. Rachel Foster was playing possum. Her nose twitched as she fought to stifle a smile.

"Miss Foster's been on some mighty powerful drugs," Kee drawled, crossing his arms over his chest. "And she's had a hard night, what with breaking and entering, beating me up, and then trying to outrun Mickey. We'll probably have to throw her into the subbasement to wake her up."

And there it was again. Another twitch. Only this time she was trying to stifle a frown.

Lord, he was enjoying this game.

It was Duncan who gasped for her. "Hell, boss, we can't do that," his second-in-command growled, his stance defensive, as if to protect their guest. "She'd drown. Let's just try getting some coffee down her."

Kee witnessed a shudder run through Rachel.

"A cold shower would work," Jason interjected, sounding slightly frantic as he looked at his watch. "Let's just get her up. The tide's rising as we speak."

Duncan reached for Rachel, and Kee simply waited. As soon as the man's hands touched the blankets, her eyes shot open. "I'm awake!" she shouted.

The two startled men jumped back.

Jason recovered first. "The tide's flooding the basement," he told her. "I can't get the water shut off."

Rachel tried to scoot into an upright position against the headboard. Duncan reached out and lifted her there. She squeaked, her eyes going wide with surprise.

"Miss Foster. Did you hear me? The basement's going to be flooded in less than an hour," Jason repeated, leaning down to look her in the eye.

Judging by her calm, if amused, expression, Kee surmised they were not in danger of drowning.

She lifted her good hand and waved Jason's concern away. "You must have found the turbine valves," she said, giving him a reassuring smile.

He answered her with a frown. "What turbine?"

"In the subbasement. When the system's turned on, Sub Rosa uses tidal water to generate power. If the tide's coming in, the reservoir is filling. The fall and rise of the tide turns the turbines, creating electricity," she explained.

Kee was impressed—with her and with her father's genius. He'd wondered what the electricity bill was going to be for this monstrosity. Thaddeus Lakeman had been rich, but he'd also been smart.

Jason's eyebrows rose into his hairline. "Sub Rosa generates its own power?" he asked, his awe as great as his glee.

Jason was the engineer in the group. Kee relied on him to keep the computers and mechanical side of his business running smoothly. Jason was a soldier first, but a damn handy one.

"Of course," Rachel answered, smiling hugely now, as if the man's joy were contagious. "It would cost a fortune to run this place otherwise. Sub Rosa's hooked into the local grid, and has been running on purchased power for the last three years. You must have accidentally started up the tidal generator."

Jason stepped closer to the bed. "Could you maybe come downstairs and show me how to get the storm shutters open?" He shook his head. "That control room looks like it belongs in a nuclear power plant."

Kee wholeheartedly agreed. He'd taken one look inside the previously locked chamber in the basement and hadn't been able to stifle a shudder. He'd quickly called Jason and left him to figure things out.

Kee stepped up to the bed. "You feeling up to a chair ride?" he asked, smiling at the way she refused to look at him.

She shrugged. "Not really."

He'd expected that answer. He started to reach for her, but stopped when Matthew came rushing into the room, out of breath and holding a squirming, hissing bundle in his arms. Peter was not two steps behind him, also carrying something.

Kee shook his head in disgust. Two more of his battle-hardened men had just bit the dust. They were both grinning like old women, their expressions so eager to please it was painful to look at.

"We found your cat!" Matthew said, just as the jacket

in his arms exploded. Fur and claws and fangs came fly-ing into the room ahead of him, leaving bloody claw tracks on his neck. An enraged cat landed on all fours and ran under the bed.

Kee looked over to see Rachel wearing the most horri-fied, incredulous look he'd ever seen. She darted a glance at Duncan, then at Jason, and then at Kee before she looked back at Matthew.

"Th-thank you," she said in a whisper. "I was very worried about him."

"He's a girl!" Peter interjected, walking up to the bed and setting his burden down more carefully. "He's got kittens."

Kee watched Rachel eye the squirming, mewling bun-dle as if she expected snakes to come slithering out of it.

"Yeah, Miss Foster. You're a mama," Matthew said, his harsh features softening as he leaned over and opened the moving jacket on the bed.

Three little faces blinked up at him.

"Their eyes are open," Jason observed, turning to stare at Rachel. "How long has your cat been missing?"

Seemingly at a loss for words, Rachel darted a look at Kee before she turned back to the kittens. "Ah . . . about . . . ah . . . ten days?" she said, ending her claim on a question.

"Then why were ya so determined to find him last night?" Duncan asked, his eyes narrowing with suspicion.

"Yes, Miss Foster, why is that?" Kee asked, making sure there was no sign of amusement in his voice.

"Ah, well, I was getting really worried about him. I mean her," she said, not looking up. "And I thought I'd have a better chance of finding him at night."

"What's his name, then?" Matthew asked, the softness leaving his face with each contradictory word she spoke.

"Mabel," she blurted, her cheeks nearly crimson now.

"So you knew he was a girl cat?" Peter asked, glaring at her with enough force to push her off the bed.

Kee almost laughed out loud. Rachel was beginning to squirm worse than the kittens. She opened her mouth to answer Peter, when the cat in question suddenly jumped up on the bed. The poor harried mother immediately curled herself around her babies, then turned unblinking, threatening eyes on the men.

"Don't you want to pat her?" Matthew asked. "You haven't seen her in ten days."

"He's—she's a little riled right now," Rachel said, balling her hands into fists and tucking them a safe distance away from the cat. "What I'd really like is for you gentlemen to leave us alone for our reunion."

Kee grabbed the wheelchair he'd brought up earlier and pushed it up beside the bed. "I think—Mabel, is it?—would be better left alone to calm down," he said, and he reached down to lift Rachel off the bed.

She squeaked and tried to swat him away, but he lifted her into his arms and straightened.

"If you want to eat, lady, you're going to have to earn your keep," he told her, ignoring her glare. "This place is like a tomb with the storm shutters closed. It's time we put you to work."

"I really *will* flood the cellar," she threatened, her mutinous eyes snapping at him.

Kee lost his humor. "No you won't." Kee set her in the wheelchair and began to wheel his guest to the hall, but stopped the moment he realized she was staring at his men.

"Oh, forgive me," he said, waving at them. "This is Duncan," he told her as Duncan nodded. "And Matthew and Peter, who found your cat," he explained as Matthew and Peter nodded. "And Jason is the one dancing from foot to foot, eager to get his hands on that control room. Gentlemen, this is Rachel Foster."

Wide-eyed, Rachel nodded with each introduction, then said rather hesitantly, "It-it's nice to meet you."

Stifling a chuckle, Kee wheeled Rachel into the hall, both of them ignoring the small parade that formed behind them. He pushed back a smile when, glancing back into the room, he saw the slowly relaxing mother cat begin to wash her babies. Rachel's lies were catching up with her. If she'd ever seen that cat before today, Kee would eat the scrawny thing.

"Where are you taking me?" she asked, trying to turn to scowl at him.

"To the stairs. Unless you're ready to show me the elevators the blueprints referred to. The choice is yours, Miss Foster, the elevator or my arms?"

"They're at the end of the hall," she snapped.

Jason turned and headed down the hall, the other men following behind. Kee rolled Rachel after them.

"There's nothing here but a blank wall," Jason said, staring at the oak wainscoting.

"Thadd didn't want to spoil the ambience of the house," Rachel explained as they came up beside the men. "He hid the elevators. Just turn the bottom of that wall sconce."

Jason reached up and gently twisted the bottom flange of the wall light, and the wooden panel they were all facing silently glided open, revealing a very modern, very small elevator car.

Four sets of male eyebrows rose, and Kee barely stifled a snort. He looked down to find Rachel grinning.

"There's not enough room for all of us," she said.

"Where does it go?" Jason asked, stepping in and looking at the control panel.

"It reaches the basement and all the way up to the third floor. There's another one just like it in the west wing."

"Jason, you and Duncan meet us in the basement control room. Peter, find Luke, and both of you see about rousting up some food. Matthew, find a box and some kitty litter for Miss Foster's pet. Where's Mickey?"

Kee saw Rachel stiffen at the mention of his own pet. He pushed her into the elevator.

"He's outside. We shut the door in his face, because he was scaring Mabel," Peter said, turning to leave.

"Leave him there, but find him some dinner as well. Then maybe he'll feel less like eating our neighbor and her cat," Kee added, just before he pushed the DOWN button and the door closed.

The nearly silent hum of the elevator was all the sound in the car for the beginning of the descent. Finally, without looking up, Rachel spoke.

"He . . . he's a wicked big dog," she whispered.

"Actually, he's a wolf," Kee explained, watching her stiffen again. "His name is Mickey Mouse, and he belongs to my daughter."

She turned her head to look up at him, her expression horrified. "You gave a wolf as a pet to a little girl? You aren't worried he'll eat her?"

Kee shrugged. "She'll probably eat him first."

Her expression turned to a haughty glare. "You don't worry much about anything, do you? Like the rules against keeping endangered wild animals and kidnaping your neighbor?"

He shrugged again, biting back a smile. "Not particularly."

"You're very arrogant."

"Thank you."

"It wasn't a compliment," she snapped, turning back to face front.

The elevator stopped and the door opened, but Kee didn't wheel her out. "What about you, Miss Foster? Do you always follow the rules?"

"Of course."

"Last I knew, breaking and entering was illegal," he said.

"Which is why I don't do it," she shot back.

He chuckled aloud as he finally pushed the wheelchair into the basement. He turned down the long, wide corridor and opened the last door on the right.

"Why have the control room for the entire house way down here?" he asked, as they entered the room full of computers and panels. It really did look like a nuclear power plant.

"There's no need to come down here that often," she answered, rolling her chair forward to reach one of the consoles. "Once Sub Rosa's up and running, everything can be controlled by the computers in the kitchen and the library. This is more like the physical plant."

"This is amazing," Kee said, walking around the room and studying the gauges. He tapped on one.

Rachel pushed buttons on the console in front of her and threw a few switches. A loud, mechanical groan sounded from someplace far beneath their feet. He watched Rachel nod, as if pleased with the results, before she began turning even more knobs. Then she pushed herself away from that console and wheeled herself to another one.

Kee hung back, not helping her with the chair. It was as if she'd forgotten he was even there, and he didn't disturb her. He had known Rachel wouldn't be able to resist bringing Sub Rosa back to life. Part of her soul lived in this house.

She started flipping switches on the new console with all the confidence of someone who had helped design it. There was a sudden *whoop* from down the hall, and Kee heard footsteps running toward the control room.

"We're in business," Jason said as he burst into the room. "The storm shutters just went up. The entire house is flooded with light."

Duncan was right behind him, grinning. "The windows are filthy," he said, not sounding the least bit upset. "It's going to take a small army to clean them."

"There's a company in Ellsworth that will do it for a small fortune," Rachel said, not taking her attention from her work.

She pushed herself away again and went to another bank of switches and started flipping them. "There. All the phones are working," she said triumphantly, shooting a satisfied look at Kee. "As well as the intercom system and the front gate remote controls. You'll find those in the vehicles parked in the garage."

"The phone company said we wouldn't have service until Friday," Jason said, looking skeptical as he eyed the switches she'd just turned.

"They've always been working. The alarm system for Sub Rosa is hooked into the phone lines, as well as other data systems that monitor the conditions inside the house. This place has been in stasis for the last three years, electronically babysat by a company in Ellsworth."

Jason was nodding as he continued to look around. "That makes sense. There's too much wealth here to leave unguarded. We were given a code for the alarm before we arrived."

"Which you must possess also," Kee interjected, finally moving from his spot near the door. He walked up to Rachel and put both his hands on the arms of her chair, forcing her to face him. "Which is why you didn't set any alarms off last night."

Her chin went up. "I don't have the alarm codes. And the security company probably changes them every few months."

"Then how were you able to slip in here without setting them off?"

"I didn't. I told you, I was looking for my cat." She suddenly smiled. "Which your men found for me."

Lord, he wanted to kiss her again.

"I'm hungry, Mr. Oakes. I've lived up to my side of the bargain. Are you going to feed me or not?"

"Certainly, Miss Foster. If I am anything, I'm a man of my word," he said, his expression changing to a simmering heat.

Chapter Six

It was very disconcerting to be pushed around willy-nilly in a wheelchair by a giant. Rachel felt slightly off-balance and very much out of control.

Keenan Oakes had stormed into her life like one of the nor'easters that came up the coast, slamming into Maine with all the force of the Atlantic behind it. She was beginning to feel like the wave-pounded rocks that held up Sub Rosa.

Rachel was wheeled back into the elevator and arrived on the first floor in the blink of an eye. Her unasked-for host then pushed her into the kitchen, where they found two of his men looking frazzled and frustrated and very much out of place.

Keenan must have thought so, too.

"I think we'll eat out on the patio," he said, turning her chair around and pushing her through the kitchen door, which one of the men hurried to open, and into the great room. "It's rather nice outside today," Kee said con-versationally.

Rachel assumed he was talking to her, but she didn't an-swer. She was too busy gripping the arms of her chair and hanging on for dear life. The man must be a terror behind the wheel of a car.

The house was indeed flooded with light, Rachel realized, as they headed for the bank of glass doors that made up the southern wall of the great room. Things hadn't changed at all since the last time she'd been there, though most of the fur-niture was covered with dust cloths. The high vaulted ceil-ing, with its heavy beams and gilded molding, looked as if it belonged in a European cathedral. The granite hearth on the west wall had a fire burning low in it, and the sunlight com-ing through the now exposed windows was indeed filtered by years of grime. Several doors opened onto a stone terrace that overlooked the Gulf of Maine, and the speed demon stopped only long enough to open one of them before he grabbed the back of her chair again and pushed her through it.

Rachel prepared herself for a blast of chilled air, but it never came. The early June air was bright with sunlight, and there was almost no breeze. She closed her eyes, lifted her face to the sun, and let out a sigh of pleasure.

She was completely unaware of the man behind her or how his hands suddenly tightened on her chair.

"Your girlfriend should be here now," she murmured, still keeping her eyes closed.

"What makes you think I have a girlfriend?"

She snapped her eyes open. "I-I just assumed you do," she said quickly. "With your money, you must have women flocking to you like sheep."

He wheeled her over to the weather-worn table, took a

seat across from her, and looked at her with eyes the color of the ocean behind him. "And what would you be knowing about my money, Miss Foster? I've only just discovered my inheritance."

She eyed him directly. "Your reputation has preceded you, Mr. Oakes, by way of a newspaper article. Word is you're an international salvager. And that you charge an outrageous fee and go after stuff untouchable by most salvagers." She lifted a brow. "Any truth to that?"

She wasn't sure, but Rachel thought his face darkened in anger. Or was it humility?

She stifled a snort. Certainly not humility. Not this man.

"I run more of a lost-and-found business than a simple salvage operation. We're hired by governments and corporations as much as individuals to find things—or people—they've lost. And yes, Miss Foster, I don't come cheap." He shrugged. "But then, I don't get the easy jobs."

"And Duncan and Jason and Peter and Matthew. They work for you?"

He nodded, never taking his eyes off her. "And Luke. You haven't met him yet. And yes, we work together. We're a highly specialized, very effective team."

Rachel nodded back. "Then you won't be staying here," she said. "You'll have a hard time finding a buyer for Sub Rosa, though. It's a rather unique piece of property."

"What makes you think I'm going to sell it?"

Rachel gave him a surprised look. "Why would you want to keep it? It's miles from nowhere. The article said you lived on your boat."

"But I can just as easily work from here." He looked up at the mansion he was facing, then back at her. "And I like Sub Rosa. It suits me."

"But it's a two-hour drive to the closest international airport," she countered, horrified at the thought that he was going to become a permanent neighbor.

He and his wolf, not to mention his merry band of brutes.

"There're plenty of grounds here to put in a small landing strip. We can go through customs in Bangor and then just fly here. Did good old Uncle Thadd have a helicopter port?"

"Yes. It's just behind the garage."

"How did he come up with the name Sub Rosa?"

"It's Latin. It means 'the roses,' " she said simply.

"Actually, Sub Rosa more literally translates to 'under the roses,' " he said, his gaze narrowing with suspicion. "It also implies 'in secret,' as if there is more than the eye can see. What can't I see, Miss Foster? Secret passageways? Tunnels leading from the house to the cliffs below?"

"Thadd named it for the roses," she said, refusing to be baited. "They grow wild here—in abundance," she added, absently waving toward the cliff.

He was looking at her as if he could read her mind. Rachel pushed one of the chair's wheels to turn herself away.

"I'll find the real blueprints, you know."

She turned toward him again. And she smiled. "They're in the library. I'll go over them with you, if you want."

His eyes narrowed again. "They won't show me the tunnels, will they?"

"No. Because there are no tunnels."

"You need lessons in lying, lady," he said, suddenly standing up.

Rachel flinched. But he only walked toward the house and took the tray Peter was carrying toward them.

Keenan set it in front of her. Rachel looked at the

food and tried to figure out what it was they intended to feed her.

Keenan took his seat across from her again, and Peter quickly disappeared. Rachel turned to see him slip back into the house. "Coward," she muttered, only to turn back at the sound of Keenan's laughter.

"Cooking is not one of their strong points," he said, poking the concoction with a fork. He shoveled some of it into a plate and set it down in front of her. "Eat, Rachel. It's about all you're going to get until I can hire a cook."

"Franny Watts is available," she said, prodding the food with her fork. It didn't jump out of the plate, so she figured it was at least dead.

"She live nearby?"

"In town," she said, tentatively scooping some of the hash onto her fork. She held it up and stared at it. "She used to cook for Thadd. She'd probably jump at the chance to have six huge men to cook for."

Her host reached out and stayed her hand before she could take a bite. He pushed on her arm until she set the fork back down on her plate.

"How about I take you into town and we find a fast-food place? It's got to be healthier than this stuff. And we'll stop by your house long enough to get you some clothes." He looked her up and down, the corner of his mouth lifting. "As cute as those sweats are, I think you'll feel more comfortable if you don't have to live in clothes you've slept in."

Rachel silently fingered the hem of her sweatshirt. The clothes were hers, and she'd been trying—really hard—not to think about how she'd gotten into them. Her last memory of last night had been of her sitting on her couch like a zombie, her eyelids getting heavy, her fear and frustration ebbing away in a cloud of fuzzy peacefulness.

She could not remember changing her clothes.

And she could not bring herself to ask Keenan Oakes if he had changed them for her.

"Why not just drop me off at my house? My sister will be home this afternoon, and your house is up and running enough for the time being."

Rachel watched, amazed if not shocked, as his entire face suddenly softened. "You can't take care of yourself, Rachel. And I called Wendell Potter this morning, and he said your sister was gone until the weekend."

He shifted in his seat and set his elbows on the table on either side of his untouched plate, steepling his fingers and tapping his chin as he stared at her. "I'll make a deal with you. I won't keep bugging you about being in my library last night if you stay here until your sister gets back."

"I . . . no, I want to go home."

"You'll have free rein of the house," he continued, as if she hadn't spoken. "I'll have an electric wheelchair delivered this afternoon, so you can get around and still let your knee heal." He smiled. "Jason may haunt you with questions, but you probably won't even see me most of the time. And you can call Franny Watts and get her to come cook for us."

Rachel didn't trust him any farther than she could spit. Keenan Oakes was all but inviting her to take another shot at his library. It wasn't sincerity she saw in his eyes—it was the calculated risk a predator was willing to take to trap its prey.

"What about your wolf?"

"I'll keep him outside."

So she wouldn't escape, was what he was really saying. Rachel surprised herself by actually considering his proposition. Good Lord. Why was she trying to talk herself out of accepting his offer? She couldn't ask for a better opportunity to hunt for Thadd's secret room. Then she could get rid of any evidence that might implicate her father's involvement in Thadd's crimes.

It was perfect. Assuming Keenan Oakes kept his word and stayed away from her.

"You'll accept the fact that I wasn't here last night if I stay?"

His eyes lit with triumph. "I won't bother you about being in my library last night," he clarified, not accepting or arguing the fact. "If you'll earn your keep."

"How?" she asked, realizing he hadn't promised not to bother her in other ways. He hadn't promised not to kiss her again.

And why did that thought send shivers racing down her spine?

"Help me get this place in working order," he said, waving his hand at the mansion. "Hire a staff. Get the windows washed. Find a crew to get that dock I inherited out of dry storage and into the water before my schooner arrives. Show Jason the ropes." He suddenly smiled. "Just put my house in order."

Her eyes widened. "Do you mind if I heal while I'm at it?"

He stood up and grabbed the back of her chair. "Not at all. But last I knew, your fingers weren't broken. Use the phones you just got working."

Rachel didn't say anything else. She was too busy holding on for dear life as Keenan raced her into the house and through the great room.

• • •

The trouble with most men, Rachel decided, as she was whisked through Sub Rosa's massive gate and onto the narrow roads of Puffin Harbor, is that they tended to be creatures who liked to take charge. They loved giving orders, and they expected them to be obeyed without argument.

"Is the motor home yours?" Kee asked as he turned Thadd's shiny red Ferrari into her yard.

"Yes. I used to use it for work."

"You used a motor home for work?"

Gripping the door handle like a lifeline as they came to an abrupt halt just behind her truck, Rachel nodded. He was a terror behind the wheel of a car, just as she'd expected. But he was a proficient one, having maneuvered the vehicle with all the skill of a fighter pilot.

"But you're an architect. How does a motor home fit into that picture?" he asked, shutting off the engine and turning to face her.

Rachel calmed her racing heart before she answered. "I used to be an architect," she corrected, "doing residential design. When I took on an assignment, I camped out on the land my clients wanted to build on. I usually spent one or two weeks there, studying the lay of the ground, the weather, and the . . . the feel of the place," she explained, ending with a small shrug. "I couldn't build until I had a clear picture of what my design would look like on that particular lot."

He seemed sincerely fascinated. And maybe surprised. He draped one arm on the back of her seat and looked at her intensely. "Is that how your father worked?" he asked.

Rachel smiled. "Yes. We camped out on Sub Rosa for nearly six months while our house was being built."

Kee turned and looked at her home. "Who designed your home?"

"I did. Dad was too busy with Sub Rosa." She waved her hand at the large Victorian structure. "This is my first independent work. I was fourteen at the time."

He turned back to her. "It's lovely."

"Thank you."

"What do you mean, you used to build homes? You don't anymore?"

"No."

He waited for her to elaborate, but when she didn't, he asked, "Why not?"

She shrugged. "Because I like being a librarian now."

His gaze narrowed. "Since when?"

"Since three years ago," she told him, giving him a pointed look in return, closing the subject.

He stared at her in silence, wise enough to end the discussion. "Do you want to wait here while I find your clothes, or should I carry you in?" he asked instead.

Well, heck. She didn't want to be carried anywhere. It was disconcerting to be in his arms. But then, she didn't want him pawing through her underwear, either.

"I have crutches in the kitchen closet."

He shook his head. "If you want that knee to finish mending properly, you'll forget the crutches for a few days at least."

It wasn't really a grin he gave her as he opened the door. It was more like a happy smirk, as if he thought that keeping her confined to a wheelchair would keep her more easily under his thumb. Rachel wanted to snort, but she refrained. She'd gotten quite good at maneuvering a wheelchair three weeks ago.

He walked around to her side of the car, and Rachel braced herself for the feel of his arms going around her back and under her legs yet again.

Carrying a person was an intimate act. She had seen her father carry her mother more than once, usually when he was headed for their bedroom.

Keenan Oakes lifted her out of the car as if she weighed no more than a bag of groceries. He strode to the house with long, powerful strides, and Rachel tried her damnedest not to notice the pleasant smell of him, or how the muscles of his arms bunched, or how his legs carried them both with fluid, easy grace. She certainly refused to notice how his hair brushed the back of her hand as he walked.

It must be hormones, she decided, as he set her down on the porch swing so he could unlock the door. That must be what was causing her traitorous senses to awaken. Hormones. The bane of every woman's existence.

He got the door open, then picked her up again and carried her into the house, traveling through the living room, then mounting the steps that led to the bedrooms.

He stopped at the top of the stairs and looked down at her.

"Which way, Rachel?" he asked, his eyes laughing at her discomfort for being carried around like a child.

"Second door on the right, Mr. Oakes," she said, emphasizing his last name as a barrier between them.

But he didn't move. "If you don't start calling me Kee, you're going to get a lot hungrier."

"Kee," she growled to get him moving.

"Now, that wasn't so hard, was it?" he said, finally walking down the hall.

"You're a bit of a bully, you know that?" she muttered, scrunching herself up to fit through the door.

"Thank you."

"It wasn't a compliment," she snapped.

He set her on the bed and headed for her bureau.

"I'll pack my things from there!" she blurted when he opened the top drawer. "Just hand me the whole drawer. I've got a suitcase in the closet."

He was grinning as he walked back to the bed with the drawer in his hand, busily examining the contents with his gaze. He set the drawer beside her, then looked down at her with the devil dancing in his eyes.

"Now, how did I guess you wore basic white?" he asked, his voice laced with amusement.

Rachel felt her cheeks get hot. "The suitcase is on the top shelf," she told him, lifting her chin and trying to glare through her blush.

He chuckled all the way to the closet. "Is there a good place in town to get a lobster feed?" he asked as he rummaged around on the top shelf. He pulled out her suitcase, brought it back to the bed, and opened it. "I'm dying for some lobster."

"There's a Lobster Pot on the pier," she told him, not moving to pack anything—not until he turned around. "If you're not looking for anything fancy, it's the best place in town. Why don't you pull some of my jeans out of the bottom drawer?"

As soon as he turned to do as she asked, Rachel grabbed a handful of panties and bras from the drawer and stuffed them in the suitcase. She quickly covered them up with a pile of socks. Then she added the jeans he brought over.

"I'm not sure those will fit over your brace," he said, eyeing her huge right leg.

Rachel sighed. Of course, he was right. She tossed the jeans out of the suitcase. "I have some looser pants hanging in the closet," she told him.

He had to return to the bureau to get her some sweaters next. But he suddenly stopped and picked up a picture that was sitting on top of it. He turned it toward the light.

"Is this your mother and father?"

"Yes."

"You look like her," he said, his gaze moving from the photograph to her, comparing them. "But you have your father's eyes." He examined the photo again. "I was expecting someone different when I pictured your father. I had Frank Foster pegged as short, balding, with glasses that kept sliding down his nose. This man is downright brawny."

"Dad wasn't a pencil pusher by any means. I bet he laid half the stones for Sub Rosa himself."

He hefted the frame in his hand. "You want to bring this with you?"

"No. I'll only be gone a day or two," she said, arranging her clothes in the suitcase.

"More like four, according to Wendell Potter," he countered, tossing the picture on top of her clothes. "Is there anything else you need?"

Rachel took the photo back out and carefully set it on her nightstand. Then she closed and latched the suitcase. "Nope," she told him. "Why don't you take this down to the car? Then you can come back and get me."

He hesitated, then grabbed the suitcase and walked out of the room. In the hall, he stopped and frowned back at her. "Don't move an inch," he said, the warning clear in his voice.

Rachel smiled at him.

As soon as she heard him on the stairs, she stood up on her one good leg and closed and locked the bedroom door. Then she slowly hobbled to the bureau and pulled out some more clothes.

She stripped off her sweats and was relieved to see that she was still wearing the underwear she'd had on last night. Maybe the Neanderthal did have some morals.

But Willow was dead right in her assessment of him. Keenan Oakes did not bother to ask a girl's permission to kiss her.

It took Rachel several minutes to change her clothes, and Kee was banging on her door by the time she was done.

"Give me a minute!" she grouched at him while she used the bureau and the door casing for support to hobble to the bathroom. "I'm getting dressed!"

"I'll help you," came his suddenly lowered voice.

Rachel snorted loudly enough for him to hear.

She sat down on the edge of the tub and pulled a small bag out of the vanity, which she began cramming toiletries into. Hooking the bag over her shoulder, she hobbled back to the bedroom and opened a small chest on her bureau. She took out three barrettes and put them in her bag. She'd braid her own hair tomorrow morning, thank you very much.

She pulled her thick braid over the front of her shoulder and stared at it. It was surprisingly well braided. Why had Keenan Oakes bothered with such a personal chore?

Rachel tossed the braid back over her shoulder. She wouldn't think about it. She wouldn't picture those strong masculine fingers gently pulling out the snarls, painstakingly weaving it into some sense of order.

She wouldn't.

Rachel tightened her grip on the bag, took a deep breath, and pasted a smile on her face before she unlocked the bedroom door. Without saying a word, he swept her up and carried her down the stairs, her bag banging into his back with every step he took.

"Wait! Set me down here, in the kitchen," she asked as sweetly as she could. "I need you to do a walk-around, to check things."

"I'll set you in the car first."

"No. Here. Just leave me here. I won't budge."

The look he gave her was almost comical. "The more you push that knee, lady, the longer you'll be carried around."

Rachel widened her smile. "I know. I won't budge an inch this time."

Because she didn't have to. Kee set her on a stool at the center island and went back upstairs to check there first. Rachel immediately reached into the drawer and found the pouch of fake emeralds she'd stashed there the night before.

She had been in immense pain, dragging herself onto the porch and into the house, but she'd still had enough wits to dump the jewelry in the drawer. She'd known she might have to call for an ambulance, and she hadn't wanted some helpful attendant to find them on her.

By God, these emeralds were going back to Sub Rosa. She stuffed the pouch in the bag with the rest of her things and had a smile on her face when Kee came sneaking back into the kitchen with that silent stride of his, looking as if he expected to catch her gone from her seat.

"Everything looks fine upstairs," he muttered, clearly surprised by her obedience. "I'll check the cellar next and then the barn. Which door leads downstairs?"

"That one," she told him, pointing to the door beside the pantry.

He disappeared again, and Rachel had a moment's worry that he would discover her workshop. But then she realized he wouldn't see anything out of the ordinary. It was just a typical workshop—but for the giant puffin sitting in the middle of it, covered with a sheet. But then, he wasn't a local, so he wouldn't know about her and Willow's gifts.

"Come on," he said, returning upstairs, shutting and locking the cellar door as he entered the kitchen. "I'll get you settled in the car, and then I'll check out the barn and your motor home."

"Thank you."

He hesitated before picking her up. He was bent over, his eyes level with hers. "You don't like being dependent on anyone, do you?" he said, his expression suddenly softening.

"Who does?"

He smiled. "That's true. I've been there, and I can tell you, it's a bitch." He scooped her up again. "I'll try to remember that when you get ornery."

Rachel grabbed the back of his neck and lifted her chin. "I wouldn't get ornery if you wouldn't get bossy."

He shrugged with her in his arms. "Then I guess we're going to butt heads on occasion," he said, walking down the stairs and into the yard. "Because I can't seem to stop."

"That's probably why you can't keep a girlfriend."

He snapped his gaze to her.

Rachel smiled at him.

He set her in the car, and it was all she could do not to laugh out loud when he closed the door and headed for the barn. It was killing him to keep his promise not to bring up last night to her.

She watched his long, muscular legs carry him to the barn—and decided then that Joan the shrew was a very stupid woman.

Chapter Seven

✦

*K*ee *knew that Rachel Foster* didn't care for his driving. The poor woman was gripping the door handle with enough force to break it.

"It's going to be quite a boon to the town budget when you get caught," she muttered, just as he pulled into the only parking spot on the town pier. It was marked by the unmistakable handicapped symbol.

Kee shut off the engine and watched as Rachel pried her fingers free and flexed them. He looked at her with one raised eyebrow, waiting for her to explain her comment.

"When they fine you for speeding, then tack on the fine for parking in a handicapped spot," she said, waving at the sign in front of them. "Not to mention driving an unlicensed car."

"I didn't want to wait," he said, lovingly running his hand over the steering wheel. "This is an amazing machine. It was all but begging to be taken out."

"But it's not registered."

He looked at her again, his eyes lighting with mischief. "That's what makes the ride all the more exciting. Come on, Rachel, let your hair down a bit."

The little prig lifted her chin at him. "It's my reputation that will get ruined when I get caught with you."

Kee looked in his rearview mirror and suppressed a grin. "Well, Miss Foster, your reputation is about to take a nose dive," he said, as he got out to face the car that had pulled up behind them.

"Good afternoon, sheriff," he said, his grin widening when he saw Rachel sinking into her seat. "I'm Keenan Oakes," Kee continued, holding out his hand to the deputy sheriff.

"Oakes? I thought I recognized the car," the officer said, not returning his smile. Or his handshake. "This is Thaddeus Lakeman's car."

"It's mine now."

"It's not registered."

"I've just been reminded of that fact, Deputy Jenkins," Kee said, reading the man's name from his badge. He pulled out his license and handed it to him. "Do you mind if I get my date settled on the pier while you write me up?" he asked, not waiting for an answer, but going around the car and opening the passenger door.

Kee thought Rachel was going to slide all the way under the dash. He leaned in to find her glaring at him. Yup. She'd heard him tell the sheriff she was his date.

Kee nearly bumped into Deputy Jenkins as he stood and turned with Rachel in his arms. Her face was scorching red now and her eyes wide with dismay, as Kee held her face to face with the ticket writer.

"Rachel!"

"H-Hi, Larry," she whispered, looking down at Larry's chest.

"What happened to you? I thought your knee was healed," Jenkins said, stepping toward her, a little red in the face himself as he darted a confused look at Kee.

Kee started walking out to the pier. He found a picnic table and set Rachel down. "I'll go order for us," he told her, "while you bring our friend up to speed."

He turned to head for the Lobster Pot window only to nearly bump into Jenkins again. The poor man looked as if he didn't know who to stay with—Rachel or the criminal he was trying to ticket.

"I'll just be a minute, deputy," he told the man. "Rachel, why don't you explain how I couldn't fit the wheelchair into the Ferrari, and so I had to take the handicapped space," he added, as he stepped around Jenkins and went to the order window.

"What will it be, mister?" the old man in the booth asked, his pencil ready to write.

"Well, I don't know. My date said you have the best lobster in town, so you tell me."

The weathered old salt squinted out the window past Kee, and his eyes suddenly widened as he snapped them back to his customer.

"You with Rachel Foster?"

Kee nodded.

"On a date?"

He nodded again.

The man whistled through his teeth, his face breaking into a wrinkled grin. "Did you mention that fact to Jenkins?"

Again Kee simply nodded.

"Well, then, young man, I hope your pockets are deep. Larry Jenkins has been trying to get one of the Foster girls to go out with him for years now."

"Is that a fact? Maybe Jenkins's pockets just aren't deep enough for Rachel Foster," Kee said, watching the old man closely. "Maybe she's got more expensive tastes."

The smile instantly left. "Then you don't know Rachel very well," he growled. "She's not a wallet chaser. She's successful enough in her own right."

"Then why hasn't she gone out with him?"

The old man eyed Kee with a speculative gaze. "Because she don't date. Period."

"She's here with me."

The man leaned farther out the window and looked in the direction of the bright red Ferrari. "She's just being neighborly," he said, shaking his head. He squinted one eye at Kee. "You can call it what you like, flatlander, but Rachel Foster don't date no one, no matter how rich they are. And I sure as hell know she wouldn't be dating anyone connected to Thaddeus Lakeman," he muttered, turning around and driving his fist into a water tank full of lobster. He pulled one out, threw it in a netted bag, and dove in for another one.

Kee knew when he'd been dismissed. He turned away from the window and watched a still red-faced Rachel trying to calm an even redder-faced Deputy Jenkins.

Suddenly the officer of the law tossed Kee's license down on the table and strode back to his car. Rachel picked it up. Kee gave her enough time to study it before he walked over and sat down across from her.

"You must be one sweet-talking lady, Miss Foster. Jenkins forgot to ticket me."

"What did you order?" she asked, glaring at him while she ignored his compliment.

"I have no idea. The guy just took one look at you and started pulling lobster out of the tank. So, what's it going to cost for getting me out of a ticket?"

"A date."

"Excuse me?"

"Larry said he'd forget the ticket for a date."

Kee felt the hairs on the back of his neck rise, much as they did on Mickey whenever the beast was angry. "A date with you or with me?" he asked very softly, his eyes letting her know he wouldn't like either answer.

He watched her grow suddenly still as she stared back at him, but then she lifted her chin again.

"With me."

"I hope you told him no."

She turned the license over and over in her fingers, not taking her gaze from his. "Do you see a ticket on this table?"

She was actually baiting him, he realized. He leaned forward and rested his arms on the table. "Why didn't you get good old Larry to take you home, then?" he asked in a congenial voice. "This was your chance to tell the law that you'd been kidnapped and were being held against your will."

She looked so disappointed that Kee nearly laughed out loud. She lowered her chin and stared at the license in her hand. Finally she tossed it onto the table toward him.

"I've decided to stay at Sub Rosa awhile," she told him, her voice subdued and cautious. "As long as you keep your promise not to bother me, I'll promise to get the place up and running again."

Kee leaned forward even more.

She didn't retreat.

He smiled. "It's going to be an interesting week, isn't it, Rachel?"

Nor did she return his smile. "Yes, Kee, I believe it is."

The diabolical jerk had kissed her again—again without asking permission. And the worst part was, not only had she let him get away with it, she had liked it.

Rachel opened her eyes and squinted against the sun coming through her dirty windows. It was day number two of this little adventure, and it was time she made some plans.

If she wanted to clean up her dad's mess, she needed to come up with a way to stay out of the clutches of one very determined male. Rachel remembered the promise she'd seen in his eyes last night as he'd dropped her down on her bed and then followed her there, kissing her soundly enough to curl her toes.

And then he'd straightened, winked at her, and left the room whistling some jaunty tune that Rachel just knew had nasty lyrics.

The arrogant man! Keenan Oakes had decided she intrigued him. He had brought her here against her wishes—initially—and now he thought he had his prey right where he wanted her.

Well, she was right where she wanted herself to be. In Sub Rosa. And *she* had the knowledge of the house's secrets.

Rachel threw back the covers and sat up, smiling at the dust particles floating through her room. The first thing she noticed as she looked around her temporary haven was the electric wheelchair sitting against the wall, plugged into an outlet.

It hadn't been there last night when she'd gone to sleep.

Rachel frowned at it and then at the door. She'd locked that door last night, just before she'd undressed for bed.

It seemed Keenan Oakes had a few secrets of his own, and he wasn't afraid to show them off. He knew she wouldn't take kindly to the fact that he could waltz into her room while she slept. And that is precisely why he'd waited to bring in the chair—just to prove that he could.

She wondered what he'd think if she snuck into his bedroom tonight and rearranged things while he slept. She could, too, if she could walk. Lord, she hated being laid up.

Rachel sighed and sat up on the edge of the bed, only to fall back on the mattress with a squeak. A similar squeak sounded below her, and she heard the scurry of tiny claws under the bed.

The kittens.

She rolled onto her stomach and lifted the bed ruffle, leaning over until she could see underneath. Four pairs of eyes blinked back at her. One of the pair was decidedly larger and narrowed. Mabel emitted a throaty growl of warning.

That damn cat. Her lie had certainly come back to haunt her, hadn't it? She was now the proud owner of a feral cat and three scruffy kittens, whether she liked it or not. She was either going to have to make peace with the growling beast or face five men she didn't want for enemies.

The sixth man, Kee, already knew she'd never seen that cat before in her life. He just wasn't in a hurry to call her bluff. He was too busy enjoying a good laugh at her expense.

"Come on, Mabel. I won't hurt you," she told the mother, her voice dripping sweetness as she reached under the bed. "I just want to pet you. Come on, kitty. That's a nice cat."

Her fingertip barely made contact with fur before she pulled her hand back with a yelp. She immediately began sucking her finger, tasting blood.

"Dammit. I'm not going to hurt you," she said, glaring at the unblinking eyes watching her. "We just have to get along for a little while. Then you can go back to your hole in the woods."

One of the kittens mewled, and Rachel's heart immediately softened. "Now, Mabel. You don't want your babies to have the hard life you've led, do you? You can come live in my barn with your family. You'll have plenty of food and good shelter, and I can find homes for your little ones when the time comes. Won't that make you feel better?"

Mabel answered Rachel with another growl and used one of her paws to push the mewling kitten deeper into the shadows.

"Fine. Be that way, you dumb cat. Maybe I'll just forget and leave my bedroom door open. And if that wolf comes snooping around, don't come crying to me," she finished with a growl of her own, dropping the ruffle and pulling herself up by the bedpost. "I hope he takes a chunk out of your tail, you ungrateful witch," she muttered, hurling herself in the direction of her new wheelchair.

She landed with a grunt. She got herself settled, pulled the plug from the wall, then began to play with the controls. The wheelchair quickly responded to her commands to go forward and back and spin around in circles that would make a top dizzy.

Her spirits immediately lifted. To heck with the stupid cat. She was independently mobile again. No more being carried around in Kee's arms or scared out of her wits as he pushed her through Sub Rosa. Her knee would heal quickly and she would find her dad's blueprints, and then she would wave good-bye to the whole motley crew of men who had invaded her peaceful world.

But first she had to call her sister.

Willow was going to be worried sick about her if she couldn't reach her at home. Rachel directed the chair to the phone by the window and punched in Willow's cell phone number. It rang several times before the voice mail kicked in. With a sigh of regret, figuring Willow was probably in a meeting, Rachel left a vague message. She told her sister not to worry if she couldn't reach her for the next few days and that she'd try calling her again that night to explain everything.

She hung up and headed for the bathroom. Once there, she unwound the bandage from her left arm and examined her wound. She saw that she was black and blue just above the wrist.

Rachel poked it. The swelling was gone, but it was still tender. She flexed her fingers and twisted her wrist, deciding that after her bath she wasn't going to rewrap it. But she was going to wear a long-sleeved shirt. It was an ugly sight.

She unfastened the brace from her right leg next. Her knee looked no better than her arm. It was swollen and stiff.

It took her nearly an hour to bathe. But in the end Rachel felt human again when she finally emerged from her room. She was clean, dressed, and ready to take on Sub Rosa.

She headed for the kitchen first.

"Oh, good afternoon, Miss Foster," the man standing at the sink said as she rolled into the kitchen. She wasn't sure, but she thought his name was Matthew.

"Afternoon?"

He nodded, his smile making up for his harsh features.

Good Lord. She'd slept the morning away. No wonder she was starving. Darn it. She wasn't taking any more of those pain pills.

"Are you hungry?" he asked, looking around for a towel, giving up and wiping his hands on his pants.

"Ah, I'll just have an apple," she quickly assured him, sending her chair over to the counter and grabbing up the only apple sitting in the bowl. "And then I'll call Franny Watts."

His face brightened even more. "Kee said you knew a cook. Is she good?"

Rachel eyed the man up and down, realizing that he probably ate more calories in a day than she consumed in a week. She nodded to him just as she took a bite of her apple. "Yup," she said once she'd swallowed. "She can feed an army with one hand tied behind her back. But I should probably warn you—she won't let anyone mess with her kitchen."

His eyes crinkled at the corners as he nodded. "That's fine with me. She can have the kitchen."

Just then, the back door opened, and a man walked into the kitchen. Along with Mickey.

Rachel spun her chair around and pushed the handle forward as far as she could. She zoomed around the counter, bounced off a stool, and shot through the door leading into the great room.

Mickey came bounding after her with a yelp.

Rachel yelped, too, and sped the chair around the great room, the huge wolf nipping at her tires. She slammed the lever to the right as she approached the hall, and Mickey went skidding into a table, upsetting it in a tangle of paws and fur and splintering wood. The two men ran out of the kitchen and nearly tripped over each other as they scrambled to escape Rachel's chair as she went speeding past the door and down the hall.

Mickey was back on his feet and after her in a matter of seconds. Rachel screamed at the top of her lungs. The chair was not fast enough to outrun the wolf.

And she was running out of hallway.

Keenan stepped into her path, looking like Zeus himself. He planted his feet and leaned over and grabbed the arms of her chair, stopping her dead in her tracks. Rachel swallowed her scream. His claws scratching for purchase on the marble floor, Mickey went skidding into the back of her chair and landed with a painful grunt. Rachel's chair shuddered with the impact.

"What in hell is going on out here!" Kee growled, sounding more dangerous than his wolf.

Rachel threw her arms around his neck and pulled herself up to the safety of his chest. He let go of the wheelchair and straightened, holding her securely.

"He's trying to eat me again!" she shouted, pulling her good left leg up and wrapping it around his waist. "Help me!"

Her whole body started shaking with the force of an earthquake, and Rachel realized her savior was laughing.

Laughing!

She smacked his shoulder. "It's not funny! He's after me!"

"Rachel. He's a wolf. He'll chase anything that moves."

She looked behind her. Mickey was sitting on the floor, one of his paws lifted to his face, and he was licking it. He stopped, his tongue still stuck on his paw, and looked up at her.

Rachel hugged Kee tighter.

Without setting her down, Kee walked into the room he'd stepped out of earlier, closing the door with his foot behind them. He walked over to a couch that had been pushed up against one of the walls and set her down.

Rachel's hair stuck to his neck and then to her own as he pulled away. She brushed it out of her face and realized it was wet. So was her cheek. And her hands.

She looked at Kee, and her eyes widened. He was dressed all in black, in pajamas, and he was a ball of sweat. She looked around the room and saw that all the furniture had been moved to the edges of the room, and even the expensive Oriental rug had been rolled up against the wall. Jason was sitting in one of the chairs, a towel around his neck, a bottle of water in his hand, and a huge grin on his face.

He was wearing pajamas, too.

She looked back at Kee, who was looming over her, his feet spread and his hands planted on his hips. Unlike Jason, he wasn't smiling.

Rachel took the offense. "You said you'd keep your wolf outside."

"He must have come in with one of the men," Kee returned softly, still staring at her with eyes that reminded her of the Gulf of Maine in winter.

"Then tie him up."

He slowly shook his head. "He's a wolf, Rachel," he repeated, as if she needed the reminder. "You can't tie him up. It would kill him."

"*I'm* going to kill him, if he doesn't kill me first."

All that declaration got her was a smile. He shook his head again. "Rachel. He won't hurt you. He was enjoying the chase."

She held up her left arm and pulled back the sleeve of her sweater, waving her injured wrist at him. "What do you call that?"

Kee sat down beside her on the couch and took hold of her hand and examined her wrist. "That was an accident," he said, gently rubbing her pulse with his thumb.

Rachel pulled her arm back, mostly because she caught herself enjoying his touch. "I don't like him," she grumbled, mad because she knew he was right. Mickey had just been doing his job. She still didn't like him.

"Jason. Open the door," Kee said, standing up and putting himself between Rachel and the door.

She squeaked and swung her legs up on the couch, knowing damn well it was a puny defense.

Jason hesitated, looking at her. Then he looked back at Kee and obeyed. He opened the door, stepped aside as Mickey trotted in, and then left the room, closing the door behind him.

Rachel decided she wasn't answering any more of Jason's questions about Sub Rosa, the traitor.

"Mickey, come," Kee said, his voice gentle and low.

The wolf trotted up to his master and sat at attention in front of him. Kee turned to Rachel, and the animal moved to heel beside him, sitting again.

Mickey cocked his head to one side, his tongue lolling out of the corner of his mouth. He looked almost civilized, his expression curious.

"Put out your hand, Rachel. Let him sniff it."

She looked at Kee in horror. "Are you nuts?"

"Wolves respect courage and pounce on fear. Hold out your hand and say his name. Let him come to you."

Rachel eyed her perfectly healthy right hand, wondering if it looked like a slab of beef to a wolf. Slowly, cautiously, and very reluctantly, she reached out. Mickey licked his lips.

"H-Hello, Mickey," she whispered.

He didn't move. Rachel saw Kee push the animal with his knee. Mickey stood up and stepped forward. The beast's tongue darted out and licked the ends of her fingers. Rachel pulled them back to safety.

"Again," Kee ordered, his voice gentle but firm. "This time, leave your hand there."

She gave the bossy giant a good glare first, then slowly obeyed. By God, she was going to make friends with this wolf. He could end up being the only thing standing in her way of finding Thadd's secret room.

Mickey took a step closer just as she reached out to him, and Rachel nearly drove her hand down his throat. She jumped. So did the wolf, only forward, not back. He landed with his front paws on her lap and reached up and licked her chin.

Rachel closed her eyes and held her breath.

"That's enough, Mickey," Kee said.

Rachel opened her eyes just as Kee pulled the animal down to the floor. "There. That wasn't so bad, was it?" he asked, taking Mickey's place by kneeling in front of her. He brushed a stray hair from her face and tucked it behind her ear. "Now you can tell people that you've been kissed by a wolf."

Rachel was thinking she'd already been kissed by a wolf—just last night. She wiped her face with the sleeve of her sweater.

"And don't run from him again. He loves a good chase, and your wheelchair is a novelty."

"You're not going to keep him outside, are you?"

"No. He's part of my package. You get me, you get my wolf."

"What if I don't particularly want either of you?"

Kee's eyes gleamed. "I don't particularly care."

"You might, if I finally lose my temper."

He gave her a horrified look. "Little Goody Two-shoes don't have tempers."

"I have one," she told him, nodding to let him know she was serious. "And I'm about to let it loose. I don't like being pushed around by large men with even larger egos, I don't like things being done to me for my own good, and I don't like wolves." She gave him her best, haughtiest glare. "And I don't like men breaking into my room at night while I'm sleeping, just to prove they can."

His face was a picture of pure innocence by the time she finished. Only the laughter in his eyes said her lecture amused him. Rachel's palm itched to connect with the side of his face.

She closed her hand into a fist to stifle the urge. This man kneeling in front of her had the power to summon her darker side with just a smirk. Or a kiss. Or a touch.

He was touching her now, though she knew he probably wasn't even aware of his action. He was slowly rubbing her hip, around and around in sensuous circles— slowly driving her nuts.

"Now what's the matter? I swear, Rachel, more emotions just crossed your face than most women show in a year. One minute you're giving me hell for being a man, and the next minute you're looking at me as if I just drowned your cat."

Rachel finally moved, but not to slap his face. She

simply wrapped her arms around Kee's neck and pulled his mouth down to hers.

Given the choice of kissing the jerk or slapping him, Rachel decided this was probably less reckless. She certainly got quite a reaction. The poor man was so surprised, he actually pulled back. Rachel didn't let go, and they both ended up on the floor. Mickey started bouncing around them as if expecting to join in the play.

Once Keenan got over his initial shock, he seemed more than willing to let her have her way with him, and even started kissing her back.

Rachel lost the big fight with herself. A sudden burst of unbidden, outrageous, and highly unpredictable lust sang through her body. She wanted him. With a fierceness she had never felt before, she wanted Keenan Oakes in a very passionate way.

She parted her lips and accepted his tongue into her mouth, grabbing his hair and turning her head to deepen the contact. His arms came around her back, and she felt the world spin. Their positions were suddenly reversed; Kee was now on top of her, nestled between her thighs, the evidence of just what he thought of her attack pushing against her.

Rachel went up in flames at the feel of his weight covering her. She tugged at the collar of his pajamas and pushed them down over his shoulders. Apparently quite willing to help, he shrugged out of the top completely, returning his weight to her, moving his lips from her mouth to her face, her chin, her neck.

She kneaded his naked shoulders and powerful arms, and kissed his jaw before gently nibbling his ear.

A warm wet tongue drove into her own ear, and Rachel's eyes flew open in surprise.

Mickey Mouse was helping his master. Rachel screamed.

At the sound of her scream, Kee reared up, his entire body tensed for a fight—or tensed with lust denied, she didn't know which.

Mickey took advantage of the opening and moved closer, washing her face again.

"Goddammit, you insatiable wolf! Get off her," Kee shouted, pushing Mickey away.

Rachel scooted out from beneath them both, wiping her face with the sleeve of her sweater yet again. She pulled herself over to the sofa, not knowing whether to laugh, cry, or scream.

Mostly, though, she just wanted to melt into the floor.

She wiped her face again, only to realize that her hand was shaking with the force of her scattered emotions—or was it her *own* lust denied?

"Lady, you're dangerous," Kee said, as he came over and sat down beside her on the floor against the front of the sofa.

They both stared across the room.

"Yeah, well, I'm sorry," she whispered, her breath just as shaky as the rest of her.

"Sorry?"

"I don't make a habit of attacking men." She pushed a stray lock of hair from her face and tucked it behind her ear. "This was . . . was . . . it was a momentary lapse in judgment," she said, waving at the spot they'd recently occupied on the hardwood floor. She was surprised to see that the wood wasn't even singed. Mickey was sitting there now, looking at them with lupine disappointment.

"I don't think I want you going out with Jenkins," Kee said, still staring at nothing.

Rachel shrugged. "I didn't really make the date for me. It's Willow you're actually indebted to."

Kee looked at her out of the corner of his eye. "Is your sister as . . ." He cocked his head and studied her. "As impulsive as you are?" he finally said. "Maybe I should warn poor Officer Jenkins."

Rachel looked back at Mickey. "What is it with your wolf?" she asked, not answering his question. Her heartbeat had finally lowered to a steadier drum, but her whole body still tingled with remembered sensations. What madness had come over her that she was so wildly attracted to Keenan Oakes that she had actually attacked him?

And what was she going to do about it?

"Mickey?" he asked, also looking at the animal. He shook his head. "That damn wolf has cost me more girl-friends than I care to count." He turned to her, gently tugging on her braid until she looked at him. "How about you, Rachel? Will Mickey scare you off as well?"

Rachel grinned at him. "There's not much in this world that frightens me, Mr. Oakes." She held out her hand to Mickey, urging him over. "Especially not anything four-legged," she added, patting the eager wolf who was now leaning against her, a blissful rumble coming from his throat as she scratched his neck.

Kee made a sound of disgust and stood up, grabbing his pajama top and shrugging back into it. Rachel sighed with regret—for no longer having his beautiful body to look at and for wanting to look at it in the first place.

Once dressed, Kee stood with his arms crossed over his chest and stared down at her with assessing sea-blue eyes. "Mind telling me what that was all about?" he asked.

"What?"

He nodded toward the spot on the floor where they'd ended up. "That kiss," he clarified. "Or should I say that second assault on my manhood in less than forty-eight hours."

She didn't like his towering over her like a god of inquisition. Nor did she like having to explain her actions, when he was guilty of the same thing only the night before.

"Just proving a point," she told him, giving him a direct stare in return.

"And that point would be?"

"That it's pointless," she countered. "Kissing me every chance you get will not help you find those passageways you seem to think exist. Nor will bringing me here and trying to lull me into trusting you make me admit to something I didn't do. I was not in your library two nights ago."

Kee reached down and scooped her up in his arms, pulling her away from Mickey and walking to the closed door that led to the hall.

"Point taken, Miss Foster," he said. "And please feel free to make that point again, anytime you wish." He set her down in her wheelchair, bending close, his arresting eyes pinning her in place. "And Rachel," he whispered thickly.

"Y-Yes?"

"The next time that particular point is made, by either of us, I intend to finish it."

"F-Finish it?"

He nodded. And grinned. And lifted her chin with his finger and softly kissed her lips. "And Rachel?"

"Y-Yes?"

"Denying passion is much more dangerous than acting on it."

Chapter Eight

Rachel was thinking, later that afternoon as she sat at the massive desk in the library, that the intensity of her attraction to Keenan Oakes seemed to vary in direct proportion to her proximity to him.

If they were in the same room, she had quite a time controlling her emotions—wanting to be close to him, smell him, touch him, and feel his lips covering hers.

Conversely, if he was in another part of the house or gone into town to register his newly inherited fleet of expensive cars, Rachel found she was better able to pretend the arresting man didn't exist.

It was confounding, the mess she'd gotten herself into. Keenan Oakes was the new lord and master of Sub Rosa. He was a billionaire. He was arrestingly handsome, infuriatingly arrogant, and a far more dangerous man than she was prepared to deal with.

He stirred her blood. He made her feel alive as they waged a silent battle over the lie she'd told him, as she tried to outwit him by finding the secret room right under his nose, and as she brought his house to life while dodging his advances and making a few of her own.

Definitely stirred. Wonderfully alive.

On the other hand, she had helped build Sub Rosa, had just enough money in the bank for a comfortable living, and was also the daughter of the man who had killed his great-uncle. (Although from Kee's point of view that tragic event may have been a favor, considering the inheritance he'd walked into.)

But most disturbing, Rachel had actually thought she could keep herself dispassionate, aloof to the point of rudeness, and uninterested in things such as smells and touches and remarkably sensuous kisses.

What had possessed her to attack him this morning? Before that foolishly impulsive act, she might have been able to go on pretending he didn't affect her that way—if not to Keenan Oakes, at least to herself.

Now she was caught, because she found she wanted him passionately. Like the great home she was coaxing out of stasis, her own emotions were being awakened by piercing ocean-deep eyes, an incredible body, and a strong-willed zeal for life that was almost addictive.

Which was why she was beginning to feel guilty for setting Kee up to face the fireworks of Thadd's crimes.

The library door opened, and the devil himself walked in, followed by Duncan and Mickey. Mickey immediately trotted over to Rachel and pushed his nose against her arm, begging for a pat. She obliged her new friend, giving him her undivided attention, determined not to let Keenan Oakes continue to affect her, not even for one minute, even if it killed her.

Rachel soon discovered, however, that she couldn't control her heartbeat, which had started to race the moment he opened the door. Yup, directly proportional to his proximity.

"Making yourself at home, I see," he said, standing in the middle of the room. He looked around, as if checking to see if anything had been stolen while he'd been gone. Apparently satisfied that she hadn't looted his home, he moved closer and gazed down at the blueprints spread out on the desk. "Ready to show me Thadd's vault?" he asked, turning the large pages, looking for the second-floor layouts.

Rachel placed her index finger on the drawing. "It's right here," she said, pointing to the outline of the vault.

Kee studied the drawing, then looked to his left, at the east end of the library. "I see a wall of books," he said, walking over to them.

Duncan followed, and both men stood examining the shelves. Rachel gently pushed Mickey away and moved the lever on her wheelchair, guiding herself over to them.

"There, Duncan," she said. "Just to your right. Pull out those last three books on the middle shelf. See the lever? Turn it clockwise."

Duncan did as she instructed, and the wall of books moved forward with a soft mechanical click. Both men stepped back and Mickey moved closer, sticking his nose in the newly exposed crack.

"Pull it open," she instructed, positioning her chair out of the way. "It's heavy, but it will slide easily."

Kee pulled on the bookshelf until it swung completely open, revealing the vault's large titanium door. "This is unbelievable," he said, his voice awed and somewhat reverent.

"No," Rachel countered, grinning at his back. "It's practical. You don't want to advertise a vault's location for would-be thieves."

Kee turned narrowed eyes on her, his expression speculative. "What's the combination?" he asked.

Rachel broadened her grin, letting him know she knew why he was asking, and shrugged. "How should I know? It's your vault. Didn't the lawyers give you the numbers?"

Kee turned back to study the door, but not quickly enough for Rachel to miss his frustration. She almost laughed out loud. It was killing him not being able to mention their supposed meeting in this very room the other night.

She watched in silence as he pulled his wallet from his back pocket and rummaged around inside it.

"Hey, while you've got that out," Rachel said, remembering all the calls she'd made earlier, "I need some money."

He looked over his shoulder at her.

"A thousand dollars should do for starters," she told him, grinning again at his shocked look. "The pantry is empty, and Franny said she can't find her recipe for stone soup. She needs to go shopping."

"What in hell's the cost of living in Maine?"

"For six large men? Oh, that should last you about a week."

He turned fully around to face her. "What?"

"She needs staples, Kee. Flour, rice, spices, butter, shortening. And meat. Lots of meat. Should I go on? It's not cheap to restock an empty pantry."

He dug into his wallet again.

"Unless you won't be staying that long," she added, her expression hopeful. "Then six hundred should be enough, just for the basics."

"This is all the cash I have on me right now. Franny will have to stretch it." Kee handed her eight one-hundred-dollar bills. "And we're staying. I'll open an account in town that you can write checks on," he said, turning back to the safe, a small card in his hand.

"No," Rachel said. She was shaking her head when he turned back to her. "I agreed to give you only a few days of my time to help you open your home. I don't need a checkbook. I'm not, nor do I want to be, your property manager. And I don't want my name linked to Sub Rosa any more than it already is. Pay your own bills, or I'll find you a property manager if you want."

He studied her in silence, and Rachel could almost see the wheels turning behind those arresting blue eyes of his. He was trying to decide whether or not this was a battle worth waging in their ongoing little war of wills.

He nodded curtly and turned back to the vault. "I don't need a manager," he said, lifting the card beside the lock to read it more easily. "I'll pay what bills you've run up already. Just put them in a pile on my desk." He began spinning the dial, smartly dismissing the subject.

But Rachel wasn't through yet. "You'll pay them promptly," she told him. "And you won't haggle over the prices. The people I've hired to put in the docks and wash the windows are hardworking folks, and they can't afford to wait a month for their money."

He stopped what he was doing and looked back at her.

"Thadd never had any problem getting work done at Sub Rosa," she continued, ignoring his raised eyebrow and darkening expression. By God, she was going to make sure Keenan Oakes understood the work ethic of Maine people. She was the one who had called them, and it was her reputation that would be hurt if they had to wait for their money.

"In fact," she added, arching her own brow, "folks were always eager to come the moment Thadd called, because they always went home with a check in their pocket the minute the work was completed. They're going to expect the same from you."

Duncan took a step back, away from Kee. Rachel kept her chair firmly planted where it was, and recklessly—and quite eagerly—continued her lecture.

"And Franny wants to be paid in cash, every Thursday by noon, so she can get to the bank and back before she has to start supper. Eight hundred dollars for her, seven hundred for her kitchen help, and another five a week for the food. For that you'll have three meals a day, six days a week. You're on your own on Sundays."

She'd give him credit. He didn't even bat an eyelash at the figures she threw out. His expression, however, darkened. And his eyes narrowed.

Rachel shot him another grin. "When's your daughter coming? Should I make arrangements for a nanny? I know a couple of high school girls who'd love the chance to earn extra money this summer."

"Mikaela will be fine," he said. "She's got Mickey to look out for her."

Rachel was horrified. "A wolf is not a babysitter."

Kee turned his attention back to the lock on the vault. "He's more reliable than most teenagers," he said over his shoulder. "Dammit. This combination isn't working."

Rachel moved her chair to the desk and gathered up the notepad she'd been using and tucked it next to her thigh. She pushed the lever again and started across the library, headed for the door. She was done here, since she wasn't having any luck pricking Kee's temper. She might as well go down to the kitchen and see if Franny had arrived yet.

Mr. Unflappable stepped out and blocked her path. "And just where are you going? I can't get the vault open," he said, somewhat accusingly, as if it were her fault.

Rachel gave him an innocent look. "Then you've got a big problem. A nuclear explosion won't crack that safe. You should probably call your lawyers and get the right numbers."

He leaned down, bracing his hands on the arms of her chair, setting his face level with hers. "I bet you know how to open it," he said softly.

Proximity. Much too close.

"You'd lose that bet."

"Come on, Rachel. Get me into my vault."

"You want me to try those numbers?"

"No. I want you to open it with the combination you already have. Up here," he added, reaching up and gently tapping her forehead.

Her heart shifted into overdrive the moment he touched her. She was close enough that she could smell the sea on him, mingled with the faint scent of roses. Her palm itched again, but not with the urge to smack him this time. She wanted to run her fingers along the strong curve of his jaw.

Or she could do something even more stupid. What if she just glided her chair over to his vault and simply opened it?

Yes, that just might prick his temper. And riling Keenan Oakes was much safer than throwing herself into his arms.

"I'll make a deal with you then," Rachel offered, quietly pulling on the lever of her chair, trying to back up.

He held the chair firmly, overriding the gears with little effort. He grinned at her futile attempt to put some distance between them. "And what would that be?" he asked.

"I'll get you into your safe if you let me hire a nanny for your daughter."

He straightened, releasing the chair. Rachel went flying backward the moment she was free. She bumped into the desk and Mickey came bounding over, grabbing at the wheels.

"Mikaela doesn't need a babysitter," Kee said, his arms crossed over his chest, his feet planted in a way that Rachel had come to recognize as his intent to be stubborn.

"She's what? Four? Five?" she asked.

"She'll be five the end of this month," he told her. One side of his mouth turned up. "And she'd probably keelhaul anyone you hired within a week."

"This isn't a place you can let a kid run wild," Rachel said, moving her chair back toward him. She could match his infuriating stubbornness with a healthy dose of her own. "Sub Rosa isn't an amusement park, nor was it designed with children in mind. There are thirty-foot drops from the cliffs at high tide, a maze of hallways and rooms that can confuse a mapmaker, and five hundred acres of woods to get lost in."

He nodded in Mickey's direction. "The wolf will keep her from getting lost, in and out of the house, and she climbs the ropes on my schooner like a monkey. I'm sure your cliffs will be more of a challenge than a danger to her."

Rachel was terror-stricken at what he was implying. "She's a child," she said, her voice rising with outrage. "She needs supervision."

"There's six men living here," he countered, leaning

over and grabbing the arms of her chair again, getting back in her face. And his voice, when he spoke, was forcefully soft. "I've been looking after my daughter since she was ten minutes old, Miss Foster, and I haven't killed her yet."

Rachel swallowed the lump in her throat. Ohh-kay. The subject of Mikaela Oakes was definitely off limits.

"Fine. Open your own safe," she said, swatting his hands away and slamming the lever on her chair to the left. The wheels spun, and the smell of heated rubber rose into the air and followed her out the library door.

It was time she got on with the business of why she was here. Thanks to Franny Watts, Rachel had finally filled her belly with enough proper nutrition that she was actually beginning to feel like her old self again. Two days of being confined to a wheelchair—and carried around like a child—had helped her knee immensely, and an afternoon of studying the blueprints of Sub Rosa had given her a few ideas of where to look for Thadd's secret room.

First, though, she had to call Willow, who was probably frantic at not being able to reach her. Rachel sent her wheelchair over to the writing table of her new first-floor bedroom and picked up the phone.

She'd changed bedrooms earlier this morning after spending last night tossing and turning in bed. Without the pain pills to knock her out, she'd found that sleeping on the third floor of Sub Rosa, even in the opposite wing from Thadd's bedroom, had been impossible. Ghosts of the disturbing kind had visited her dreams. Memories and emotions had invaded her thoughts so vividly that three years and even two floors of marble and granite would probably still not be enough to keep them at bay.

So instead of trying to sleep tonight, she was going to keep the ghosts away by going on a treasure hunt.

"Where in hell have you been?" was Willow's greeting when she answered the phone after only two rings, letting Rachel know she'd probably been sitting by the phone waiting for this call.

"Hi, sis," Rachel answered cheerfully.

"Don't 'Hi, sis' me. Where have you been? I've been calling the house for two days."

Rachel took a deep breath, preparing herself for the firestorm that was about to erupt, and decided it was best simply to plunge headfirst into the middle of it.

"I'm at Sub Rosa."

"What!"

"Now, Willy. It's not what you think. Well, it is, but it's not why you think."

"I don't care what it is. Get out of there. Now."

Rachel gripped the receiver more tightly and carefully tempered her lie with a small part of the truth. "Do you remember how Mom came to possess the emerald earrings and necklace you have?" she asked.

That diverted Willow's attention. She was silent for several seconds, and when she did finally speak, her voice was less angry but no less confused. "Daddy gave them to her. For their twentieth anniversary."

"That's the story you know," Rachel told her, softening her voice with compassion. "But that's not exactly the whole truth," she added, crossing her fingers and closing her eyes, hating the half-truth/half-lie she was about to tell. "Actually, the emeralds had come from Thadd. He gave them to Dad to give to Mom."

Silence again.

Rachel took a calming breath. "They're worth over a million dollars, Willy," she told her. "And there are no papers of transfer for them. They're still legally part of Thaddeus Lakeman's estate."

"How do you know this?" Willow asked, the anger returning to her voice. She was not pleased to discover that the jewelry she cherished had not belonged to their mother but to Thadd.

Yes. How did she know this, Rachel thought? Whatever story she told would have to contain enough of the truth that Willow would not get suspicious.

"The article in the *Island Gazette* started me thinking about Thadd's estate and all, and your wearing the emerald earrings made me remember," Rachel began. "Those pieces of jewelry were never in Mom and Dad's wills specifically, and I realized that they probably still belonged to Thadd's estate."

It was a weak story, and Rachel cringed at the realization that she had just started down the slippery slope of compounding lies.

"That doesn't explain what you're doing at Sub Rosa," Willow snapped, obviously pained by the news.

"I'm here to return the emeralds."

"That takes about five minutes. And you don't even have to do it in person. Wendell could have returned them for you."

"A million dollars, Willy," Rachel reminded her. "And they've been in our possession for three years. Thadd's lawyers probably reported them stolen when they inventoried the vault and couldn't find them."

"It was innocent," Willow pointed out. "They're not going to charge us with theft. Wendell can corroborate your story that Thadd gave them to Dad."

"Then call me cautious," Rachel countered. "We don't know anything about this Keenan Oakes guy, and we don't know much about Thadd's lawyers, for that matter. What if they don't want to hear the truth? And why even bother to take that chance? Especially now, with you just starting your new job. The publicity alone could be detrimental to your career."

Silence again on the other end of the phone. "What are you saying?" Willow finally asked. "What are you planning to do?"

Rachel sat up straighter and gripped the receiver painfully tightly. "What if I just slip the emeralds into Thadd's vault when no one is looking? I'll stick them in something—one of his antique boxes, maybe—and when they're discovered, everyone will think they've been there all this time. That they had simply been overlooked before."

"No. It's too risky, Rachel. This isn't like replacing a beat-up old mailbox. It's breaking and entering. If you get caught—especially if you still have the emeralds in your possession—you'll be charged with grand larceny."

"Spoken like a true attorney general," Rachel said, smiling now. "You know I can do it, Willy. I can get in and out of that vault without anyone knowing."

Silence again. Finally: "Ah, if I remember right, you have to go through the tunnel that runs directly from Thadd's bedroom into the vault if you don't want to be seen. Do you really want to do that?" Willow asked, her voice gruff. "Are you prepared to put yourself through that?"

"Heck, no," Rachel replied truthfully. "But I will, if it makes this mess go away. Besides, I can get close enough to the library, and then just sneak into the vault while everyone is sleeping. That's why I'm here, Willy."

"Just give the emeralds to Wendell. He can find an anonymous way to return them."

"No." Damn. She was into this lie up to her knees, she might as well jump in up to her neck. "There're also some other items that actually belong to Thadd that we have at home," she confessed. Heck, it would help explain their disappearance. "That painting over the mantel, for one," she continued. "And the ring Dad gave me for my birthday."

"Oh, Rachel," Willow softly wailed. "Not your ring? Why would Dad have given us gifts that didn't even belong to him?"

"Because he trusted Thadd," Rachel quickly prevaricated, trying to soothe her sister's disappointment. "He wasn't thinking about papers of transfer. But you and I know better, and now we've got to make this go away quietly."

"I don't like it."

"Neither do I," Rachel shot back, getting angry, more at herself than anyone else.

Or was it Frank Foster she was really mad at?

"We'll come back to this in a moment," Willow said, sounding very much like a lawyer. "You still haven't explained what you're doing at Sub Rosa."

"Keenan Oakes arrived early," Rachel told her. "And he showed up on my porch and asked for my help opening the house."

Well, that was the truth. She didn't need to mention that the man had showed up at two in the morning and taken her back to Sub Rosa without her consent. But those were minor lies of omission compared with the whoppers she was telling now.

"And I decided to help him because it would give me an excuse to be in the house."

"That doesn't mean you have to actually stay there," Willow said, obviously not liking Rachel's reasoning.

"But it will make things easier. I slipped and hurt my knee again. Not badly," Rachel rushed to assure her. She rubbed her forehead. This lying business was giving her a headache. "It was my idea. I can't hobble up the cliff path and through all the tunnels to return the items. This way I just have to disappear into a wall and come out in Thadd's library."

"I still don't like it."

It was time to end the conversation. Rachel suddenly pitied anyone who dared cross the citizens of Maine. Once started, Willow could argue a point until her opponent folded from sheer frustration.

"I have to go now, Willy. I promised Jason I would show him how to fill the saltwater swimming pool."

"Who's Jason?"

"He's one of Kee's apostles," Rachel answered, smiling.

"Kee? Apostles?"

"Keenan arrived with a small army," Rachel explained. "And three of them are named after the apostles, so that's what I call them."

"Dammit, Rachel. You're enjoying this."

Rachel was taken aback by her sister's tone. "No I'm not," she assured her. "But that doesn't mean I can't be civilized about this. The men are really nice, Willy."

Rachel remembered meeting Luke, and how Matthew and Peter had helped her today, to move Mabel and the kittens down to her new bedroom. The two men had left wearing bloodstains and several Band-Aids.

"You called him Kee. That's sounding a bit chummy to me," Willow said, no trace of chumminess in her voice.

"That's his name."

"I'm coming home. Tonight. I'm leaving here in ten minutes, and I'll pick you up at the front door in two hours. Be ready, because I'm not getting out of the car."

Rachel rubbed her forehead again. "No. I don't want you coming here, Willy. I've got everything under control. I'm going to return the stuff tonight, after everyone's gone to bed."

Silence answered her. Rachel wanted to slam the receiver down in its cradle, but wisely refrained from adding to her sister's anger. Willow would be at Sub Rosa within an hour if she did, and she wouldn't stay in the car as she threatened. No, she'd be racing down Sub Rosa's halls, shouting for Rachel and charging through anyone who got in her way.

For a baby sister, Willow could be downright scary sometimes.

Rachel took a calming breath and counted to ten before she spoke again. "Willow," she said more softly. "It's okay. I'm okay. Just let me get rid of Thadd's things tonight, and I'll return home tomorrow morning, first thing."

"What if you get caught?"

"I won't. Nobody but you and I knows about the tunnels."

"What did they do with Thadd's collections?" Willow asked, sounding calmer now but still not convinced. "It wouldn't all fit in his vault."

"No. Most of it is still in place, but I think the more expensive, larger pieces are locked in a room on the third floor. That would have been my choice. It's a secure location, and it's climate-controlled because Thadd kept his tapestries in there. And when I tried the door today, it was locked."

"Then that's where you should take the emeralds and

painting. There's a direct tunnel from the great room. Can you walk well enough to climb three flights?" Willow asked, now obviously resigned to Rachel's illegal operation.

Rachel was impressed with her sister's deviousness. She should have thought of the room herself three nights ago, instead of the vault. It was a much simpler solution.

"Then that's what I'll do," she told Willow, her headache magically disappearing. "I can make the climb okay. And I'll be back home by noon tomorrow."

The receiver in her hand suddenly jerked, and Rachel looked down to see a kitten hanging from the phone cord dangling near her feet. The little bundle of fluff was accompanied by its two litter mates, and they were all trying to attack the cord. She smiled at their awkwardness.

"Oh, by the way," she said into the receiver, holding it firmly. "For the record, we own a cat."

"We do?" Willow asked, obviously confused by the sudden change of subject.

"Actually, we own four cats," Rachel told her. "I had to make up an excuse for being someplace I shouldn't have been, and the only thing I could think of was that I was looking for my cat."

"Where were you?"

"On the cliffs, near the tunnel entrance."

"Dammit, Rachel. You're going to get in trouble."

"No I won't." She laughed out loud when one of the kittens began attacking the lacing on her sneaker. Some of the tension she was feeling suddenly eased. "It turns out there really was a cat, sis. I don't know where they found her, but two of the apostles showed up with her in their arms. And she's got three kittens. You just have to remember that her name is Mabel."

"This isn't going to work," Willow cried, her worry returning. "Wait until I get back and can help you. I'll go along with your plan—just wait for me."

Rachel decided she should have hung up ten minutes ago. "For the love of God, Willow," she said, her patience gone. "This isn't rocket science. Nor does it require two people. I'm here *now*, and I'll stash the emeralds and be home tomorrow."

Silence again.

"I have to go. Jason's waiting for me. Good-bye, Willy. Call tomorrow at noon, and I promise to answer the phone."

"Wait!" Willow said, obviously not ready to hang up. "What did I see in the paper about a boat burning in Fisherman's Reach? What happened? The article said it was a lobster boat named *Norway Night*. Do you know who it belonged to?"

Rachel went deathly still. "What did you say the name was?" she whispered.

"*Norway Night,*" Willow repeated. "The paper said it appears to be arson."

For the life of her, Rachel couldn't speak. "Norway night" was a boat? Her father's dying words had been the name of a boat?

"Rachel? Did you see the fire? Do you know what happened?"

"Ah, yeah, I did," she said, forcibly pulling herself back to the conversation. "But I don't know anything about it. Did the paper say where the boat was built?"

"No," Willow answered, sounding somewhat confused. "It didn't even say who the *Norway Night* belonged to. That's why I asked. I thought you might know more about it."

"I don't. But I'll try and find out. I gotta go, Willy.

Jason's waiting." Rachel rubbed her forehead again, letting out a tired sigh. "I can't stop you from worrying, sis," she added softly. "I can only promise that I'll be careful. Good-bye," she said again, more gently this time. "I love you."

Rachel waited until Willow quietly repeated the declaration before she softly set the receiver in its cradle. She closed her eyes, rubbed both of her hands over her face, and blew out a calming breath.

Norway Night was a lobster boat. And lobster boats often traveled beyond the sight of land to tend traps, and would be a perfect way to inconspicuously meet up with another boat at sea and bring stolen art back into port. No one would be suspicious because lobstermen were as common, and just as ignored, as seagulls around there.

Great. Just great. Another mystery had just been added to this blasted mess, further complicating things. Now she had to find out why her father's dying words had been about the *Norway Night,* whether it had been built by Thadd's shipyard, and if Frank Foster's name was on the designs.

Willow had said they suspected arson. Lord, she hoped it was payback from a rival lobsterman in a trap war, or maybe even an insurance burning.

Just as long as it wasn't connected to her father in any way.

Rachel stood up and tested her right knee. It was only tender now, and felt surprisingly stable, but she wasn't pushing it any further this evening. She sat back in her wheelchair and glided over to the bedroom door. She was going to find Jason, fill the saltwater pool, and then get rid of the fake emeralds, just as soon as Kee and his men went to sleep.

Chapter Nine

But instead of finding Jason at the pool, where they'd agreed to meet, Rachel ran into him and Kee and Duncan in the huge three-story, tall, glass-domed foyer. Kee had a thick three-ring binder tucked under one arm, and all three men were holding plastic-covered sheets of paper.

They were also frowning hard enough to hurt their faces.

Kee looked up as her wheelchair softly whirred toward them, and Rachel's hand suddenly slipped off the lever, Kee's piercing glare bringing her to dead stop a full ten feet away. If she weren't mistaken, that glare was filled with anger and . . . and accusation.

Kee walked toward her, his eyes stormy, his stride filled with purpose, his mouth set in a thin line that spoke of impending disaster.

Rachel's first thought was to spin around and race

back to her room, but she held her ground even though a flock of butterflies had taken flight in her stomach.

Duncan and Jason also strode forward, and when Kee stopped in front of her, they moved to flank him on either side, the three of them forming an imposing wall of testosterone.

Rachel darted a glance at the papers in their hands, wondering what had them so riled. Matthew came into the foyer just then, followed by Luke. Peter entered from the south wing. They also held plastic-covered papers and were also frowning.

"Two of the items on my list are missing," Matthew said as he approached. "And a sixth-century urn from Greece is shattered to pieces."

Rachel snapped her gaze to Kee, but his only reaction to Matthew's news was to lift his left brow at her.

"Unless there's been one hell of an earthquake, that urn didn't jump out of its nook all by itself," Matthew continued. "Somebody helped it along. I found it clear across the room."

Kee's stare remained on her—and remained accusing.

The butterflies in Rachel's stomach turned to angry bees.

"Three of the items on my list are missing," Luke said.

"I found everything on mine," Peter interjected, glancing at his papers. "Except for a painting that was supposed to be hanging in the upstairs hall of the south wing."

"What's going on?" Rachel finally asked, lifting her own brow inquiringly.

"We're taking inventory," Kee said, his voice neutral. "And it appears that someone's been helping themselves to my inheritance over the last three years."

Rachel lowered her gaze back to the papers in his hand. Items were missing from Sub Rosa? And Kee thought she was responsible.

She looked at the other men. "That's impossible," she told them. "A mouse couldn't get into this house without having the security codes."

"Then explain how several items on the inventory list are missing," Kee demanded.

"They can't be missing. They're just . . . they're only misplaced. Have you checked the tapestry room on the third floor? It's a secure room and climate-controlled."

Kee was shaking his head before she even finished. "We've checked. We found two of the items in there, but that still leaves over thirty unaccounted for."

"Thirty!"

Kee gathered the sheets from his men, opened the three-ring binder, and started putting them inside.

"What about the vault?" Rachel asked. "Did you finally get it open? Maybe they're in there."

He snapped the binder closed and looked at her. "I got in. Everything is accounted for, and none of the missing items are there. But this did puzzle me," he added, reaching into his pocket and then opening his hand toward her.

It took every bit of control Rachel possessed not to react.

"The odd thing is, I found it on the floor," he said, holding the emerald earring between his fingers. "And there was already a set of earrings in one of the safes, along with a matching necklace." He dangled the glittering emerald in front of her. "I'm not that well acquainted with women's jewelry. Is it common to have three earrings in a set, Rachel?"

"Ah . . . I don't know much about jewelry myself," she whispered, darting a glance at the silent men. She looked back up at Kee. "I don't wear jewelry."

He nodded. "I noticed that. Except for a ring?"

Rachel looked down at her right hand, touching her thumb to her naked middle finger, and saw the faded band of skin where her ring used to be. "I . . . I do own a ring, but it's being cleaned."

A stark silence settled over the foyer at that. A silence pregnant with distrust, accusation, and, if Rachel wasn't mistaken, disappointment.

Kee thought she was a thief. He'd caught her in his library two nights ago, things were missing from Sub Rosa, and a third emerald earring had turned up. Dammit. He'd never believe she had been trying to add to Sub Rosa's treasures, not steal from him.

Rachel didn't know if she was more disappointed with Kee or with herself. She was head over heels in lust with a man who blamed her for his missing inheritance.

"I'm . . . I'm tired," she said, without looking up. "I'll help you hunt for the missing items in the morning." She pushed the lever on her wheelchair, turned herself around, and started back out of the foyer.

She was almost to the great room when Kee spoke. "Rachel," he said with quiet authority.

She stopped and looked over her shoulder. "Yes?"

He hesitated the briefest of seconds before gently waving her away. "Sleep well."

"Ya cannot be thinking our Rachel is responsible," Duncan said into the silence broken only by the whir of Rachel's disappearing wheelchair.

Kee turned from watching his houseguest's tactical re-treat and faced his men. Every damn one of them looked as if he were accusing their mothers of prostitution.

"And just when did she become 'our' Rachel?" he asked.

"You have to admit she's been working awfully hard to help us open this house," Duncan rebutted. "And that can't be easy for her, considering what happened here three years ago."

Kee tossed the binder down on the foyer table, crossed his arms over his chest, and faced his men squarely. "And that very fact doesn't ring any bells for you? Are you not wondering why she so easily agreed not only to help us, but to stay here?"

"She can't walk," Matthew interjected. "It makes things easier."

"It makes it very easy," Kee agreed, nodding. "If she's trying to finish what she started two nights ago, before we arrived unexpectedly."

Duncan scowled. "If Rachel is responsible for the missing items—and I'm still not convinced she is—why not just stop, now that we're here? Why risk continuing right under our noses?"

"Maybe because of this," Kee suggested, opening his hand to reveal the emerald earring. "It's a forgery, and was part of a fake set that was listed to be in the vault. But the emerald necklace and earrings I found in safe number sixteen are real."

He closed his fist over the earring. "And that set, worth well over a million American dollars, was stolen from the Grenier estate in France almost seventeen years ago."

"So what are you saying?" Luke asked. "That Rachel was exchanging the fake emeralds with real ones two nights ago? That doesn't make any sense."

"Aye," Duncan agreed. "If she had the real emeralds, why exchange them for fakes?"

"That's what I'm trying to find out," Kee said. "But more important, where did she get the real ones to begin with? They've been missing for sixteen years."

"How come Thaddeus Lakeman had a forged set, anyway?" Peter asked. "That doesn't make any sense, either."

Kee shrugged. "It's not uncommon to have duplicates of famous jewelry. Nor is it illegal."

Duncan let out a frustrated sigh, wiped his hand through his hair, then kneaded the back of his neck. He eyed Kee speculatively. "Are ya thinking that if we just wait, the missing items will mysteriously reappear? That Rachel's agreed to help us in order to replace the stuff she's stolen? Hell, man, that makes the least sense."

"All I know is that she was in the library the night we arrived," Kee said. "And that she's had access to this house with complete autonomy for three years. She built Sub Rosa, and she knows every one of its secrets."

"That doesn't make her a thief," Jason said. "In fact, it makes her an asset." Jason shifted anxiously, holding up his hand to stop Duncan from speaking. "Think about it. What if someone other than Rachel has been helping himself to Thaddeus Lakeman's estate? She could show us the tunnels he's obviously been using."

"You mean the tunnels she claims don't exist?" Kee asked.

"She just doesn't trust us," Luke interjected. He suddenly grinned. "But we can change that."

"How?" Kee asked, lifting one brow.

"By trusting her first," Duncan quickly added, nodding agreement with Luke. "By not acting like we think she's looting our home. Did ya not see her reaction when she realized things were missing? She was shocked."

"Yeah," Matthew said, rubbing his hands together. "You've said it yourself, Kee. She feels proprietary toward this place. If we involve her, she'll become an asset, just like Jason said."

"It could also put her in danger if there is a thief who is still nosing around," Kee pointed out.

Duncan waved that away. "We can protect her." He suddenly stiffened. "What about Mikaela? When's she due to arrive? Watching out for Rachel is one thing, but two females running loose around here is a bit more of a problem."

Kee couldn't help but smile. "Our little angel is due to arrive in about three days."

Jason groaned. "Duncan's right. Radio the *Six-to-One Odds* and have Ahab take the scenic route up the coast to buy us more time."

Kee snorted and tucked the emerald earring in his pocket. "I talked with our good captain this morning, and he's pushing the wind as it is. One week is about all Ahab can take of Mikaela. He threatened to put her in the dinghy and tow her behind them if she didn't stop rerigging his sails. I spent twenty minutes on the radio trying to convince her that schooners were not designed to fly spinnakers."

"You do know you're raising a tyrant," Jason said, smiling approval.

"Not by myself," Kee shot back, giving first Jason and

then the rest of his men a good glare. "She has every one of you wrapped around her little finger."

And her father most of all, Kee silently admitted to himself. Mikaela Oakes was spoiled rotten, and every man in this room, and every member of the *Six-to-One Odds* crew, was guilty of contributing to the problem.

Kee pitied the teacher who got Mikaela in school this fall.

At only ten minutes old, the tiny, wide-eyed bundle had been placed in his arms, and Kee had felt a blow to his chest that had nearly brought him to his knees. But that had been nothing compared to his men's reaction when he'd introduced his daughter to them not ten minutes later.

Kee may have provided the seed for Mikaela's conception, but she actually had six proud, doting, and overly protective fathers. And Duncan was the worst of the lot. The battle-hardened mercenary had taken the twenty-minute-old Mikaela in his arms and immediately turned into a mother hen.

It was Duncan who'd come home with a small wolf cub no bigger than Mikaela herself three and a half years ago, claiming that every kid needed a pet. But Kee knew Duncan had more likely been getting yet another protector for their daughter.

The men had named the wolf Rex Regum, the King of Kings.

Two years ago Mikaela had renamed him Mickey Mouse.

The wolf didn't seem to care what he was called; like his two-legged counterparts, he was also deeply in love with their tyrannical little angel.

If Mikaela got punished—which was always harder on the men than on her—it was Mickey who curled up with her in her bunk and patiently kept her company for the time-out.

And when Mikaela got sick—which was always harder on the men than on her—everyone, including the wolf, went into a state of panic.

Their daughter was God's greatest blessing and their worst nightmare. It was a wonder the six of them had been able to keep the precocious, curious, and often exasperating child from killing herself.

"We have three days before Mikaela arrives," Kee told them. "Let's make the most of it. Let's solve this mystery and get on with the business of settling in here." He looked at each of his men. "It's time we put down roots. Mikaela needs to be enrolled in school, and I like the idea of raising her here in Puffin Harbor."

"But Kee," Duncan said softly. "Ya know we can't stay."

Everyone shifted uncomfortably at that declaration.

"What about Rachel?" Jason asked into the ensuing silence. "What do we do about her?"

Kee eyed each of his men in turn. "You just solve the problem of Thaddeus Lakeman's missing art. I'll take care of Rachel."

Rachel had her own problems to take care of, and they seemed to be compounding exponentially. If finding out she'd inherited millions of dollars of stolen art wasn't enough, now she was suspected of stealing legitimate art as well.

Rachel fluffed the lump of towels under her blankets, shaping it into a curve that looked like her body. She smiled, realizing this was the oldest trick in the book and was probably the first place Kee would check.

That thought quickly sobered her. Kee wouldn't be checking anything, because he wouldn't be coming to steal any kisses—not after tonight's not-so-subtle encounter in the foyer.

Rachel straightened, heaving a pitiful sigh. So much for Kee's warning that denying her passion was a dangerous thing. She had finally decided that a hot and steamy, old-fashioned affair might be a good idea after all—that maybe this little attack of lust she was having was actually healthy.

It should certainly be safe. Keenan Oakes didn't seem to get emotionally attached to women, if his attitude toward Joan that first night was any indication. He hadn't even taken the time to get over their breakup. In fact, he'd turned his attention—and kisses—to Rachel rather quickly, now that she thought about it.

And what about Mikaela's mother? There had never been any mention of her—from any of the men, for that matter. Not that Rachel had asked, though she did wonder if Kee was widowed or divorced.

But did she really care? Nope. She just wanted to jump the guy's sexy bones, not build a life with him.

Rachel sat down on the bed next to her lumpy likeness and absently massaged her knee. Who was she kidding? It wasn't simple lust she was experiencing, but full-blown, unadulterated, undeniable passion. She'd been living like a nun too long, and her newly awakened hormones had zeroed in on Mr. Arresting Oakes.

Not that it mattered now.

It was time to go home. Sub Rosa was up and running, finding Thadd's secret room had just bottomed out on her list of priorities, and her need to gather the rest of her dad's contraband—and discreetly dispose of it—had risen to the top.

If she couldn't locate Thadd's secret room, Kee certainly wasn't going to, even if he lived here for the rest of his life. And whoever had been stealing from Sub Rosa was Kee's problem now. As long as the Foster name couldn't be tied to any illegal activities—past or present—then she and Willow were safe.

Bolstered by her reasoning, Rachel looked at her watch for the tenth time. Good Lord! While waiting for the house to quiet down, she'd spent more than four hours taking a bath, shaving her legs, covering every inch of her body with lotion, giving herself a manicure and pedicure, washing and drying and brushing her hair until it shone, and then weaving it into a single thick braid fastened with a barrette shaped like a moose and a pine tree.

It was after midnight. Surely the men were asleep by now.

Rachel stood up and checked to make sure she had the fake emerald necklace and single fake earring in her pocket. She still couldn't believe she'd lost one of the earrings and that—just her luck—Kee had found it. Which only proved yet again that she must never consider becoming a professional burglar.

She started toward the door, spotted her cane standing in the corner of her bedroom, and stopped and shifted most of her weight to her right leg. Her knee felt surprisingly sound, with barely a hint of pain, so Rachel decided the cane would be more of a nuisance than a help. She picked up the flashlight instead, which she'd pilfered from the kitchen earlier, and opened the bedroom door.

She nearly tripped over Mickey.

"Are you waiting to see me?" she whispered, bending down and patting the yawning wolf on the head. "Or are you hoping to sneak in and eat my cat?"

Mickey yawned again as he sat facing her, then cocked his head in lupine inquiry. Had Kee put the wolf on guard by her door, just as he had that first night, or was Mickey only looking for some female company?

Rachel found herself in a quandary. Did she dare bring Mickey into the tunnels with her? Damn. If she did disappear into the wall without him, he'd likely scratch the panel raw trying to follow her.

"Oh, come on," she whispered, limping down the hall toward the great room. "I'm about to let you in on a very big secret, but you have to promise not to tell anyone."

Mickey silently padded beside her all the way to the great room until Rachel stopped in front of the huge granite hearth on the west wall.

"Now, this is important," she told her companion. "You have to know just which stone to push."

Rachel applied pressure to one of the granite stones until she heard a click come from the wall on the right side of the hearth. Mickey immediately stuck his nose in the crack.

Rachel pulled the panel all the way open.

Mickey disappeared into the dark void.

Rachel snapped her flashlight on and followed, stopping only long enough to close the panel behind them.

Dust immediately assaulted her nose. Mickey was already exploring the passage, well out of the beam of her flashlight.

"Get back here," she whispered, walking down the narrow passage. "You're going to get lost."

Her only answer was the faint vibration of the electrical turbines humming in gentle echoes through the tunnel.

Great. Another contrary male with a mind of his own.

Rachel continued down the passageway, deciding that it was Mickey's responsibility to find her, and didn't stop until she came to an intersection of tunnels. To the left was a set of stairs that led all the way up to the third floor and came out in the tapestry room. Straight ahead led to another intersection that would bring her to the foyer. And if she went right, she'd end up in the tunnel that came out on the cliffs just above the Gulf of Maine.

Rachel lowered the beam of her flashlight to the floor, looking for paw prints that would tell her which direction Mickey had taken.

What she found, though, besides Mickey's prints heading up the stairs to her left, were several human footprints, mostly traveling from the cliff tunnel and continuing up to the third floor. She leaned over and set the beam of her light on the clearest print.

It was definitely male—a size eleven or twelve, maybe—and looked like a sneaker tread. She moved the light again, stopping on another print, this one smaller—definitely that of a woman.

Rachel straightened and stared into the darkness. Two sets of footprints: one male, one female.

Dammit. Who else knew about these tunnels?

"Think," she absently whispered to herself. "Who could possibly know about these passageways? Female. Female," she softly repeated, trying to picture all the women who had visited Sub Rosa when Thadd was alive.

Her mother, for one. Marian had certainly known about the tunnels. Rachel aimed the flashlight back at the floor. But these footprints were fresh, not three years old. There was almost no dust covering some of them.

"Come on, Rachel. Who else?"

Mary Alder, Thadd's girlfriend, might have known about the passageways. Had Thadd and Mary been close enough that he'd trusted her with such a secret?

Maybe. But if she did know, why would she be visiting Sub Rosa now, after all these years?

Rachel considered Mary Alder. It was sad what had happened to Mary after Thadd's death. The once proud, vibrant, and beautiful woman who'd enjoyed the status of being Thadd's girlfriend had become a recluse after the tragedy. She was seen walking in town, only occasionally and usually at night, in a state of disarray, mindless of those around her and usually talking to herself.

Which was why Rachel doubted these footprints belonged to Mary. And even if they did, that didn't explain the male footprints.

Mary did have a son. Mark Alder. He'd been running the Lakeman Boatyard for nearly eight years now.

"Naw," Rachel said to herself. "Not Mark. He's weirder than his mother."

About six months after her parents had died, Mark started asking Rachel to go out with him. It had taken nearly a year of gentle refusals for Mark to finally get the message that she wasn't interested.

For lack of a better term, Mark Alder was a dork, and an odd dork at that. He was a mama's boy, still living at home at the age of thirty-three, and he rode a rusty old bicycle to work even in winter. He'd been two years ahead of Rachel in high school, and even then he'd worked at Thadd's boatyard as a painter.

Naw. They couldn't be Mark's footprints. Besides, Mark had never liked Thadd—he always thought Thadd should have married his mother instead of just stringing her along.

Maybe . . . maybe Willow had been here.

Rachel aimed her flashlight back on the smaller footprint. It wasn't a sneaker tread, like the larger one, but a dress shoe.

Willow wore dress shoes. And she knew about the passageways. But she hated Sub Rosa.

But did she hate it enough to pilfer its treasures?

Nope. Not Willow. Besides, she'd been too focused on law school and pursuing her new career.

Rachel sat down on the bottom granite step and absently massaged her knee. "Think. Who else?"

What about the workers who had built Sub Rosa? Rachel remembered discussing with her dad her worry that they would know about the secret passageways since they were actually building them. Frank Foster had thought he'd solved that problem—or at least minimized it—by bringing in a crew of stonemasons from Guatemala.

But they could have told someone.

Rachel suddenly tensed at a thought. Raoul Vegas. What about the dealer her dad had mentioned in his letter, who was in the business of "redistributing" stolen art? Could he possibly know about the tunnels?

He might, if he'd dealt directly with Thadd.

Rachel aimed the beam of her flashlight down the tunnel that led to the cliffs and hugged herself against the sudden shiver racing down her spine. She didn't know much about criminals—that was Willow's department—but she doubted they were very nice people.

Had Raoul Vegas been quietly helping himself to Sub Rosa's wealth for the last three years?

Rachel shook that thought away, dismissing the idea—or rather hoping—that an international criminal had not been sneaking around here. Or that he might still be in the area.

Besides, it still didn't explain the smaller footprints.

Well, heck. The more she thought about it, any number of people might know about the passageways.

Rachel snorted. Here she was trying to keep her "big secret" from Kee, when a virtual parade of people had obviously been using the tunnels on a regular basis.

Maybe when she left Sub Rosa later, she should simply leave one of the panels open. Kee would find the passageways and discover the footprints just as she had and know that someone besides his neighbor was roaming through his house at will.

Something bumped against her back. Rachel jumped up and spun around, holding her flashlight like a weapon, only to find Mickey standing on the stairs above her, his tail wagging and his eyes gleaming like silver stars.

Rachel covered her racing heart with her hand and took a calming breath. "Dammit. You scared me," she scolded in a whisper. "Give a girl some warning, will you? Make a little noise next time."

Seemingly oblivious to her fright, Mickey turned and trotted back up the stairs. Rachel followed at a much slower pace, favoring her knee.

And again she lost the wolf. She continued climbing, passing several intersecting tunnels on the second floor, and finally reached the panel that opened into the tapestry room.

"Pssst. Here, Mickey." She softly whistled. "Come on, boy. It's time to go back to the real world."

She continued to call, then finally gave up and slowly pushed on the panel. A warm current of air rushed into the room from the tunnel, creating an eerie moan.

She pushed the panel all the way open, and Mickey brushed past her leg.

"Will you cut that out!" she hissed, stepping out of the tunnel and sweeping her flashlight around the room. "You're going to get us cau—"

Rachel swallowed her words the moment the beam of her flashlight landed on a pair of leather-shoed feet, crossed at the ankles, attached to a shadowed but definitely male body sitting in a chair on the other side of the room.

Chapter Ten

*M*ickey *was sitting facing the chair,* his wagging tail sending wisps of dust sparkling through the narrow beam of her flashlight. Rachel clicked off the flashlight, dropped her head, and sighed. Damn. She definitely needed a new career. Sneaking around Sub Rosa was becoming an exercise in futility.

And just as before, Keenan Oakes had nothing to say.

Rachel lifted her head, squared her shoulders on a deep breath, and tried to see past the stark moonlight cutting through the room. "I'm not a thief," she firmly whispered. "I have never taken anything from Sub Rosa."

The shadow stood.

Then slowly started toward her.

Rachel took a cautious step back. "I'm not a thief."

He stopped just six paces away, the moonlight slicing across his body, illuminating the broad stance of his legs while keeping the upper half of him in shadow. She couldn't see his hands, and assumed he had his arms crossed over his chest—as he was in the habit of doing whenever he was in a speculative mood.

"I'm not a thief," she repeated, just in case he hadn't heard her the first two times.

"I know," came his soft reply from the darkness.

She took a step closer. "You know?"

He also moved a step closer. "But you do like to trespass."

"I'm not trespassing. I'm a guest here."

He took another step forward, the moonlight now reaching his crossed arms. "You're a guest who's standing in the middle of a locked room."

Well, there was that. "I was looking for you," she lied, staring directly at his face, pretending she could see him.

"And why is that?"

"To tell you I'm not a thief."

"And it couldn't wait until morning?"

"I couldn't sleep, with you and everyone else thinking I've been taking things from Sub Rosa."

"They don't think that, Rachel. They're as . . ." He uncrossed his arms and held his hands away from his sides in a gesture of acquiescence. "They're as charmed by you as I am."

Charmed? He was charmed?

That was good, wasn't it? That she'd charmed him into believing she wasn't a thief?

"That's not how it looked earlier in the foyer."

He took another step forward, which brought him close enough that she could actually feel the heat of his body. And smell him. And—oh, God—she could practically taste him.

"You didn't stick around long enough to find out what

we thought," he said, his whisper sending a succession of shivers down her spine.

Rachel was back to her proximity problem. Her palms itched, and it was all she could do not to reach out and touch him.

"Do you remember what I told you in our workout room, right after you kissed me?" he asked, reaching behind her and gently lifting her braid, pulling it over her shoulder.

"I . . ." Rachel swallowed and tried again. "I don't remem—what did you say?" she asked hoarsely, trying to see his face through the shadows. She couldn't see a damn thing, so she looked down—and could only watch, mesmerized, as he deftly opened the clasp, pocketed her barrette, and then slowly twined the freed ends of her hair around his fingers.

"I told you that the next time we reached this point, I intended to finish it."

"And we . . . we're at that point now?"

Slowly, and with such gentle precision that Rachel tingled all the way down to her toes, Kee began unraveling her braid.

"We're past that point, Rachel."

Her skin tightened in awareness.

The braid slowly unfurled, and his hand moved higher.

Breathing became difficult.

And when his fingers finally reached the nape of her neck, he cupped her head, leaned down and brought his lips to hers—not kissing her, not quite touching her—just close enough to bring every nerve in her body alive in anticipation.

"Either smack me with your flashlight, Rachel, or kiss me."

The flashlight clattered to the floor.

Rachel threw herself against him, wrapped her arms around his neck, and kissed him so fiercely that even a dead man would get the point.

He lifted her off her feet, his hands cupping her bottom to hold her against him, as he took several steps forward. Kee pushed Rachel back against the oak panel she'd come through, and her only escape banged shut with resounding finality.

Not that she cared at the moment, with her mouth so busy feasting on his. She wrapped her legs around his waist while canting her head to deepen the kiss, pulling the taste of pure heaven into her mouth. He braced one hand on the wall, his other hand still holding her securely, and obligingly parted his lips.

Years of denied passion exploded inside her. Rockets went off in her brain. Her heart raced, her skin heated, and the shell of protection she'd carefully built suddenly shattered with deafening glory.

Kee thrust his hips forward, pressing her against the tapestry room panel, and reached for the buttons on her blouse. His lips moved from her mouth to her cheek, then lower and to the side, until he was nuzzling a deliciously sensitive spot below her left ear.

Rachel moaned her pleasure, just to let him know he was driving her crazy in a very good way.

She couldn't think, couldn't seem to move other than tremble. There was something . . . something she wanted to do.

The first button on her blouse gave way, then the next, and the next one.

Ah, yes. That was it. She wanted to undress him and

run her hands over every inch of his body. Tension and heat and passion radiated from him, battering her like the ocean waves pounding the granite cliffs outside.

He was finishing it, he'd told her. Tonight. Now. Here. God, she hoped so.

She reached down to the hem of his shirt and tugged, wiggling it up his ribs, only to moan again when his lips captured her earlobe. His tongue teased and probed and promised even more.

"Help me," she whispered, tugging at his shirt. She needed to touch his bare skin, the fever inside her beginning to spiral out of control.

He leaned back, his hips keeping her firmly planted against the wall, and with one deft movement, his shirt disappeared.

Rachel made a sound of thanks and leaned into him, laying her face on his chest and wrapping her arms around his now naked torso. His heart thumped against her cheek with the power of a locomotive. His skin was moist, the hair on his chest soft and sensuous, tickling her lips in a most delicious way.

She licked his nipple, and was rewarded with a moan so male in nature it sent shivers of pure feminine delight racing through every cell of her body.

He pushed her blouse off her shoulders, pulling the straps of her bra with it. "Help me," he demanded rawly, trying to peel her clothes off, too.

Rachel let go of him long enough to unclip her bra and slip her arms free, then immediately went back to touching him, tracing each powerful muscle on his shoulders and arms and neck, reaching up to kiss him again.

The contact this time was hotter, more frenzied—and

maybe just a bit desperate. Her nipples engorged as they brushed his chest hair, making them supersensitive. He pressed heavily against her, the bulge of his arousal burning through her jeans.

Rachel's insides convulsed. She couldn't take much more of this torment. She yearned—hurt—to have him inside her.

"Finish it," she whispered beside his ear, letting her tongue linger, feeling a shudder run through him.

He stepped back, set her on her feet, and attacked the zipper of her jeans. Rachel quickly slipped out of her shoes and went for his belt, the task overly difficult because her hands wouldn't quit shaking.

Their breathing grew labored, their urgency palpable.

He shoved her jeans down to her ankles at just the same time as she pushed down his. He lifted her up, moving her back against the wall as before. Rachel wrapped her legs around him, this time gasping at the shock of having nothing between them.

Nothing but glorious, quivering heat.

He positioned her higher, then stopped suddenly, the tight muscles of his arms twitching, his eyes closed, breaths rasping from his lungs.

Rachel realized he was fighting for control.

She didn't want that. She dug her nails into his skin to make him look at her, and stared up past the angular planes of his face in the moonlight into dark-blue eyes blazing with primordial need.

"It's not trespassing if you've been invited," she told him, shooting him a crooked smile. "Or do I need to clarify that point as well?"

A shudder ran through him, shaking them both.

Rachel tilted her pelvis, relaxing her thighs to lower herself until she could feel the tip of his shaft probing the wet folds of her opening.

And still he held back.

"I've always had a thing for cavemen," she whispered.

His eyes burned at her reference to their first meeting, his nostrils flaring and his hands biting into her thighs. He swore, grabbing a fistful of her hair as he braced one forearm on the wall behind her and captured her mouth in a hard and consuming kiss. He moved that kiss to her cheek, then her throat, then buried his face in the crook of her neck and thrust forward, and upward, not stopping until she was fully impaled.

Rachel sucked in her breath at the deep invasion. She took advantage of his stillness to adjust to his size, willing her inner muscles to relax, to yield and accept him.

"I need to move, Rachel," he growled, his mouth hot and wet, his teeth rasping her neck—then his lips soothing her skin.

But still he waited, her noble caveman. Rachel arched against him, buried her own face in his shoulder, and lightly bit her permission.

He moved with the force of a hurricane, fast and hard and completely out of control. Rachel cried out, not in distress but in triumph. She rode the storm she'd created, joyously meeting each powerful thrust of his hips.

The wall at her back, the room, the house, the world—it all slipped away in a haze of erotic smells and tastes and sensations. She welcomed each thrust with small moans of encouragement, matching his own grunts of pleasure.

She climaxed quickly, bucking against him, consumed

by convulsions that exploded from her in a scream of fulfillment.

He pounded deeper and harder and faster, then suddenly stopped. She felt him come then, embedded all the way up inside her, his shaft pulsing against her seizing muscles.

He dropped his head to her shoulder, his huffing breaths pushing his sweat-soaked chest against hers. Their hearts pounded as tiny shudders continued to ripple through each sensitized nerve of her body. She clenched on a lingering spasm that pulled him even deeper inside her.

His head snapped up, his gaze narrowed on hers. He thrust forward slightly, retreated, then forward once more, this time with deliberate purpose, closing his eyes on a curse that was more groaned than spoken.

He straightened abruptly, pulling her away from the wall, and stood in the middle of the room, holding her in their erotic embrace—Kee still deeply seated inside her and Rachel only able to cling like quivering jelly.

He started for the door, and the movement embedded him deeper, the sensation causing Rachel to clench involuntarily around him.

He stopped, and growled, and changed direction.

"If you keep bouncing me around, I'm going to come again," she warned through gritted teeth, desperately trying not to.

He stilled, staring directly into her eyes with a heat so intense, she melted right there in front of him and climaxed again.

He made a sound—half wounded animal, half angry lion—and dropped to his knees, laying her down on the rug without breaking contact, driving deeply into her with a pounding force that sent her climax into hyperdrive.

He reared up, threw his head back, and entered the storm again.

And finally they were finished.

Point made.

Driven home quite soundly.

Rachel lay on the dusty carpet—Kee half on her, half off her—and stared at nothing, the silence broken only by heavy breathing and thumping hearts. She could count on one hand the number of men she'd been with. Heck, she could count on her fingers and toes the number of times she'd actually done it.

She'd never done it like this, though, with such . . . such . . . dammit, with such *need*. If she hadn't felt him inside her, she would have just died. Or gone crazy.

Hell, she had gone crazy. She was lying on the floor with a demigod sprawled across her, and she'd just climaxed twice—the second time *by just looking at him*.

The genie was out of the bottle.

Passion had finally won over good sense.

He levered himself up on one elbow to stare at her, his large, utterly masculine, slightly trembling hand brushing the tangle of hair off her face.

"I'm locking you in the south tower and keeping the key around my neck. You're one dangerous lady."

She wouldn't look at him. Couldn't. Not while her palms still itched to touch him, and definitely not while her whole body still throbbed with erotic sensations.

She was a danger, all right—to herself.

"I wouldn't be there long. There's a tunnel out of the south tower," she told him, staring up at the dark ceiling that she knew was exactly twelve feet, nine inches away.

His sigh moved through her hair and cooled her sweaty face. He lifted himself up on his hands, straddling her head with his arms and kneeling between her spread legs, replacing her view of the ceiling with his broad chest, powerful shoulders, hard-muscled arms—and his damned arresting blue eyes and a mouth made for driving women crazy.

"If you don't quit looking at me like that," he said rawly, his eyes narrowed in warning, "we're not going to make it to a bed this time, either."

Every cell in her body went on full alert. But before she could react, Kee pulled her upright, stood, and swept her into his arms.

Where did the man get his strength? She couldn't even lift her own arms enough to wrap them around his neck.

He headed for the door to the hallway.

"We're naked," she thought to remind him. "You're not carrying me through Sub Rosa like this."

He stopped long enough to open the door, and then they were out in the hallway. Rachel blinked at the sudden brightness from the blazing wall sconces set exactly ten feet apart.

Kee carried her into the bedroom across the hall from the tapestry room, headed for the bed, pulled back the covers—God only knew how he could do that without dropping her—then dropped her onto the cool sheets and landed on top of her.

"Are you on the pill?"

"No."

He whispered a curse, then took her by the chin and made her face him. "When's your period due?"

"In a couple of weeks."

He swore again, a bit cruder and with even more feeling. Rachel pulled her chin away, but he grabbed it back. He leaned in close and said softly, "You'll tell me the minute you start, because I'll be on you every day until we know if you're pregnant."

How . . . chivalrous of him.

The glow of their lovemaking—or rather their wild frenzy—died a quick death. He was actually angry. At her? Hell, he'd started it. He should have left her damned hair alone.

Rachel tried to get up.

But he rolled her onto her back and pinned her to the bed with his weight. "And just where are you going?" he asked softly.

"Home." She hesitated, thinking she should probably say something else. Something nice, maybe. "Ah, thank you. I had a . . . a wonderful time."

The look he gave her was confounded, almost comical, before he suddenly snorted, dropped his forehead to hers, and shook them both with his laughter.

Rachel's temper flared. She shoved at him and was surprised when he cooperated. But instead of rolling off her, he only leaned to the side far enough to reach the drawer in the bedside table. He opened it, pulled out a string of packets, and quickly returned his weight over her.

It was a little late to close the barn door, wasn't it? The cow had gotten out ten minutes ago—twice! Rachel couldn't decide if she was angry or excited.

"We're finishing it, by God," he growled, setting the packets on the pillow beside her.

"We . . . we're not finished?"

"Dammit, Rachel. I've come twice and I haven't even touched you yet. Here," he whispered, tracing one finger down the length of her neck to between her breasts. "And here," he said, his voice turning raw as he trailed that maddening finger up to one engorged nipple. "And here," he continued, settling beside her and running his finger down over her ribs, dipping into her belly button, then continuing on.

Her stomach muscles quivered. Her insides clenched. Moisture gathered again between her thighs, and Rachel could only close her eyes as his journey continued even lower.

"And . . . here," he whispered gutturally, his mouth tracing the path of his finger.

Rachel gripped two fistfuls of his hair, undecided whether to stop him or help him. But he suddenly found just the right spot, and made just the right sound of appreciation.

With a heartfelt curse of her own, Rachel arched up and said in a near shout, "Okay, we can finish."

Chapter Eleven

*T*he *man* *was* *insatiable*. The first hint of dawn
had crept through the windows by the time they'd used
the last of the condoms, and he still wouldn't quit. His
tongue was now making its way up her arm, after lavish-
ing kisses over every inch of her right hand—which she
was simply too weak to lift away.

She couldn't move.

Didn't want to.

Rachel decided she would just lie in this bed forever
and die a happy woman—happy and completely satisfied.
Heck, she had actually reached that point somewhere
after the fourth time.

That's when she'd quit counting.

"You're going to have to do it without me this time,"
she muttered into her pillow, attempting to gather the
energy to swat him away. "I'm dead."

She was answered by a weak grunt from someplace

on her left, and a pitiful whine near her now wet right shoulder.

Rachel's brain finally kicked in. Mickey.

She still didn't open her eyes. "I'm locking your wolf in the dungeon, Oakes, if you don't teach him some manners."

Another grunt from her left, this one sounding pained.

Rachel was proud of herself. It was damned hard work bringing a demigod to his knees.

Mickey finally got Rachel to open her eyes by licking her cheek. She didn't know where she found the strength, but she swatted him away and rolled off the bed, taking the sheet with her, using the momentum to wrap it around herself.

She stood on rubbery legs, wonderfully numb from the neck down, and stared back at the bed. She blinked . . . once . . . twice . . . but still couldn't focus. She ran a shaky hand over her face only to have to brush a tangle of hair out of the way. Ah, now she could see, and the view was magnificent.

Her demigod was sprawled on his back, either shamelessly comfortable or dead. Rachel started her eye's journey at his toes, deciding to drink in the vision of him in an orderly fashion so she could tuck the memory away for a rainy day.

The bottoms of his feet were callused, his knees—ahem—looked a bit rug-burned, and his thighs were long and sinuous and wonderfully muscled. She continued higher, and his—ahem—well, he was definitely sated. She quickly moved on to his stomach, which had more ripples than a whole bag of potato chips. His chest was covered with soft curls, and his thick neck had a couple of red spots she hoped he had enough manners to pass off as razor burns.

Rachel continued onward and upward, eager to feast on his arresting face, only to find him silently watching her. She hoisted her sheet higher and lifted her chin.

He waggled two fingers at her, not even able to lift his hand off the bed. "Come here, so I can wipe that look off your face," he said hoarsely.

"You can't even wipe your own face."

"Come back to bed, Rachel, before you fall down."

She noticed the watch on his arm then. "What time is it?"

"I don't know," he said, trying to lift his arm but failing. "You got a hot date to get to?"

She made the mistake of leaning over to look at his watch. He suddenly bolted upright and dragged her down beside him. "That's better," he said, tucking her firmly against his side.

"You faker. You're not dead."

"I am now. That finished me," he muttered, flopping an arm over her so she couldn't escape. "Go to sleep, Rachel. It can't be noon yet."

Noon . . . noon . . . she needed to do something at noon.

"Willow!" she cried, sitting up. "She's going to call!" She turned and pushed at his arm still holding her. "If I'm not home, she'll come here, and God save us then!"

He threw his flopping arm over his face with a pitiful groan. "Mickey will have to save us. God's busy watching my boat." He moved that arm up to his forehead and gazed at her curiously. "Are you afraid of your sister?" His eyes widened. "Should I be afraid of your sister?"

Rachel nodded. "She can be a terror when she's mad."

"And she'll be mad . . . why? You're a big girl, Rachel. You can spend the night at a guy's house if you want."

"Not this house. And not with you."

With another groan and what seemed like a rather heroic effort, he sat up, scrubbed his face with his hands, twisted his shoulders as if trying to get the kinks out, then softly cursed.

Rachel gathered up the ends of her sheet and turned and hobbled to the door. She stopped, leaned past the doorjamb, and peeked down the hall in both directions. "Ah, where do you suppose everyone is?"

"If they're smart, they're not in this wing," he said, coming up behind her, totally naked, completely shameless.

Rachel scooted across the hall, tripping into the tapestry room when Mickey rushed in ahead of her. Kee stepped on her trailing sheet, bringing her to an abrupt halt.

"I am capable of getting dressed without helpers," she snapped, tugging the sheet free and going in search of her clothes.

She could see her blouse crumpled against a table, her pants—in a fireman's heap, ready for her to step into—on the floor by the wall, and her bra was a good six feet past her blouse. She could only see one sock beside both sneakers, and couldn't find her panties anywhere.

"Mickey has something for you," Kee said.

She turned and looked at Kee first, heat instantly flushing her cheeks. He was standing in the middle of the room, still shamelessly naked, holding his pants.

She looked for Mickey then and found him sitting by the door, his tail kicking up a cloud of dust and her panties dangling from his mouth.

She limped over to the wolf, and after a brief tug of war got her panties back, along with a bit of canine slobber. She pulled the sheet up over her shoulders, faced away from Kee, and awkwardly slipped into them.

She picked up her bra next, turning again and slipping it on under the sheet. Mickey brought her blouse over, and Rachel wiped away a bit of drool and then slipped it on and finally let the sheet fall to the floor.

Kee finally had his pants on and was just reaching for his shirt when a small thud sounded by the wall.

Mickey had her pants in his mouth—and sitting on the floor in front of him was that damned emerald necklace.

Rachel stared at the necklace, unable to move.

Kee had no such problem. He walked over, patted Mickey on the head, picked up the necklace, and silently turned to Rachel.

Rachel grabbed her pants from the wolf and put them on. She gave up on her lost sock and sat down in a chair and put on her sneakers, tucking the one sock in her pocket as she stood.

Her hand came out with the remaining emerald earring. She walked over to Kee, dropped it in his palm beside the necklace, then continued over to the wall she'd come through last night. She twisted a piece of molding, and the panel popped open.

"Whenever you come to a panel in the tunnels, just push on the edge and it'll open," she told Kee, watching Mickey disappear through the wall. "The best way to find them is from the tunnel side. From the room side, most open with either a twist of the molding or a push on something nearby."

She finally turned and faced him. "As you explore the passageways, you'll find some fairly fresh footprints. Most lead from the cliffs below up to this room. I found prints of both a man and a woman. The small sneaker prints are mine."

She waited, but Kee had nothing to say, so she continued. "Obviously others know about the tunnels, and have been coming and going for quite some time now. I suggest you padlock the gate down by the cliffs. Or dynamite it shut," she added, heading for the hallway.

Kee stepped in front of her, still holding the emeralds. "Do you really expect to just walk out of here without explaining these?" he asked, holding them toward her.

"Yes, that's exactly what I expect to do."

"Dammit, Rachel. They were locked in the vault. In safe number sixteen." He stepped closer, shoved the emeralds in his pocket, then took hold of her shoulders. "But now the set in number sixteen is worth over one million dollars."

She smiled up at him. "Congratulations. Your inheritance is growing by leaps and bounds."

He shook her, his face darkening around his narrowed sea-blue eyes. "They were stolen from an estate in France almost seventeen years ago. I want to know where you got them."

"But I don't 'got' them. You do."

He shook her again, a bit more roughly, then suddenly stopped, let her go, and stepped back. He ran a hand through his tousled hair, eyeing her speculatively, then let out a sigh so harsh that her own mess of curls actually moved.

"It's grand larceny, Rachel," he said softly.

"I am not a thief."

"Where did you get them?"

Rachel sighed. "You can ask me a thousand times, and my last answer will be the same as the first one. I can't tell you, Kee. I have no idea who stole them originally, nor do I care."

"Just tell me where you got them."

"No. Final answer. End of discussion. So either let me leave or take me to the police station and press charges." She lifted her chin. "Although I can't think what those charges would be, since the stolen emeralds are sitting in your vault."

He took her chin in his hand and leaned his face into hers. "This isn't a game, Rachel. And walking out of Sub Rosa won't make your problem go away. Whomever it is you're protecting isn't worth the trouble I'm going to cause you. Instead of fighting me, let me help you."

Rachel said nothing.

Kee tightened his fingers on her chin. "I know you had nothing to do with stealing the originals. You would have been—what?—fourteen at the time? But if those footprints belong to the people who did, shutting me out could be dangerous."

"I'm not shutting you out, I'm shutting myself out. I'm done, Kee. I'm going home and getting on with my life."

"I'm part of your life now," he said softly.

Rachel's eyes widened. "Because of last night?"

He nodded.

She reached up and took hold of his chin in an exact parody of his hold on hers and squeezed. "Last night was remarkable. In fact, it was the best night of my life. But it was not a commitment of any kind, for either of us."

He stepped out of her grasp and slipped his sweatshirt over his head, then stood staring at her for several seconds, not saying anything. He suddenly bowed at the waist and swept his hand toward the door in dismissal.

Rachel didn't wait for him to change his mind and quickly headed for the hallway.

"Rachel," he said, just as she reached the door.

She stopped and looked over her shoulder. "Yes?"

"If you turn up pregnant, we're both committed."

Kee emerged from the tunnel into early afternoon sunshine, moving out of the way so Jason could also step through the iron gate. They joined Duncan and Luke, who were already standing on the cliff, Duncan facing Sub Rosa and Luke scanning the rocks below.

"I can't see how anyone could land a boat here," Duncan said, turning to Kee. "They had to have come in on foot."

"Maybe there's a lower tunnel that reaches the tide. It'll take weeks to explore all these passageways," Jason said, shaking his head. "It's quite an elaborate system."

Kee stared at the pine-studded bluff the mansion stood on. "But the tunnels do have a certain methodology. They seem to be laid out with one major artery and several side tunnels leading to various points in the house."

"These look like skid marks," Luke said, hunched down about ten feet away, examining the ground. "Here," he added, pointing to the base of a young pine tree. "Someone fell right here."

Kee walked over to Luke and saw where the moss had been scraped off the granite in several places, rosebushes were broken, and patches of sea grass had been pulled up by the roots.

He walked farther down the cliff, following the skid marks as they continued right up to the edge. He leaned forward and silently stared down at the churning water a good thirty feet below, and his insides suddenly turned cold.

Rachel had fallen.

She had nearly slid off the cliff in her flight from the library that first night. Dammit, she could have drowned—assuming the fall wouldn't have killed her first.

Kee turned hard eyes on Duncan, who had come to stand beside him. The look on Duncan's face said he understood the markings as well as he did.

"Rachel Foster needs a keeper," Kee said. "And starting now, she's got six. I want her watched around the clock. If that suicidal woman so much as chips a fingernail, I want to know about it."

He turned to include Luke and Jason. "The plan has changed. I thought we were coming here to search for a dead man's stash of stolen goods, but the footprints we found in the tunnels just turned this little treasure hunt into a man hunt."

"It's not safe for Mikaela," Duncan interjected, still staring over the cliff, then looking at Kee.

Kee nodded agreement, then gave Duncan a perverse grin. "Then you radio Ahab and tell him not to dock."

Duncan held up his hands and snorted. "Not me. That lunatic's liable to turn his cannons on us. And Mikaela will be reloading for him." He shook his head. "She'll swim to shore if she has to. She misses us."

"It's more likely the other way around," Kee muttered.

Hell, they all missed their little angel.

"She could stay with Rachel," Jason suggested. "Since

we'll be watching her anyway, we'll just keep an eye on both of them."

Kee raised a brow at Jason. "That's assuming Rachel won't bring her back to us in a burlap sack. Mikaela doesn't have a very good track record when it comes to dealing with women."

Duncan waved that away. "That's because the women you've been bringing around are like Joan. Rachel's different." He hesitated, giving Kee a speculative look. "It might be good for both of them," he said softly. "Mikaela's getting to the point where she needs some feminine input."

"And Rachel?" Kee asked.

Duncan's grin was more diabolical than genial. "Rachel might as well get to know our little girl." He hesitated only a heartbeat, then said, "After last night."

Kee's eyes narrowed in warning. "And what happened last night?" he asked softly.

Duncan shrugged. "Ya turned up missing till noon. And as it happens, so did Rachel. Ya said she needs a keeper. Why not see if ya might keep her a bit longer than the others?"

Kee's heart stopped for the briefest of seconds, then started thumping with the force of a sledgehammer. He glanced at Jason and Luke, only to find them smiling like simpletons, nodding agreement with Duncan.

"My love life is not open to majority rule," he snapped, turning to glare at Duncan. "And have you forgotten that Rachel Foster is in this mess all the way up to her lying little neck?"

Duncan waved that away as well. "Bah. She's obviously protecting someone."

"Not another man," Jason said.

"What makes you so sure of that?" Kee asked.

"How do you think Mickey got into your bedroom this morning?" Jason asked in answer.

Kee's growl of warning for his men to butt out of his love life would have done the wolf proud. He turned on his heel and headed back into the tunnel.

"Maybe it's her sister," Duncan said as they walked single-file up the tunnel. "Willow, isn't it? She's a lawyer or something. Maybe Rachel's protecting her."

Kee stopped and turned his flashlight on Duncan. "According to Rachel, her sister is more than capable of taking care of herself," Kee told him. "I agree, she's protecting someone, and our first order of business is to find out who."

"You want me to secure the end of the tunnel so we don't get any more visitors?" Jason asked.

Kee aimed his flashlight back toward the entrance to the tunnel and shook his head. "No. Rig some sort of warning device instead that will let us know when our visitors arrive."

Jason rubbed his hands together. "Yeah," he said. "I've got something that will work. How about a pager system for our belts? That way it'll be silent."

Kee nodded. "Get Matthew to help you. And try and cover our own tracks in the tunnels. No need to warn them we've been here."

"What about Mikaela?" Duncan asked. "Are ya going to let the *Six-to-One Odds* dock?"

Kee thought about that, torn between wanting to protect his daughter and wanting her with him. He blew out a frustrated breath and rubbed the back of his neck.

"They're still two days out. She can dock, and I'll ask Rachel if she wants a little company for a few days." He looked at Duncan for agreement. "But if things get dicey, both Rachel and Mikaela are getting packed aboard the *Six-to-One Odds* and shipped out to sea."

"And if Rachel doesn't want to go?" Duncan asked.

Kee smiled. "It might take two or three of us, and a length of rope, but I think we can get her on board."

Duncan made the sign of the cross over his chest. "Ahab's going to slit our throats in our sleep," he muttered, walking deeper into the tunnel, Jason and Luke following him.

Kee stood where he was and broke into a cold sweat. Mikaela and Rachel together—now, there was a scary thought.

Rachel had stayed in the shower until every last drop of hot water was gone, using nearly a whole bottle of conditioner trying to get the snarls out of her hair. Then she'd spent twenty minutes looking for her lobster boat barrette, only to realize she'd lost it the night Kee had found her in his library.

He'd taken her moose barrette last night, too. The guy was amassing quite a collection of her hair clips.

Now she was flopped on the sofa of her living room, staring at the empty space over the fireplace where the picture of the castle used to hang and trying to assess her situation.

It didn't look good. By showing Kee the tunnels, she'd lost any hope of finding Thadd's room and her dad's blueprints for the smuggling boats. Kee also knew that she'd been in his vault and had exchanged the fake emeralds with the real ones.

What had possessed Frank Foster and Thaddeus Lakeman to give her mother a set of stolen emeralds? Hadn't they been afraid someone would recognize them?

Rachel snorted. In Puffin Harbor? Heck, her mother could have worn the crown jewels of England and nobody would have realized. The most prestigious place Marian had worn the emeralds was to a fund-raising supper in Ellsworth for the local hospital. Which only proved that the safest place to hide something was in plain sight.

Rachel looked at the grandfather clock in the corner. Three o'clock, and Willow still hadn't called. And Rachel had forgotten her appointment with Dr. Sprague. Betty Potter had left three messages on the answering machine.

She had to get her life back under control. And that meant she had to stop thinking about sexy blue eyes, a night of lovemaking that had left her insides in more knots than her hair, and this damnable urge to run back to Sub Rosa and do it again.

It wasn't just lust, she was finally beginning to realize, or even the satisfaction of ending a long sexual drought. Keenan Oakes intrigued her. What she saw is what she got. No pretense. No trying to charm her socks off. But especially no asking permission to kiss her.

She liked that. A lot.

For the first time in her life, Rachel felt she could simply be herself with a man. Comfortable. Safe. She didn't have to put on an act for fear of scaring the guy away.

She doubted anything scared Keenan Oakes.

The man could actually handle her passionate nature. Heck, he *had* handled it—over and over and over last night.

And afterward, in the tapestry room, when he'd found the fake emeralds, he had simply let her walk away. He hadn't pushed for answers, or gotten angry at her for not telling him where she got them, or resorted to threats.

Oh, she knew it wasn't the end of it, by any means. But Kee seemed to respect her enough to let *her* pick the time for the truth.

Which she would—eventually.

A car drove into the yard, but Rachel didn't move from her spot on the couch, recognizing Willow's always-in-a-hurry arrival. She smiled, not the least bit surprised. Willow hadn't called at noon because she'd decided to come home and lecture Rachel in person.

The screen door slammed, and Willow came storming in, shouting Rachel's name as she strode through the kitchen. She stopped in the doorway of the living room, her beautiful hazel eyes on fire, and waved a paper in the air.

"This is not a speeding ticket," she snapped. "It's Larry Jenkins's home phone number. It seems I have a date with him tomorrow night."

"I owe you."

"You owe me?" Willow repeated, clearly surprised by Rachel's answer. "So Larry wasn't just making it up? You really did promise I'd go out with him?"

Rachel slowly rose from the couch, every muscle in her body protesting. Who would have known lovemaking was such strenuous work? She walked over to Willow, hugged her nonplussed sister, and gave her a crooked smile.

"Larry owns a pickup truck, Willy. And if you're real nice to him tomorrow night, you could probably borrow it."

"Why do I want to borrow Larry's truck?"

"For Puffy. How else are we going to get him into town?"

Willow stepped back, incredulous. "You want me to

borrow a deputy sheriff's truck to sneak an illegal statue into the town square?"

Rachel nodded.

Willow sighed and finally found a tentative smile. "It would serve him right if his truck is recognized leaving the scene of our crime. What's Larry got on you that he's stooping to blackmailing me for a date?"

Rachel headed into the kitchen, deciding she needed a cup of tea—no, something stronger—for the fireworks that were about to begin.

"Rae?" Willow questioned, following her.

"I offered to go out with him first," Rachel thought to clarify, getting the rum down from the top cupboard. "But apparently I don't hold the appeal I used to," she added with a snort, going to the fridge and opening the door, looking for some soda. "He said it had to be with you, or he was writing the ticket."

"A ticket? You?" Willow gasped, her eyes rounded in mock horror.

"Not me," Rachel said, popping her head out of the fridge long enough to roll her eyes at Willow. "It was Keenan Oakes he was threatening to ticket."

"Keenan Oakes! I'm going out with Larry Jenkins so Keenan Oakes doesn't have to pay a ticket? Rae, the man's a billionaire! No, here, give me that," she said, taking the soda from Rachel. "I have something better in the car. Get out the blender and some ice."

Willow was out the door, the soda bottle still in her hand, before Rachel could even ask what she was talking about. So she got out the blender, set it on the counter, and plugged it in.

Willow used her foot to open the screen door and

came back in carrying four boxes overflowing with plump, deep red strawberries. Rachel squeaked in delight and immediately grabbed one of the berries and popped it in her mouth.

"Oh, man. It's strawberry season," she moaned, squishing the succulent fruit between the roof of her mouth and her tongue.

"No," Willow said, popping a berry into her own mouth. "It's strawberry *daiquiri* season."

Rachel went to the fridge and pulled out two trays of ice cubes, dumped one in the blender, and poured in a healthy amount of rum. "Quick. Get the hulls off those puppies," she urged, getting a knife and starting on them herself.

More of the berries from the first quart went into their mouths than into the blender. "I have four more quarts in the car," Willow said around a mouthful. "I couldn't resist when I saw Bickford's roadside stand. I think I ate a whole quart on the way home."

Rachel hit the button on the blender, and the berries and rum and ice swirled into a tornado of bright red decadence. Willow got down two daiquiri glasses and stood watching the whirlwind with Rachel. "It's done," she declared, holding out the glasses.

Rachel hit the switch and poured both drinks, then took one of the glasses and held it up for a toast. "To strawberry season," she said, clinking her glass to Willow's.

"And to sisters," Willow replied.

Each took a sip and both moaned in unison.

"Now," Willow said, giving Rachel a threatening glare that was thoroughly ruined by her strawberry mustache. "I believe you were about to explain why I'm paying Keenan Oakes's ticket."

"It's . . . complicated," Rachel said, going to the table and sitting down. She waited until Willow was seated across from her before she continued. "It just sort of happened. Kee was driving Thadd's Ferrari, which is unregistered, and he parked in a handicapped zone on the pier."

"And you were with him . . . why?"

"I was hungry. He offered to take me out for lobster."

"Sounds chummy," Willow muttered over the rim of her glass before taking a sip. "I thought we agreed you would stay away from him."

"He was rather insistent," Rachel whispered, quickly taking her own sip. "And that's when we made the deal that I'd help him reopen Sub Rosa. And Larry . . . Larry just showed up, and before I knew what I was doing, I promised him a date."

"How thoughtful of you."

"Hey, we do need a truck for Puffy. It's a win–win deal. See if you can get it for tomorrow night." Rachel suddenly frowned. "You are staying, aren't you? It is Friday, isn't it?"

"What in hell have you been doing all week?" Willow asked, eyeing her suspiciously.

"I've been opening Sub Rosa."

"And returning the emeralds?"

"Ah . . . well . . . sort of." Rachel quickly decided that this was not the time to lie to Willow—at least not a full lie. "Kee found them. But he didn't say anything," she rushed to explain. "It turns out they were fakes."

"The emeralds were fakes?" Willow echoed in a whisper, leaning closer. "All that worry, and they were fakes?"

"Do you have any idea how much a good forgery

costs?" Rachel asked her. "A couple hundred thousand bucks at least. Either way, I wanted them off our hands."

"And he didn't say anything?" Willow asked in disbelief, leaning even closer. She suddenly sat back in her chair, her eyes widening in horror. "You slept with him!"

"What!" Rachel choked, spitting out a mouthful of strawberry daiquiri. "How can you think that!"

"You did!" Willow shouted, standing up and pointing her glass at Rachel. "I'm gone less than four days, and you run right over there and jump into bed with the man!"

Rachel also stood. "Will you calm down? It's just . . . I didn't mean for it . . . oh, dammit, so what if I did! I'm a big girl," she said, repeating Kee's words from this morning. "I'm entitled to a bit of fun. And you know what? It was the best damned fun I ever had!"

Rachel wanted to smack herself in the forehead the moment she heard her own words. Willow was staring at her in stunned silence.

"Willy," Rachel said quietly. "I've never met anyone like him. He's . . . he's real."

"Puffin Harbor has real men," Willow countered, just as softly.

"I know. But haven't you ever looked at a guy and your insides just turned to mush? Or found yourself looking into eyes so beautiful that you just melted? Have your palms ever itched so much, Willy, that you think you'll just die if you can't run them over his face?"

Willow could only stare at Rachel and slowly shake her head. "Oh, man," she whispered. "You've been so careful, so . . . so protective of yourself." One corner of her mouth slowly lifted. "I'm happy for you, Rae. Really, I am. I've been so worried these last three years, watching you shrivel up inside yourself and not being able to help you."

She moved around the table and stopped in front of Rachel. "But does it have to be Keenan Oakes? Couldn't you get all hot and bothered over someone a bit . . . a bit safer?"

"He's safe, Willy. He's real."

"He's going to break your heart."

"Probably," Rachel quietly admitted. "But isn't that better than feeling nothing? How does that saying go? 'Better to have loved and lost than never to have loved at all'? "

Willow sipped her drink, staring at Rachel over the rim of her glass, her eyes clouded with concern as she contemplated Rachel's question.

"And what if he doesn't break my heart?" Rachel quietly asked. "What if I run from this? Wouldn't wondering what might have been be worse than never experiencing it at all, even for a little while?"

Willow let out a shuddering breath. "I don't know, Rae. Maybe. Probably. I just don't want you to get hurt. You were so devastated after Mom and Dad died. A second blow to your heart might be fatal."

"You know what I think?" Rachel asked.

"What?"

"I think it's going to take all eight quarts of strawberries and a whole bottle of rum to answer my questions," she said, going over to the counter and dumping the second tray of ice cubes into the blender.

Chapter Twelve

*L*uke sat on the ground in the shadow of a giant maple tree, grinning like the village idiot as he listened to the rhythm of quiet conversation, a whole lot of giggles, and sudden bursts of laughter coming from Rachel Foster's porch.

It was ten o'clock and fully dark, and just cool enough that mosquitoes weren't a problem, thank God. His shift had started the moment Kee had decided Rachel needed watching, and wasn't due to be up for another two hours. But even if he wasn't on duty, he wouldn't have missed this show for the world. He'd been contemplating whether or not he should call and tell Kee, but hadn't been able to decide whether Rachel's privacy took precedence over Kee's need to know what was happening.

"Come on, Rae," the woman said, jumping up and running down off the porch with a glass full of what Luke now knew was ice and rum and strawberries.

They'd brought out the blender about an hour ago and started making the daiquiris right on the porch so they wouldn't have to keep running back inside every twenty minutes.

"It'll be like old times," she urged. "Come on, push me!"

Luke had watched her arrive earlier, and assumed the woman was Rachel's sister, Willow. They looked quite a bit alike, though Willow's hair was stylishly cut at shoulder length, and her clothes were more businesslike.

Well, not at the moment—Willow was growing noticeably more disheveled with each passing hour. Hell, so was Rachel, for that matter. They'd both tossed off their shoes quite a while ago, Willow's suit jacket was inside out and hanging over the railing, and both their shirts were untucked and covered with strawberry stains.

Luke shifted to get a better view as Rachel came teetering down the steps, also with a glass in her hand, following her sister to the swing tied in an old oak tree on the ocean side of the house.

Aw, to hell with nobility. Kee and the others needed to see this, if only as a reminder that life was still full of surprises. Other than Mikaela's antics, it had been eons since any of them had seen such impulsive and completely unrestrained joy—especially from grown women.

Luke pulled out his cell phone and punched in Kee's number.

"What?" Kee said.

"I'm calling to thank you for the supper you sent down," Luke said, covering the phone's mike when Willow screamed in laughter as Rachel spilled her drink down her back trying to push her in the swing.

Kee's sigh came over the phone. "Hell, I'm sorry.

We've been exploring the tunnels all afternoon. I'll send Peter with some food. Everything okay down there?"

"Ah, you said you wanted to know if she so much as chips a fingernail, but does getting rip-roaring drunk count?"

There was a heartbeat of silence. Then two. Then three.

"Excuse me?" Kee whispered. "Did you say drunk?"

"Her sister arrived home a little after three," Luke said.

"Did you say drunk?" Kee repeated, even more softly.

"There was a bit of shouting at first," Luke said, continuing his report. "But then Willow came running back out to her car and carried several boxes of strawberries inside. And then there was some more shouting, and then it went quiet."

"Luke," Kee growled in warning.

"Willow Foster's quite a looker," Luke continued. "And a happy drunk. And Rachel gets to giggling so hard she ends up snorting. I swear, boss, if I wasn't a disciplined man, I'd be tempted to join the party."

The phone suddenly went dead. Luke smiled and shifted again, settling more comfortably against the maple tree in a position with a better view of the women. His stomach let out an impatient growl just then, and he hung his head at the realization that he wouldn't be getting any supper tonight.

Utterly speechless, Kee could only crouch in the bushes and watch Rachel and Willow Foster throw rocks at the ocean. Fog was slowly inching its way shoreward, and even though the floodlights on the front of the house were enough to illuminate the entire lawn, the women couldn't see their impressively launched missiles hit the water.

There would be several minutes of searching for just the

right rock, a bout of bragging when one was found, then a collective silence as the rock sailed through the air. There would be a whoop of triumph when it hit the water with a muted plop, and then a rather animated discussion about whether or not it went farther than the previous one.

The contest had been going on for nearly twenty minutes.

"Your woman can't hold her liquor, I'm afraid," Duncan whispered from beside him, amusement ruining his insult.

Kee looked toward the house and counted five empty ice cube trays, seven empty strawberry boxes, and two empty bottles of rum littering the ground and the porch. He looked back at Duncan. "Hell, *I* can't hold that much liquor." He shook his head. "They'll be paying a painful price tomorrow."

Kee turned to Luke, the floodlights barely reaching him in the shadows. "Could you make out any of the shouting when Willow arrived? Do you know what they were arguing about?"

"Something about a date with some guy named Larry Jenkins," Luke said, the slash of his grin perfectly visible. "And I heard your name shouted once or twice."

Kee stifled a snort. He just bet his name had come up.

Mickey whined and tried to inch forward through the bushes toward the women. Kee grabbed a fistful of fur and held him in place. "No," he said in a firm whisper. "Let them have their fun."

"Have ya noticed how partial he's become to Rachel?" Duncan asked.

"I've noticed," Kee admitted with a sigh. Even the damn wolf had fallen under her spell.

"They say animals are good judges of character," Duncan continued, his voice soft. "Children have that gift as well. I wonder what Mikaela will think of Rachel."

Kee didn't rise to the bait. The women were finally winding down from their marathon of daiquiris, rock throwing, and general disorderly conduct. They were stretched out on the grass now, their arms thrown out in exhaustion, staring up at the stars slowly disappearing behind the fog and quietly talking to each other.

"If they fall asleep, they'll catch colds," Duncan worried in a whisper—in his typical mother hen mode.

Luke's stomach growled, and he finally stood up, keeping in the shadow of the maple tree. "I'm hungry," he said, rubbing his belly. "And it looks like the show's over. I'm headed back. You want me to send Matt down to keep an eye on things?"

Kee had told Luke he could leave more than an hour ago, when he and Duncan and Mickey had arrived, but Luke hadn't said anything and hadn't left.

"No, I'll cover this shift," Kee told him. "Duncan, take Mickey back up with you."

Duncan also stood, but hesitated. "You'll want a jacket."

Kee shook his head. "I'll be warm enough on Rachel's couch."

"Ya plan to sleep inside?"

Kee nodded toward the women. "You really think they'll know I'm there?" he asked. "Once their heads hit their pillows, an army could camp out in their house and they wouldn't know it."

Duncan tapped the side of his leg and clicked his tongue. "Come on, then, Mickey. Let's go home."

Mickey looked at Duncan, then back at the women, and whined.

"Go," Kee said, nudging him with his knee.

In the end, Duncan had to grab the wolf by the scruff of the neck and drag him back up the path to Sub Rosa.

Kee turned and settled himself against the maple tree Luke had been using, saw that the women were now sitting up and still talking, and shook his head with a chuckle.

Rachel Foster was certainly full of surprises. When she wasn't trying to make the world think she was a nice, demure, worthy member of society, she was attacking him in the library, lying like a Trojan, and then attacking him again with that hot and delicious and very passionate mouth of hers.

But for as many surprises as she had, she also had secrets.

Kee agreed with Duncan that Rachel was probably protecting Willow. The bond between the two sisters was obvious, especially after tonight's little demonstration. And as near as he could tell, from his background check and subtle inquiries in town these last few days, there simply wasn't anyone else in Rachel Foster's life close enough to warrant such a grand charade.

No, the only thing that could have made Rachel return to Sub Rosa—considering what had happened there three years ago—was a powerful and unconditional love for her sister.

And Kee was pretty sure he knew what she was protecting. She hadn't been stealing from him that first night— she'd been returning the emeralds, a valuable painting, a ruby and gold ring, some silver items, and a bronze Asian statue, all stolen years ago. He'd found everything in the vault, and none of them had been there when good old Uncle Thaddeus had died.

Yes, it was sisterly love that had compelled Rachel to

set up the new heir of Sub Rosa for a very unpleasant fall.

Kee actually admired her cunning.

It was nothing personal—she had no idea *who* was inheriting Sub Rosa. Rachel was just trying to protect Willow's political future by making sure the scandal of Thaddeus Lakeman's illegal doings could never be linked to the Foster name.

And wouldn't he do the same thing for someone he loved?

Damn right. He would walk through the fires of hell for Mikaela. And dammit, wasn't he compromising his own personal code to protect Rachel right now, by not demanding she tell him how she'd gotten the stolen items?

Kee stood up and moved deeper into the shadows as Rachel and Willow finally tottered to their feet and made their way back to the house. Rachel's gait was an exaggerated limp, and Willow was trying to support her, both of them so drunk it was amazing they could stand up at all.

He watched them stagger up the stairs and into the kitchen, right past the mess they'd made on the porch, then heard a chair slide across the floor and hit something, a curse, more giggling and laughter, and then silence.

He moved in the shadows of the tree line until he was even with the screen door, and watched—incredulous if not somewhat angered—when they ambled into the living room and turned and started up to their bedrooms without even closing, much less locking, their kitchen door.

Dammit. They both needed keepers.

Kee sprinted across the lawn to the bottom of the porch stairs, watching through the screen door as they slowly mounted the interior stairs, still holding each other up.

He crept onto the porch, opened the screen door, and stepped into the kitchen. He quietly closed the inside door, locked it, and then walked over and grabbed the last quart of strawberries off the island counter. He righted the overturned chair and sat down, then popped a large, juicy strawberry into his mouth. Someone bumped into a wall overhead, there was another rather nasty curse, and then even more laughter.

Kee ate the entire box of strawberries waiting for things to settle down upstairs. After a good twenty minutes, satisfied they were both dead to the world, he finally slipped out of his shoes and headed for the stairs himself.

He passed a strawberry-stained blouse on the third step, and wondered which Foster sister it belonged to. Not that it mattered, because he passed another one four steps later.

He picked up the bra thrown over the banister at the top and stepped over a pair of pants left in a heap at the beginning of the hall. By the time he made it to the first bedroom door, his own pants were becoming rather uncomfortable.

He peered into the first room, with its overhead lights blazing brightly, and saw a softly snoring Willow flopped facedown on the bed, her satin baby-blue-panty-covered butt left out to the breeze. Unlike her sister, Willow had a bit more imagination when it came to her underwear.

Kee tossed her matching baby-blue bra into the room, reached in and shut off the light, and quietly closed the door.

He headed for Rachel's room, suddenly deciding that the couch downstairs had looked a bit short to him, and that maybe Rachel's bed would be more comfortable.

It would definitely be warmer.

Kee stepped into her bedroom only to find himself rendered speechless for the second time tonight. Rachel was also flopped on her bed, but she'd had a much harder time getting out of her clothes. Her pants were stuck at her knees, and her bra straps were wrapped tightly around both elbows like a straitjacket.

Kee ran an unsteady hand over his face, wiping away a fine sheen of sweat on his forehead, and tried to remember if he'd put two or three condoms in his pocket this morning.

The fact that he was contemplating jumping the little drunkard's bones, and that it might not be a very gentlemanly thing to do, didn't particularly bother him. Rachel had given herself to him last night, completely and rather passionately, and this was his chance to return the favor.

Besides, being drunk might actually slow her down. Mellow her out. And, he hoped, calm the urgency that seemed to explode between them whenever they touched.

He really would like to make love to Rachel slowly and not let her work him into a sexual frenzy with her wonderfully feminine hands, her hot and delicious mouth, and that damned head of wild hair that turned his cock to stone every time he touched it.

Kee wiped a trembling hand over his face again. What was it about her that she had gotten under his skin so quickly and so completely?

It wasn't just her wildly passionate nature, or even the sexy body that passion came packaged in. No, it was all of her—her courage and intelligence and spunk. It was her willingness to stand up to him, to lie right to his face and smile while she did, and her loyalty to her sister that was so strong she was willing to put herself in an impossible position.

But mostly, he thought, it was her spunk.

Kee turned and quietly closed the bedroom door, but left the light on. There would be no groping in the dark tonight; it would be a slow and tender lovemaking with both of them able to see and appreciate each other.

He pulled his shirt off over his head and tossed it on the floor, and, with much difficulty, unsnapped his jeans and took them off. He carried his pants with him, taking out the three condoms and placing them on the table beside the bed.

He slowly worked Rachel's pants off her legs, stopping long enough to look at her right knee. It seemed pretty well healed, with only two small red scars dotting each side.

News in town was that she had torn her cartilage hiking Gull Mountain. It was also being bantered about that she'd given the rescue team hell the entire trip down.

Rachel muttered something unintelligible and tried to wave her trapped arm in the air, as if swatting at a fly. Kee smiled, sat down on the bed beside her, and went to work on her bra.

Of course it had to be one of those damn bras that hooked in the back, and he had to lift her up and hold her against him with one hand and undo the clasp with the other.

She made a sweet little noise that sent blood rushing straight to his cock, and her hot little lips brushed over his chest and zeroed in on his left nipple.

Sweat broke out on his forehead again, and Kee ended up using both hands to rip the bra hooks apart. He quickly untangled her arms, tossed the ruined bra on the floor, and gently pulled her mouth from his chest only to find her eyes open and watching him.

She smiled. "I've never met anyone with more beautiful eyes," she told him in a slurred whisper.

"Can you even see my eyes right now?" he asked, staring into hers, which appeared glazed with one too many daiquiris. There was a strawberry stain on her cheek, and a hull from the fruit was stuck in her hair.

"I don't have to see them," she whispered dreamily, letting her head fall back. "They're forever imprinted on my brain," she trailed off in a mumble, rolling until she was snuggled against his side, one of her now free hands tucked uncomfortably close to his groin.

"I want to make love to you," he said, shaking her slightly.

"Okay," she mumbled into his thigh, her warm breath sending tremors coursing through him.

"I kind of need your help, Rachel." He chuckled desperately, turning her onto her back. He covered one beautiful breast with his hand, his blood starting to simmer at the feel of her nipple pushing into his palm. "You need to stay awake," he rawly petitioned.

He darted a glance at the bedside table. Maybe he should just put the condom on now, while he could still think. He stood up, grabbed one of the foil packs, and ripped it open with his teeth.

"No, come back," she moaned from the bed, flopping her arm toward him. "I'll stay awake, I promise."

Holding the foil pack in his hand, Kee looked over at Rachel, then down at his cock, then up at the ceiling.

"Damn," he growled, tossing the packet back on the table. She couldn't even keep her eyes open.

Kee walked to the door, snapped off the light, and walked back to the bed. He picked Rachel up, pulled back the covers, laid her down, and crawled in beside her.

It was a tight fit. "Why in hell is a grown woman still sleeping in a twin-sized bed?" he muttered, yanking her up against him, sucking in his breath when she snuggled her bottom into his groin.

Teeth gritted, Kee repositioned his cock so it didn't get any ideas of its own, and he even went so far as to tuck the blanket between them. He threw one leg over Rachel, more to anchor himself than to hold her, and wrapped his arms around her with a deep-winded sigh.

It was going to be a very long night.

Chapter Thirteen

She was ungodly hot. And she must have forgotten to braid her hair before she went to bed, because it was tickling her nose.

Only it didn't smell like her hair usually did, or even like her shampoo. She sniffed. It was a familiar smell . . . like a spice of some sort, with a hint of strawberries.

Good God, she was hot. Had she left the furnace cranked on high? And she'd gotten all tangled up in the blankets and couldn't move.

But it was the dull pounding in her head that finally made her remember. Strawberry daiquiris. Willow. Rum, and even more rum. Drunken, fragmented conversations.

Rachel refused to open her eyes because she just knew it was going to hurt. Hell, she already hurt. It felt as if a Mac truck was sitting on her chest, and something was poking her thigh.

And something else was softly breathing by her head!

Rachel snapped open her eyes and found herself nose to chest with Keenan Oakes. She knew it was him—his smell, his feel, the very essence he exuded, and the fact that every nerve in her body was wide awake, once again proving her proximity problem.

Well, wasn't this a pleasant surprise? It wasn't every day she woke up to find a demigod sleeping on top of her.

What to do. . . .

What should she do . . . ?

She could poke him in the ribs and push him out of bed, and then give him hell for having the audacity to come sneaking in here while she slept.

Or . . . or she could just make love to him until he woke up, and then see if they couldn't put whatever was poking her in the thigh to good use.

"If you keep that up, I'm going to pounce without asking permission," he whispered, lifting his chest away from her mouth.

Rachel hadn't realized she'd been running her lips back and forth over his soft, sensuous chest hair.

He leaned up even further, so he could look her in the eye. "How's the head feel?"

"Pounding."

"So," he said on a sigh. "It's only our second date, and already you're complaining of a headache."

"This is a date?"

He nodded.

"Ah . . . did I have fun on this date?"

"Not yet. But I can fix that." His eyes tenderly searched hers. "Though it might be hard with a headache."

"But my head will ache whether I'm having fun or just lying here being miserable, right?"

His beautiful Atlantic-blue eyes sparkled in the stingy morning light trying to push through the window. "Having fun might even help that headache go away," he suggested.

"An old family remedy?"

He nodded. "Passed down from my father's father."

Rachel wiggled her arm until she could free one hand, and immediately ran her finger down the side of his face, tracing the angle of his jaw, feeling the rasp of his stubble, and then moving on to his bottom lip, rubbing it back and forth.

"I'm not up for athletics," she warned. "But a slow romp in the sheets sounds like wonderful medicine."

His smile was warm and tender as he carefully moved to free the blankets from around them. He settled back beside her, his wonderfully naked, searing hot body pressed full-length against hers. She tickled his shins with her toes and wrapped her arms around his neck while kissing his throat, rubbing her nipples through his chest hair with a moan of pure pleasure.

He shifted, leaning more fully over her and laying one leg across her thigh. "This is going to take some finesse," he whispered. "It's a damn small bed you sleep in, Miss Foster."

"It wasn't built for demigods," she mumbled into his neck, just before she lightly nipped his shoulder.

"A demigod, huh?" he repeated, running his fingers through her hair as he rained kisses over her face, her eyes, her nose. "Are demigods better than cavemen?"

"Oh, yes," she whispered, sliding her hand down the length of his back until she came to one finely muscled butt cheek and squeezed, eliciting a very male groan. "In fact, if you cross a caveman with a demigod, the results can be quite amazing."

"For instance?" he asked, his question turning to a groan when she pulled his hips forward—that little thigh-poking problem now poking her belly.

Rachel's insides tightened as a succession of shivers raced down her spine. She couldn't get enough of him. Would *never* get enough of him. He was so . . . so intrinsically male, in a wonderfully lustful way.

His velvety skin covered such unyielding strength. His hands—oh, God, his hands—were so large and strong and tender, leaving tingles of salacious pleasure in their wake as he moved them over her with deliberate care.

Heat built inside her and moisture gathered between her thighs. She became restless and eager, anticipating where his hands would explore next.

And his mouth. He whispered wildly erotic things to her as his mouth moved over her face and throat and shoulders, kissing and nipping and then soothing each shiver he created.

Her own mouth played over his skin, sipping the dew of his own building heat, and she flexed her fingers into his back as she lifted her hips up, yearning to feel him inside her.

"For instance?" he repeated, nibbling her earlobe.

"Wh-what was the question?" she gasped, when one of his roaming hands found one of her nipples.

He tugged, soothed, and then rolled it between his fingers, teasing it to a sensuous peak that made Rachel moan in ecstasy and bury her face in his chest.

"I can't remember." He chuckled in a pained whisper. "Something about demigods and cavemen. I want you, Rachel," he said, his voice raw, as he lowered himself down her body until his head was even with the breast he'd been tantalizing.

Rachel arched up when his mouth found its target, keening her pleasure as he gently suckled her nipple. He centered his hips between her thighs and began attending to the other nipple, pushing her breasts together, feasting first on one and then the other.

Rachel went wild, bucking her hips as he pleasured her to the point of torment. The hot, bulbous tip of his shaft pressed against her moist folds, enticing, probing, and then slowly entering her.

He flexed his hips, only slightly, moving just a bit deeper as he nuzzled the sensitive outside of one breast. Rachel felt herself stretching, the mounting pressure causing every nerve in her body to hum. Need and want and building passion sparked like fireworks through her mind, making her dizzy, making her yearn for more.

She moaned as his shaft teased her entrance, withdrawing then returning, each time a little bit deeper. She splayed her fingers through his hair, gripping him fiercely as the tension mounted, her own head thrown back on the pillow until she was drawn as taut as a bowstring.

His tongue traced a maddeningly erotic path back to her nipple, and he suckled, and nipped, and tugged with his teeth until she clenched in a spasm of desire.

He drove into her fully, exploding her orgasm into a million fragments of pulsing sensations, tearing a cry of surprised joy from her throat. She floated, suspended, for the merest of seconds, riding the passionate storm of his pounding thrusts, and then crested again—this time with a violence so powerful he was pulled into the maelstrom with her.

He shouted his own pleasure, his release pulsing deep and hot and hard, his muscles ridged with virile strength, his whole body trembling with his powerful orgasm.

Rachel could only look up at him in wonder, at this demigod who had invaded her room—and who was dangerously close to invading her heart.

"You little witch," he whispered, smiling through gritted teeth, still holding himself rigid as tiny echoing pulses clenched her insides around his shaft. "You did it to me aga—"

There was another sudden shout just as something crashed over his shoulders, exploding in splinters of wood and ceramics that rained down over them both.

Rachel screamed as Kee fell limply against her, his dead weight pushing the breath out of her. Another crash landed on his back, the violence of the blow making him hit the floor with a sickening thud.

Rachel scrambled off the bed after him, rolling to face the threat, and the room suddenly flooded with light. She blinked—then blinked again at the sight of Willow standing by the light switch, her hair tangled around her angry red face, her eyes wild, holding the remains of the lamp that had been on the bureau.

They both started talking at once.

"Oh, my God, Rachel! Are you okay? Did he hurt you?"

"What are you doing!"

Willow pointed at the floor. "He was . . . he broke in here and was . . . he was assaulting you."

"He was what?"

"I heard you scream. You screamed!" Willow yelled, stepping closer to the bed, holding the broken lamp threateningly. "It woke me up, and I came in here and saw this shadow on top of you, and I . . . dammit!" she shouted, only to quickly grab her head. She took a deep breath. "I thought he was trying to kill you," she whispered, her eyes clouding with pain. She dropped the lamp and clutched her stomach. "Oh, God. The room won't stop spinning."

The room was spinning for Rachel as well. And her head throbbed like the devil, and her stomach roiled.

"It's Kee," she hoarsely told Willow. "You just assaulted Keenan Oakes."

Willow clutched her robe to her neck and stepped closer, peering over the edge of the bed. Her eyes widened. "He's . . ." She looked at Rachel, then back at Kee. "He's . . . No wonder you can't keep your hands off him. He's . . . oh, my," she finished with a moan, grabbing her head again.

Rachel looked down and quickly pulled the sheet over Kee's hips. "I can't believe you hit him," she muttered, cupping his face. She looked over her shoulder at Willow. "Are you telling me you can't tell the difference between a scream of terror and one of passion?"

Willow walked around the end of the bed and knelt down on the other side of Kee. "How in hell am I supposed to know what you sound like making love? It's not like you're in the habit of sneaking men into the house."

"I didn't sneak him in," she said, gently patting his face. "Oh, God, Willy, you killed him."

"I did not," Willow defended, prodding him in the shoulder.

Kee groaned, shook his head, then suddenly exploded into motion. He grabbed Rachel and threw her to the floor, rolling until she was behind him and he was kneeling to face the threat.

"No!" Rachel screamed, groping for his arm. "It's Willow!"

His hand stopped in midswing, and he let out a curse foul enough to singe the air. That lethal hand changed direction to cup the back of his neck. "Sweet Jesus," he growled, lightly poking the lump beginning to rise just below his hairline. "What in hell did you hit me with?"

Willow, her eyes rounded in stark fear, her face pasty white with tinges of green around the mouth, only squeaked as she sat pressed against the wall.

Rachel reached up with a corner of the sheet and dabbed the cut oozing blood down his neck. Kee turned, scowled hard enough to knock her over, and grabbed the sheet and wrapped it around his waist as he stood up.

He tucked the sheet into a precarious knot, then crossed his arms over his chest, planted his feet apart, and stared down at the two of them.

Willow's clouded hazel eyes widened even more, and she scooted along the wall until she bumped into Rachel.

Rachel put her arm around her trembling sister and smiled up at Kee. "I'd like for you to meet my sister, Willow. Willow, this is Keenan Oakes."

Willow squeaked again, darting a frantic look at Rachel. Rachel patted her arm. "He only looks like a caveman, Willy," she assured her. "He won't bite. I promise."

"I might," he growled.

But he sighed instead, and rubbed the back of his neck, closing his eyes and slowly shaking his head. "I'm beginning to think the safest place for Mikaela is right here with you two deadly little Amazons," he muttered.

He looked back at them, glaring again. "Willow, go to the bathroom and throw up. And Rachel, get some clothes on!" he snapped, spinning on his heel and stalking around the bed, grabbing up his pants and shirt and striding out of the room.

Willow still wasn't breathing. Rachel hugged her and

rocked her back and forth. "It's okay, Willy," she whispered. "He's not mad at you. He's mad at himself for getting caught with his pants down," she ended with a chuckle that turned into a moan, as her head started pounding with the force of a jackhammer.

Willow hung her own head in her hands, covering her face and letting out a shuddering breath. "God, my head hurts," she croaked. "I'm never eating another strawberry."

Rachel snorted and took hold of the side of the bed and stood up. "I don't think it's the strawberries giving us headaches," she told her. "I think it's two bottles of rum."

Willow also stood, took down Rachel's robe from the peg by the closet, and tossed it to her. "What time is it?" she asked.

Rachel looked at the clock by the bed. "Hell, it's only four-thirty."

Willow was also looking at the table by the bed, and her eyes rounded again. She walked over and picked up the three foil packets, turned, and held them out to Rachel.

"Three?" she asked in awe, only to suddenly frown at her hand. "They're all here." She looked at the floor near the bedside table, then back at Rachel. "All three are here."

Her eyes widened in horror again. "And if I remember right, he wasn't wearing anything when I . . . when . . . Rachel! You didn't use anything!"

But before Rachel could answer, Willow was stalking out the door. Rachel chased after her in a running limp, but Willow was headed downstairs. By the time Rachel caught up with her, her sister was just entering the kitchen, shouting Kee's name.

Standing by the sink, holding a towel under the faucet, Kee shut off the water and slowly turned and faced her.

Willow threw all three packets of condoms at him, and Rachel could only watch, speechless, as they bounced off his chest and fell to the floor.

"You do not have unprotected sex with my sister," she told him, carefully enunciating each word. She stepped forward and pointed her finger at him. "And so help me God, if you get her pregnant, Mr. Oakes, I will come after you with a shotgun. Got that?" she snapped, taking another threatening step forward.

Kee merely nodded.

"Hey, now wait a min—" Rachel started.

Willow whirled on her. "No, you wait, you idiot! You do not have unprotected sex!"

"Oh, for the love of God, Willy." Rachel hissed.

Willow whirled again, this time at the sound of Kee's laughter. "It's not funny, Mr. Oakes!"

He held up his hands in supplication. "I know it's not. It's just that the two of you make such a pair, fearlessly determined to protect each other."

Rachel gasped and slit her hand across her throat at Kee behind Willow's back. Willow turned and caught her. "What is he talking about?" she demanded, stepping toward her. "What are you protecting me from?"

Rachel shook her head at Willow while glaring at Kee. "He's not talking about anything, Willy. He's just still mad at being blindsided."

"I'm talking about a million-dollar set of stolen emeralds suddenly appearing in my vault," Kee said, drawing Willow's attention. "And millions of dollars of art being stolen from Sub Rosa over the last three years."

"What?" Willow whispered, looking at Rachel, then back at Kee. "And you think Rachel is responsible?"

Kee shook his head. "No. But she's into it up to her pretty little neck, and she's trying to protect you by not telling you about it."

"How is she into it?" she asked, turning and asking Rachel her question. "You said the emeralds were fakes."

"Not the set we had," Rachel explained. "I found the fakes in the vault when I returned the real ones." She shook her head in self-disgust. "I should have just left all of them there."

Willow turned back to Kee. "This is all a misunderstanding. We didn't steal those emeralds from Thadd. He gave them to our father to give to our mother for their anniversary."

"I realize that. Thaddeus Lakeman is the one who stole them," Kee explained. "Along with a few other items," he added, looking past Willow at Rachel. "A painting of a Scottish castle, a bronze statue, a ruby ring—the list goes on."

Rachel glared at Kee, but he just kept on talking. "Your sister brought everything to Sub Rosa the night I arrived and caught her in the library."

Willow turned to Rachel. "Did you know Thadd had stolen the emeralds?" she asked, stepping toward her. "And you're trying to protect me? Why? From what?"

Rachel walked to the cabinet beside the fridge and took down a bottle of aspirin. She shook three pills into Willow's hand, and three into her own. "From our name being linked with stolen goods, Willy," she quietly told her. "It could ruin your political future."

The aspirin clutched in her fist, Willow turned back to Kee. "Thadd was a thief?" she asked in disbelief. "But why? He had more money than God. He didn't have to steal anything."

Kee shrugged. "People like Thaddeus Lakeman don't steal for profit. It's the fun of possessing, and the excitement and challenge not to get caught."

Kee held the towel up to the back of his neck and continued. "And I doubt he did the actual stealing. He likely commissioned it done."

Rachel took down two glasses from the cupboard, walked over to the sink, and glared at Kee until he moved out of her way. She filled the glasses with water and carried one over to Willow.

Willow sat down at the table with a tired sigh, and Rachel sat down beside her. Kee moved closer, but leaned against the center island.

Willow took her aspirin, then stared at her empty glass. "You said someone's been stealing from Sub Rosa for the last three years," she said without looking up. "Is all the stuff in Thadd's house stolen?"

"No. Everything there is legitimate. The only stolen items I found were the ones Rachel put in the vault."

Willow looked up at Kee, her eyes worried. "Are you going to press charges against her?"

"You tell me, counselor. What can I have her charged with? I'm the one in possession of stolen goods."

Willow found her first, tentative smile. "That is true." She looked at Rachel. "How did you know the emeralds and painting and other stuff were stolen?"

That question put Rachel in a quandary. What to say? How much should she say? "Wendell Potter brought me Dad's strongbox the other day," Rachel told her. "He'd forgotten to give it to me when he died."

She reached out to Willow, squeezing her arm and smiling into her suddenly misting eyes. "There was a letter in the box from Dad, Willy, that told me the items were stolen. He asked that I not tell you or Mom, but just quietly dispose of them."

"Dad knew?" Willow whispered. "He knew Thadd was giving him stolen goods and he accepted them?"

"It was a game, Willy. The two of them were just playing a game that they thought was harmless."

"I want to see the letter."

"I burned it," Rachel told her. "I read it, burned it, then gathered up all the items and took them to Sub Rosa."

"To protect me."

"Yes," Rachel softly admitted, squeezing her arm again. She looked up at Kee as she continued talking to Willow. "All Kee has to do is crate them up and send them to whatever authority is in charge of recovering stolen goods—no return address, all fingerprints wiped clean. That way nobody has to know anything."

"Why didn't you do that?" Kee asked.

Rachel just stared at him, stunned. "I . . . I don't know," she finally said. "I thought of taking everything to Portland and leaving it on the police station steps, but I was afraid I'd get in an accident and get caught. I . . . I guess I wouldn't know how to go about shipping something anonymously. Everything today has a paper trail a child could follow."

"But you don't mind my taking the risk," he returned, his expression benign. "But the stolen items in the vault are not our most pressing problem at the moment," he said. "The fact that Thadd's legitimate art is being stolen is what concerns me."

Willow's defenses rose. "Rachel has nothing to do with that," she said fiercely.

Kee shook his head. "I don't believe she does. But somebody knows about the tunnels, and has been coming and going quite regularly."

"Then call the police," Willow snapped. "And leave Rachel out of it."

"I intend to. It's your sister we need to convince." He looked at Rachel. "I have a favor to ask you, but first I need your promise that you'll stay away from Sub Rosa, the tunnels, and anything that has to do with any of this."

Rachel glared first at Willow, then at Kee, only to realize that glaring made her headache worse. "What's the favor?" she asked softly.

"Mikaela," he said. "She's due to arrive tomorrow, and I don't want her at Sub Rosa."

"Then make her stay wherever she is."

He shook his head with a self-abasing grin. "I can't. Ahab will have our throats if he has to put up with her another day."

"Ahab?" Rachel asked, lifting one brow, only to realize that hurt, too.

"He's my captain. And his real name is Jonathan French, but somebody read *Moby Dick* to Mikaela a year ago, and she renamed him Ahab—and it stuck."

"And you want me to babysit your daughter, whom Mr. French can't take any more of," Rachel repeated, just to make sure she'd gotten it right. "And you think she'll be safe here with me."

"You won't be alone. Mickey will be here, and there will always be one of us with you."

Rachel looked down at the table and frowned. Kee walked over and lifted her chin.

"She's my whole world, Rachel," he said softly. "And I

want her safe and happy and protected. I want both of you protected until we can find out what's happening at Sub Rosa."

"I don't know anything about little girls."

His smile was warm and tender. "She's not a little girl. Mikaela's just a tiny adult. You can bake cookies or something," he suggested. "And take her to the library and into town for ice cream. Just hang out with her, doing . . . doing female stuff."

"She's a heathen, isn't she?" Rachel asked with a grin.

"No, she's a tyrant," he returned, his own grin more proud than debasing. "But you're going to love her anyway."

"She'll watch Mikaela," Willow interjected, standing up and taking her glass to the sink.

"I will?" Rachel asked.

Willow filled her glass, then turned back to face them. "You'll do it because Mikaela needs a safe place to stay," she said. "And because I like the idea of your not being able to stick your nose in this mess." She directed her attention to Kee. "Someone will stay here at all times?"

Kee rubbed the back of his neck where Willow had hit him. "Only if I get a promise from you as well," he said. "Not to attack my men."

Willow's cheeks flushed. "I heard her scream," she defended, lifting her chin.

Kee looked at Rachel. "Yeah, I heard her, too," he said softly, his eyes heating with remembered passion.

Rachel pushed her glass away, folded her hands on the table, and dropped her head onto her arms with a pain-filled groan.

Chapter Fourteen

*I*t should have taken them only an hour to shower and dress and clean up last night's mess, but it had been four hours since Kee had left, and all they'd managed to do was take showers. Rachel hadn't even dried her hair, but had simply braided it wet. They were on their third pot of ginger tea, and their stomachs still wouldn't settle down, and their heads still ached.

The strengthening morning sun helped, and the loungers on the ocean side of the porch were so damned comfortable that nothing seemed pressing enough to make either of them move.

Willow pushed her sunglasses up on her nose and yawned. "Do you think Larry will notice if I nod off on our date tonight?" she whispered.

"I'm sorry I set you up," Rachel said, also whispering in deference to the sledgehammer in her head.

Willow softly snorted. "I understand, after meeting

Keenan Oakes. I probably would have done the same to you if I had met him first."

Rachel lifted her sunglasses and looked over at Willow, her eyebrows raised in surprise. "He scared you spitless."

Willow also lifted her glasses. "The man was naked, Rae, and trying to kill me."

Rachel dropped her glasses back on her nose, snuggled deeper into the soft cushion of the lounger, and stared at the ocean. "Only after you nearly killed him," she said. "But you didn't stay scared very long. You threatened to take a shotgun to him."

"I was mad. And you can't be mad and scared at the same time. I think it's impossible or something. Why did Dad leave the letter only to you?" she asked softly.

"Because of your hopes for a political career," Rachel told her. "And to protect Mom. He left the letter with Wendell two years before he died."

"That was quite a burden to dump on your shoulders."

Rachel shrugged, still watching the ocean, and wondered how much she should tell Willow. Maybe mentioning the blueprints for the smuggling boats would be okay, since she could use some help finding them. But the secret room in their own house?

No, she needed to get inside the room first and see what was there, and then decide whether or not to expose something that might possibly be incriminating.

"Do you remember that Dad dabbled in boat designs?" she asked, shifting on the lounger to face Willow.

Willow lifted her glasses again. "Yeah. Why?"

"I think they were special designs, Willy—for boats with secret compartments for smuggling in the stolen goods to Thadd."

Willow sat up in her chair. "Smuggling boats? Dad?" She shook her head. "He wouldn't do something like that. Daddy was not a criminal."

"No, but he was an architect," Rachel returned, also sitting up and taking off her sunglasses. "And he wouldn't have been able to resist redesigning a lobster boat with hidden compartments." She swung her feet over the lounger and sat facing Willow, leaning toward her. "When I found him, he said something to me, Willy, just before the paramedics arrived."

"He told you he'd killed Mom. You said he told you something about Las Vegas and that he'd killed Mom."

"He also said 'Norway night,' and 'see dancer,' . . . and 'find her.' I thought he meant I should find a dancer in Las Vegas, but it sounded so silly I ignored it. But I can't ignore that he said 'Norway night.' "

"Norway night," Willow repeated, mouthing the ear-piece of her sunglasses. Her eyes widened. "That's the name of the boat that just burned." She suddenly frowned. "Why didn't you tell me this three years ago?"

Rachel looked down at her hands, twirling her own glasses through her fingers. "I don't know. It didn't make sense to me at the time, and I just figured it was nothing." She looked back at Willow. "But if he was referring to the lobster boat the *Norway Night*, why was it important enough to be his dying words? Do you think it's because his name is on the designs and that he wanted me to find them?"

"It could be," Willow whispered. "What about the letter? Did he mention the *Norway Night* in that?"

Rachel shook her head. "He only said that he'd designed three boats for Thadd." She finally stood up. "We have to find those blueprints before someone else puts two and two together."

Willow also stood, facing Rachel across the lounger. "You gave your promise to stay out of this."

"I promised to stay away from Sub Rosa," Rachel rebutted, lifting her chin. "I did not promise to sit here and do nothing while the Foster name gets tangled up in this mess and your future gets ruined."

"My future is not worth the risk," Willow said fiercely, her face flushing with anger. "It's not worth you getting in trouble."

"Then help me."

"Help you? I thought you wanted me out of this, to protect my future?" she said, her own chin lifted provokingly.

"But don't you see? You and I can go to the Lakeman Boatyard without it being suspicious. You still have your Boatyard shares. We can go see Mark Alder and you can offer to sell them to him. And while you two go for a walk to talk about it, I can snoop around."

"No."

"And while we're there, we can ask how his mother is doing."

"No."

"I found a woman's footprints in the tunnels, Willy. I think they might be Mary's."

"You promised!"

"But Mark's not dangerous. He's a dork."

"But he's a very smart dork," Willow countered. "And he's not going to just leave you alone in the office while we go out for a 'talk.' "

"It's just an office," Rachel said, waving that away.

"And he wasn't even managing the boatyard when Dad would have designed the *Norway Night*. But the blueprints are probably still there."

"Or they could be in storage only God knows where," Willow argued.

"This is too important to let slide, Willy. What harm could there be in just checking it out? And you do want to get rid of your shares. It's a perfect plan."

Willow crossed her arms under her breasts, leaning back on her hips and eyeing Rachel. "Then let's just run this plan by Kee and see what he thinks of it," she softly suggested.

"No."

"I didn't think so."

"We can do this, Willy. It's not dangerous. It will be broad daylight, and it's Mark Alder."

"And what if you do find the blueprints? Then what?"

"Then I steal them and destroy them."

"No."

"Willy," Rachel entreated, stepping around the lounger and taking hold of her arms. "They're all that's left to link us to Thaddeus Lakeman. And you've worked so hard, and have a good position now, with a bright future. Please don't let this one thing hang over our heads."

"And if you can't find the designs at the boatyard, you'll let it go?" she asked.

Rachel nodded. "If they're not there, then they can't come back and haunt us. It will mean Dad already took care of them."

"But why say what he did when he was dying?" Willow asked.

"Maybe he was referring to the boat itself, not the

designs," Rachel speculated. "Maybe he just wanted me to be aware of it. Remember, he wrote the letter two years before he died. He may have destroyed the designs in between."

"I wonder what the other boats' names are?"

"I don't know. But give me at least twenty minutes in Mark's office, and I'll know if Dad's designs are there or not."

"And just when do you plan for us to go there?"

"What's wrong with right now? It's Saturday, and there won't be any workers there."

"Then what makes you think Mark will be there?"

Rachel snorted, walked back around the lounger, and headed toward the screen door. "Mark all but lives there since I sold him my shares two years ago, making him a one-quarter owner," she said, going into the house.

Willow followed her, and they both took three more aspirin and went upstairs to change. Twenty minutes later they were in Rachel's SUV and headed to the Lakeman Boatyard.

"Give him a good price on the shares," Rachel suggested. "He all but jumped up and down when I offered him mine for fifty cents on the dollar."

"Shouldn't I be offering them to Keenan Oakes first? He's half owner now."

Rachel waved that away. "According to the will, Thadd left 52 percent to his heir and 24 percent to each of us. Kee will still hold a controlling interest."

"What were you saying about Mary Alder being in the tunnels? Do you really think she's been stealing from Sub Rosa?"

"I don't know." Rachel looked over at Willow. "She

would know about the tunnels. She and Thadd were quite close."

"But he took care of her in his will," Willow said, staring out through the windshield. "Enough to live comfortably without having to steal from his estate."

"There was also a man's set of footprints. A large sneaker tread. We'll check out Mark's feet while we're at it," Rachel added, slowing down as she entered town.

She pulled to the edge of the street beside the village green, shut off the engine, and looked at the grassy park shaded by huge maple trees and littered with park benches, a number of people and children, and several dogs.

"Where should we put Puffy?" she asked. "By the bandstand or by the Veterans' Memorial?"

"I think he should be by himself," Willow said, pointing to their right. "There, in that grassy area between the two paths. We can just set the base you made on the ground. It should be enough to support him."

"Maybe if everyone likes him enough, they'll have a fund-raiser and buy him a granite base," Rachel said, liking that idea. "And a plaque thanking the benevolent, anonymous donor."

"How are we going to get him out of the cellar?"

"I've thought about that. We can wrap him in blankets and lay planks on the outside cellar stairs and just winch him into the back of the pickup. Then when we get here, we'll ease him off the truck and onto the base."

"It's going to take *manpower*," Willow said. "Your knee's not healed enough for tugging on a three-hundred-pound puffin."

"How about a couple of apostles?" Rachel suggested.

"We could probably buy their silence with a strawberry pie. Those men do love to eat."

"I'm never touching another strawberry," Willow hissed. "We're both so hungover we can't see straight, and you've got us breaking and entering and spying on Mark and Mary Alder."

"We're not breaking, we're only entering. And the spying is just a bonus."

Willow looked at her through narrowed eyes. "You're enjoying this."

"I am not. I'm trying to protect our name. And as of tomorrow I'm out of it, when Mikaela the little tyrant arrives."

"Do you know anything about Mikaela's mother?"

Rachel silently shook her head.

"And you haven't thought to ask?"

"I've thought about it. But that's getting too personal."

"And having sex isn't?" Willow shot back, eyebrows raised.

"No, sex does not automatically imply a relationship. I told you, I have no intention of getting any more involved with Keenan Oakes than I already am. I'm having a . . . a fling," she said, waving her hand in the air. "Yeah, a fun little fling. Stretching my wings. Sowing my oats. That sort of thing."

"And Kee feels the same way?" Willow asked.

"He's a guy," Rachel said with a laugh, rolling her eyes. "Of course he feels that way."

She started the car and pulled back onto the street. They drove in relative silence until they came to the fire station—and the catcalling and whistling morons. Willow, of course, couldn't resist and rolled down her window, matching their catcalls with a few inventive ones of her own, leaning out the window and making a general fool of herself.

But it was short-lived. As soon as they were out of sight of the fire station, Willow was holding her head and cursing her outburst.

Three miles down the coast, they finally pulled into the Lakeman Boatyard. It was an impressive operation that had flourished under Mark Alder's care these last eight years. And two years ago, when Rachel had sold her shares to Mark, he'd started sprucing up the place—painting, installing a new sign, and landscaping the entrance. He'd also put his name on the sign: MARK ALDER, OWNER/OPERATOR.

Rachel was glad she'd sold her shares to Mark and that Willow was going to do the same. With his mother still taking Thadd's death so hard, Mark at least deserved the recognition that came with being a solid businessman in the community.

Mark might be a dork, but he was a really nice dork.

Rachel only hoped he hadn't been visiting Sub Rosa with his mother. Unless . . . unless he'd been going there to fetch her.

"Hey, maybe they *are* Mark's footprints in the tunnels," she said. "And it's something as innocent as him chasing after Mary to bring her home. Maybe she's been going there since Thadd died because she just can't let him go."

"There's still the problem of the missing items," Willow reminded her. She suddenly perked up. "Maybe Mary's been taking them. Not to sell, but to possess. People do really weird things when they're grieving."

"Okay," Rachel said, stopping Willow from getting out of the car by grabbing her arm. "We check out Mark's feet, and if he's anywhere near a size twelve, we take our theory to Kee."

"That's the first intelligent thing you've said today," Willow said with a sassy smile.

Rachel gave her a haughty glare. "There're still the boat designs," she warned. "We still need to find them."

"Twenty minutes is all I'm giving you. And if you don't find them, it's over and done with."

Rachel nodded and opened her door.

"Well?" Willow asked as they pulled away from the Lakeman Boatyard.

"I couldn't find anything. But the drawer where they should have been had fingerprints smeared in the dust. Someone was in there recently."

Willow sighed and closed her eyes, leaning her head on the headrest. "So we didn't gain a damn thing," she said tiredly.

"Mark said his mom was here last week, and he sounded like that was a rare occurrence," Rachel reminded her. "I'm wondering . . . the *Norway Night* burned the same day the article about Keenan Oakes came out in the *Island Gazette* saying that the Lakeman heir had been found."

"So?"

"So what if the article somehow disconcerted Mary Alder? What if she knew about the *Norway Night* and the other two boats? She could have taken the blueprints. That might be why she visited the boatyard."

"To what end?" Willow asked, rolling her head and

looking at Rachel. "Do you really think the boat burning is tied to Keenan Oakes's arrival?"

"It's quite a coincidence if it isn't."

Willow sat up. "If Mary did burn that boat, maybe she's just trying to protect Thadd's name, just as you're trying to protect Dad's. And Mark's feet are large, but he was wearing work boots, not sneakers," Willow added with a sigh. "Which doesn't prove a damn thing, either."

Rachel pondered the problem of Mary Alder, the *Norway Night,* and the missing designs. Nothing made sense. If the boat burning had been precipitated by the article in the *Island Gazette,* who had burned it?

"Why hasn't Kee just called the police and reported his missing stuff to them?" Willow asked.

"That's a good question," Rachel said softly.

"Unless he thinks you really are involved," Willow speculated.

Rachel remained mute.

Willow leaned against her headrest again. "How did he know that the emeralds were stolen in France seventeen years ago and that they're worth a million dollars?" Willow continued. "And the other stuff you put in the vault. How come he knew it was all stolen?"

Rachel started to say something, but smiled instead, pulling the SUV over to the side of the road, watching in her rearview mirror as the sheriff's car, lights flashing, pulled up behind them.

"What time's your date?" Rachel asked.

"It's set for seven."

"Maybe he's canceling," she said, nodding behind them.

Willow turned and looked out the back window and snorted. "From your lips to God's ears."

"We need his truck, Willy," she reminded her. "Tonight."

Larry walked to Willow's side of their SUV, and Rachel pushed the button to lower Willow's window.

"Hi," he said, leaning on the door.

"Are we still on for tonight?" Willow asked.

"I'm sorry, but I have to cancel," Larry told her, shaking his head. "I'm stuck pulling a double shift. I'm sorry. Are you coming back next weekend?"

"Ah, no. I'm going to try and organize my new apartment. Larry, you have a pickup, don't you?" Willow asked.

Rachel watched as Larry's chest actually puffed up. "Yes, I do. It's a brand-new Chevy with an Isuzu turbo diesel, a five-speed Allison tranny, and leather interior." He lowered his voice and leaned closer to Willow. "You want me to move you down to Augusta?"

Rachel looked out her own window so Larry wouldn't see her roll her eyes. Machismo was alive and well in Puffin Harbor, and it drove big trucks with five-speed transmissions. Heck, lobster boats were even bigger objects of male one-upmanship. A lot of the lobstermen had more money tied up in their boats than they did in their homes.

"Ah, thank you, Larry. I'd like that," Willow said. "Are you off tomorrow?"

"Yup. As of seven in the morning."

"Then maybe I should just bring your truck to our house tonight. Rachel and I and a couple of town boys can load it up this evening. Then tomorrow you can go home and have a little nap and then we can head to Augusta in the afternoon."

Larry suddenly paled.

"I promise not to scratch it," Willow whispered, laying

her hand on his arm. "It's a beautiful truck. Green, isn't it?"

Larry nodded, still looking worried. "Forest green with aluminum mag wheels."

Willow patted his arm, and Rachel would bet her kayak her sister was batting her eyelashes and making good old Larry's knees knock with her killer sweetheart smile. "You'll be tired after working a double shift, so it only makes sense that Rachel and I load the truck ourselves. That way you'll only have to unload it in Augusta."

Yup, that sweetheart smile did them in every time. Larry reached into his pocket, took out his truck keys, and handed them to Willow, folding her fingers around them in her hand, his own large hand lingering possessively.

Though Rachel wasn't sure if it was Willow he was clinging to or his truck keys.

"I'm really sorry about our date tonight," he said, still holding her hand. "Maybe I can make it up to you tomorrow night. We'll find a nice lounge in Augusta that has a band."

"Sounds great. It's a plan, then," Willow said, gently freeing herself. "Rachel can drop me off at your house now, and I'll drive your truck back to ours. Thanks, Larry. I'll see you tomorrow noon, then," Willow said, tossing the keys in her purse.

Larry hesitated, darting a glance at Rachel, then looked back at Willow and smiled. "Yeah. Tomorrow," he said with a nod, finally lifting his arm off the passenger-side door and walking back to his squad car.

Rachel watched Larry in the rearview mirror as he shut off the flashing lights and pulled around them onto the road. "You are going to fry in hell," she said with a chuckle.

Willow smacked her in the arm. "Hey, it's not my fault men are easy. Besides, I like Larry. He's sweet. I am not just stringing him along."

Rachel was about to respond when she spotted the boat through the sparse trees, less than half a mile from shore and obviously heading in.

"Aw, hell," she muttered, digging in the glove box and pulling out the small binoculars. She leaned in front of Willow, focusing the binoculars on the boat. "Dammit, that's a schooner. Miss Mikaela the tyrant is not arriving tomorrow," she said as she zeroed in on the little blond girl standing at the rail, waving both arms and shouting. "She's arriving today."

She lowered the glasses and looked at Willow. "There go our plans for Puffy."

Willow took the binoculars from Rachel and looked at the schooner, then turned and smiled and shook her head. "Naw. We'll just bring her along. She'll love it. It'll be women's night out on the big town of Puffin Harbor."

"Five-year-olds cannot keep secrets. In two days everyone will know it's us."

"I was five when I caught you kissing Mike Johnson at the Lobster Festival."

"I threatened to cut your hair while you slept if you told," Rachel reminded her, finally starting the truck and pulling onto the road, turning, and heading back toward Larry's house.

"Then that's what we'll use to threaten the tyrant," Willow said, putting her sunglasses on and leaning back against the headrest with a tired sigh.

Chapter Fifteen

⬙

*T*he *Foster* home *hadn't been* this full since Marian and Frank Foster's funeral service. But while three years ago it had been neighbors and friends all speaking softly, grieving, and still somewhat in shock, tonight it was one wolf, seven men, and a little blond cherub, all speaking loudly and at once, happy to be reunited.

Well, except for Jonathan French—a.k.a. Ahab. He was just happy to be getting rid of his charge and seemed much more interested in the bowl of strawberries he was gobbling down than in the reunion.

They had appeared like an invading army half an hour ago—Kee holding Mikaela in his arms and smiling proudly, Duncan carrying her bags, Matthew carrying a huge stuffed animal that looked like a giraffe with wings, Luke carrying four bottles of wine, and Jason and Peter loaded down with at least ten quarts of strawberries.

Willow had taken one look at the strawberries, turned green, and run upstairs before Rachel could even introduce her to the apostles.

Rachel had been playing hostess ever since, hulling strawberries, setting out bowls and spoons, and pouring wine. She had refilled the sugar bowl three times already, until finally giving up and just plunking the sugar canister in the middle of the table.

Kee was sitting at the table, Mikaela in his lap, and the two of them were getting more strawberry juice on themselves than in their mouths.

"You tell your daddy what you done, young lady," Ahab said, pointing his spoon at Mikaela. "And what I want him to do about it."

Wiping her hands on her apron, Rachel inched closer in the suddenly silent room and watched as Mikaela looked up at Kee with the largest, brightest blue, most beguiling eyes Rachel had ever seen.

"I broke the compass," she whispered, her long blond eyelashes blinking once . . . twice . . . her expression downright pitiful. She turned just enough to snuggle into Kee's chest, tucking her head under his chin as she faced the others at the table. "And Ahab wants you to beat me."

"I did not say 'beat,' " Ahab declared, glaring at Mikaela, then looking at Kee. "I said 'spank.' There's a mighty big difference. And if you'd take a firm hand to her naughty little bottom once in a while, we might come through the next fifteen years with our sanity intact," he defended.

Not showing any reaction to either Mikaela's or Ahab's statements, Kee turned his daughter back around to face him, took hold of her chin, and lifted her face up to his. "What do you think I should do?" he asked.

"I think I've been punished enough, Daddy," she said, her eyelashes batting again. "A whole week of missing you . . . and . . . and everyone," she added, her voice quivering as she tried to look at the others at the table.

Kee wouldn't let her, holding her facing him. "How did the compass get broken?"

"The boom fell on it."

"And what made the boom fall?"

Her large blue eyes finally started to show some worry. "It might have fallen when I untied the rope," she whispered.

"You untied the rope even though you're not allowed to touch the rigging," Kee said quietly.

Mikaela nodded. "I was trying to get to you faster, Daddy."

Oh, she was good, Rachel decided. Miss Mikaela Oakes could give lessons to a courtesan. Rachel inched closer, noting the expressions on all the men's faces.

Ahab's eyes were glazed with resignation, apparently having witnessed this display of feminine wiles once too often. Duncan was frowning hard enough to damage his face, Luke was holding in a laugh, and Jason and Peter and Matthew were nodding agreement with Mikaela.

"Do you know what can happen to a boat without a compass?" Kee asked.

Mikaela slowly shook her chin back and forth in his fingers.

"It can get lost. If not for Ahab being such a good captain, you could be sitting in France right now instead of with us here in Maine."

"I won't touch the rigging again, Daddy."

"No, you won't," Kee softly declared. "And you're going to buy Ahab a new compass."

"I don't got any money."

"Then you'll have to earn some. Whatever Ahab pays his man to polish the brass on the *Six-to-One Odds*, he'll pay you. And when you have enough money for the compass, you'll buy him one."

Unbelievably, her eyes got even bigger. "But that's hard work," she declared, pulling her chin free and crossing her arms over her chest. "I'm only a little girl."

"If you're strong enough to untie rigging, you're strong enough to polish brass," Kee said, cupping her face between his large hands and kissing her loudly on the forehead. He stood up and set her in his place on the chair, pushing the bowl of strawberries toward her. "Eat up. You can start tomorrow."

Not at all happy with how things had turned out, Mikaela knelt on the chair and cuddled her bowl of strawberries to her chest, her shoulders hunched as she alternated between eating and shooting accusing glares at Ahab.

Ahab refilled his own bowl with strawberries, covered them with at least half a cup of sugar, and finished his feast with a satisfied smile on his face.

"Can I talk to you outside?" Kee asked, coming over to Rachel and placing a hand at her back, then guiding her out the screen door and off the porch and across the lawn toward the ocean.

"She's adorable, Kee," Rachel said as soon as they reached the pebble beach in front of her house. "She's beautiful—and simply a treasure."

"She's a hellion," he said, fierce affection and pride

deepening his voice. "It's a wonder we don't all have a drinking problem." He smiled and shook his head. "The last five years have been the longest years of my life, and I swear I've aged at least ten."

He reached up and ran his knuckles gently down over her cheek. "But they've been the best years of my life, and I wouldn't trade them for the world," he softly declared, taking her in his arms, lifting her enough to bring her face up to his.

His mouth captured hers with heart-stopping possession.

Rachel wrapped her arms around his neck and parted her lips to give his strawberry-sweetened tongue complete access. His own arms held her so tightly against him that she could feel his heart thumping against her breasts.

One of his hands captured her braid, winding it around and around until he reached the nape of her neck and used it to cant her head and deepen the kiss.

Rachel's reaction was immediate, her blood simmering and her nerve endings coming alive, humming with desire. His heat permeated her clothes all the way to her skin, flushing her with salacious warmth. And his mouth—oh, his wonderful mouth—teased her passionately, sending erotic images through her mind of them together, naked, in bed, touching and loving and arousing each other senseless.

He lowered his free hand down her back, cupping her bottom and pulling her into him, and Rachel felt his own desire pushing against her. He broke the kiss, trailing his lips across her cheek to nibble her ear, causing her to shudder with need.

And then he straightened and set her away, his hands

gripping her shoulders—which was a good thing, considering her legs were filled with jelly. "There," he declared softly, taking a calming breath. "That's better."

Better? Better than what, a root canal? Hell, she'd been better before he'd started boiling her blood.

"Now, about Mikaela," he said, letting her go and crossing his arms over his chest. "Can she stay with you?"

"Do I have a choice?"

He shrugged. "I can put her back aboard the *Six-to-One Odds* and hope Ahab doesn't take her out to sea and throw her overboard," he offered.

"Oh, come on," Rachel said with a snort. "She can't be that bad. She's only five years old."

"Going on sixty," he clarified, rubbing a hand down over his face with a deep sigh. "She could use a bit of female company, I suspect. She's been surrounded by men her entire life."

"But what about her mother? Doesn't she ever see her?"

His eyes hardened, and he shook his head. "No. Mikaela's been mine since she was ten minutes old."

"Is her mother . . . is she dead?" Rachel asked in a whisper.

"No. So do we have a deal?"

Apparently the subject of Mikaela's mother was not open to discussion. "Could our deal start tomorrow instead? Willow and I have a little errand to do tonight."

His brow lifted in question, and he nodded toward the green pickup parked in the yard. "Does this errand have anything to do with Larry Jenkins's truck?"

"How do you know it's Larry's truck?"

"I know a lot of things. I know that you went to the

Lakeman Boatyard this afternoon, and that while Willow distracted Mark Alder, you went snooping through his files. What were you looking for, Rachel?"

Rachel crossed her own arms under her breasts. "You had me followed."

He nodded. "I told you I'd be keeping an eye on you, for your own protection."

"It wasn't supposed to start until after Mikaela arrived."

He stepped forward and took hold of her shoulders. "It started the moment I realized you nearly fell off the cliff that first night," he said, tightening his hands when she tried to pull free. "What are you and Willow doing tonight?"

"I had a life before you showed up here, you know," she said, glaring at him. "Willow and I have had this thing planned for months."

"What thing?"

"That's none of your business. Just keep Mikaela tonight, and she can come here tomorrow morning. And quit following me. I am more than capable of taking care of myself."

He pulled her against his chest, wrapped his arms around her with a growl, and kissed her soundly on the mouth. "I can take care of you better," he whispered, trailing his lips across her cheek. "You could have broken your neck or drowned."

Rachel leaned into him and tucked her head under his chin, breathing in his wonderful smell with a sigh. "Can your daughter keep a secret?" she asked.

She felt him nod. "When she's motivated to," he told her.

Rachel leaned back in his arms and looked up. "Willow and I have to sneak an eight-foot puffin into the town park tonight, and we could use a little manpower, I guess."

"An eight-foot puffin?"

"We made a wooden statue of a puffin," she told him, nodding. "As a gift for the town. But it has to be an anonymous gift." She shrugged in his embrace and smiled. "For the past two years Willow and I have been leaving little surprises around town. Everyone's been getting into the mystery of where they're coming from, and who's doing it. And tonight Puffy is making his debut."

His expression suddenly changed to one of understanding. "The statue in your basement," he said with dawning awareness. "I saw it the day we picked up your clothes. You made that for the town? And the birdhouses and mailboxes on the workbench—you've been setting them out all over Puffin Harbor, haven't you? I've passed one or two mailboxes like them and thought they looked familiar. But why?"

"For fun," Rachel told him. "To give everyone something to talk about."

"But why?" he repeated.

"I believe it's called entertainment," she told him with a laugh. "There's not a whole heck of a lot to do around here in the winter, so Willow and I decided to create a mystery for the townspeople to solve."

His smile slashed through the darkening twilight. "And you borrowed a sheriff's truck for your clandestine operation," he said in wonder, shaking his head. "And you want to take my daughter on this little adventure."

"Only if she can keep our secret."

Kee pulled her back against him, rocking her gently. "Maybe we'd better wait until she falls asleep, and leave Jason or Luke here with her. Duncan and I will go with you and be your muscle and lookout. Are you going to tell me what you were looking for at the Lakeman Boatyard?"

Rachel blinked at the sudden change of subject. "I was looking at Mark Alder's feet," she said.

He leaned back and looked down at her. "His feet," he repeated evenly.

"And to ask how his mother is doing, and to sell him Willow's shares in the boatyard." She gave him a brilliant smile. "You're partners with Mark Alder now instead of with the Foster sisters. We both sold Mark our shares."

"Why were you looking at his feet?" he asked.

"To see if they were the same size as the prints I found in the tunnels. I think the smaller prints might belong to Mary Alder, Mark's mother. And maybe the larger prints are Mark's, and he'd gone to Sub Rosa to get her."

"Do you think Mary Alder's been taking the items?"

Rachel nodded. "Willow and I came to that conclusion this afternoon. Mary's been . . . well, she's been acting strange ever since Thadd died, and people do funny things when they're grieving."

"So if you believe that's all that's going on here, why were you were rifling through Alder's files?"

"How do you know what I was doing?"

"That's what Matt said," he told her, shaking his head and smiling. "You really aren't a very good burglar, Rachel. You should close the blinds before you start snooping. And when you're hiding in a closet, wait at least ten minutes after you think the coast is clear before you try and sneak out."

"Thanks for the advice," she said sweetly, patting his chest. "I'll remember that the next time."

His arms tightened around her. "There won't be a next time," he growled. "Did you find what you were looking for?"

"Where?"

His sigh moved her hair. "At the boatyard," he said, squeezing her.

"Oh. No. No, I didn't."

He pulled her back to his chest, resting his chin on her head and tucking her tightly against him with another deep, long-suffering sigh. "You need to trust me, Rachel," he whispered.

"I trust you just as much as you trust me," she whispered back, snuggling into his embrace.

His chest shook with a chuckle. "What in hell kind of answer is that?"

"An appropriate answer, considering."

"Considering what?" he asked, pushing her away again—just enough to glare at her.

"Considering that I've known you less than a week."

That was the wrong answer if his expression was any indication. He looked so confounded, Rachel had a moment's worry that he might take a lesson from Ahab and throw her in the ocean.

"Are you in the habit of sleeping with men you don't trust?" he asked softly.

"I'm not in the habit of sleeping with men at all," she shot back, getting defensive. "Do you sleep with women you don't trust?"

She snorted and pulled free, holding up her hand. "Never mind. That was a dumb question to ask a guy."

She turned and started back to the house, but stopped, turned again, and walked back to him.

"Let me ask you this instead. How come you knew the emeralds I put in the vault were real, and that they're worth over a million dollars and had been stolen seventeen years ago? And how come you knew the other items were also stolen?" she asked, crossing her arms under her breasts again, waiting for his answer.

"I'm in the lost-and-found business, Rachel," he explained, his smile almost—but not quite—indulgent. "They weren't on Sub Rosa's inventory list, and it was a simple matter to log on to a database of stolen and unrecovered art."

She took a step closer, uncrossing her arms in surprise. "So there really is a database for that stuff?"

"Yes. And there's a reward. A ten percent finder's fee is the standard, payable to anyone returning stolen items to the insurer of record."

She stepped even closer. "And how does one go about returning stolen items without any questions being asked?" She suddenly frowned and stepped back. "And why didn't you mention this little finder's fee this morning, when you and I and Willow were discussing it in the kitchen?"

He shrugged. "It's not like it's a big secret or anything. Why? You want your stuff back?"

"No," she said fiercely, turning on her heel and heading for the house again. "You are more than welcome to it."

He caught her before she'd taken three steps. "Rachel," he said, turning her around and pulling her back into his arms so he could kiss the tip of her nose. "I'm giving you my daughter. Doesn't that say I trust you?"

"No. It only says that you trust I would never do anything to endanger her, and even then it comes with six watchdogs and a wolf. But it's also a very convenient way for you to tie my hands and keep me out of the way." She made a face, lowering her voice. "Put the womenfolk together and circle the wagons, and let the menfolk take care of business."

He threw back his head in laughter, pulling her tightly against him and hugging her fiercely. "You little impostor," he said with a bearlike growl. "You hide behind a nunlike demeanor, but you are a little feminist who is royally pissed that you've found a mystery but have promised to stay out of it."

He kissed her now flushed-mad forehead, refusing to let her wiggle out of his arms. "I don't think you're trying to protect Willow nearly as much as you're enjoying the adventure."

"That's not true."

"Then tell me right now, Rachel, that sneaking into my library and opening that vault didn't get your blood humming," he softly entreated. "And that you didn't enjoy bringing Sub Rosa back to life while disappearing into the tunnels right under our noses. And still that wasn't enough. Today you rifled through Mark Alder's files while spying on his mother."

He lifted her, bringing his mouth down on hers in a kiss so consuming that Rachel's senses reeled. She clung to him, kissing him back just as fiercely, wishing she could simply crawl under his skin and put out the fire raging in the pit of her stomach.

"Sleeping Beauty's been awakened," he whispered as he continued to rain kisses over her face. "And she doesn't want to go back to bed."

Oh, yes she did. Right now, to Keenan Oakes's bed, with no wolves or sisters or apostles to disturb them. And definitely no five-year-old hellions.

"How about giving me a tour of your boat?" Rachel suggested.

"There're two crewmen on watch," he told her. "How about you show me your camper instead?"

There was a sudden scream from the house, something crashed to the floor, and the screen door slapped open. Willow came running out onto the porch and down the steps.

Mickey was one step behind her, and Duncan was one step behind the wolf. Mikaela ran onto the porch, hopping up and down and waving her spoon, yelling at Mickey.

Willow ran to her car, jumped in, and slammed the door shut, peering out through the window with eyes the size of dinner plates glowing in the porch light.

Rachel wasn't sure if it was Mickey that had Willow so riled or Duncan. Willow was looking from one to the other, shaking her head. She pushed down the car door lock.

Which meant it must be Duncan.

Kee set Rachel away with a sigh and went to the rescue. Rachel trailed behind and walked over to the passenger's side of Willow's car and climbed in.

"Hi," she said to her startled sister.

"Lock your door," Willow all but shouted, and pushed the button on her side of the car that locked all of them. "You left me alone in a house full of strangers," she accused. "And you could have warned me they had a wolf. And this brute," she added, nodding toward Duncan, who was now leaning down and grinning in the window.

"Actually came upstairs looking for me. And he had a bowl of strawberries with him and was muttering something about eating the hair of the dog that bit me."

"That's Duncan," Rachel told her, waving at him past Willow. "And he and Kee are going to help us put Puffy in the town park tonight."

"We don't need his help!" Willow snapped. "He's a brute."

"Yeah, but you said we need *manpower.*"

"That is not a man. That is a mountain of testosterone. He's probably got muscle where his brain should be. He . . . he came into my bedroom," she whispered.

"Oh, come on, Willy. We'll go back inside, and you can just ignore Duncan, and I'll introduce you to the others. They're very civilized, I promise. And you'll meet the tyrant and Ahab."

"The whole house smells like strawberries," Willow said. "And the table has enough sugar covering it to frost a cake. And it's *full.*"

"What's full?"

"The house! It's full of men."

Rachel patted her arm. "You're an assistant state's attorney general, Willy. You can handle it. Just think of them as a jury you're determined to charm."

"They all look like they should be behind bars," she said softly, finally lifting one side of her mouth in a half smile. "I think I'll run background checks on them."

Mickey reared up and set his paws on the window, his tongue lolling out the side of his mouth, his head canted inquisitively. Mikaela had come down from the porch and was now in Kee's arms, and the others had come out of the house and were all gathered around the car, watching.

"Bet you wish your date hadn't fallen through," Rachel said, unlocking and opening her door. "Come on. I'll make the introductions, we'll get Mikaela settled in bed, and then we'll load up Puffy."

Willow's tentative smile suddenly turned brilliant. "Maybe Puffy will fall on the brute and kill him," she said, finally unlocking and opening her own door, taking a deep breath, and then getting out of the car.

Rachel had just walked around the hood to stand by her sister and start the introductions, when several of the men suddenly stiffened. They all grabbed their belts at their sides, and Duncan swore softly under his breath.

Kee handed Mikaela over to Rachel and turned to Luke. "Luke, you and Ahab stay here. Matt and Peter, head to the front of the house and wait for my signal. Jason, you go in through the terrace. Duncan and I will use the cliff tunnel."

"What's happening?" Rachel asked as they turned to leave. "What's going on?"

"Daddy!" Mikaela demanded loudly.

Kee turned and took hold of Mikaela's shoulder. "You stay with Rachel, sweetheart. We'll be back in a little bit." He looked at Rachel. "Someone's in the tunnels," he said softly, pulling a vibrating pager off his belt, holding it up for her to see and then shutting it off. "We're just going to check it out," he said, somewhat absently, already turned and heading toward the cliff path.

Rachel handed Mikaela to Ahab and ran after Kee. "Wait," she said, catching up with him at the edge of the trees. "It might be Mary. You're going to scare her to death. I'm coming with you. She knows me."

Kee shook his head. "It might not be Mary," he said evenly, taking her by the shoulders and turning her around. "Go inside with the others, Rachel. Now," he ordered curtly, one large hand nudging her along when she didn't move fast enough.

Completely disconcerted by the don't-mess-with-me-now tone in his voice, Rachel crossed her arms and hugged herself as she walked toward her house without looking back. Dammit, it was probably only Mary.

Then again, it could be the owner of the male footprints.

And that meant Kee and Duncan and the others were heading straight into danger.

She spun back around, but Kee had already disappeared into the woods. A large warm hand touched her shoulder.

"Come on, Rachel," Luke said, gently pulling her back toward the house. "They'll be fine."

"Why doesn't he just call the police and let them handle this?" she asked.

He chuckled softly. "That's not how we work." He stopped her when they reached the porch. "He'll call the police, Rachel, when it's time. Until then, let him have his fun."

"This is not fun," she snapped. "It's dangerous."

He waved that away. "Naw, it's definitely fun," he said, smiling—somewhat longingly—as he looked toward Sub Rosa.

"And you're mad because you're stuck here with us," she said, drawing his attention again.

He shook his head. "I'm right where I need to be, Rachel. I can tell you from personal experience that pulling guard duty can get pretty exciting all by itself," he said, rubbing his ribs just below his chest.

"What kind of personal experience?" Rachel asked softly.

He stared at her, his expression uncertain, then suddenly he sighed and rubbed his ribs again. "Six years ago I was left to watch a woman and her three children while Kee and Duncan and Peter went looking for her husband's kidnappers," he quietly stated. "Only the kidnappers weren't at the camp like we'd been told. They were watching the house."

"What happened?" Rachel whispered hoarsely.

"I spent the next month recovering in a hospital in Brazil."

"And . . . and the woman and her children?"

He smiled apologetically. "She spent a month in the same hospital. The children didn't get a scratch on them."

"And what happened to the husband?"

"Duncan came walking out of the jungle with him two days later."

"And . . . and the kidnappers?" she asked, hugging herself against a shiver.

Luke merely shook his head and opened the screen door.

Rachel mutely walked into the kitchen ahead of him. Luke walked in behind her only to stop her by the shoulder again. "That's why Kee left me here, Rachel," he said softly, his voice not reaching the others gathered in the living room. "Because he knows I never make the same mistake twice. Please don't worry. Everything will be okay. They'll be back before you know it, hopefully with the answer to our little mystery."

Chapter Sixteen

�֍

Luke's "*back before you know it*" translated into two hours. Three of the men reappeared as suddenly and silently as they'd left. Rachel walked into the kitchen to get a plastic cup to fill with water for Mikaela, only to find Kee standing at the sink, dabbing a wet towel on the back of Jason's neck. Duncan was standing beside them, softly imparting the news that he didn't think it needed stitches.

All three men looked over when she walked in and Jason smiled sheepishly. "I tripped and fell on a rock," he said.

"You did not," Rachel said, waving his lie away and taking the towel from Kee. "Someone hit you."

She pulled Jason down by the shoulder and looked at the cut on the back of his neck. "I have some butterfly bandages," she told him, slapping the towel to his chest and turning toward the downstairs bathroom. She stopped and looked up at Kee, being careful to keep her expression neutral. "Any other injuries I should know about?"

Kee's smile was lopsided and definitely reassuring. "You got anything in your medical kit for dented egos?"

"Yours . . . or mine?"

He pulled her into his arms with a laugh and hugged her tightly. "We're all okay, Rachel. Matt and Peter stayed at Sub Rosa to keep an eye on things. And it's Jason's ego that needs tending. He was taken by complete surprise."

"The threat was supposed to be coming from inside the house," Jason defended. "Not from outside on the terrace."

Still firmly ensconced in Kee's embrace, and in no hurry to leave it, Rachel looked over at Jason. "Someone was hiding on the terrace?"

Jason nodded. "I must have ran right past him."

"It was a 'him'? You're sure?"

He nodded again, holding the towel on his neck. "Unless women in Puffin Harbor have beards," he told her. "He was about five-nine or five-ten, wiry, with dark hair and a full beard. That's all I saw before my face kissed the terrace."

"Does Mark Alder have a beard?" Kee asked, drawing her attention.

"No. And he's taller." She shook her head. "I don't know anyone fitting that description. But lots of men around here have beards, though most usually shave them off come summer."

"I do remember the distinct smell of rotten fish," Jason added.

"A fisherman?" Duncan interjected. He looked at Rachel. "What kind of working boats do you have here? That would give us a direction to look."

"Lobstermen, deep-sea charter fishermen, haddock and scrod boats, and scallop draggers. Heck, he might only work on the docks. Basically, he could be anyone."

"Then we still have nothing," Duncan said with a snarl.

Kee gave her a quick kiss on her frowning forehead and turned her toward the bathroom. "Get the bandages," he said, patting her bottom to get her moving, then going to the cupboard where she kept the aspirin and tossing the bottle to Duncan.

"Wait," Rachel said. "What about your alarm in the tunnels? Did you find anything?"

Kee shook his head. "Our small-footed friend did come for a visit tonight, but he or she obviously knows their way around the tunnels. We didn't so much as catch a glimpse. Where's my daughter?" he asked, heading toward the living room.

"Upstairs. But take her a glass of water," Rachel told him. "I have plastic cups in the cupboard over the stove. She's in the guest bedroom with Ahab and Luke and Willow." She smiled and shook her head. "Willow's reading her a bedtime story, and Ahab and Luke seem more interested than Mikaela. Duncan, could you please go outside and plug the phone line back in at the junction box? It's just around the side of the house."

"It's unplugged?" he asked, looking confused.

Rachel nodded. "I saw Luke sneak out when he heard Willow say that we should call the police." She picked up Willow's purse and pulled her cell phone out of it. "And you might want to remind him there's more than one way to dial 911."

Kee turned from getting the glass down from the cupboard and looked at Rachel with shining Atlantic-blue eyes. "Thank you," he said softly. "For not interfering tonight."

"Gee," Rachel said, shooting him a brilliant smile and then walking into the bathroom. "Ain't trust a fickle thing."

• • •

Puffy did not fall over and kill Duncan, much to Willow's dismay. He was finally loaded in Larry's truck, it was midnight, and they were finally headed into town—but only after a ten-minute discussion about who was riding where.

Duncan thought they could all ride in the front, with Willow on his lap and Rachel in the middle. Willow thought she should drive, Rachel should have the shotgun seat, and the two men should ride in the back with Puffy.

Willow won.

"I swear he's doing it on purpose," she said as she slowly pulled out of their driveway and onto the main road.

"Who is doing what on purpose?" Rachel asked.

"Duncan. He keeps pushing my buttons, trying to get a rise out of me."

"He's just teasing, Willy."

Willow held her hair away from her face and leaned toward Rachel. "Do I have a sign on my forehead that says 'redneck'?" she asked. "Or maybe it says 'camp follower' or something. Look real hard, Rae, and tell me the truth."

Rachel leaned over and made a production of looking at Willow's forehead. "It says 'assistant state attorney general,'" she told her. She rubbed Willow's temple. "And if I look real hard, I can just make out the word *governor* under it."

Willow leaned back and smiled. "Thanks, sis. That's just what I needed to hear," she said gruffly, slowing the truck as they came into town. She drove right past the park, then turned right while making sure the coast was clear, as was their normal routine whenever they were putting out their gifts.

"Pull over there," Rachel suggested, pointing to the left. "Just between Annie's Coffee Shop and Brigham's Grocery."

Willow pulled up to the curb and backed into the small alley between the buildings, then shut off the engine and killed the lights. The truck rocked as the two men jumped out of the back, and Duncan appeared at Willow's door and Kee at Rachel's.

Willow turned the key just enough to roll down the windows.

"I don't suppose ya could have found a truck that made a little more noise?" Duncan asked. "With maybe a bit more chrome so that everyone could see us better?"

Willow ignored him and pointed out the windshield as she spoke to Kee. "We're thinking of putting Puffy right there, on that grassy section between the two paths."

Kee looked at where she was pointing, then headed across the street. Rachel got out and followed, noticing that Willow slid across the seat and got out the passenger door to avoid Duncan. The four of them climbed over the low rail fence, walked into the park, and stopped between the paths.

"So we just set that huge wooden base on the grass and then set Puffy on it?" Kee asked, moving around until he found a level spot the size of the base. He looked at Rachel. "It will support him? If he topples over, he could kill someone."

"I've thought of that," Rachel told him. "That's what the steel rods are for. We bolt Puffy to the base, then drive the rods into the ground through the brackets I've already attached to it. The rods are four feet long. That should hold him against anything short of a hurricane."

"Can you back the truck up here?" Duncan asked, visually scanning the park for access. "Is there a place in the fence wide enough?"

"There's a gate on the other side of the bandstand," Rachel said, pointing. "With a chain across it."

Kee chuckled. "I wondered what the bolt cutters were for." He raised an eyebrow, crossing his arms over his chest. "You're turning into quite a criminal, Rachel. Only this time you're taking not only your sister down the perilous path with you, but your new neighbors as well. We haven't even been here long enough to register to vote, and already we're accessories to a crime."

"We brought a new padlock," Willow defended. "And what can they charge us with? It's a public park, and we're the public. We can bring a puffin with us if we want."

"Breaking and entering," Duncan began, holding up his fingers to count on. "Destruction of public property and—"

Headlights suddenly appeared at the north end of town, moving toward the park. Kee grabbed Rachel around the waist, picked her up, and ran to the nearest maple tree. She heard Willow squeak in surprise, and looked over to see Duncan grab her sister and run in the opposite direction.

"We really have to stop meeting like this," Kee whispered, pressing her against the tree, his mouth mere inches from hers. "I'm beginning to worry that life with you is going to be one adventure after another."

Rachel sucked in her breath.

Kee had been wondering what life with her would be like?

He pressed even closer, shifting them deeper into the shadow of the tree, covering her head with his large hand and tucking her face into his chest as the lights slowly moved closer.

He'd been wondering what life with her would be like?

Rachel couldn't seem to catch her breath. She could

feel sweat breaking out on her forehead, her heart was racing a mile a minute, and her insides started to churn with mixed emotions.

He'd really been wondering what life with her would be like?

Dammit. She didn't know if she was thrilled by that or scared out of her wits.

They were having a fun little fling, was all.

They'd known each other only a week.

He owned Sub Rosa.

She owned a room full of stolen art.

"You're trembling," he whispered, lifting her face to his. "And I know you're not scared."

Yes she was! She was scared spitless.

"So it must be me making you quiver," he said, lowering his mouth to hers, kissing her gently, coaxing her to respond.

And it dawned on her then that he didn't even realize what he'd said—that he had no idea what he had revealed to her with those simple words and no clue about how they'd affected her.

So Rachel dealt with the problem the only way she knew how, by opening her mouth to his wonderful taste and kissing him back.

A sharp floodlight slashed across them.

Kee quickly turned to hide her identity. "Keep kissing me," he whispered in her ear. "And maybe good old Officer Jenkins will go away."

Rachel heard a car door open and close, and the light beam narrowed to that of a flashlight. "Come on, people," Larry said, walking toward them. "Go get a room. This park is closed."

Kee sighed and kissed her forehead, then turned to Larry, keeping Rachel tucked behind his back. "Officer Jenkins," he said, nodding.

"Oakes?" Larry asked, clearly surprised. "What are you doing here?"

"I'm trying to talk my date into going home with me," Kee said, masculine amusement lacing his words.

Rachel pinched him—really hard—in the small of his back.

"Who you got back there?" Larry asked, moving to his left.

Kee turned slightly, and Rachel sidestepped to stay hidden. Lord, she was too old to be caught necking in the park! She frantically scanned the area, looking for Willow and Duncan, but she couldn't see either one of them.

That was all they needed, for Larry to find Willow in the park at two in the morning with another man. He'd haul them all off to jail just out of spite.

Rachel stepped out from behind Kee. "Hi, Larry," she said, lamely waggling her fingers at him.

"Rachel! What are you doing out here at this hour?"

"I . . . ah . . . Kee and I were just out for a walk. It's such a beautiful night."

Larry looked from her to Kee, then back at her, the streetlights illuminating his face enough for her to see his shock. He also seemed to be at a loss for words.

"I didn't realize they closed the park at night," Kee said, drawing Larry's attention back to him. "We'll head home then." Kee took hold of her hand and started to lead her toward the street.

"Wait," Larry said, shining his flashlight directly at her face. "Rachel? Have you been drinking?"

"No, of course not," she told him.

"Maybe I should just give you a ride home."

"I'm fine, Larry. But thanks for the offer."

He darted a look at Kee, then back at her. "I'll call Willow and have her come—"

The radio crackled to life in Larry's squad car, and a woman's voice came over the speaker. "Domestic disturbance on Hollow Hill Lane," the radio blared. "Possible shots fired."

Larry cursed, already turning toward his car. He stopped and looked back at Rachel. "I'll check in on you later," he said. "So don't panic when I come to your door."

"No! It's okay, La—"

He had already reached his squad car. He tossed his flashlight in the front seat, jumped in, and put the car in gear before his door even closed.

Rachel smacked Kee in the arm. "Thank you for telling him you were trying to get me in bed!"

"Hey, I didn't hear *you* offering any excuses for your tongue being down my throat."

She was just about to smack him again when a muffled scream came from the bushes about fifty yards away, then a very loud grunt, and the bushes started shaking, and Willow came scrambling out of them.

"You try that again, you overgrown bear, and I promise you'll never father children," Willow hissed as she got to her feet and started brushing down her clothes.

"I was just making sure that wee little snake didn't scare a scream out of ya," Duncan said, crawling out of the bushes.

"I am not afraid of snakes."

"Now, how was I ta know that?" he asked, standing up and rubbing his ribs as he plucked a leaf from her hair.

Willow swatted his hand away and started marching toward the truck. And of course Duncan was one step behind her, grinning like the village idiot.

"Your sister scares me," Kee said, smiling as he rubbed his neck where Willow had brained him with the lamp that morning. "Actually, so do you. You Foster women are hard on men."

Rachel patted his arm. "I think you and Duncan will survive," she assured him, heading after her sister.

"How's the knee holding up?" he asked, helping her over the fence.

"It's only a little lame. How lucky for us that Larry got that call," she said, walking around to the back of the truck and picking up the bolt cutters.

Willow pulled her cell phone out of her pocket and waved it at Rachel. "That wasn't luck," she said. "That was me."

"You called in a false alarm?" Rachel asked. "Hey, doesn't Wendell live on Hollow Hill Lane?"

Willow shrugged. "I think so. Come on, let's get moving. We'll have maybe an hour before Larry gets out there, realizes it was a hoax, and gets back to our house to make sure Rachel's home in bed—alone," she finished, shooting Kee a pointed look.

Kee took the bolt cutters from Rachel. "Bring the truck to the gate," he told her, "while I go destroy public property."

"You're scared to death of snakes," Rachel reminded Willow as soon as they climbed in the truck and started to pull out of the alley.

Willow looked over at her and smiled, nodding at the men walking along the fence toward the gate. "Yeah, but he doesn't need to know that. He's one of those guys, Rae, who doesn't ask permission to kiss you."

"Duncan kissed you? Just now, in the bushes?"

Willow nodded. "And like an idiot, I kissed him back," she admitted, shaking her head in disgust. "I don't even like large men with more brawn than brain."

"Duncan has a brain."

Willow snorted. "Too bad it's below his belt."

"Willy!"

Willow stopped the truck and put it in reverse, turning in her seat to back through the now open gate. She looked over at Rachel and grinned. "Okay. He's not that bad. But if he tries to kiss me again, I am going to 'brain' him."

"Would ya at least turn out your headlights, woman," Duncan shouted through Willow's closed window, trying to be heard over the rumble of the loud diesel engine.

And with that resounding dictate, Willow and Rachel's covert little mission of goodwill really turned into an adventure.

Willow got the truck stuck, burying it all the way up to its axles in the children's sand pit. They had to spend ten precious minutes rocking it out of the sand, and as if that weren't enough, when the truck finally did come spinning out of the pit, it headed straight into a park bench, splintering it to pieces.

Duncan opened Willow's door then, and without saying a word, he plucked her out of the truck, carried her over to a picnic table, set her down, and then walked back and got in behind the wheel himself.

"Your sister drives like she kisses," he growled to Rachel, who could only stare at him, unblinking. "And she needs lessons in both."

Rachel silently opened her door and got out, and went over and stood beside Kee. "I think they like each other," she told him, watching Willow glare at Duncan from her perch on the picnic table.

"Duncan's just having some fun with her because he knows she doesn't like men with more brawn than brain."

"You heard that!"

"Your window was down," he told her, going over and opening the tailgate of the truck.

Duncan jumped in the back and handed the base to Kee.

"Slide Puffy to the edge of the tailgate, and I'll bolt the base to him," Rachel instructed. "Willy, come help."

"I was told to stay put," Willow called back.

"And you're doing a very good job of it," Duncan said.

Willow instantly jumped down from the picnic table and ran over to Rachel, grabbing one side of the base and helping Kee wiggle it over the bolts sticking out of Puffy's feet.

Rachel could only find three of the four nuts she needed to secure him to the base.

"Damn. I lost a nut." She looked around the bed of the truck, checked all her pockets, and then finally started walking around the truck. She stopped and stared at the back right wheel.

"Oh, no you don't," Willow said through gritted teeth. "You are not cannibalizing Larry's truck."

"But it looks like the exact size," Rachel said, bending down and fingering one of the eight lug nuts holding the wheel on. "He'll just think it came loose and vibrated off."

Finally, thanks to Larry's stolen lug nut, they got Puffy secured to the base and lowered to the ground. Willow walked back ten paces and gave directions to the men to move the statue until she was satisfied that Puffy was level.

"I hope ya're enjoying yourself," Duncan said with a winded growl after five minutes of Willow's barked instructions, straightening to glare at her. " 'Cause I'm about to teach you how to properly kiss a man if ya don't quit being so fussy."

"He's perfect," Willow snapped.

Kee took one of the rods from the bed of the truck, knelt down, and threaded it through the bracket at the base. Duncan grabbed the sledgehammer and started pounding it into place.

They had just finished the third rod when an alarm suddenly screamed through the night. The large doors on the fire station one block away went up, every light in the building came on, and even the one signal light in the center of town changed from flashing yellow to flashing red.

"Shit," Kee said, grabbing the last rod and quickly threading it through the bracket. "Come on, finish it," he told Duncan. "Rachel, get that truck back in the alley."

Willow beat her to Larry's truck. She jumped in, brought the rumbling engine to life, and went spinning across the grass, weaving around the sand pit and park benches, scattering the bolt cutters and blankets they'd used to wrap Puffy all over the park.

Duncan stopped pounding the rod and straightened, staring in awe when the rear wheel of Larry's truck lifted off the road as Willow squealed around the corner and into the alley.

Duncan turned incredulous eyes on Rachel. "Was she dropped on her head as a child?" he asked.

Rachel smiled back, then ran after her scattered possessions. The fire trucks came screaming out of the station, and she dropped to the ground in the shadow of a bush, watching them speed by in the direction of the harbor. She was just about to get up when Larry's squad car shot past, his sirens blaring as he also headed toward the harbor.

"Come on, Rachel," Willow said, climbing over the fence and running to one of the blankets. "Let's get out of here."

"What's that smell?" Rachel asked, standing and brushing herself off. "Smoke?"

"Gee, let me guess," Willow said in a singsong voice. "Fire trucks . . . something that smells like smoke—do you suppose there's a fire?"

"Watch it, sis!" Rachel snapped, picking up the bolt cutters. "I'm going to tell Duncan you really, really like him if you don't cut it out. You're getting cockier every time we go on one of these little adventures."

"I can fix that," Duncan said, coming up behind Willow and throwing a blanket over her head. He spun her around, and, ignoring her muffled scream of outrage, he tossed her over his shoulder and headed back across the park. Rachel gasped when he slapped Willow's wiggling bottom, and burst into laughter when his hand lingered, and patted, and then squeezed.

"My God, she's going to kill him," she told Kee as she fell into step beside him.

Kee wrapped his arm around her shoulder and tucked her against his side. "Want to bet on who wins?" he asked, bending down and giving her a quick kiss on the mouth. "You Foster girls sure do know how to liven up a date. Any more surprises in store for us tonight?"

"Oh, I don't know," Rachel whispered, reaching over

and squeezing his butt. "I still haven't given you a tour of my camper."

Kee couldn't remember the last time he'd had this much fun in the company of women. But he did know it had been years since he'd seen Duncan in such a playful mood.

Kee set the bolt cutters in the bed of the truck, then walked back to the front of the alley to stand beside the others as they looked toward the harbor.

The harbor was a scene of utter chaos, with men running in every direction, shouting to be heard over the whine of the noisy truck engines. Black smoke billowed into the night sky, reflecting off the red flashing lights of the fire trucks and the blue and white strobes of the sheriff's car. An ambulance came racing past the park just then, its blaring siren only adding to the urgency of the drama.

"It looks like another boat is burning," Duncan said. "Just like the first night we arrived."

Kee saw Willow and Rachel glance at each other, their expressions horrified, as something unspoken passed between them. Rachel began to fidget nervously, and Willow hugged herself and rubbed her arms as if overcome by a sudden chill.

"Let's go see," Rachel whispered to Willow.

The two women started walking toward the harbor.

"I do believe we've been dismissed," Duncan said, rubbing his ribs. "I feel so cheap. They used us, and now that they don't need our muscle anymore, they just walk away."

"Didn't you see the look they gave each other?" Kee asked, starting after them, keeping a comfortable distance between them. "They both seemed pretty upset.

And it wasn't just neighborly concern I saw on their faces, but fear."

"Of the boat burnings?" Duncan asked. "Do ya think they know something about them?"

"Rachel did rifle through Alder's files," Kee reminded him.

"And ya didn't think to ask her what she was looking for?"

"She said she was looking for Mark Alder's feet. She and Willow are convinced that Mary Alder, Mark's mother— who was also Thaddeus Lakeman's old girlfriend—is the one using the tunnels at Sub Rosa. And that Mark Alder was probably going there to bring her back home."

"And were Alder's feet in his files?" Duncan asked.

Kee chuckled and shook his head. "Rachel wouldn't tell me what she was looking for in the files."

Duncan also shook his head. "It's a sad state of affairs when one slip of a female can run circles around a man. You're losing your touch, my friend."

"There's a female at home who's been running circles around the six of us for the last five years," Kee shot back. "Do you think the boat burnings could be tied to Sub Rosa's missing art?"

"How?" Duncan asked. "And to what end? It's probably just a turf war between fishermen."

They were approaching the harbor, and Kee watched Willow and Rachel walk up to Larry Jenkins.

"If you don't want to start another turf war," Kee warned Duncan, "over a woman instead of a fishing spot, then keep your distance from Willow in front of Jenkins."

Duncan snorted. "Why are women always attracted to men in uniform?"

"You tell me, Captain Ross," Kee shot back with a

grin. "I remember when you had to beat them off with a stick."

Townspeople had started to gather on shore, some in only their bathrobes, all watching in horror as the fishing boat, not two hundred yards out, burned on its mooring. The whine of the fire engines drowned out their comments as they labored to pump water through the hoses being dragged out to the burning boat by firefighters in another, much smaller boat.

There was a sudden explosion, a collective flinch from the audience, and Kee saw Larry Jenkins pull Willow and Rachel into the shelter of his arms to shield them with his body.

Kee gritted his teeth and stood where he was.

"I can make sure Jenkins's truck is missing more than just a lug nut," Duncan offered, scowling at the deputy sheriff, who was taking his damned good time to release the women.

Kee shook his head and moved into the crowd. He watched the firefighters quickly pull back from what was left of the burning hull as debris from the explosion rained over them, the water, and the remaining boats in the harbor.

Another boat with four firefighters was dispatched, and the two boats then focused their efforts on putting out the small fires on the other moored boats caused by the falling fireballs of debris. Several fishermen in rowboats started out from the docks, desperate to save their livelihoods.

Rachel stepped away from Jenkins and scanned the crowd of onlookers. She looked startled when she spotted Kee, as if she'd forgotten about him. She pivoted and started walking toward one of the fire trucks.

"Look for anyone with a beard who fits Jason's description, and keep an eye on him," Kee told Duncan before heading after Rachel.

"Ronald, do you know the name of the boat?" Kee heard Rachel ask a firefighter standing beside one of the fire trucks.

Ronald turned from watching the gauges on the truck, his face suddenly lighting into a smile. "So you're talking to me again?" he asked loudly, to be heard over the rumble of the engine. "How's the knee?"

Kee kept his distance and looked out at the harbor, as he continued to listen.

"It's fine," he heard Rachel say. "Do you know the name of the boat that's burning?" she repeated, even more loudly. "And is the owner here? Has he been notified?"

"What are you, a reporter now?" Ronald asked.

Kee turned just enough to see Ronald give Rachel a calculated grin. "Have breakfast with me later, and I'll give you an interview."

"We're losing water pressure!" someone yelled from the shoreline.

Ronald snapped to attention and turned back to his gauges. "It's the *Sea Dancer*," he shouted over his shoulder as he turned a valve. "I don't know who owns it, but I think the guy's on the dock."

Rachel took off in the direction of the dock. Kee caught up with her just before she reached it, grabbing her shoulder to stop her. She turned around with a gasp of surprise.

"Kee," she said, looking past him toward the crowd. "I thought . . . what . . . where's Duncan?"

"You need to stop, Rachel," he softly told her, guiding her away from the crowded dock and the noise of the fire engine. "The last thing I want is for you to draw attention to yourself."

"I'm not. I live here. It's normal that I'd be curious. And why is my drawing attention to myself the last thing *you* need?"

"Because whoever is burning these boats won't like you asking questions," he quietly explained. "What's going on, Rachel? Why are these boat burnings so important to you?"

"They're happening in my town."

Kee shook his head. "Not good enough. Why were you rifling through Alder's files today? You were looking for the blueprints of the boat that burned last week, weren't you?"

She crossed her arms under her breasts, stared up at him, and remained mute.

Kee took hold of her shoulders. "Rachel, asking questions about arson can be dangerous."

He looked out at the harbor, then back at her. "How are the boats tied to—" He suddenly stiffened. "Dammit. This does involve Sub Rosa," he whispered, leaning down to look her in the eye. "They're smuggling boats, aren't they?"

She still said nothing.

"And you and Willow know that for a fact, and you're trying to . . . to what, Rachel? Even if you know they're smuggling boats, what do you hope to accomplish by looking through Alder's files and talking to the owner of the boat? What are you looking for?"

When she still said nothing, Kee shook her. "Dammit, Rachel, you have to trust me! You have to tell me what's going on so I can protect you."

"I am not in danger," she finally said, her expression defiant. "I want to find Willow and go home."

"Everything okay over here?" Larry Jenkins asked, walking up to them. "Your sister's looking for you," he said, darting an accusing glare at Kee before giving his attention back to Rachel.

"I was just going to find her," Rachel said, pulling out of Kee's grip and turning toward the crowd. "We're leaving."

"I can't walk you home," Larry said. "I have to stay here."

"I'll see they get home safely," Kee interjected, nodding to Jenkins, who didn't seem to care for his offer.

The chaos in the scene suddenly turned frantic. Desperate shouts rose above all the noise, and the crowd of onlookers, some of them pointing, collectively moved down the shore.

"Someone's in the water!" one man yelled. "There! He's floundering!"

Kee started to run and could see that Duncan was already swimming out into the harbor, ahead of a couple of other men. Kee reached the water's edge, Jenkins and Rachel beside him, just as Duncan reached the person.

The ambulance crew pushed through the crowd, and Kee pulled Rachel out of the way. Willow came over and stood beside them as they watched Duncan start back with the now seemingly listless swimmer.

Jenkins and one of the paramedics waded into the water and took the victim from Duncan, carrying the person to the gurney on shore.

Rachel gasped, her hand on her chest. "It's Mary!" she cried, grabbing Kee's arm. "It's Mary Alder. Oh my God, Mary," she whispered, going to her.

Kee stopped her, pulling her so that her back was against his chest, wrapping his arms around her protectively. "You can't help," he said softly. "You'll just be in the way."

Duncan waded out of the water and came over to them. He pulled his shirt off over his head, wrung it out, then used it to wipe down his face and hair before slipping it back on. He walked a bit farther away from the crowd, herding Kee and Rachel and Willow with him.

"She's dead," he said softly, his tone even, giving Rachel and Willow a sympathetic glance before looking back at Kee. "But she was alive when I reached her. She said something." He shrugged. "I barely understood, but it sounded like 'Find' or 'Find her,' or something like that."

Kee tightened his arms around Rachel when she stiffened.

Duncan leaned in closer and lowered his voice even more. "She was burned some, but that's not what killed her. She'd been shot."

Rachel lifted her hands to her mouth on a soft wail, and turned in Kee's arms to bury her face in his chest. Kee held her tightly as shivers racked her body.

Willow bent at the waist, hugging herself, and Duncan swept her into his own embrace, whispering useless words of comfort.

"You're freezing wet," Willow said, suddenly lifting her head. "You're going to catch a chill."

She broke free and ran to the ambulance, leaving Duncan empty-armed and looking confounded. But his frown quickly turned to a grin when Willow came running back with a blanket.

"Thank you," he said, bending down so she could wrap it around his shoulders. He looked at Kee. "I'm thinking we should get ourselves home," he softly declared. "And it just might be time to find that strong length of rope." He looked from Kee to Willow, then back to Kee. "Maybe two lengths of rope."

Kee stared at him, confused, until he remembered his vow to tie Rachel up if he had to, to get her on board the *Six-to-One Odds*. He nodded to Duncan.

"What do you need rope for?" Willow asked.

Duncan wrapped one arm around her, covering her shivering body with the blanket, and turned and started toward the road. Kee saw Willow stiffen, then let out a sigh and meekly go with him.

He peeled Rachel off his chest enough to look into her eyes. "I'm sorry about Mary," he told her. "But we need to go home."

She looked over at the ambulance, saw they were loading Mary into it, then straightened and turned to follow Duncan and Willow.

Before she'd taken three steps, Kee swept her off her feet and into his arms. "You're limping. You've worn out your knee tonight."

"I'm too heavy," she said with a gasp, grabbing his neck. "You can't carry me—it's over a mile home."

He settled her into a more comfortable position and kissed her blushing cheek. "I could carry you to the moon, Rachel."

Chapter Seventeen

❖

Rachel woke up with what felt suspiciously like another hangover. Her head throbbed and her body ached. But unlike yesterday morning, this morning she was alone in her bed.

She could hear somebody talking downstairs, and realized it was Mikaela chattering nonstop, a deep male voice breaking in every so often.

Last night came back to her in a rush—the boat burning, the horror of the scene, and Mary.

Mary Alder was dead.

Shot, Duncan had said.

Murdered.

Kee and Duncan had wasted no time hustling her and Willow home then, not even bothering to get Larry's truck from the alley. Kee had carried her into the house and straight up to bed, then given her a quick kiss on the cheek and turned around and left.

Rachel had rolled over and cried herself to sleep.

Something crashed to the floor downstairs, there was a moment's silence, then male laughter and little-girl giggles rose up from below. Rachel caught herself smiling. Little-girl giggles were such a wonderful sound—precious and heartwarming and so endearingly innocent.

Rachel blew out a heavy sigh, slowly sat up, and swung her legs over the side of the bed. The room didn't spin, and the throbbing in her head increased only a little. She looked at the clock, discovered it was nearly ten, and stumbled her way to the bathroom.

Willow was already there.

"Good morning," Willow said softly, looking only a little better than Rachel felt. "Are you okay?"

"I'm fine," she assured her. "Why are we whispering?"

Willow nodded toward the hall. "Kee's still asleep in Mikaela's room."

"I thought Luke slept in the other bed?"

"He did," Willow confirmed, smiling. "When I peeked in on the way to the bathroom at five this morning, Luke was in one bed with Mikaela's giraffe, and Kee and Mikaela and Mickey were in the other bed. It was the cutest thing. Kee was flat on his back, Mikaela was sprawled across his chest, and Mickey was curled up beside them with one of his paws lying over Mikaela's leg."

"But they're twin beds in that room," Rachel pointed out with a smile of her own. "We have another spare room with two more beds in it, and Mom and Dad's room."

Willow shrugged. "Duncan and Ahab used the spare room. I guess Kee just wanted to be with his daughter."

"Good God. Our house is full," Rachel whispered with

a crooked smile, then suddenly sobered. "What was Mary doing in the harbor last night?"

Willow's smile disappeared just as quickly. "I don't know. Do you suppose she burned those boats?"

"Mary?" Rachel asked, thinking about that. "I guess she was capable of it. Physically, I mean. But why?"

"For the same reason she took the designs from the boatyard," Willow suggested. "To protect Thadd."

"You don't commit arson to protect a dead man. There's got to be another reason. How about Mark? Could she have been trying to protect Mark?"

"From what?"

"Dammit," Rachel said in a whisper. "I don't know. Maybe Mark's the one who's been stealing from Sub Rosa and Mary was trying to stop him before he got caught. Maybe he was using the boats just as Thadd did."

Willow nodded slowly. "That would make sense. But who shot her?" she quietly asked. "Not Mark," she said, shaking her head. "I don't even see him smuggling art. He's simply too straitlaced for something like that."

"Did you hear what Duncan said?" Rachel asked. "Mary said 'Find her.' That's the same thing Dad said to me just before the paramedics arrived."

" 'Find her,' " Willow repeated, staring out the bathroom window, then back at Rachel. "Find who? Is the smuggler a woman?"

"I suppose it could be a woman," Rachel quietly agreed. "But do you remember a guy who used to visit Sub Rosa every so often?" she asked, still whispering. "Neither of us liked him. You said he looked like he should be selling snake oil."

Willow's eyes widened. "I remember him. Why?"

"Looking back, I'm pretty sure he was the smuggler Thadd dealt with. Remember how Dad used to make us stay away from Sub Rosa whenever he visited? I think it was because he didn't want us to overhear anything."

"It's been years since the guy's been around here," Willow said, hugging herself. "Do you suppose he's come back? And that he could have shot Mary?"

"It's possible. He would definitely know about the stolen art if he helped smuggle it in. And he would know it's just been sitting here for the last three years." Rachel shrugged. "It's the perfect crime. He'd be stealing something that no one even knows exists. And while searching for it, he probably helped himself to some of the legitimate art. That would explain the missing items."

"But why now?"

"I don't think it's been only recently. Someone's been using the tunnels for years. He's probably been looking for it ever since Thadd died."

"Looking for what, exactly?" Willow asked.

Rachel leaned into the hall and checked both ways, then stepped back into the bathroom and quietly closed the door. "Think about it, Willy. If we had those stolen things in our house, what kind of stuff do you suppose Thadd had in Sub Rosa?"

"But where is it?"

"In a secret room Thadd had built."

"There's a secret room in Sub Rosa? Where?"

"I don't know. But I think Dad built it the summer you and Mom and I went to Paris. He certainly didn't want me to know about it, so he waited until I was gone."

"Then how do *you* know about it?"

"It was in the letter, Willy. Dad mentioned the room in the letter he left with Wendell."

"Dammit. You shouldn't have burned it."

"It was incriminating."

"You should have showed it to me first."

"You would have done something about it."

"Of course I would have. You're talking about millions of dollars in stolen art!" she whispered tightly.

"And that's exactly why I burned it," Rachel shot back.

Willow stared at her, her arms crossed under her breasts. "So we're back to that," she said softly. "All this sneaking around and putting yourself in danger to protect me."

"Why are you and Kee insisting I'm in danger?"

"You've been roaming through the same tunnels a smuggler's been using," Willow started, holding up her fingers to count off her reasons. "You nearly broke your neck escaping from Sub Rosa the night Kee arrived."

"Who told you that!"

"You snooped through Mark Alder's files," Willow continued, ignoring Rachel's outburst. "And you were running around last night trying to find out who owned the boat that was burning."

"Duncan talks too much."

"And," Willow hissed, glaring at her, "you plan to go back to Sub Rosa and find Thadd's secret room."

"You don't know that."

"I damn well do," Willow snapped. "That's why you haven't told Kee about it and why you never intended to tell me."

"Willy," Rachel said softly, taking her sister by the shoulders. "I can't tell him about the room because it will bring us into this mess by implicating Dad."

"How?"

"That room is only half the story," Rachel explained. "I'd have to tell Kee about the boat designs, and that we had the stolen art all this time."

"It's gone beyond protecting our name," Willow said softly. "Mary was murdered."

Rachel looked into Willow's beautiful, worried hazel eyes and realized that keeping their father's crime a secret was hurting her sister far more than the secret itself would.

"But there's more stolen art," she finally told her. "More than what's in Thadd's secret room. And it's here, in this house someplace," she said, nodding at the wall.

"What?" Willow gasped, stepping back.

"That's what Dad's letter was really about," she gently told her. "Dad built a secret room in our house, too, Willy. And he listed several more pieces of art that should be in it. Don't you see? This isn't just knowing about Thadd's crimes, it's about being part of them. We still possess some of the stolen art."

Willow covered her face with her hands, shaking her head. "Oh, God," she whispered with a sob. "Dad really was a thief."

"He wasn't a bad man, Willy," Rachel softly declared, pulling her sister into her arms, rocking her trembling body. "He was just . . . he was stupid," she said. "He and Thadd were both stupid."

Willow looked up. "Where's the room? What's in it?"

"I don't know," Rachel quietly admitted. "I know where it is, but I can't find a way to get inside."

"You got the letter over a week ago."

"But I haven't been alone in this house since. I just

need some time, Willy. I need to get in that room and see what we're dealing with before I say anything to anyone."

Willow grabbed Rachel's arms with desperate strength. "What if that smuggler knows about our stuff? He might come here."

Rachel shook her head. "He can't know. We haven't had one single problem in three years. And our door is unlocked more than it's locked."

"I'm not leaving you alone this week," Willow said, puffing up with sisterly determination. "I'm calling the office and telling them I have a family emergency."

"No. You can't do anything here," Rachel told her. "And I already have more guards than the county jail. Besides, you can use your office to check on what the procedure is for returning stolen art anonymously. Kee said there's a database. See what you can find out."

"I don't want to leave you."

"I'll be fine. I promise. And I promise not to go any-where near Sub Rosa," Rachel added, holding up her hand in a scout's salute. "I'll just get into the room in this house, and I'll wait and let you see what's in it. Then we'll decide together what to do about it."

Willow thought about that, then reluctantly nodded.

"Do you remember what he looked like?" Rachel asked. "The guy who used to come to Sub Rosa? All I remember are his eyes. They were . . ." She shivered involuntarily. "They were creepy. Like he was undressing me in his mind."

"I only saw him once, and that was only briefly," Willow said. Her eyes widened. "I think I heard Thadd call him Raoul."

"Raoul?" Rachel repeated, stepping back. "Then he is

the smuggler. Daddy told me in his letter about a dealer by the name of Raoul Vegas."

"Dammit. I could kill you for burning that letter, Rachel! It was the only evidence we had."

"It was a confession," Rachel snapped. "An admission of Dad's guilt written in his own hand."

"You have to warn Kee about the smuggler," Willow said.

Rachel nodded, not liking it but knowing Willow was right. "Okay. I'll tell him this guy used to visit Sub Rosa when Thadd was alive, but that we haven't seen him in years."

"Give him the name Raoul Vegas, too."

"I will."

There was a knock on the door, and both Willow and Rachel jumped and turned to face it.

"I need to get in," Kee said through the door.

"There's another bathroom off the bedroom down the hall," Willow told him.

"Where's Rachel?"

"She's . . . ah . . . she's in here," Willow admitted, smiling sheepishly as she shrugged at Rachel.

"That sounds . . . interesting," he said.

Neither of them had anything to say to that, but they did hear Kee sigh and slowly pad down the hall. Rachel covered her mouth with her hand to contain a horrified giggle.

" 'That sounds interesting,' " Willow mimicked, lowering her voice to sound like Kee. She snorted. "Only a man would find two women in a bathroom interesting," she said, opening the door and walking out.

She ran straight into Duncan.

"What's interesting?" he asked, lifting an eyebrow when Rachel walked out behind her. "Now, that's interesting," he said, lifting his other brow.

Willow smacked him on the arm as she walked past. "Try growing an upper brain, you overgrown bear."

Duncan grinned at Rachel. "She likes me, doesn't she?"

Rachel patted his arm where Willow had smacked him. "Almost as much as she likes snakes," she assured him.

By the time Rachel got showered and dressed and felt she could face the world with some sense of decorum, her house was completely empty again. She came down the stairs, walked through a surprisingly tidy living room and sparkling clean kitchen, and ended up on the porch before she finally found everyone.

They were standing around Larry's truck, which was already loaded with the furniture Willow was taking to Augusta. Kee and Duncan and Luke and Willow were gathered near the front of the truck, staring at the bumper.

"I'm telling Larry you came tearing into the dooryard and skidded into his truck with your car," Willow said, smiling sweetly up at Duncan.

"And I'm going to tell him ya need lessons in kissing," Duncan returned, his smile sinister.

Luke ran his hand over the scratch on the bumper where Willow had smashed into the park bench. "We might be able to rub it out and he won't even notice."

Mikaela was perched on Kee's shoulders, and having set her winged giraffe on her daddy's head, was whispering to it. Mickey was sitting at Kee's feet, staring up at Mikaela, his tail wagging in the gravel and his tongue lolling out the side of his mouth.

"Can Mickey and I go throw rocks in the water?" Mikaela asked, bending over to look Kee in the face.

Kee lifted her off his shoulders. Mickey immediately headed for the beach, and Mikaela shot after him just as soon as her feet touched the ground, clutching her stuffed toy to her chest.

"She should have a life vest on," Rachel said, walking toward them as she watched Mikaela grab a rock and run to the edge of the water.

Kee and Duncan and Luke turned to her, their expressions nonplussed. "Why?" Luke asked.

"Why?" Rachel repeated. "It's the ocean. With *waves*," she emphasized. "She could get swept into the water."

"She won't stay in it long," Duncan said, shuddering. "It's damn cold."

"Mickey's with her," Luke added. "He's better than a life vest. If she falls in, he'll just pull her out."

"She's five years old!" Rachel growled, pivoting toward the beach. Dammit, if they weren't going to watch Mikaela, then she would.

Kee caught up with her just as she reached the edge of the lawn. He sat down on a driftwood log next to the giraffe his daughter had set there, pulling Rachel down beside him and putting his arm around her shoulders to hold her in place.

"She's grown up on the ocean," he told her. "She's as safe playing on your beach as she is sitting in your house."

Rachel watched the little girl run the length of the wide beach, Mickey trotting beside her and barking excitedly whenever Mikaela stopped to pick up a rock.

"She needs to run," Kee continued, smiling at his

daughter. "She's been cooped up on the *Six-to-One Odds* for over a week."

"Does she wear a life vest on the boat?"

He looked down and hugged her against him reassuringly. "It's not a conventional vest because they're too cumbersome to live in all day," he told her. "She wears a tube that sits around her neck and runs down to her waist, where it's strapped on tightly. It has a CO_2 canister and a sensor, so that if she falls overboard, it pops open and inflates."

"Oh, I've seen those," Rachel said, relaxing against him. "Some of the fishermen wear them."

He kissed the top of her head. "But thank you for caring enough to give us hell," he said softly, lifting her chin to look at him. "How are you this morning?"

"I . . . I'm fine."

"I'm sorry about Mary Alder. But more than I'm sorry, I'm worried. She was murdered, Rachel."

He turned on the log to face her more squarely and cupped her face between his large hands, forcing her to look at him. "And that's why I'm giving you two choices this morning. You either give me your promise you'll stay completely out of this, or you and Mikaela go aboard the *Six-to-One Odds* for a nice little sail until this is over."

Taken completely off-guard, she tried to pull back, but he only tightened his hold. "This is not negotiable, Rachel. You'll promise to stop asking questions, or you'll be out to sea before you can call good old Larry to come save you."

His thumbs caressed the sides of her face. "You have five minutes to decide. And Rachel?"

"Y-yes?"

"Trust is no longer an option but a fact, for both of us. I trust you to keep your word, and you trust me to keep your secret safe."

She did trust him. She trusted all the men.

It was the circumstances she didn't trust.

"I really don't know what's going on," she told him. "But my father left me a letter," she began, slowly telling Kee the whole story. But she stopped short of mentioning the room in her own house, because she and Willow had agreed they would find out what was inside it first.

She did tell him about Thadd's secret room, so he could be on guard. And she told him about Raoul Vegas—that she thought he was back here trying to find Thadd's treasure and that he might have been the one who shot Mary. She even told him about her father's role in designing the smuggling boats, that there were three of them that she knew of, and that two of them were now burned.

"You don't know the name of the third boat?" he asked.

She shook her head. "I think Dad was trying to tell me their names when he was shot. He named the *Norway Night* and the *Sea Dancer*, but he grew too weak. His last words to me were 'Find her.' I didn't know what he was talking about until Wendell brought me the letter."

" 'Find her' is what Mary said just before she died," he whispered, more to himself than to her, staring off at the horizon, his face unreadable.

He finally looked back at her, taking hold of her face again and kissing her tenderly on the forehead. "Thank you," he said softly. "A lot of it makes sense now. I can see why you were trying to get yourself out of this mess quietly. It very well could turn into a scandal that would ruin Willow's future."

"I'm sorry I set you up to take the fall for the stolen items," she told him. "But I didn't know what else to do."

He smiled. "I probably would have done the same thing. If you just could have gotten in and out of Sub Rosa and replaced the emeralds and other items, you would have been home free."

"That's what I thought. But then the boat burnings started, and that meant we could still get dragged into this, if the designs were found with Dad's name on them."

"And you didn't find them in Mark's files?"

"No. But Mark said Mary had been at the boatyard last week, and I think she took them."

Kee was silent again, watching Mikaela and Mickey before turning back to Rachel. "You really have no idea where that secret room is in Sub Rosa?"

She shook her head. "I've gone over all the blueprints, including the ones I have here. Daddy built it the summer I went to Paris with Mom and Willow. It could be anywhere."

"What would it take for you to find it?"

That question surprised her. "I would have to spend time at Sub Rosa, measuring rooms against the blueprints and checking out every one of the tunnels."

He shook his head. "That's out of the question, at least for now." He took hold of her chin, his deep, dark Atlantic-blue eyes looking directly into hers. "Do I have your promise to let me handle things from here on out?"

"You don't think we should call the police now?" Rachel asked. "Because of Mary?"

He shook his head. "Not yet. Let me find out what's really going on, so I can figure out how to keep you and Willow out of it before we call them."

Rachel nodded. "Okay. I promise."

His smile made her insides melt. He wrapped both his arms around her and lifted her onto his lap, squeezing her so tightly she squeaked. Mikaela came running up, slid to a stop in front of them, and put her hands on her hips and stared.

"What?" Kee asked her.

"Is Rachel your girlfriend now? What happened to Joan?"

"Joan decided Europe was more interesting than I am," Kee told her. "And yes, Rachel's my girlfriend."

Rachel quit breathing.

"So I gotta be nice to her and not scare her off?" Mikaela wanted to know, her expression fierce.

Rachel finally found her breath and her voice. "I don't scare easy," she told the five-year-old, reaching out and tugging on the hem of her shirt. "I survived growing up with Willow. I think I can survive anything you dish out."

Mikaela's eyes narrowed. "I like Willow," she said, her stance defensive. "She reads good, and makes faces and voices that match the story."

"I like Willow, too," Rachel quickly assured her. "And just so you know, I'm the one who taught her to read like that."

Mikaela's posture relaxed slightly as she looked from Rachel to her father. "Luke said Ahab's waiting for me on the *Six-to-One Odds* and that he's got a whole mess of polishing rags," she said, her lower lip sticking out far enough to hang a hat on. "Can Rachel help me polish the brass?"

"Rachel didn't break the compass," Kee told her.

Mikaela turned her calculated look on Rachel. "Can you bake? Cookies and cakes and stuff?"

"Nope. I can't even boil water."

Rachel didn't know who was more surprised, Kee or Mikaela.

"You can't cook?" he asked, leaning to the side to look her in the eye.

"But I can run a skill saw," she told him, turning her smile on Mikaela. "And I can show you how to build beautiful birdhouses."

"That's not women's stuff," Kee said, drawing her attention again. "You're supposed to show her women's stuff."

"I'm a pretty good shopper," Rachel offered, turning back to Mikaela. "We can go to Ellsworth and buy you some pretty new clothes."

Mikaela scrunched up her face. "I don't like ruffles."

"No ruffles," Rachel agreed. "How about barrettes?" she asked, touching one of Mikaela's perfectly braided braids. "I know an artist in Blue Hill who crafts beautiful hair clips."

The little girl eyed Rachel's own long braid hanging over her shoulder. She reached out and touched the clip on the end of it. "I like barrettes," she whispered, looking up at Rachel. "Does the guy make earrings? I would like some earrings."

"You would?" Kee asked, lifting a brow in surprise. "You've never mentioned wanting earrings before."

Mikaela lifted her chin. "Dangly ones," she said. "With pretty stones in them."

Kee rolled his eyes. "What is it with females and jewelry? Is it genetic or something?"

Rachel nodded, trying very hard not to smile. Kee was looking at Mikaela again, his expression confounded, as if seeing her for the first time—or just realizing that he'd fathered a female.

Rachel looked at Mikaela's tiny earlobes. "You would need to get your ears pierced," she warned her.

Kee answered for Mikaela, quickly and with quiet finality. "No," he said, setting Rachel back on the log and then standing up. "No one is poking holes in my daughter."

Rachel fingered her own earlobe. "I'll get my ears pierced, too," she told Mikaela, ignoring the warning growl that came from Kee's chest. "I'd like some dangly earrings, too."

"No," he repeated, this time with more desperation than authority.

Mikaela grabbed her giraffe off the log and looked up at her father with a smug smile. "I want a vote," she told him.

Confused, Rachel watched as Kee suddenly relaxed. "Okay, we'll vote. But it's going to be six-to-one for 'No.'"

And she knew then where Kee's schooner had gotten its name. For the last five years it had been six men constantly finding themselves at odds with one little girl.

"Do I get a vote?" Rachel asked, standing up.

"No."

"She can vote, Daddy. She's your girlfriend. And I want Willow to vote, too."

"What am I voting for?" Willow asked, walking up to them, Duncan one step behind her.

"I'm getting my ears pierced," Mikaela said, running up and throwing herself against Duncan.

He lifted her up until her face was even with his. "No," he said succinctly.

Mikaela nodded. "We're going to vote."

Duncan sighed hard enough to move wisps of her hair. "Now, why would ya want someone to poke holes in your head?" he asked.

"So I can wear dangly earrings." She tucked her giraffe between herself and Duncan's chest, then grabbed hold of Duncan's face with her two little hands, making him look her straight in the eye. "I want earrings and a dress and girl shoes."

She leaned in closer, her nose almost touching his. " 'Cause I'm a girl, Dunky," she whispered softly.

Duncan looked as if he was going to burst into tears.

Mikaela Oakes wasn't a tyrant, or a hellion, or any more a manipulator than any other five-year-old child. She was a little girl with six daddies who were scared to death. They knew—they just knew—she was going to grow up into a beautiful woman and fall in love with a man, and break their collective hearts.

"Dunky?" Willow said, obviously reaching the same conclusion as Rachel and trying to lighten the mood. "Dunky?" she repeated, only louder, canting her head and shooting Duncan a diabolical smile. "Well, Dunky, if we don't get started for Augusta soon, you'll be unloading the truck in the dark."

"What happened to Larry?" Rachel asked.

"He called and said he got pulled back on duty because of . . . because of last night," Willow told her.

"But he just worked a double shift."

"They gave him a few hours to get some sleep, but he's back on as of two o'clock. Larry said they needed the manpower to canvas the town for anyone who might have seen something."

Still looking quite rattled, Duncan gave Mikaela—and her giraffe—a long and emotional bear hug and then set her on the ground. Mikaela immediately went over to her daddy and silently looked up at him. And just as silently, Kee picked her up and cradled her and her giraffe in his arms, and walked toward the house.

Chapter Eighteen

Rachel sat on her couch, staring across the room at nothing, and realized it was the first time in more than a week that she was alone in her house. Jason was driving Larry's truck to Augusta, and with a stop in Ellsworth to buy a booster seat, Willow and Duncan and Mikaela were leading the way in Willow's car.

Rachel was surprised Kee had let his daughter go to Augusta, and had asked him about it. With a heart-stopping smile and his arresting blue eyes all but igniting her on the spot, he had said Mikaela made a very good chaperone, but that he'd rather Mikaela chaperone Duncan and Willow instead of the two of them.

Rachel had wholeheartedly agreed, and even though they had the house to themselves, she'd finally given Kee a tour of her camper.

Kee in turn had given her a rather memorable tour of

his beautiful body, which had ended with her cuddled up in his arms for a two-hour nap.

The nap had ended more than an hour ago, and Kee was out mowing her lawn—which Rachel thought was a very domestic thing for him to do.

She sighed, hugging a couch pillow to her chest. Being Keenan Oakes's girlfriend had some great advantages. It came with certain implied privileges, such as having access to all that muscle and heat and caveman charm, and the freedom to indulge her own passionate nature with abandon.

But it also came with responsibilities, such as putting up with his proprietary dictates, dealing with his overwhelming presence—her proximity problem had somehow expanded to when he wasn't even with her now—and conceding to his powerful drive to solve the mystery of Sub Rosa's missing art while keeping her safe.

But the greatest responsibility appeared to be Kee's need for her to trust him.

Frank Foster had been the only man Rachel had ever trusted, and that trust had ended with unspeakable tragedy, a house full of stolen art, and the realization that her father was not only a murderer, but also a thief.

And no matter how she looked at it, passion had been the ruling force—and ultimate destruction—of Frank Foster.

So how was she supposed to control her own passion and keep it from destroying her life? By bottling it up and pretending it didn't exist?

That hadn't worked. Her passion had exploded the moment Sub Rosa's heir had walked into his library.

So could she at least control it? Maybe indulge it just enough without giving herself over to it completely?

Nope. Too late.

She was in love with Keenan Oakes.

Rachel had realized it was love the moment she'd given Kee her trust that morning. And she had felt it again that afternoon in the camper. For all of her abandon, their lovemaking had been different. She had known, as he had entered her body with such consuming desire, that she'd fight to the death for his love.

So the Neanderthal had better watch out. This was one girlfriend who would not walk away—or be walked away from. If she had to paddle her kayak after him, she'd hunt him down and make him sorry he ever left her in the first place.

He wondered what life with her would be like? It would damn well be a never-ending affair! She was in love with him, and he was stuck with her, whether he liked it or not!

"Sweet Jesus, who are you wanting to kill?"

Rachel looked up with a start and found Kee standing in the doorway of her living room, watching her.

"What are you talking about?" she asked, getting off the couch and facing him squarely.

"I walk in here and find you looking like you want to murder someone," he told her. "And I was just wondering who."

"You."

"Excuse me?" he said softly.

"I was just thinking about you."

He crossed his arms over his chest and relaxed back on his hips. "Mind telling me *what* you were thinking?"

"That you're going to break my heart."

He straightened, his hands falling to his sides, his eyes widening in shock. "What!"

Rachel balled her own hands into fists and lifted her chin. "But I'm not going to let you," she growled, taking a step toward him. "I am not Joan the shrew. I'm not walking away, and I won't let you walk away, either."

He slowly started toward her, his dark blue eyes pinning her in place, his entire body suddenly coiled with portentous energy. He stopped three feet in front of her, looking so provoked that Rachel took a step back.

"That possibility ceased to exist," he said softly, "the first time you exploded in my arms."

He closed the final distance between them, and though he didn't touch her, the heat of his body wrapped around her like fingers of fire. "As God as my witness, neither of us is ever walking away," he declared rawly, sweeping her into his embrace and claiming her mouth with indisputable possession.

Rachel's heart swelled to double its size. She felt light-headed, dizzy with happiness, and so free she could soar through the sky without wings. She wrapped her arms around his neck when he picked her up, and curled her legs around his waist as he walked up the stairs.

"Say the words," he demanded gruffly, carrying her into her bedroom.

She remained silent as he set her on the bed and stretched out beside her, still saying nothing as he started caressing her cheek with knuckles that trembled with need.

"I love you," she finally whispered. "Forever."

He kissed her again, this time with such tender care, Rachel quietly started to sob.

"Ssshhh," he crooned, feathering his thumb over her

cheek. "You don't tell a man you love him and start crying, sweetheart," he whispered, nuzzling her chin. "It
might dent his ego."

"Cavemen have egos of granite," she whispered. "And
I'm crying because I love you, and because I don't know
if you even realize what you're getting. "

He moved his lips over her cheek and across her damp
lashes. "I'm getting a beautiful and passionate woman I
want to grow old with."

"If . . . if I don't kill you first."

He looked deeply into her eyes, his own eyes dark
with concern. He suddenly smiled at her. "You can't kill
a demigod. We're indestructible."

"My father killed my mother," she whispered. "He
loved her so passionately that he shot her and then put
the gun to his own head."

Kee reared up with a growl, resettled his hips between
hers, and pinned her to the bed with his body. He took
hold of her hair on either side of her face, forcing her to
look directly into his eyes. "You will not measure what
we have against your parents," he said, his voice harsh
with emotion. "Passion is not what drove your father to
do what he did, Rachel. It was fear. Frank Foster feared
life without your mother, and he killed her when he
found her with another man."

"F-Fear?"

He nodded, kissed her nose, then smoothed her hair.
"I know you adored him, Rachel. And I know his betrayal wounded you and Willow very deeply. But you're
not your father, sweetheart."

He cupped her face in his hands. "You don't fear life,
Rachel," he told her with quiet authority. "You embrace it."

286   *Janet Chapman*

"But I am afraid."

His smile was warm and tender. "You don't have your father's flaw, Rachel. You would never take the coward's way out." He kissed her nose again, lowering his head to nuzzle a sensitive spot just below her ear. "Just love me, Rachel," he gently entreated, nipping her earlobe. "Give me your passion, and I promise to keep us both safe."

With the trust of a woman finding herself deeply in love with a demigod, Rachel turned her head to capture his mouth and gave him a kiss that forever sealed their fates.

Their lovemaking was slow and tender and so wonderfully erotic that nothing existed outside themselves. And as the lengthening afternoon shadows moved through the room, Kee took advantage of her declaration and teased and tasted and became terribly bold.

Desire stirred deep inside her as his hands moved over her body with purposeful, painstaking care. Rachel became restless, shuddering, gasping, moaning encouragement while trying to remember what it was she wanted to do.

He entered her slowly—so maddeningly slowly—and she climaxed with the force of a nor'easter hitting shore. Kee rode the wave of her orgasm with the strength of a god determined to hold back the tide.

Finally he moved, rocking her gently, building her up again with lusty words and gentle caresses that inflamed her beyond reason. He made love to all five of her senses, giving her everything, yet refusing her the same privilege by trapping her hands over her head, not letting her touch him.

Yes. That's what she wanted. She wanted to touch him.

And she suddenly realized, through the haze of a second powerful orgasm, that Kee was saying the words back to her the only way he knew how. This was his declaration of love—his promise to cherish her, to give her his heart, and to keep her forever in his.

The sun slowly set, turning her bedroom into shadows and reflections of reds and oranges and purples.

And the lovemaking continued.

And the passion Rachel had felt churning inside her for more than a week finally settled into a deeper, more comfortable, and far more manageable emotion.

She would be okay.

They'd be okay.

Because she trusted Keenan Oakes—part demigod, part caveman—to keep her safe.

Chapter Nineteen

Rachel spent the next four days in a fog of surreal chaos.

She had become quite comfortable living alone, with Willow gone away to school most of the time. But suddenly her life was full—with a wolf and seven men coming and going at all times of the day or night, taking turns guarding Rachel and Mikaela and Sub Rosa.

Ahab turned out to be the biggest pest. He slept on the *Six-to-One Odds,* but came over every morning at seven, ate breakfast with them, then took Mikaela back to the boat to polish brass until noon. Which was fine, except that for the last three afternoons, the old sea salt had insisted on going shopping with them.

Rachel had never shopped with a five-year-old who couldn't decide what it was she wanted and two grown men who had more opinions than the United Nations. On their first day out, Matthew had wanted Mikaela to buy a yellow dress and white sandals, but Ahab had voted for a pink dress with brown sandals. They'd come home with nothing, and the next day Peter had tried to talk Mikaela into a blue dress and straw bonnet covered with half a garden of flowers.

They'd returned empty-handed that day as well.

Except for Ahab. He'd bought a shirt so outrageously loud that it hurt to look at him.

Kee and Duncan had both joined them the day before, and Mikaela and Rachel had finally gotten their ears pierced. All three men had silently walked out of the shop the moment the clerk had put the hole puncher to Mikaela's ear. And ten minutes later, when Rachel and Mikaela emerged wearing their little gold studs, they'd found the men sitting on a bench, silently staring at the ground, passing around the flask Ahab always carried in his back pocket.

Rachel had decided they would stay home this afternoon, since shopping by committee was proving impossible.

"They're called ants on a log," Mikaela said, kneeling on a stool at the island counter and carefully placing raisins on the peanut butter she'd smeared on stalks of celery.

Rachel eyed the gooey concoction with trepidation.

"Munky says they're good for my gut," Mikaela continued, completely unaware of Rachel's horror. "He makes them for me every time he comes home from a job."

Rachel had learned Mikaela had funky names for all the men. Apparently they'd planned for her to call them uncle, but two names had been too much of a mouthful for a toddler. Mikaela had turned Uncle Matt into Munky, Uncle Duncan into Dunky, and so forth.

The names had stuck, and the men didn't seem in any

hurry for Mikaela to change them now that she'd mastered speech.

"Do all of you live on the *Six-to-One Odds?*" Rachel asked, filling a glass with milk for Mikaela and pouring a glass of wine for herself, thinking it would probably take more than wine for her to get down the peanut butter and raisins and celery.

Mikaela nodded, holding up a log of ants for Rachel. "I got my own bunk, but Mickey and I sleep with Daddy whenever he's on board."

Mikaela stared expectantly while Rachel carefully took a bite, chewed, swallowed, and then took another bite of the surprisingly tasty treat.

"Good, huh?" Mikaela said, taking a bite of her own stalk. "Do you think it's bad that I sleep with Daddy?" she asked.

Rachel stopped from taking another bite. "No. Why would it be bad?"

" 'Cause I'm a girl and Daddy's a man. Joan said it's wrong." She scrunched up her face. "I been sleeping on Daddy's chest since I was borned. What's wrong with that?"

"Absolutely nothing," Rachel quickly assured her, wishing she could get her hands on Joan the shrew for just five minutes.

"Until you decide you'd be more comfortable sleeping by yourself, then you should sleep wherever you want," she told Mikaela. "I used to hop in bed with my mom and dad every time there was a thunderstorm."

Mikaela nodded, giving Rachel a satisfied smile. "I think Joan didn't like it when she stayed on the *Six-to-One Odds,* 'cause she had to sleep in a bed by herself."

Rachel had also been sleeping by herself these last

three nights. But she didn't mind, pleased that Kee had such a sense of morality when it came to his daughter.

Rachel grabbed another stalk of celery and popped it into her mouth just as the screen door opened and Kee and Duncan strolled into the kitchen.

The men came to a sudden stop, took one look at the mess on the counter, and collectively shook their heads. Rachel was sure she saw an involuntary shudder run through Kee.

Duncan picked up Mikaela and carried her to the sink—holding her away from himself as if she were a bomb—and turned on the faucet and ran her hands under the water. Kee remained standing at the other end of the island counter, his arms crossed over his chest, watching in horror as Rachel took another huge bite of gooey celery.

"I have an errand in town that will take me right past the ice cream shop," Duncan told Mikaela as he washed her hands. "And I might have just enough money in my pocket to buy us a real treat."

"Mickey wants to come, too," Mikaela proclaimed, wiggling down to her feet and wiping her hands on her pants. "And Rachel," she quickly added, looking at Rachel.

"I'm pretty full from the wonderful lunch you made me," Rachel told her, patting her belly, thinking this might be a great chance to look for the secret room.

"And I'm not really in the mood for ice cream," Kee added, staring at Rachel with his dark, piercing eyes.

Rachel slowly took another bite of celery as she stared back at him—and watched, fascinated, when he shuddered again.

Mikaela picked up her giraffe from one of the stools, then tugged the fur on Mickey's neck. "Come on, Mickey," she said, heading for the door. "Maybe they got your favorite—caramel swirl. And waffle cones," she added as she pushed through the screen door ahead of Duncan and after Mickey.

Rachel stopped chewing and could only blink at the closing screen door. The wolf liked caramel swirl ice cream? And waffle cones?

She looked back at Kee, and her proximity problem suddenly swelled her chest, making it difficult to swallow. Kee was emitting enough raw energy to melt glass—to melt *her.*

Rachel's insides tightened. It had been four days since they'd declared their love. And they were suddenly alone in a house full of beds, and Kee was staring at her with such . . . such *want* that it was almost frightening. Rachel grabbed her wine and emptied the glass in one gulp.

She needed to calm down. Surely she could be in the same room with this man and hold a civilized conversation without jumping his beautiful bones. Couldn't she?

"Tell me about Mikaela's mother," she said without thinking, desperately trying to slow her thumping heart.

But her heart raced even faster when Kee's eyes darkened to nearly black. He crossed his arms over his chest again, his entire body strung tight, his posture defensive.

"There's nothing to tell," he said. "I've had custody of Mikaela since she was born."

Rachel refilled her wineglass with an unsteady hand, wondering what had possessed her to bring up Mikaela's mother now. But dammit, she wanted to know. She was in love with Keenan Oakes, and this past week she'd fallen in love with his daughter.

"She just walked away from her baby?" she asked softly.

Kee studied her in silence across the messy counter, the muscles in his shoulders and neck bowstring tight, his face hard, and his eyes cold. "She walked away with a small fortune in her pocket," he finally said, his voice even. "Leaving us in debt to the tune of one and a half million dollars."

It took every bit of willpower Rachel possessed not to show her shock. He had *paid* for his daughter?

"But that's . . . is that legal?" she whispered.

He didn't move. Didn't say anything. He just kept looking at her with dark, unreadable eyes.

And she suddenly understood, only too well.

He wasn't mad she'd probed into his past—he was scared.

"So you borrowed a million and a half dollars to pay off Mikaela's mother, and in return you got a daughter."

"I could only raise a million. Duncan and Jason and Luke and Peter and Matthew chipped in the rest."

Looking back at her wineglass, Rachel picked her next words very carefully. "I think it was a very noble thing you did," she told him, looking up. "Unconventional maybe, but sweet."

"There was nothing sweet about it," he said. "Pamela was four months along when she told me and was betting on my response. She was more mercenary than maternal."

"You can't get an abortion at four months," she said, truly horrified now.

"You can if you want one badly enough."

Rachel sighed. "What do you want from me, Kee?"

"Understanding," he whispered thickly.

"You want me to understand why you went over your head in debt for your child?" she asked. "Kee, your full inheritance from Thadd wouldn't have been enough for your daughter. I think you got a damn good bargain."

She stood up and walked around the counter and stood in front of him. "I love you," she fiercely declared. "Even more, if that's possible."

He moved with the speed of a striking cobra, pulling her into his arms with desperate need and burying his face in her neck. Rachel clung to his trembling body, clutching his head to her chest and kissing his hair, whispering words of love and assurance.

It was then she resigned herself to the fact that a civil conversation between them might never be possible. Not when actions could speak louder than words.

Kee must have thought so, too. He swept her into his arms and turned and carried her through the living room toward the stairs.

The screen door opened and shut with a bang.

Kee stopped with his foot on the bottom step and cursed.

"Hello the house!" Luke shouted.

Kee lowered Rachel until her feet were on the second step, cupped her face with his hands, and kissed her soundly on the mouth. "I'll be right back," he promised. "I'm just going to shoot Luke, and then we'll go upstairs."

Rachel laughed and pushed him away, scooting under his arm and running through the living room. She skidded to a stop just inside the kitchen door—and stared, utterly speechless.

Luke looked like hell. And he smelled even worse.

The man reeked of cigarette smoke and alcohol.

Luke rubbed his hands over his face and pulled them away to reveal an apologetic smile.

"Are you drunk?" Rachel asked, looking straight into

his eyes. She frowned and turned to Kee. "What's going on?"

"I spent the afternoon at the Drop Anchor," Luke said, drawing her attention. "And I learned some pretty interesting things."

"Like what?" Rachel asked.

"Like the fact that Mary Alder probably is responsible for burning both boats," he said gently, moving his completely sober gaze from her to Kee. "Accelerants were found on her hands and clothes. And she was shot, close range, with a nine-millimeter, possibly a Glock."

"What did they do, post the autopsy report at the Drop Anchor?" Rachel asked.

Luke shook his head. "No. But apparently somebody in the sheriff's office likes his beer." He shrugged. "You know how it is in small towns. People like to tell what they know, if only for five minutes of fame.

"There was something else," Luke added, looking at Kee. "They found two cans of diesel fuel in Mary Alder's garage, one of which was empty. They matched the can found floating in the harbor last Sunday morning. And they found boat designs burned in the fireplace."

Rachel quietly sucked in her breath.

Kee looked at her, then back at Luke. "Were they readable?"

Luke shook his head. "Not according to the rumors. But they knew they were designs from some of the unburned edges. The state police detectives spent yesterday going through files at the Lakeman Boatyard."

Rachel pulled out a stool from the island and sat down, hugging her belly.

"I don't suppose you wore gloves while you snooped through Alder's files?" Kee asked her.

Rachel mutely shook her head.

"Anything else?" Kee asked Luke.

Luke suddenly smiled. "The town's new puffin statue is a big hit. Everyone's going nuts speculating on who put it up."

"Do you know when they're going to release Mary's body?" Rachel asked. "So Mark can bury her?" She stood up. "I should go see him. I should have done it before now."

Kee took hold of her shoulders and sat her back down. He picked up the bottle of wine still sitting on the counter, filled her empty wineglass, put it in her hand, wrapped her fingers around it, and nudged it toward her mouth.

"What about men with beards?" Kee asked Luke. "Or the name Raoul Vegas? Did it ring any bells?"

Luke shook his head. "If he has half a brain he's using an alias. And hell, there must be over a dozen men fitting the description Jason gave us who live around here."

Luke smiled, scratching his chest. "I told them I didn't know his name, but that I was looking for a guy who helped me change a flat tire the other night and wanted to pay him back with a rack of beer. That got me at least ten names right off the bat, two of which somebody said lived in Fisherman's Reach."

He pulled a wrinkled napkin out of his pocket. "I wrote the names down as people thought of them. It actually turned into a contest to see who could think of guys matching my description. I'll get Jason and Matthew, and we'll start nosing around."

Luke turned and walked to the screen door but stopped and looked back. "There was one more thing," he said, darting a glance at Rachel before looking back at Kee. "They found a Fabergé egg in Mary Alder's bedroom that was stolen eight years ago from a home in Austria."

"Any of Sub Rosa's legitimate art found?" Kee asked.

Luke shook his head. "Not that I heard. Only the egg."

Luke turned and left a lot more quietly than he had arrived.

Kee took Rachel's hand, tugged her off the stool, and headed out onto the porch.

"Where are we going?" she asked, following meekly.

"Duncan's idea of an ice cream suddenly sounds good. We'll sit in the park to eat it and watch people's reaction to Puffy."

Chapter Twenty

It was already Friday, and Rachel still hadn't been able to find a way into her dad's secret room, mostly because she hadn't been left alone long enough to hunt for it. And Willow was coming home tonight and would be expecting answers.

But this morning Mikaela was polishing brass on the *Six-to-One Odds,* Peter and Luke were outside scraping the trim on the house, Kee and the others were only God knew where, and this was her chance to get into that room.

And since she couldn't find the secret door, she'd decided simply to cut through the damn wall.

Rachel slipped on her safety glasses, knelt on the floor in her parents' walk-in closet, and set the small battery-powered skill saw to the plasterboard just above the bottom molding, not daring to cut any higher because she might cut into some zillion-dollar piece of art. She started the saw, wincing at the high-pitched sound of the motor echoing off the walls, and could only hope the men outside couldn't hear it.

She quickly cut a six-inch square in the plaster, then took the claw of her hammer and pried it away to expose the four-inch space between the two walls.

She clicked on her flashlight, leaned down, and shined it in the hole, only to gasp. The beam of her light wasn't hitting the plasterboard of the opposite wall as it should be, but bouncing off solid steel!

Rachel sat back on her heels and stared at the hole. Dammit. Had her father lined the room with plate steel? She picked up the skill saw and stood back up, moved to the left three feet, and cut another six-inch hole at shoulder height. She took the hammer and pried out that piece of plasterboard, and then tapped on the wall through the hole, only to hear the *ping* of metal hitting metal.

"Dammit, Dad. You built a vault!"

Rachel spun on her heel and walked out of the closet, through the bedroom, and into the guest bedroom Kee and Mikaela had been using. She went into that closet and pushed aside the winter clothes hanging there, and without even bothering with the saw this time, drove the hammer straight through the plasterboard with one violent thrust. It bounced off the interior steel wall with a resounding *ping*, vibrating so painfully that she dropped the hammer and shook her hand with a curse.

Rachel could only gape at the wall, mentally trying to picture the room on the other side of the plate steel. By her estimate, it was about eight feet by eight feet square and sat between Willow's bedroom, this spare bedroom, and her parents' closet.

She spun on her heel and headed to Willow's bedroom, stopping in her parents' room only long enough to pick up the drill she'd brought up from her workshop along with the other tools. She went into Willow's room, climbed up on the bed, took down the picture, and started drilling.

Sure enough, the drill sped through the plaster, then the four-inch air space, and started screeching the moment it hit solid steel.

"What's going on in here?" Luke hollered up the staircase. "Are you okay, Rachel? I heard a loud bang, like you fell or something," he said, walking down the hall, his voice moving in and out of rooms.

Rachel quickly replaced the picture and stuffed her drill and safety glasses under Willow's pillow, jumping down from the bed just as Luke stuck his head in the door.

"You okay?" he asked.

"I'm fine," she assured him, leaning over to smooth the blankets. "I was just changing Willow's bed before she gets home tonight.

"What's that white stuff all over you?"

Rachel looked down, saw that she was covered in plaster dust, and started brushing it off. "I . . . uh . . . I dropped the laundry detergent earlier, when I put Willow's sheets in the wash."

"What's that fine dust floating in the air?" Luke asked, waving his hand.

"I was sawing boards so Mikaela and I can build birdhouses this afternoon. I must have left the cellar door open." She smiled at him. "It creates a terrible dust that lingers forever," she said, waving her own hand.

Luke eyed her suspiciously. "This isn't one of your 'I'm looking for my cat' stories, is it?" he asked, narrowing his eyes at her, stepping fully into the room, and looking around.

Rachel strode past him with a smile and headed downstairs, Luke following hot on her heels. And when they walked into the kitchen, and Rachel filled a glass of water from the sink and turned to lean on the counter to drink it, Luke was still eyeing her suspiciously.

"What kind of trouble can I possibly get into in my own house?" she asked. "Or are you just suspicious by nature?"

Luke smiled sheepishly. "I guess it's just my nature," he admitted, going to a cupboard and taking down two glasses. "It comes with the job."

"What is your job, exactly?" Rachel asked, turning on the faucet for him and then moving out of his way. "I'm still not sure what it is you guys do."

His smile turned crooked, and he shrugged. "I guess you'd call us men of opportunity." He waved his hand negligently. "We do anything from sea salvage to kidnaping negotiations. We're hired by both governments and individuals, and sometimes by corporations who want us to track down embezzlers living off their money on small islands somewhere."

Rachel softly whistled. "Wow. How long have you all been together?"

Luke shrugged again. "We've evolved over the last eight years, with a few men coming and going. We started out with just Kee, Duncan, me, and Peter. Matt and Jason came in about six years ago. Kee bought the *Six-to-One Odds* when Mikaela was born, to give her some sort of stability." His smile broadened. "We inherited Ahab with the boat."

"Then how come you didn't name it the *Seven-to-One Odds?*"

"Ahab said he didn't want any part of raising a kid."

Luke snorted. "That lasted about six months. The crusty old salt is worse than the rest of us."

"So you just roam the world doing odd jobs," Rachel said in conclusion. "How do you find these jobs?"

"We don't. They find us now. We've built a reputation for getting things done with the least amount of . . . notoriety."

"Notoriety?"

Luke took a long drink of water and nodded. "Governments have to play by the rules, but we don't. We can just go in and get someone out, quietly, and collect our fee upon delivery."

"So you're bounty hunters."

Luke refilled his glass and turned to her. "Naw, not really. Bounty hunters catch first and ask questions later. We're hired for specific jobs. Even the sea salvage. We're hired by individuals mostly, wanting us to raise their sunken boat or at least dive for their personal belongings if it can't be raised."

Rachel shivered and rubbed her arm against a sudden chill. "It sounds very dangerous," she whispered, pointing her glass at his chest. "You got shot."

"That was a long time ago," he told her, picking up the second glass and filling both with water before turning back to her. "We're a lot smarter now." He smiled. "Having Mikaela to come home to also made us more choosy about the jobs we take."

He walked toward the door with both glasses in his hand. "Try not to get into trouble on my shift, will you?" he said as he disappeared off the porch.

Rachel just stared at the screen door. No wonder Kee was reluctant to call the police. These men thrived on intrigue, and weren't used to local authorities interfering.

Wow. She'd fallen in love with an adventurer.

How . . . interesting.

Rachel set down her glass and headed back upstairs, wondering if Kee would let her go on some of his adventures. She pulled the drill and her safety glasses from under Willow's pillow and carried them back to her parents' bedroom. Yeah, it would be exciting to have the world for a playground, to sleep on the schooner, and to be one of the gang.

"I'm home!" Mikaela shouted from downstairs, the screen door slamming behind her.

Rachel heard little-girl feet and wolf paws running through the living room and up the stairs. She quickly covered her tools with blankets and boxes and stepped out of the closet and into the doorway of her parents' bedroom.

"Did you miss me?" Mikaela yelled, screeching to a halt in the hall, Mickey barely stopping before he ran into the back of her. "Are we going to build birdhouses today?"

"We sure are," Rachel promised, opening a door next to the linen closet in the hall. "But first we have to go up in the attic and look for things to decorate the birdhouses with."

Mickey immediately ran over to the door and disappeared into the attic. Mikaela adjusted her giraffe under her arm and walked over to her. "What sorts of things?" she asked softly, peering up the dark attic stairs.

Rachel reached in and flipped on the light. "Anything that you think would look good on a birdhouse," she told her, moving up the stairs and then reaching back for Mikaela's hand. "Who brought you home?"

"Ahab," Mikaela said, taking her hand, her lovely blue eyes—the mirror image of her daddy's—rounded in curiosity. "But he said he was walking to town to see someone about a dropped anchor."

"Who braided your hair this morning?" Rachel asked, trying not to laugh as she led Mikaela into the attic.

"Punky," Mikaela said, fingering her crooked braid. "He gets confused sometimes and messes up."

"How about we find our decorations, then I'll fix your hair? I'll lend you one of my clips until you can get your own."

"Okay," Mikaela said, walking over to Mickey, who had his nose pressed up against the attic window, watching Peter scrape the trim on the nearby eave.

Rachel opened the window, and Mikaela leaned out. "Hi, Punky," she said, waving at him. "You got paint chips on your hair. Rachel and I are going to build a birdhouse."

"In the attic?" Peter asked in surprise.

"No, in the cellar," Mikaela told him. "We're just looking for stuff to decorate it with. If we want the birds to come live in it, the house has to be pretty."

Peter nodded sagely. "That makes sense." He looked at Rachel. "I found the kayak you said was in the garage at Sub Rosa and brought it down this morning, so Willow can have her kayak back if you both want to take a paddle."

"Thanks," Rachel said. "But do you really think it's necessary for one of you to always come with us? Willow and I have been paddling this coast since we were kids."

"It's necessary," was all he said, turning his attention back to the trim.

"How about this?" Mikaela asked.

Rachel turned from the window to find the little girl almost buried in a box of Christmas decorations.

Mikaela straightened and held up a red tinsel garland. "Birds will like it, won't they?"

"Too shiny," Rachel told her, shaking her head. "It might scare them off. Let's try over here," she suggested, leading Mikaela to a large trunk. "Here are some old postcards and gardening books to look through. We'll paste the pictures on the house for decoration. You sit here," Rachel told her, setting her down on another box, "and look through this whole pile."

Rachel waited until the girl became absorbed in her work, then walked to the area over the secret room downstairs. "I'm going to look for stuff over here," she said, pushing a few boxes and an old chair out of the way.

She studied the roof rafters and the floor, and visually measured the distance from the chimney to where the secret room was. She continued to move items until she had an eight-by-eight-foot spot cleared off, then got down on her knees and studied the floor more closely.

A perimeter of boards had been disturbed.

But two minutes later, after prying up several of the boards, Rachel only found more plate steel covering the room's ceiling. "Damn," she whispered under her breath, sitting back on her heels.

"Daddy makes anyone who cusses in front of me swim around the boat," Mikaela said, coming over with her arms full of torn-out pages and postcards. She visibly shivered.

"What happens if your daddy catches you cussing?"

"I only gotta jump in, and they pull me out by a rope tied around my waist." She shot Rachel a smug smile. "I only cuss when we're in warm water. Did you find some pictures, Rachel?" Mikaela asked, looking around. "None of the boxes are open."

"I was looking for a special box. But I think you have enough there. Let's head downstairs."

Rachel walked over and closed and locked the attic window, seeing that Peter had already moved his ladder to the other side of the eave. She picked up Mikaela's pictures and giraffe, then led the little girl back down the stairs.

Dammit. If the floor of the room was plate steel, as the walls and ceiling seemed to be, she was going to need a bomb to get inside.

The birds would have to be either very desperate or drunk to move into the birdhouse Rachel and Mikaela made. The lumber was covered with postcards and colorful pictures in a hodgepodge of psychedelic patterns that made Ahab's new shirt look tame. The house tilted to the left quite a bit, and several nails had been driven only halfway in, the top half of them pounded flat by the powerful determination of a five-year-old refusing help.

Willow arrived home two hours early, just in time to help cover the birdhouse with a coat of exterior polyurethane finish. And to speed up the process, since Mikaela insisted they set the house out this evening in case any birds might be shopping for a new home tonight, they turned a fan on to help it dry.

The three of them emerged from the cellar to find Kee and Duncan and Luke sitting at the table in front of a huge stuffed turkey, a large bowl of mashed potatoes, and an even larger tossed salad.

"Where'd all this come from?" Rachel asked, leading Mikaela to the sink to wash their hands.

"Franny said she was tired of having only half of us show up for supper," Kee told her, filling a plate for Mikaela. "She's feeding Matt and Jason and Peter and Ahab and his crew, and sent this down for us."

"Oh, God. It's been years since I've had Franny's cooking," Willow said, drying her wet hands on her pants, sitting down at the table, and reaching for the salad.

Duncan beat her to the spoon, and without skipping a beat, Willow changed direction and reached for the mashed potatoes.

"I'll get a platter to set that turkey on," Rachel said, determined to be more civilized, wiping her hands on a towel as she headed for the pantry.

She entered the small room just off the kitchen and stopped and looked around for the platter. It had been years since they'd had a feast requiring large serving dishes.

It was as she was scanning the floor-to-ceiling shelves full of pots and pans and cooking appliances that Rachel realized she was standing in a room that was exactly eight-by-eight feet square.

And she was standing directly under the secret room!

She snapped her gaze to the ceiling, letting her eyes run from corner to corner, along the molding and back to the center light fixture.

When had that light been changed from a brass fixture to a square fluorescent light? She was sure it had been a two-bulb brass receptacle when the house had been built. But then, who paid attention to lights in pantries?

An architect intent on hiding a secret entrance, that's who.

Rachel nearly shouted with joy. She'd found it! She had finally found the way into the secret room!

She pulled the step stool into the center of the room and climbed up, grabbed the square fixture, and wiggled it.

It wiggled back.

"Never mind the platter, Rachel," Duncan hollered. "We can eat right out of the roaster."

Rachel snapped her gaze to the pantry door. Damn. "I'm coming," she hollered back, jumping down from the stool. She pushed the stool into its nook, wiped the excitement off her face, and walked back to the table.

Dinner took forever.

And washing and drying the dishes took even longer.

And the three men, their bellies full, were in no hurry to leave. Dammit. She had to get them out of the house.

"Your birdhouse should be dry by now," Rachel offered, smiling at Mikaela. "Maybe your daddy and Duncan and Luke can help you put it up outside."

Mikaela immediately jumped down from her stool at the island, where she'd been talking to her giraffe, and headed toward the cellar. "Come on, Daddy. We got to get it up before the birds come out."

Kee gave her a quick kiss on the lips. "Remind me to thank you later," he whispered.

"Come on, Daddy! The paint is dry," Mikaela hollered from the cellar.

Duncan came up from the cellar with a tall stake in one hand and a hammer and nails in the other. "Where do you want us to put it?" he asked.

"Anywhere," Rachel said, gently extricating herself from Kee's embrace. "Let Mikaela decide where she thinks a bird would like to live."

"I can promise it won't be in that house," Duncan whispered with a shake of his head, moving out of the way so Kee could go downstairs and get his daughter and the birdhouse. "Were ya both drunk when ya built it?"

Willow came into the kitchen dressed in several layers

of clothes. "I'm going paddling," she said, taking down two life vests from the pegs behind the door. "Rachel, why don't you come with me?"

Luke, who'd been rubbing his overstuffed belly, sighed. "Give me five minutes to change, ladies."

"Why do you have to change?" Willow asked.

"Because we can't go kayaking without a babysitter," Rachel explained before Luke could, making a face. "Boss's orders."

Kee, who was just stepping out of the cellar and had heard Rachel's answer, lifted a brow at Willow's glare. "You either play by the rules or don't go," he said softly.

"I could take ya into town for an ice cream instead," Duncan offered.

Willow snorted and pulled down another life vest for Luke. "In your dreams," she muttered. "Come on, Rachel, go change."

Rachel eyed the pantry door, then took off her apron and headed upstairs to change.

Dammit. She was so anxious to get into that secret room, it was all she could do not to scream in frustration. She pulled a sweater over her blouse, then slipped into a fleece jacket and zipped it up. She changed into thick fleece socks and water sneakers, and dug her paddling gloves out of the bureau before heading back downstairs.

Well, at least she'd found the entrance, and surely she and Willow would get some time alone this weekend. If not, then they'd have to take turns distracting the men while they checked out the room one at a time. Either way, they were going to find out what was in it that weekend.

Chapter Twenty-one

The tide advanced toward shore in undulating swells and a gentle south wind that pushed waves over the bow of Rachel's kayak as she paddled after Willow. Luke, still new to the sport of sea kayaking, trailed behind them a good two hundred yards, paddling fiercely, too proud to ask them to slow down.

Willow had always been a mad dasher for the first leg of their paddling jaunts, and Rachel powered her strokes to catch up with her sister. "Wait up," she finally said as she closed the distance between them. "I have something to tell you."

Willow laughed and stopped paddling, resting her paddle across the cockpit of her boat and wiping the sea spray from her face with the back of her gloved hand. "You're getting old, big sister," she teased as she gently rode the swells like a baby being rocked in a cradle.

Rachel looked back over her shoulder at Luke and saw

that he was working hard to catch up. "I found the way into the room," she quickly told Willow. "It's the light fixture in the pantry. It pulls down and probably releases a ladder."

Willow sobered. "What's in the room?"

"I don't know," Rachel told her, keeping an eye on Luke. "Daddy lined it with plate steel, and I spent all day looking for a way in. I just found it this evening, when I went after the turkey platter in the pantry."

Willow also glanced toward Luke, then started paddling again, this time at a slower pace that would eventually let him catch up. "When are we going to get a look inside?" she asked. "There's somebody around all the time."

"We may have to take turns. You'll have to create a distraction while I look, and I'll keep everyone busy while you look," Rachel suggested.

"What about tonight, when everyone's asleep?"

Rachel shook her head. "The room is right beside Kee and Mikaela's. And Mickey would definitely hear us and start nosing around."

With a nod of understanding, Willow stopped again, letting her left paddle trail in the water to turn her kayak crosswise to Luke's approaching boat. "Not bad," she told him with an encouraging smile. "Especially considering that old kayak weighs more than you do."

It was Thadd's old kayak. It was almost twenty-one feet long and made of thin cedar strips curving in classic lines that gave the boat its artistic grace—and a whole lot more weight than their modern fiberglass kayaks.

Labored breaths bellowing from his lungs, Luke glared at Willow, who turned again and started paddling toward the island that lay four miles offshore and three miles to the east of Sub Rosa. "If we hurry, we'll make it in time to watch the sunset," she said, powering her strokes again.

Rachel hung back and paddled her seventeen-foot kayak just off Luke's port side.

"Is your sister always this driven?" he asked. "Or is she really a sadist?"

Rachel laughed. "Officially, she's the terror of the Mid-Coast Kayak Club. She's won the Crane Island Kayak Race six years running."

Luke was about to respond when something to the right of Willow, who was now a good two hundred yards ahead of them, caught his attention.

Rachel turned to where he was looking and gasped. A lobster boat, running at full throttle, was heading directly for Willow.

Rachel and Luke shouted at the same time, digging their paddles into the water as they watched Willow stop and wave her own paddle in the air at the approaching boat. The boat turned at just the last minute, pushing a giant wave broadside into Willow's kayak, sending her rolling backward into the water.

The boat turned sharply again, still at full throttle, and circled back toward Luke and Rachel.

"Shit!" Luke growled, dropping his paddle and reaching under his life vest, his hand emerging holding a gun. "Get the hell out of here!" he shouted to Rachel, raising his gun in both hands to aim at the boat now bearing down on them.

Rachel's scream was drowned out by the sudden barrage of gunfire coming from both Luke's gun and the boat. The boat turned again, straight into Rachel's path. The thrust of its bow wave slammed her defenseless kayak just before its stern clipped her with such force that the kayak's nose shattered on impact. Rachel was tossed into the water, her body twisting and bobbing like flotsam in the churning wake.

She surfaced to the sound of rapid gunfire coming from the boat as it continued its circle and headed back toward Willow. The powerful diesel engine suddenly throttled back, and Rachel swam to the top of a swell and looked toward Luke, only to see him floating—unmoving—beside his overturned kayak.

She started swimming toward him, but stopped at the sound of Willow's screams. The lobster boat had stopped, and the two men on board were trying to pull her out of the water. Willow was fighting them, bracing her feet on the side of the boat and trying to shove herself away.

One of the men reached down and grabbed Willow by the hair, violently tugging her up as the other man grabbed hold of the shoulder strap of her life vest.

Rachel spun and started for Luke again. She reached him just as she heard the diesel engine rev back to life.

"Luke," she whispered, turning him toward her. "Luke!"

She let go of his life vest and put both hands on his face. Her hands were covered with blood.

"Luke!" she shouted, glancing behind her.

The lobster boat was slowly approaching, one man driving and the other man standing on deck, leaning over the rail and pointing a rifle at them. Willow was nowhere in sight. Rachel kicked at the water, putting Luke's bullet-riddled kayak between them and the boat.

The lobster boat turned sideways twenty yards away, and the engine was cut, the nightmare suddenly turning silent as the two men stared at Rachel. The man raised his rifle and aimed it at her.

"Take off his vest," he said.

"No!" Rachel screamed, moving Luke behind the feeble protection of his kayak.

The second man suddenly bent at the waist and straightened with Willow, holding her semiconscious body by her hair with one hand, his other arm wrapped threateningly around her neck.

"Take off his vest," the gunman repeated.

Rachel looked at Luke. His face was ashen, his lips starting to turn blue as the cold gulf water drained heat from his weakening body. She didn't know where he'd been shot or how many times.

She only knew that he was dying, and that if she took off his life vest, he would simply slip under the surface and drown.

"Hey," the gunman grunted, drawing Rachel's attention.

The moment she looked at him, he took the back of his hand and slapped Willow across the face so violently that her head snapped back against her captor and she cried out in pain. The gunman then lifted his rifle and stuck it against Willow's chest.

"Take off his vest," he repeated, "or your sister joins your friend."

Her hands shaking violently, more from the horror of what she was doing than from the cold, Rachel slowly unbuckled Luke's vest and slid it off his shoulders.

"Bring it with you," the gunman ordered, his rifle still pressed into Willow's vest. "And hold up your hands as you swim over here so I know you haven't got his gun."

She couldn't let him go. She just couldn't open her

hands and allow Luke to sink helplessly below the surface. They crested a swell, and Rachel looked toward shore. It was more than two miles away. She could see Sub Rosa sitting high on the cliff four miles to the west, and could just make out the masts of the *Six-to-One Odds* tied up to the dock. And her house, to the left, looked small and so far, far away.

She gasped as the rifle boomed and flinched when a bullet slammed into the kayak beside her, splintering wood against her. Rachel spun back to face the boat in time to see the gunman lowering the rifle back in Willow's direction.

Both men also scanned the area shoreward and seaward.

Satisfied they were alone on the water, the gunman nodded to the man holding Willow, who pulled back her head by her hair until she cried out in pain.

"Let him go, and swim over here," the gunman demanded, putting the barrel of his rifle to Willow's cheek this time. "Now, Miss Foster. My patience is gone."

Rachel turned back to Luke, and with tears streaming down her cheeks, she kissed him gently on the lips, forced herself to open her fingers, and helplessly watched as he drifted away and slowly sank below the surface.

The engine of the lobster boat started, the rhythmic idle bubbling water around the exhaust. The driver put it in gear and backed it slowly toward her, closing the distance they'd drifted apart.

And through blurry, tear-soaked eyes, Rachel read the name painted in large black letters across the stern.

Finders Keepers. Out of Trunk Harbor.

Finders. Find her. Mary Alder's and Frank Foster's

dying words, a warning to look for an enemy living in their midst.

The gunman hauled Rachel aboard with callous indifference, throwing her trembling, freezing body roughly onto the deck against Willow. He wrenched her hands behind her back and tied them and her feet with quick efficiency.

The gunman waved to the driver, telling him to get going, and then tied up Willow, who was listless and moaning and trembling from the cold. He picked up a burlap bag and tossed it over Willow's head, then hunched down beside Rachel with another bag. But instead of covering her, he stared at her for several seconds, then grabbed her braid and lifted her head to look at him.

"It's been a few years, Miss Foster," he said, his dark snake eyes narrowed and his beard curved with amusement. "You remember me?"

"No."

His hand on her braid tightened. "I think you do. Such a dedicated little architect you were then, following your father around like an adoring puppy." His feral smile broadened. "How protective Frank was of you." He nodded toward Willow. "Of all his women, especially his dear Marian."

He pulled Rachel's head up by the hair to look her more closely in the eye. "But in the end, Frank couldn't protect her or even himself." He shook his head and *tsk-tsked*. "And Thadd. He was worse than your father when it came to keeping me away from you girls."

He leaned in real close. "Your father begged for his life like a baby, you know," he softly said. "Will you do the same?" He shook his head again. "No? How about for your sister's life? Frank got down on his knees and begged me to spare Marian."

Rachel twisted to free herself from his hold and tried to bite his arm. His hand clutching her braid tightened painfully, and he pulled her face back to his, his eyes filled with amusement.

"Ah, you are shocked. You believed your father murdered your mother and Thadd, and then shot himself." He nodded. "A crime of passion is so easy to stage. It only takes one woman and two men in a bedroom, and the police fill in the rest."

He straightened, grabbed her by the strap of her life vest, and dragged her across the deck into the wheelhouse. He sat her up against the side.

"Forgive me," he said, hunching down to face her again. "For forgetting my manners. I am Raoul Vegas, Miss Foster," he said, nodding his head in greeting. "And we have met, although I am sure neither Frank nor Thadd ever mentioned me by name. What? You have nothing to say?"

He shifted to his knees, lifting her chin with bruising fingers. "Ah, you are mourning your friend." He cocked his head at her. "I was not close enough to see. Was it Keenan Oakes I dispatched to hell?"

"You killed my parents."

"Yes, I guess I did. I only intended to kill Thadd, you know, because the fool suddenly got a conscience in his old age. But your father arrived quite conveniently, and allowed me to make a clean sweep of my dealings here in Maine." He shrugged. "Marian was just a bonus, to make the scene complete."

"And you killed Mary Alder. Was she going to burn this

boat next?" Rachel glanced toward the bow, then back at him. "It has a compartment for smuggling stolen art, doesn't it? That's what you did for Thadd, and what you've been doing since he died. You've been stealing from Keenan Oakes," Rachel said. "You've been using the tunnels."

"Yes, I've used the tunnels for three years now. But it's not Oakes I'm stealing from, but the new heir of Sub Rosa."

"Keenan Oakes is the heir."

Raoul Vegas threw back his head in laughter. "I read that article in the newspaper," he said, looking back at her, still chuckling. "And I laughed myself silly. If Keenan Oakes is Sub Rosa's heir, I am king of England."

Rachel just stared in confusion, her mind trying to take in the horror of what was happening—of what she was hearing. This man had murdered her parents, and Thaddeus, and Mary. And Luke. And now he was telling her that Kee wasn't who he said he was.

He shook his head. "Keenan Oakes is only after what I am, Miss Foster. He's here on the pretense of being the heir, but it's really the Cup of Virtue he's after."

"The lawyers wouldn't have let him near Sub Rosa unless he was the heir," Rachel defended. "He has the codes. And complete access."

Vegas shook his head. "The true heir is an international banker living in Geneva with a wife and five teenage kids. Oakes merely made a deal with him to come here first and find Thaddeus Lakeman's lost treasure." He leaned in closer. "The greatest part of which is the Cup of Virtue."

He stood up and looked down at her. "And you, Miss Foster, are going to help me find it." He kicked her thigh. "Was it Oakes I shot?"

"Yes."

He nodded. "Then the others will be of no conse-
quence, at least while they are searching for him." He
looked up to see where they were, then hunched down
beside her again and took her chin in his hand. "Mary
had convinced me that you didn't know where Thadd
hid his stolen treasures, and that is why I used her these
last three years. But her death has put me at a disadvantage, considering that Oakes had full run of Sub Rosa.
Was he getting close to finding it?"

"He found it already. There was a hidden room my
father built, and Kee found it."

"He did not," he snapped. "He would not have been
here still. Oakes gets in, gets what he's after, and is gone
before anyone realizes he's even been there."

"Are you saying he's—he was—a smuggler?"

He shook his head. "The reward being offered for the
Cup of Virtue alone would have made him rich. No, I
learned that he had worked out a deal with the real heir
to sweep Sub Rosa clean of stolen art before the man
took possession. Chances are Oakes was in contact with
the various insurers as well."

His sinister smile returned. "We were after the same
prize, only for different reasons."

Raoul Vegas shoved her down to the deck, stood up
again, grabbed the burlap bag, and threw it over her head.

Rachel's world turned black, all but suffocating her in
the sickening smell of rotten fish. Her chest ached with
heart-crushing pressure as the boat cut through the waves
with amazing speed, obviously taking them far, far down
the coast.

Luke was dead. One minute they'd been laughing at

Willow, the next minute he'd been floating in Rachel's arms, the life draining from him.

And her parents. Murdered by Vegas. And Thadd. Her mother had not betrayed her father. All these years she and Willow—everyone—had believed it to be a crime of passion.

Instead it had been nothing more than the greed of one man.

And Kee. He wasn't the heir to Sub Rosa. He was an impostor. An opportunist. A liar.

He'd lied to her about who he was. He'd brought her to Sub Rosa not to help him open his house, but to use her to help him find Thadd's stolen treasure—for profit.

She'd been nothing more than a means to an end.

A titillating, amusing bonus.

She'd been a fool to let passion blind her to the truth.

Chapter Twenty-two

They heard the gunshots. That unmistakable sound had traveled across the water, the direction impossible to pinpoint as it skipped over waves and echoed against the shore like rolling thunder.

But Kee knew—he knew—the barrage of gunfire had come from the direction Rachel and Willow and Luke had gone.

He dropped the hammer he'd been using to hang the birdhouse, grabbed up Mikaela, and started running behind Duncan. Mickey led their way up the narrow path to Sub Rosa. At the base of the mansion they continued straight along the cliff, arriving at the ramp to the dock just as Ahab was giving the order to lower the power launch off the *Six-to-One Odds*. The crew of three men worked quickly as Ahab barked orders. Matt and Jason and Peter arrived, running down from the house.

Kee handed Mikaela to Peter and took the binoculars Jason held toward him. He scanned the open water in a sweeping arc, then returned to a lone lobster boat speeding east. He backtracked and saw a yellow kayak bobbing in its wake, the setting sun hitting it as swells raised it one second and dropped it out of sight the next. Another kayak, its white belly turned up, drifted on the tide, and the nose of another, wood-grained, rose out of the water as it started to sink.

Kee tore his gaze away and looked down at the dock. Ahab lowered his own sea scope, then turned and looked up at Kee.

"I saw two men pull the women aboard," he shouted. He looked at the men standing behind Kee, as if taking a mental roll call before shaking his head. "There's no sign of Luke. When I heard the gunshots I started looking, but I couldn't see him once his boat rolled over. There was a scuffle of some sort in the water before the second woman—I couldn't tell which—was pulled on board."

Kee lifted his binoculars back up and trained them on the fleeing boat. Willow and Rachel were in it, and Luke was . . . Luke was out there somewhere. He scanned back to the kayaks, searching for movement, then lowered the glasses and watched as Ahab and one of his crew climbed into the launch and headed out.

"Jason," Kee barked, pivoting toward him. "Check that list Luke gave you, and find out which of the names live in any town east of Fisherman's Reach. Peter, you take Mikaela on board the *Six-to-One Odds*, and get her out to sea. Matt, go up to the house and send Franny and the others home, call an ambulance and the coast guard, then help Jason."

"Daddy!" Mikaela cried, reaching out against Peter's hold.

Kee took a calming breath and cupped Mikaela's face in his hands. "I need your help, pumpkin," he said gently. "You have to steer the *Six-to-One Odds* because Ahab can't go out with you now. Rachel and Willow and Luke had a boat accident, and I have to go find them. But I need you to steer the schooner and follow Peter's directions. Can you do that?"

"If Peter gives me the numbers, I can steer." Her face suddenly fell. "I broke the compass, Daddy," she whispered.

"You know port from starboard. Peter will call out, and you'll steer. The crew is cut in half, and we need your help."

"Are we gonna go look for Luke?"

"No, baby. You're going to sea and wait until I call you."

"Mickey can look for Luke. He can smell him."

Kee kissed her on the nose and nodded. "Mickey can help me. He's got a good nose and good eyes."

He kissed her again, then nodded to Peter to head down the ramp and get aboard the schooner. Jason and Matt were already running up the path to Sub Rosa, and Duncan was now holding the binoculars up to his eyes, watching the retreating lobster boat and then scanning back toward the kayaks.

"They might not find him," Duncan said softly, lowering the glasses and looking at Kee.

"They'll find him," Kee growled. "The bastard has more lives than a cat."

They stood side by side with Mickey sitting between them, silent sentinels waiting and watching and growing impatient, helpless to do anything until they knew exactly what they were dealing with.

Kee had learned a long time ago that waiting might be the hardest thing to stomach, but it was better than rushing in without direction or purpose. The odds were good it was Raoul Vegas who had taken Willow and Rachel. The moment Rachel had given Kee his name last Sunday, he had realized just how dangerous the situation had become.

He'd been minutes away then from packing Rachel and Mikaela aboard the *Six-to-One Odds* and shipping them out, but in his arrogance, and after discussing it with his men, he'd thought they had everything under control. Raoul Vegas was after the art hidden in Sub Rosa, and as long as the women were tucked away safely at Rachel's, Vegas shouldn't have been a threat to them.

But Mary Alder's death had put the smuggler at a disadvantage. He'd been using Mary to help him through the maze of tunnels, and with her dead, he needed Rachel now. Willow was the most likely leverage to gain her cooperation.

They'd crossed paths with Vegas before, if only indirectly. Vegas had stolen a Renoir from a museum in Italy, but had botched the job, killing a guard and wounding the curator. The curator's daughter had been taken hostage for their run out of the country.

Kee and his men had found the girl, who was only nineteen, in Brazil. When Vegas hadn't needed her anymore, he'd sold her to a warlord deep in the Amazon.

Kee had stolen her back, and the warlord wouldn't be buying any more women for his amusement. The Renoir and Vegas, however, had gotten away clean.

"Tell me what ya're thinking," Duncan said, lowering the binoculars to look at Kee.

"I'm thinking we don't belong in this game anymore," he said softly. "When we reach the point we can't even protect what's ours, we sure as hell have no business involving innocent people."

Duncan sighed, scratching his chest and then raising the glasses again. "We had no reason to believe Vegas would go after Rachel."

Kee stopped watching the launch, which had just circled one of the kayaks and was heading to another one, and turned to look at Duncan. "We should have seen it coming. Vegas is after the Cup of Virtue, and Rachel is the only one who can help him find it. It's common knowledge she knows that mansion like the back of her hand. Vegas has obviously been living here, posing as a lobsterman and making forays into Sub Rosa for years now."

"Then why hadn't he taken Rachel before this?" Duncan asked, still looking through the binoculars.

"Mary Alder," Kee said succinctly. "He had her help until last week. She must have convinced him she could help him better than Rachel could. And she did, until he killed her."

"Aye," Duncan said softly, lowering the glasses and looking at Kee. "We don't belong in this game anymore."

The *Six-to-One Odds* was moving west under diesel power, already about two miles out. The mainsail was just being unfurled, and Kee took the binoculars from Duncan and looked at his schooner and smiled. His little girl was standing at the wheel, which was taller than she was, her attention focused on Peter. Kee could actually picture her beautiful little face, her bottom lip stuck out in concentration, her wispy locks blowing in the sea breeze as she executed her duties with the determination of a lion cub.

Kee turned his gaze to the launch and stiffened. "They have Luke," he growled. "Ahab just went into the water."

Duncan shifted nervously. "Can ya tell if he's alive?"

"No."

Jason and Matthew came running down the path from the mansion. "Raymond Bishop in Trunk Harbor or Paul Bean in Maplehead," Jason said as he came to a stop beside them. "Do they have him?" he asked, looking toward the launch.

"They have him," Kee answered, lifting the glasses again. "But he's not moving."

The beat of chopper blades moved in from the west at the same time as a siren sounded up on the road. The coast guard and an ambulance had arrived.

"Jason, call Peter on the *Six-to-One Odds* and have him radio the chopper and let them know what's happening. Have him tell them it was a hit-and-run, and send them after the lobster boat. Maybe they can find out its destination."

"Do you have any idea how many boats are out there?" Jason asked, taking out his cell phone. "The coast guard won't know which one they're looking for."

"It's a long shot," Kee admitted. "But it's better than nothing. Matthew, guide the paramedics down here."

"I already opened the gate," Matt said, turning back to the mansion.

Kee held up the glasses again to see Ahab cradling Luke, waving a thumb in the air as the launch sped toward shore.

"He's alive," Kee said, breaking into a relieved smile as he nodded to Jason and Duncan.

Jason turned away to hear Peter on the cell phone,

and Kee listened as Jason gave his instructions. The coast guard chopper hovered over the kayaks, then moved over the launch, taking in the situation.

"Tell them everyone's out of the water," Kee told Jason, who relayed that message to Peter, which Peter would then relay on the marine radio.

The chopper hovered another minute, then banked east and took off in that direction, the sound of its powerful rotor blades quickly fading into the distance.

Jason and Duncan and Kee trotted down the long ramp to the large floating platform, Jason bending to catch the nose of the launch as it docked.

Duncan lifted Luke off Ahab's lap. He handed him over to Kee and Jason, and they laid him out on the dock. Duncan tore open Luke's shirt, then pulled down his pants.

"Two shots," he said. "One in the thigh and the other in his side." He rolled him slightly, then took off his own shirt and held it tightly against Luke's side. "Both bullets are still in him. This one may have nicked a rib."

Kee stopped Mickey from washing Luke's face, replacing the wolf's tongue with his own hands. "Open your eyes, Luke," he demanded. "Look at me."

Luke's eyelids flickered, then slowly opened to mere slits, his mouth turning up in a slight, drunken grin. "It took you guys long enough," he whispered weakly. "I thought I'd freeze to death before I bled out."

"Give me something, Luke," Kee said softly. "Anything."

"*Finders Keepers*," he whispered, shivering, and closed his eyes again. "Out of Trunk Harbor."

Kee ran a gentle hand over Luke's forehead, brushing his wet hair out of his face. "Good man," he told him. "Good man."

The paramedics came down the ramp with their equipment. Kee moved out of the way, reaching out to help Ahab climb onto the dock. He patted the wet, shivering man on the back. "How was your swim?" he asked, walking with him up the ramp.

Once at the top, Ahab turned and looked out to sea. "Who stole my boat?" he growled.

"Peter," Kee told him. "Mikaela's steering."

Ahab headed back down the ramp. "Untie that damn launch!" he shouted to his crewman. "We got a boat to catch before those idiots run her aground."

Duncan and Jason came up the ramp and turned to watch the paramedics working on Luke. Matthew was standing over them, flinching every time one of them poked something into their friend and glaring every time Luke groaned.

"Any ideas?" Kee asked the two men beside him.

"I'll go after Willow," Duncan suggested, looking Kee in the eye. "While you and Jason and Mickey wait for Vegas and Rachel."

"So we've decided it's Vegas?" Jason asked. "And that he took Rachel to help get him into Sub Rosa?"

Kee nodded. "Willow's his leverage."

Jason scanned the horizon. "It'll be dark in about an hour." He looked at Duncan. "Can you have Willow by then?"

"How far is Trunk Harbor?"

"Twelve miles up the coast," Jason told him. He pulled a paper out of his pocket and read something on it. "Raymond Bishop lives at Twenty-four Drew Lane." He held the paper out to Duncan. "I downloaded this map when I did the Internet search."

Duncan studied the map. "Drew Lane runs down to a cove where he could moor his boat." He looked at Kee. "He might leave Willow alone if there's only two of them. I'll call as soon as I find out and let you know the number of guests to expect."

That said, Duncan turned and ran up the wide cobblestone path to Sub Rosa. Matthew came up the ramp from the dock, helping the paramedics wheel Luke up. Deputy sheriff Larry Jenkins arrived just in time to stop them and peer down at Luke.

"Boating accident?" he asked.

"Gunshots. Two," one of the paramedics said, pushing Luke past the stunned sheriff.

Jenkins turned to Kee. "What the hell happened here?" he asked, pulling out his notepad. "I was told this was a boating accident."

Kee looked Jenkins in the eye. "A lobster boat ran down our friend and started shooting at him. We don't know why, and we don't know who."

"Anyone else involved?" Jenkins asked.

Kee shook his head. "Luke was alone. But he was conscious when they brought him in. If you go to the hospital, you might get something from him."

Jenkins narrowed his eyes at Kee. "Is Rachel around?"

"She's home," Kee said, turning toward the cliff path. "Watching my daughter. I'm going to tell them what happened and then I'm headed to the hospital." He stopped and looked back at Jenkins. "Matt went in the ambulance with Luke. He knows as much as we do," he added, turning again and heading along the path. "Jason, bring the car to Rachel's."

Jenkins called his name, but Kee kept walking, eventually breaking into a jog. Jason would escort the deputy to his squad car and then meet Kee back in Sub Rosa's tunnel.

The last thing any of them needed was help from the local law. Jenkins seemed to be a good man, but dammit, Rachel's life hung in the balance and Kee wasn't about to let anything or anyone get in his way.

He stopped at the entrance to the cliff tunnel and turned and looked back out to sea, taking a deep breath and willing his pounding heart to calm down.

God, he should be shot for being so stupid.

This was it. He was done. Just as soon as he got this mess cleaned up, he was settling down with Rachel and Mikaela, here in Puffin Harbor, and opening a lobster stand or something.

Jason emerged from the tunnel five minutes later and quietly stood beside Kee. Together they watched the *Six-to-One Odds*, under full sail now, disappear around a large point of land.

Kee spotted the small launch returning, breaking through the waves and sending sea spray over its lone passenger.

Jason chuckled. "Peter isn't about to miss any of the fun."

Kee pulled his cell phone from his pocket and called the ship's phone. Mikaela picked up on the first ring.

"Daddy!"

"Ahab told you we found Luke, sweetheart. He's going to be okay. But he is banged up a bit and had to go to the hospital. I'll take you in to see him tomorrow."

"Can I come back now? Did you find Rachel and Willow?"

"Not yet. We're going to go get them right now. You be good for Ahab, baby. Sleep tight."

"Daddy?"

"Yes?"

"When you find Rachel, will you tell her I love her, too?"

Kee closed his eyes again, this time fighting for control. "That's the first thing I'll tell her," he said softly.

"I gotta go. Ahab's hollering at the crew again. I gotta go save him. 'Bye, daddy."

The line went dead before Kee could respond. He softly closed his cell phone and stared at the horizon.

"Any toys in particular you want me to dig out?" Jason asked. "Night vision? Infrared?"

Kee watched the launch approaching the dock. "I'm thinking we should use rubber bullets," he said, looking at Jason.

"We don't want to tap Vegas on the shoulder, we want to kill the bastard," Jason snarled.

"But we can't risk Rachel in the process."

"I haven't forgotten how to hit what I'm aiming at," Jason countered.

"Rubber bullets, with lethal loads for backup," Kee ordered. "And percussion grenades."

Jason rubbed his hands together. "Now you're talking," he said, turning back to the tunnel entrance. "I'll meet you and Peter in the foyer."

"Check the trip wires on your way through. I want to be able to tell which tunnels they're using."

Jason stopped and looked back. "Do you think Rachel knows where the room is?"

Kee hesitated, then shook his head. "She was telling me the truth last Sunday."

"Then Vegas is going to be piss-faced mad when he realizes she can't help him."

"She'll bluff him along, knowing we'll be waiting."

Jason suddenly brightened. "Yeah, she will. She's got brass," he said, disappearing into the tunnel.

Kee turned back to the ocean, lowering his hand to Mickey's head and ruffling his fur. He could just make out the reflection of one of the kayaks as the sun sank into the horizon, reflecting off it every time the small boat rose on a swell.

What a hell of a mess.

"How's Luke?" Peter asked, running down the path from the dock.

"He'll make it," Kee assured him. "He was shot twice, once in the leg and once in the side. He lost blood, but he was talking when he left here."

"And Rachel and Willow?"

"Duncan's gone after Willow. It's Raoul Vegas, and we're expecting him and Rachel to arrive sometime after dark."

Peter simply nodded, then smiled. "Mikaela did good. She's growing up fast."

"Too fast," Kee said, turning and entering the tunnel. "We're using rubber bullets, and lead for backup." He looked back at Peter. "We stop Vegas here, tonight, either by catching him or killing him—I don't give a damn which."

Peter whistled. "He tugged the wrong tiger's tail this time," he said, closing the gate behind them.

Chapter Twenty-three

*S*he *was right where she had* begun almost two weeks ago, except this time it wasn't the demon of Sub Rosa's past she had to deal with, but the demon now holding the gun at her back.

Willow's life depended on Rachel's being able to lead Raoul Vegas to Thadd's secret room and then get him safely back out with his precious Cup of Virtue without Kee's interference. She knew the tunnels were wired, but she didn't know how. She only understood that if they didn't return to the house where Willow and the other man were waiting by sunrise, Willow would die.

"The tunnels are under surveillance," she told Vegas as she carefully opened the cliff gate. "But I don't know how."

"I do," he said, prodding her with his gun. "Mary tripped a wire when we came here last Saturday. I'll lead the way. You stay directly behind me, and don't touch anything, not even the walls." He crowded past her, stopping and holding the barrel of the handgun against her cheek, his flashlight turned to illuminate their faces. "If Oakes is dead, Sub Rosa's treasures are the least of his men's worries. If not, then think hard before you do anything foolish. Your sister's life depends on our returning by sunrise."

That said, he turned and walked down the tunnel, confident that he had her cooperation.

"Why did you kill Mary?" Rachel asked, following along in his footsteps, hugging herself to keep from touching anything.

"Mary was willing to help me only as long as Sub Rosa was empty. But the article in the newspaper spooked her, and she started burning the boats and anything else that might tie the Foster name to the stolen art."

Rachel stopped walking. "Mary was protecting *us?*" she asked. "But why?"

Vegas stopped and shone the flashlight back at her, making it impossible for Rachel to see his face. "She told me only last week that she had been granting your father's wish these last three years," he said with a sinister chuckle. "As he sat dying on the floor of the bedroom, Frank Foster asked Mary to look out for you."

"Mary was there?"

"I actually had the gun to her head at one point," Vegas said. "But she told me I would never find Thadd's room on my own—that she would help me if I spared her."

"For three years? You and Mary have been searching for Thadd's room for three years?"

"Not consistently. I still had my own lucrative trade to look after. I only searched a few months each summer so that I could pose as a lobster fisherman," he explained, turning and continuing down the tunnel.

"Why didn't Mary just go to the police?" Rachel asked, following him again.

"Because of her promise to your father," he reminded her. "She knew you had inherited some of the stolen art without even being aware of it. She was protecting you."

"Then if you know we didn't realize what my father and Thadd were into, what makes you think I know where the secret room is?"

He stopped and shone the light back at her. "You've had almost two weeks to think about it, since you first came here to replace some of the stolen items you had. I'm sure you've figured it out by now."

"You knew I came here?"

She barely made out his nod. "I was just about to head into the tunnel myself that night, but you went limping in with your backpack full of stolen art. It was all I could do not to burst out laughing. I couldn't believe my eyes—that I was watching someone breaking into a house to return stolen treasure."

"I'm still not certain where Thadd's room is," she warned him. "I'm only taking an educated guess."

"Where?" he asked, taking a step toward her. "Where do you think it is?"

"On the third floor."

"We've covered every damn inch of that third floor," he said, angrily waving the flashlight. "And the second, and first, and even the basement. It's got to be down here, deeper into the cliffs."

"I'm betting Willow's life that it's on the third floor," Rachel said, moving toward him and then brushing past. "But we have to go in through Thadd's bedroom."

He pulled her back behind him and aimed the light at

the floor of the tunnel as they walked. "What's in Thadd's bedroom?" he asked, turning at an intersection and carefully making his way up the stairs.

"A secret entrance to his vault."

Vegas stopped and spun toward her. "Mary told me there was none. That the only way in was through a thick titanium door."

Rachel shrugged. "She lied."

With a curse, Vegas turned and started climbing again.

Rachel hugged herself, her still damp clothes sending shivers down her arms. At any point she could simply slip through one of the panels and into the mansion before Vegas even realized what she was up to. And then she could disappear into another tunnel and could keep up the game of cat and mouse until she could make her escape.

But she'd been blindfolded earlier and didn't know where Willow was, so escaping was not an option—not if she wanted to see her sister alive again.

They reached the panel to Thadd's bedroom, and Rachel balked. The last time she'd been in that room it had been littered with dead and dying people she loved—killed by the monster she was helping now.

"What?" he sneered, prodding her with the barrel of his gun. "You afraid of ghosts?" he asked with a laugh, pushing her into the room.

Rachel stumbled in with her eyes closed, the horror of three years ago still vivid in her mind. Strong hands grabbed her shoulders and pulled her out of the way, her scream of terror drowned out by the sudden explosion of gunfire.

The room suddenly flooded with light, and just like

that—in mere seconds, really—it was over but for Rachel's screaming.

"No!" she shouted, running to Vegas and pushing Jason out of the way. "No! Don't kill him! He knows where Willow is!"

"We have Willow," Kee said softly, coming up behind her and lifting her away.

Jason rolled Vegas onto his stomach and quickly tied his hands behind his back, then tied his feet, straightening and giving him a harsh kick in the ribs.

Rachel struggled against Kee. "Willow!" she continued, not hearing what he was saying. "We only have five hours!"

Kee turned her around to face him, shaking her to get her attention. "Willow's safe, Rachel. Duncan is taking her to the hospital right now. He thinks she has a concussion."

Rachel stopped struggling. "She's safe?" she whispered, looking deeply into Kee's eyes. "Duncan found her?"

He nodded. And smiled. And he pulled her up against him and hugged the breath right out of her. "God, I'm sorry," he whispered into her hair. He leaned back and looked at her. "This has been the longest three hours of my life."

His smile suddenly disappeared. "What's the matter? I promise you, Willow's safe, sweetheart."

It was the *sweetheart* that did it—that term of endearment used by lovers.

Rachel broke free and stepped back, only to nearly trip on Vegas. She turned, drew back her foot, and kicked the bastard as hard as she could in the ribs. And she kicked him again, and then threw herself down on top of him and started pummeling him with her fists, screeching every foul name she could think of. She shouted Luke's name, punching Vegas in the face, cursing him for making her kill Luke.

"Easy there," Kee said, pulling her back. "Luke's not dead, sweetheart. He just got out of surgery and will be back in fighting form in a month."

Rachel spun in Kee's arms and smacked his chest with her fist, trying to pull out of his grasp.

"Don't call me 'sweetheart'! And I'll kill him!" she shouted, twisting to get free. "He murdered my parents. And Thadd and Mary. He murdered my mother and father!"

Kee opened his arms. "Then have at him," he said softly, nudging her forward. "You may not kill him, Rachel, but I sure as hell won't deny you some satisfaction."

Rachel became aware of Peter and Jason standing nearby, silently watching.

She couldn't continue. Vegas might be able to slap a semiconscious woman across the face, but she simply couldn't continue.

Well, maybe just one more.

She drew back her foot and drove it into the monster's belly with enough force that he vomited. And she stepped back, hugged herself, and looked at the three men in silence.

"Remind me never to piss you off," Jason said, suddenly relaxing with a smile.

Kee moved to take her in his arms, but Rachel stepped away.

He looked at her, his eyes unreadable.

Rachel walked over to another panel in the south wall

and punched the wainscoting. A new panel popped open. Rachel disappeared into the dark void, the three men silently following her.

"Vegas?" Jason asked softly.

"He's not going anywhere," Kee said from behind her.

Rachel stopped on the bottom step and touched the tunnel wall to her right. A small door slid open, and she punched the month, day, and year of her birthday into the lighted electronic keyboard. The door in front of her slid open, and Rachel stepped into Thaddeus Lakeman's huge vault.

Kee stepped in behind her, then Peter, then Jason.

Peter whistled under his breath. "Old man Lakeman liked to keep his options open, didn't he?"

"Why didn't you use this passageway the night I arrived?" Kee asked, his eyes dark and probing.

"Because I didn't want to go through Thadd's bedroom."

"Why have you brought us here?" he asked. "Is this where you were bringing Vegas?"

Instead of answering, Rachel looked up at the light in the ceiling. It was a good two feet larger than the light in her pantry. She looked around, found a stool tucked in the corner, and pulled it to the center of the vault. She stepped up the two steps, reached up, and was just able to grasp the fixture by the edges and open it.

She quickly hopped off the stool as the fixture swung open, and a light automatically came on in the overhead room as a folding ladder lowered into the center of the vault.

All three men collectively sucked in their breath. Rachel stepped out of the way and waved her hand for Kee to proceed.

"So you did know where it was," he said, not looking up at the room but at her.

"No. I only figured it out today."

"How?"

"I realized that my father would have built it more like a vault than a room, and that it would probably have to be climate-controlled." She shrugged. "The infrastructure was already here because of this vault, and the foundation and walls below us were built to support the weight of the titanium walls and door, so they definitely could have supported another armored room. It was the only logical place to put it."

"And in order to enter the secret vault, you would have to get into this vault first," Jason said, putting his foot on the first step of the ladder. He looked at Kee, Kee nodded, and Jason went up and Peter followed.

Kee remained below, staring at her.

"So now you've found what you were after," Rachel said, hugging herself again. "You'll be able to collect the reward and turn Sub Rosa over to the rightful heir."

Kee didn't move, didn't say anything for several heartbeats. "Vegas told you," he finally said.

"He told me that the reward for something called the Cup of Virtue alone will make you all rich men."

"Rachel."

She held up her hand to stop him. "How did you know we'd be coming out in Thadd's bedroom?"

"Mickey has a hell of a nose. He could tell where you were in the tunnels from the moment you stepped through the cliff gate. He followed your progress through the walls."

"Where is he now?"

"Locked in the hall. We didn't want him in the room. He could have ended up in the middle of something nasty."

"Speaking of which, how come Vegas isn't dead?"

"Rubber bullets. You get hit by several of them and, believe me, you're down for the count."

"It's empty, people," Jason said through the opening in the ceiling.

"What?" Rachel gasped, going over to the ladder and looking up. "Empty?"

Jason nodded and moved out of the way so Rachel could climb into the room. Kee followed, and the four of them stood in silence, staring at the huge, completely empty room. Rachel turned in a circle, gawking.

"Where is everything?" she whispered.

Nobody said anything.

It was gone. All gone. But where?

Raoul Vegas hadn't taken it.

"Mary," Rachel whispered, looking at the men. "Mary Alder must have moved everything."

"But where?" Peter asked. "Could there be another hidden room in the mansion?"

Rachel blinked at him, unable even to consider that.

Kee sighed.

And Rachel decided she had had enough. She wanted to go see Willow.

She climbed down the ladder, walked to the large vault door, spun the interior lock to open the huge titanium door, and walked out into the library.

"And just where are you going?" Kee asked from behind her.

"To the hospital to see my sister."

"I'll take you," he said.

"No," she countered, walking toward the hall door. "I'll take myself."

"Rachel!"

She stopped and looked back.

"We agreed that neither of us is walking away."

She lifted her chin. "I remember saying that," she told him. "But I believed I was making that promise to someone else. You called me an impostor, while you really are one, Mr. Oakes. Peter can come and get Mikaela's things tomorrow. But I don't ever want to see you again," she finished, walking out into the hall.

She'd made it to the top of the grand staircase when he spoke. "I'm not going away, Rachel. And this isn't over."

"Yes it is," she said, looking back down the hall at him. She waved at Sub Rosa's walls. "Enjoy your treasure hunt."

Chapter Twenty-four

Rachel dropped the bundle of clothes she'd brought for Willow and pulled her sister into her arms, hugging her fiercely as they broke into quiet sobs, so happy to see they both were okay that they couldn't speak.

The nurse had to break them apart.

Rachel stood to the side, wiping her cheeks dry of tears, and watched the nurse help her bruised and battered sister slowly get dressed. "I have to go find Luke, Willy."

"He's in ICU," Willow said, wiping away her own tears. "Duncan and Matt are with him."

"I have to go see for myself he's okay," Rachel told her. "Then I'm coming right back here and taking you home."

"Take your time, Rae. I'm not going anywhere."

Rachel got directions to ICU, and found Duncan and Matt standing outside Luke's room. "I need to see him," she whispered, touching Duncan on the arm. "Thank you for saving my sister."

Duncan nodded, then went and spoke to a nurse.

The nurse led Rachel into Luke's room. "He's heavily drugged, but can probably hear you, although I don't know if what you're saying will make any sense to him," she told Rachel. "I can only give you five minutes."

Rachel nodded, her eyes glued to Luke. He was flat on his back, as white as the sheets covering him, but he still looked a damn sight better than the last time she'd seen his beautiful face. She walked over to the side of his bed.

"Kiss me again," he whispered.

"You're awake," Rachel said on an indrawn breath.

"Kiss me."

With relief bubbling inside her, Rachel leaned down and kissed him right on the lips, just as she had in the water.

"I'm so sorry," she whispered. "Can you ever forgive me?"

"For?"

"Taking off your vest and letting you . . . letting you go."

His eyes opened to mere slits. "You saved my life."

"I almost killed you. I left you to drown."

"Playing possum," he whispered, his words labored. "So they'd leave."

Rachel brushed the side of his face. "Look at me, Luke," she softly demanded.

He cracked open his eyes again.

"If I ever hear of you guarding anyone ever again, I'll hunt you down and shoot you myself." She smiled at him. "You suck at it, my friend. You keep getting shot, and one of these days you're not going to wake up in a hospital."

"I just need practice," he whispered, his attempt to smile back at her turning into a groan of pain.

"Quit talking and just listen," Rachel told him, brushing his hair back, gently wiping her tears from his face. "As soon as they let you out of here, you're coming to stay with me. I'll feed you until you're fat, make you strawberry pie, and we'll walk the woods looking for my cat."

She knew he heard her, because he fell asleep with a smile curving his lips.

Rachel wanted to cry every time she looked at her sister and saw her swollen, battered face. The two of them had gone into their parents' bedroom the moment they returned to their once again empty house. Cuddled side by side in the darkness, in the security of their parents' big bed, Rachel had told Willow what had happened at Sub Rosa, that Raoul Vegas had killed their parents and Thadd and Mary Alder, and she told her about the room over Thadd's vault and that it was empty.

And then she told her about Kee's deception.

Neither of them slept much that night, and what sleep they did get was fraught with nightmares, both new and three years old. By daybreak they finally gave up, and both stumbled downstairs. Rachel made ginger tea, and Willow just stood in the pantry, staring up at the ceiling.

"I'm afraid to look," Willow finally admitted.

"It's probably empty, just like Thadd's room."

"Or everything that was at Sub Rosa is here," Willow countered. "And we are in possession of millions of dollars in stolen art."

Rachel snorted. "That would be the final irony."

Willow rubbed her hands together and shifted uneasily. "Open it," she urged.

Rachel set their cups of tea on one of the shelves and

pulled the stool out of its nook. She climbed up, swung open the light fixture, then jumped down as a light came on in the overhead room and a ladder folded down into the pantry.

Willow leaned over and looked up. "It's not empty," she whispered, slowly climbing the ladder. She gasped as soon as her head rose above the ceiling. "Oh, my God. It's a treasure trove. A virtual museum."

Rachel prodded Willow to keep climbing and climbed up after her. They stood in the small room, turning in slow circles, speechless, their mouths hanging down to their chests.

Their perusal ended with them facing each other, both wide-eyed and unable to take it all in. "Why did they bring everything here?" Rachel whispered, feeling she was in the presence of something sacred.

"Maybe Thadd and Daddy realized that Vegas had become a danger to them. We have to turn this in, Rachel," Willow said. "We can't pretend it doesn't exist and hope it goes away."

"And exactly how do we do that without creating the biggest media circus this state has ever seen?"

Willow reached out, opened a glass display case, and picked up the small cup inside. "Is this the Cup of Virtue?" she asked.

Rachel took it from her, turning it around in her hand. "I don't know. But it looks very old. How can this simple cup be worth the lives of four people we love?"

"Kee could tell us. And he'll know what to do with all of this," Willow said, waving her hand at the walls and benches filled with treasure.

"He could if we tell him about it," Rachel agreed. "But

since I'm never speaking to him again, then I guess we'll have to come up with another plan."

Willow set down the cup and looked at her. "You love him."

"Loved. Past tense."

"You don't stop loving someone just like that. You're only mad at him right now." Willow shrugged. "You'll get over it."

Rachel gaped at her. "He lied to me. He used me. He expected me to trust him, and he couldn't even trust me enough to tell me who he really was."

"He was on a job," Willow pointed out. "And he didn't use you—he was trying to protect you."

Rachel snorted.

Willow's bruised face darkened with angry impatience. "He loves you," she snapped. "And you love him, and you've also fallen in love with Mikaela."

"It was just lust," Rachel countered, more to convince herself than Willow. "Raging hormones or a chemical imbalance or something." She straightened her shoulders and glared at her sister. "I'm fine now. There's nothing like a good old-fashioned lie to bring a girl to her senses."

Willow sighed. "Dammit, Rachel. Have you forgotten that you've done nothing but lie to the man for the last two weeks?"

"That's different. He knew I was lying."

"Will you listen to yourself? You're expecting to fall in love with a saint?"

"No, a demigod," Rachel whispered. "And they're not supposed to lie to you."

"Demigods are not infallible—hence the prefix 'demi,'" Willow returned just as softly. "You're not nearly as angry as you are hurt, Rae. But you hurt Kee, too."

"How?"

"You've been running your own charade. You haven't been completely up front with him, either," she said, waving at the room full of treasure. "You didn't trust him enough to tell him about this room."

"I was protecting you."

"No, dammit, you weren't," Willow snapped, her face flushing with anger again. "I am tired of being a convenient excuse for you to justify your actions of the last two weeks. It may have started with the intention to protect me, but it turned into a grand adventure for you. You loved the mystery. And you let your passion get you into this mess, and now your stubbornness is going to stand in the way of your happiness."

"Gee, when did you get a second degree in psychology?"

Instead of snapping back, Willow smiled at her. "You've met your match, big sister. Keenan Oakes is just as passionate and probably a whole lot more stubborn than you are. He's not going to go away, Rachel."

Rachel took one last look at the treasure and started down the ladder, stopping just long enough to glare at Willow. "We're not telling him about this room," she told her. "It's been sitting here for over three years, it can damn well sit a while longer, until I figure out how to get rid of it."

Willow slowly nodded. "Okay. I'll give you one month. Then it's my decision."

Chapter Twenty-five

Willow's prediction that Keenan Oakes was not going to go away proved disconcertingly true. The *Six-to-One Odds* was moored in Puffin Harbor, and Ahab was serving beer at the Drop Anchor. Near as Rachel could find out, Ahab's crew had dispersed to parts unknown. Peter and Matthew and Jason had also disappeared, and Luke and Duncan were living with Kee and Mikaela on the far side of town in a house they were renting.

Mickey, at least twice weekly, would come scratching at Rachel's door just around sunset and insist on sleeping in Rachel's tiny bed with her. Then he would silently disappear the next morning.

Mickey was the only one of the gang she'd had any direct contact with these last three weeks—except for one visit from Luke, who'd hobbled out of a shiny new truck and into her house with the use of a cane two days ago. He'd said he was wanting his strawberry pie and a short walk in the woods to look for her cat. And while he'd sat there and watched, she'd baked him his pie and they'd talked about unimportant things, and then about Mikaela getting signed up for school in the fall.

But the biggest news of the last three weeks was that Sub Rosa's true heir had finally arrived. Almost every light in the house was on every night, and loud music and laughter could be heard coming from the terrace most evenings.

Rachel would sit out on her porch in the evening and look at Sub Rosa, filled with happiness to see her old friend so alive, the heart of the mansion all but singing its joy.

Frank Foster had his granite memorial. Sub Rosa finally had its soul back, bigger and better than ever. It was full to brimming with people, a family who would love it, grow old with it, get married in it, and bring grandbabies to run through its halls.

Sub Rosa was no longer an opulent museum, but a home.

Rachel sat on her swing on the porch and sipped her glass of wine as she watched the shadows lengthen with the setting sun and the lights slowly come on in Sub Rosa. She was sort of expecting Mickey to visit again, but a truck pulled into her dooryard instead. Luke climbed out and hobbled up and joined her on the swing.

He pushed the swing gently with his good leg, sitting beside her in silence, and also looked up at Sub Rosa. Loud, punk-rock music started blaring from the terrace.

Luke chuckled. "Five teenagers," he said, shaking his head. "Have you met them?"

Rachel nodded. "The day after they moved in. I went

up and introduced myself and gave them a quick tour of the control room. I've been back two or three times since, when Sub Rosa did something that scared the hell out of them."

"Like what?"

Rachel looked over at Luke and smiled. "Like when that huge glass dome in the foyer suddenly rotated."

"It spins?"

"It adjusts to the seasons. And on the eve of the summer solstice, it turns so the sunrise will hit one special prism and send light shooting down to the calendar built into the marble floor. What's the Cup of Virtue, Luke?"

He looked at her. "It's supposed to be the cup Socrates drank from, filled with hemlock, to carry out his death sentence," he told her. "He was sentenced to death for impiety against the church."

"That's—it's over two thousand years old."

Luke nodded. "It dates from 399 B.C., to be exact. Has Willow told you anything about Raoul Vegas? Will he stand trial here first for the murder of your parents and Thadd and Mary?"

Rachel nodded. "The murders take precedence over larceny," she assured him. "How's Mikaela?"

He stared for a minute, then finally said, "If you want the truth, she's miserable."

"Miserable? Why?"

"She's having a hard time adjusting to living in a house. She says it's too big. And she doesn't like that the bed doesn't rock at night, like on the *Six-to-One Odds*."

"She did okay here."

"But did you notice that she only ran on the beach? She never once got in your swing," he said, nodding to the swing in the oak tree down on the lawn. "And the woods behind the house we're renting scare her. She keeps thinking bears are going to come out and eat her. She won't go out and play unless Mickey or one of us is with her."

"She needs to have some kids come over," Rachel suggested.

Luke shook his head. "She's scared of the kids, too. When Kee took her to sign up for school, she hugged his leg and wouldn't let go. She's never been around kids." He shrugged. "We never thought to expose her to any. It's just been Mikaela and a bunch of men."

"Then you've got to bring her to the library for story time. You can stay with her, and she'll get used to being around children. If not, she's going to throw a hissy fit her first day of school."

"I've told Kee that. But he's putting it off." Luke cocked his head, giving her a crooked grin. "I think the first day of school's going to be harder on him than on Mikaela. When are you going to stop this nonsense?"

Rachel looked at him in surprise. "What nonsense?"

Luke shook his head. "It's not even stubbornness anymore, is it? It's pride. Kee's too proud to come to you, and you're too proud to go to him."

"I didn't break our trust," she snapped.

"Kee sees it differently."

"Then that's his problem, isn't it?"

Luke shook his head again. "Pamela's his biggest problem right now."

Pamela. Pamela. Why did that name sound familiar? "Who's Pamela?" she finally asked.

Luke eyed her speculatively. "Mikaela's mother," he said softly. "She arrived in Puffin Harbor yesterday."

"She's here?" Rachel asked on an indrawn breath. "Why?"

Luke's eyes hardened. "Why else? She's out of money."

"She spent a million and a half dollars in five years?"

Luke nodded. "It appears so. And now she's asking for more."

Rachel just stared at him.

"Another million," Luke clarified. "Or she's taking Kee to court for custody of Mikaela."

"On what grounds? She *sold* her. She can't just take her back."

"She has a lawyer who says she wasn't in her right mind five years ago. That hormones or something," he said, waving his hand, "impaired her judgment."

Rachel stood up, her hands balled into fists at her side. "Kee better not pay her."

"He hasn't got a choice, Rachel. He can't risk a court battle."

"And what happens in another five years when Pamela comes looking for more money? Kee can't keep paying her off. He's in debt now."

"We'll raise the money," Luke whispered, looking out at the ocean, then back at her. "Kee put the *Six-to-One Odds* up for sale. And this time he'll have the custody sanctioned by a court of law. It won't happen again."

"It's not right," she snapped.

"We won't lose Mikaela," Luke said, standing up and leaning on his cane. "And we'll do whatever we have to to stay out of a court battle. It will be too unsettling for her."

Rachel scrubbed her face with her hands, blowing out a frustrated breath. "He's selling the *Six-to-One Odds?*"

"It's not near enough," Luke told her. "But it'll help. And Jason and Peter and Matt are on a job right now that should bring in a hundred thousand, if all goes well."

"What kind of job?" Rachel asked, peering at him through her fingers.

Luke shrugged. "An embezzler living on one of the Cayman Islands. His company wants its money back." He reached out and pulled her hands down from her face. "It shouldn't involve guns, Rachel. Embezzlers are quiet little bookworms."

"Has Mikaela . . . has she seen her mother?"

Luke shook his head. "Pamela's staying at the Red Boot Inn in town and met Kee at the Drop Anchor. She's agreed to stay away from Mikaela as long as Kee agrees to pay."

Rachel let out a relaxing breath. "At least she has that much decency."

Luke snorted. "It's not decency, it's greed. Kee told her that if she tries to see Mikaela, she won't get a dime."

Luke carefully walked off the porch and to his truck, but stopped before opening the door. "I'll try and bring Mikaela around to the library soon. When's story time?"

"Nine in the morning, Wednesdays and Fridays."

He nodded. "Mickey should be arriving soon. He snuck off about half an hour ago," he told her, opening the truck door and climbing in. He waved good-bye, backed up and turned around, and slowly pulled out of her driveway onto the main road.

Rachel turned and had just walked into her house when Mickey appeared at the screen door and gave a soft *woof*. She opened the door, sat down on the floor, and buried her face in his fur.

● ● ●

There were instances, Rachel decided as she walked down the side of the darkened road, when stubbornness was a virtue instead of a flaw, when passion was an ally instead of a foe, and when pride was just plain stupid.

She was sorely tired of being stupid. But more important, she was glad that Keenan Oakes was more stubborn than she was.

He was never going to go away.

"What do you think, Mickey?" she asked, shifting the box to her other arm so she could pat the wolf on the head. "Will this fix everything or only make things worse?"

Mickey trotted beside her in silence. Rachel stopped with a sigh, awkwardly reaching for the watch on her left wrist to light up the dial while trying not to drop the box.

Three in the morning. One hour to sunrise.

She looked at Keenan Oakes's rented house. The tug on her heart was definitely stronger, with only a few hundred yards between them. Damn, but she missed his smell. And his taste. She missed the way her heart thumped when he looked at her, and the way her skin tingled when he touched her.

She had nearly been as stupid as Joan the shrew.

Nearly, but not quite. She'd come to her senses, thank God, just in time.

At least, she hoped she was in time.

With a fortifying breath, Rachel adjusted her grip on the box and marched through the night to Kee's house with all the anticipation—and determination—of a woman about to set off a nuclear explosion.

Chapter Twenty-six

It wasn't a nuclear explosion—it was more a hard blow to the chest that started his heart racing the moment Kee opened the kitchen door and found Mickey and the box on his porch.

Mickey sat up with a yawn, stretched back on his haunches, then trotted past Kee and down the hall toward Mikaela's bedroom.

Kee stood in the doorway and stared down at the box.

Now what was her game?

He knew the box was from Rachel; his name was scrawled across the top in bold black letters formed with the precision of an architect. He looked out at the road beyond, barely visible in the early morning light, then back at the box.

He was tempted to give it a good kick and send it flying.

What was she up to that she couldn't deliver the box in person? Kee bent over and picked it up, somewhat surprised by how light it was. He carried it into the kitchen and set it on the table.

Duncan strolled into the kitchen. "What's that?" he asked with a yawn, coming to stand beside Kee.

"It's from Rachel," Kee said, not taking his eyes off the box.

"Ya don't seem in much of a hurry to open it," Duncan softly observed. He chuckled. "In fact, you're looking as if ya think it's going to explode in your face."

Kee looked at Duncan. "That possibility did occur to me."

Duncan waved that away with another chuckle, walked to the counter and pulled a knife from a drawer, and came back to the table. "I'll open it then," he said, slitting the tape and lifting the top flaps.

Kee brushed him aside, pulled out the packing paper on top, then stared into the box.

Duncan sucked in his breath on a whistle.

With a slightly trembling hand, Kee reached in and pulled the item out of its nest of packing paper.

"The Cup of Virtue," Duncan whispered. "She's had it all along."

Kee set the dull-patinated chalice on the table, pulled the folded piece of paper out of its bowl, and read the note.

I thought this might help solve your little financial problem, so that you won't have to sell the Six-to-One Odds. But you should probably change its name to the Six-to-Two Odds.

Kee took Rachel's porch steps two at a time and, without knocking, strode into her house, shouting her name.

He found her sitting on the couch, her feet curled beneath her, sipping what looked like a glass of orange juice.

Kee stood in the living room doorway and crossed his arms over his chest—mostly to keep his hands from shaking.

Rachel took another sip of juice.

"You're pregnant," he whispered, proud of the fact that his voice hadn't cracked from saying it out loud.

She shrugged. "I promised to tell you," she said with maddening calm, setting down her drink and standing up. "I'm not just guessing. I took a home pregnancy test."

Kee's ability to speak utterly and completely failed him.

Rachel, apparently, had no such problem. "But this child is going to cost you a bit more than Mikaela, I'm afraid," she told him, crossing her own arms over her chest.

He still couldn't speak, probably because his heart was stuck in his throat. But he did manage to lift one brow.

She shrugged again. "Although that depends on how you measure cost." Her chin lifted. "I don't wear jewelry, so a simple wedding band shouldn't set you back too much." She took a step toward him. "And this house was designed for a family, but I will be just as happy living on a schooner."

Kee's heart slowly started to settle back down in his chest, but was still pounding with the force of a runaway train.

"Your greatest expense, the way I see it, will be passion," she continued, taking another step closer. "And that might cost you more than you're willing to pay."

She stepped even closer. "I won't compromise on this,

Kee. I will swallow my pride, apologize for being a stupid fool, give you my trust without question, and beg forgiveness. But I will not give up passion."

She took another step closer, bringing her mere inches from him. "Can you afford that?" she whispered. "Can you afford to love me?"

Kee finally found his voice. "I believe I can manage that," he said softly. Carefully, gently, he pulled her into his arms, cradling her head against his chest, against his still racing heart. "If you let me swallow my own pride, apologize for being a stupid fool, accept my trust without question, and allow me to beg forgiveness, I can promise you a lifetime of passion."

She wrapped her arms around his waist and let out a deep sigh as she snuggled even closer against him. Kee used her braid to tilt her head back and found himself looking down into beautiful hazel-green eyes shining with promise.

"I love you," she whispered.

"I love you, too," he told her back.

Her face suddenly flushed. "Promise to remember that when I show my treasure trove of stolen art."

"All of it?" he asked.

"Every damn last item from Sub Rosa, near as I can tell," she confirmed, trying to wiggle away. "It's in a secret room my dad built over the pantry."

Kee wouldn't let her go. He swept her into his arms and, instead of heading to the pantry, started up the stairs to her bedroom. "You can show me later," he said thickly, taking the steps two at a time.

He strode into her bedroom and gently set her down on the narrow bed, quickly covering her body with his and kissing her cute little nose. "It's not every day a demigod gets a marriage proposal from a goddess."

He felt her chest puff up against his. "A goddess?" she whispered, wrapping her arms around his neck.

Kee kissed her nose again, then nodded. "A passionate goddess. And there is no greater treasure, Rachel, than knowing you're carrying my child."

Kee finally kissed her full on the mouth, deeply and passionately, showing Rachel exactly what a treasure she was.

And he would wait, he decided, to tell her that she'd had only one more week before he'd stolen her away on the *Six-to-One*—no, the *Seven-to-Two Odds*—and proposed to her himself.